The Widow

www.**transworldbooks**.co.uk

THE
WIDOW

FIONA BARTON

BANTAM PRESS

LONDON · TORONTO · SYDNEY · AUCKLAND · JOHANNESBURG

TRANSWORLD PUBLISHERS
61–63 Uxbridge Road, London W5 5SA
www.transworldbooks.co.uk

Transworld is part of the Penguin Random House group of companies
whose addresses can be found at global.penguinrandomhouse.com

Penguin
Random House
UK

First published in Great Britain in 2016 by Bantam Press
an imprint of Transworld Publishers

A CIP catalogue record for this book
is available from the British Library.

ISBNs 9780593076217 (hb)
9780593076224 (tpb)

Typeset in 11/15pt Giovanni Book by Falcon Oast Graphic Art Ltd.
Printed and bound by Griffin Press

Penguin Random House is committed to a sustainable
future for our business, our readers and our planet. This book
is made from Forest Stewardship Council® certified paper.

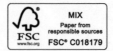

3 5 7 9 10 8 6 4 2

www.randomhouse.com.au
www.randomhouse.co.nz

For Gary, Tom and Lucy,
without whom nothing would mean anything.

The Widow

Chapter 1

Wednesday, 9 June 2010

The Widow

I CAN HEAR THE SOUND of her crunching up the path. Heavy footed in high heels. She's almost at the door, hesitating and smoothing her hair out of her face. Nice outfit. Jacket with big buttons, decent dress underneath and glasses perched on her head. Not a Jehovah's Witness or the Labour party. Must be a reporter, but not the usual. She's my second one today – fourth this week, and it's only Wednesday. I bet she says, 'I'm sorry to bother you at such a difficult time.' They all say that and put on that stupid face. Like they care.

I'm going to wait to see if she rings twice. The man this morning didn't. Some are obviously bored to death with trying. They leave as soon as they take their finger off the bell, marching back down the path as fast as they can, into their cars and away. They can tell their bosses they knocked on the door but she wasn't there. Pathetic.

She rings twice. Then knocks loudly in that rap-rap-rappity-rap way. Like a policeman. She sees me looking through the gap at the side of my net curtains and smiles this big smile. A Hollywood smile, my mum used to say. Then she knocks again.

When I open the door, she hands me the bottle of milk from the doorstep and says, 'You don't want to leave that out, it'll go off. Shall I come in? Have you got the kettle on?'

9

I can't breathe, let alone speak. She smiles again, head on one side. 'I'm Kate,' she says. 'Kate Waters, a reporter from the *Daily Post*.'

'I'm—' I start, suddenly realizing she hasn't asked.

'I know who you are, Mrs Taylor,' she says. Unspoken are the words: *You are the story*. 'Let's not stand out here,' she says. And as she talks, somehow, she's come in.

I feel too stunned by the turn of events to speak and she takes my silence as permission to go into the kitchen with the bottle of milk and make me a cup of tea. I follow her in – it's not a big kitchen and we're a bit of a squeeze as she bustles about, filling the kettle and opening all my cupboards, looking for cups and sugar. I just stand there, letting it all happen.

She's chatting about the units. 'What a lovely fresh-looking kitchen – I wish mine looked like this. Did you put it in?'

It feels like I'm talking to a friend. It isn't how I thought it would be, talking to a reporter. I thought it would be like being questioned by the police. Thought it would be an ordeal, an interrogation. That's what my husband, Glen, said. But it isn't, somehow.

I say, 'Yes, we chose white doors and red handles because it looked so clean.' I'm standing in my house discussing kitchen units with a reporter. Glen would've had a fit.

She says, 'Through here, is it?' and I open the door to the living room.

I'm not sure if I want her here or not – not sure how I feel. It doesn't feel right to protest now – she's just sitting and chatting with a cup of tea in her hand. It's funny, I'm quite enjoying the attention. I get a bit lonely inside this house now that Glen is gone.

And she seems to be in charge of things. It's quite nice really, to have someone in charge of me again. I was beginning to panic that I'd have to cope with everything on my own, but Kate Waters is saying she'll sort everything out.

All I have to do is tell her all about my life, she says.

My life? She doesn't really want to know about me. She hasn't walked up my path to hear about Jean Taylor. She wants to know the truth about him. About Glen. My husband.

You see, my husband died three weeks ago. Knocked down by a bus just outside Sainsbury's. He was there one minute, giving me grief about what sort of cereal I should've bought, and the next, dead on the road. Head injuries, they said. Dead, anyway. I just stood there and looked at him, lying there. People were running round finding blankets and there was a bit of blood on the pavement. Not much blood though. He would've been glad. He didn't like any sort of mess.

Everyone was very kind and trying to stop me seeing his body, but I couldn't tell them I was glad he'd gone. No more of his nonsense.

Chapter 2

Wednesday, 9 June 2010

The Widow

THE POLICE CAME TO THE hospital, of course. Even DI Bob Sparkes turned up at A&E to talk about Glen.

I said nothing to him or any of the others. Told them there was nothing to say, I was too upset to talk. Cried a bit.

DI Bob Sparkes has been a part of my life for so long – over three years it is now – but I think perhaps he will disappear with you, Glen.

I don't say any of this to Kate Waters. She sits in the other armchair in the living room, nursing her mug of tea and jiggling her foot.

'Jean,' she says – no more Mrs Taylor, I notice – 'this last week must have been terrible for you. And after all you've already been through.'

I say nothing, just stare at my lap. She has no idea what I've been through. No one has, really. I've never been able to tell anyone. Glen said that was best.

We wait in silence, then she tries a different tack. She stands up and picks up a photo of us from the mantelpiece – both of us laughing at something.

'You look so young,' she says. 'Was this before you got married?'

12

I nod.

'Did you know each other a long time before that? Did you meet at school?'

'No, not at school. We met at a bus stop,' I tell her. 'He was very good-looking and he made me laugh. I was seventeen, an apprentice at a hairdresser's in Greenwich, and he worked in a bank. He was a bit older and wore a suit and good shoes. He was different.'

I'm making it sound like some romantic novel and Kate Waters is lapping it up, scribbling in her notebook, peering at me over those little glasses and nodding as if she understands. She isn't fooling me.

Actually, Glen didn't seem the romantic sort at first. Our courtship was mainly in the dark – the cinema, the back seat of his Escort, the park – and there wasn't much time for talking. But I remember the first time he told me he loved me. I prickled all over, like I could feel every inch of my skin. I felt alive for the first time in my life. I told him I loved him, too. Desperately. That I couldn't eat or sleep for thinking about him.

My mum said it was a 'fascination' on my part when I mooned around the house. I wasn't sure what it meant, 'fascination', but I wanted to be with Glen all the time and back then he said he felt the same. I think Mum was a bit jealous. She relied on me.

'She relies on you too much, Jeanie,' Glen said. 'Not healthy to be going everywhere with your daughter.'

I tried to explain about Mum being frightened of going out on her own, but Glen said she was being selfish.

He was so protective, picking a seat for me in the pub away from the bar – 'Don't want it to be too noisy for you' – and ordering for me at restaurants so I tasted new things – 'You'll love this, Jeanie. Just try it.' So I did and sometimes the new things were lovely. And if they weren't, I didn't say anything in case I hurt his feelings. He would go quiet if I went against him. I hated that. Felt I'd disappointed him.

I'd never been out with someone like Glen, someone who knew what they wanted in life. The other boys were just that – boys.

Two years later, when Glen proposed, he didn't go down on one knee. He held me very close and said, 'You belong to me, Jeanie. We belong together . . . Let's get married.'

He'd won Mum over by then, anyway. He'd come with flowers – 'A little something for the other woman in my life,' he'd say to make her giggle and he'd talk to her about *Coronation Street* or the Royal Family and Mum loved it. She said I was a lucky girl. That he'd brought me out of myself. Would make something of me. She could see he'd take care of me. And he did.

'What was he like, then?' Kate Waters asks, leaning forward to encourage me. Then. She means before all the bad stuff.

'Oh, he was a lovely man. Very lovey-dovey, couldn't do enough for me,' I say. 'Always bringing me flowers and presents. Said I was the one. I was blown over by it all. I was only seventeen.'

She loves it. Writes it all down in a funny scrawl and looks up. I'm trying not to laugh. I feel the hysteria rising but it comes out like a sob and she reaches her hand over to touch my arm.

'Don't be upset,' she says. 'It's all over now.'

And it is. No more police, no more Glen. No more of his nonsense.

I can't quite remember when I started calling it that. It had begun long before I could name it. I was too busy making our marriage perfect, beginning with the wedding at Charlton House.

My mum and dad thought I was too young at nineteen but we persuaded them. Well, Glen did, really. He was so determined, so devoted to me, and in the end Dad said 'Yes' and we celebrated with a bottle of Lambrusco.

They paid a fortune for the wedding because I was their only one and I spent my whole time looking at pictures in bridal magazines with Mum and dreaming of my big day. My big day. How I clung to that and filled my life with it. Glen never interfered.

'That's your department,' he'd say and laugh.

He made it sound like he had a department, too. I thought it was probably his job; he was the main breadwinner, he said. 'I know it sounds old-fashioned, Jeanie, but I want to look after you. You're still very young and we've got everything in front of us.'

He always had big ideas and they sounded so exciting when he talked about them. He was going to be the manager of the branch, then leave to start his own business. Be his own boss and make lots of money. I could see him in a posh suit with a secretary and a big car. And me, I was going to be there for him. 'Never change, Jeanie. I love you just the way you are,' he'd say.

So we bought Number 12 and moved in after the wedding. We're still here all these years later.

The house had a front garden, but we gravelled over 'to save on cutting the grass,' Glen said. I quite liked the grass, but Glen liked things neat. It was hard at the beginning, when we first moved in together, because I was always a bit untidy. Mum was forever finding dirty plates and odd socks in the fluff under my bed at home. Glen would've died if he'd looked.

I can see him now, clenching his teeth and his eyes going all narrow, when he caught me brushing crumbs off the table on to the floor with my hand after we had tea one night, early on. I didn't even know I was doing it – must've done it a hundred times without thinking, but I never did it again. He was good for me in that way, taught me how to do things right so the house was nice. He liked it nice.

In the early days, Glen told me all about his job in the bank – the responsibilities he had, how the juniors relied on him, the jokes the staff played on each other, the boss he couldn't stand – 'Thinks he's better than everyone, Jeanie' – and the people he worked with. Joy and Liz in the back office; Scott, one of the counter staff, who had terrible skin and blushed about everything; May, the trainee who kept making mistakes. I loved listening to him, loved hearing about his world.

I suppose I did tell him about my work, but we seemed to drift back to the bank quite quickly.

'Hairdressing isn't the most exciting job,' he'd say, 'but you do it very well, Jeanie. I'm very proud of you.'

He was trying to make me feel better about myself, he told me. And he did. It felt so safe being loved by Glen.

Kate Waters is looking at me, doing that thing with her head again. She's good, I'll give her that. I've never spoken to a journalist before, apart from telling them to go away, never mind let one in the house. They've been coming to the door for years, on and off, and no one has got inside until today. Glen saw to that.

But he's not here now. And Kate Waters seems different. She's told me she feels 'a real connection' with me. Says she feels like we've known each other for ages. And I know what she means.

'His death must've come as a terrible shock,' she says, giving my arm another squeeze. I nod dumbly.

I can't tell her how I started lying awake, wishing Glen was dead. Well, not dead exactly. I didn't want him to be in any pain or suffer or anything, I just wanted him not to be there any more. I would fantasize about the moment when I'd get the call from a police officer.

'Mrs Taylor,' the deep voice would say, 'I'm so sorry, but I've got bad news.' The anticipation of the next bit almost used to make me giggle. 'Mrs Taylor, I'm afraid your husband has been killed in an accident.'

I then saw myself – really saw myself – sobbing and picking up the phone to ring his mum and tell her. 'Mary,' I'd say, 'I'm so sorry, I've got some bad news. It's Glen. He's dead.'

I can hear the shock in her gasp. I can feel her grief. I can feel the sympathy of friends at my loss, gathering my family around me. Then the secret thrill.

Me, the grieving widow. Don't make me laugh.

Of course, when it actually happened it didn't feel nearly as real. For a moment, his mum sounded almost as relieved as me that it was all over, then she put the phone down, weeping for her boy. And there were no friends to tell and just a handful of family to gather around me.

Kate Waters chirps up about needing the loo and making another cup of tea and I let her get on with it, giving her my mug and showing her the downstairs cloakroom. When she's gone, I look around the room quickly, making sure there's nothing of Glen's out. No souvenirs for her to steal. Glen warned me. He told me all the stories about the press. I hear the toilet flush and she eventually reappears with a tray and starts up again about what a remarkable woman I must be, so loyal.

I keep looking at the wedding picture on the wall above the gas fire. We look so young we could've been dressing up in our parents' clothes. Kate Waters sees me looking and takes the photo off the wall.

She perches on the arm of my chair and we look at it together. September the sixth, 1989. The day we tied the knot. I don't know why but I start to cry – my first real tears since Glen died – and Kate Waters puts an arm round me.

Chapter 3

The Reporter

KATE WATERS SHIFTED IN her chair. She shouldn't have had that cup of coffee earlier – what with that and the tea, her bladder was sending distress signals and she might have to leave Jean Taylor alone with her thoughts. Not a good idea at this stage of the game, especially as Jean had gone a bit quiet, sipping her tea and gazing into the distance. Kate was desperate not to damage the rapport she was building with her. They were at a very delicate stage. Lose eye contact and the whole mood could change.

Her husband Steve had once compared her job to stalking an animal. He'd had a glass too many of Rioja and was showing off at a dinner party.

'She gets closer and closer, feeding them little bits of kindness and humour, a hint of money to come, their chance to give their side of the story, until they are eating out of the palm of her hand. It's a real art,' he'd told the guests round their dining-room table.

They were his colleagues from the Oncology department and Kate had sat there, wearing her professional smile and murmuring, 'Come on, darling, you know me better than that,' as the guests laughed nervously and sipped their wine. She'd been furious during the washing up, sloshing suds over the floor as she threw pans into the sink, but Steve had put his arms around her and kissed her into a reconciliation.

'You know how much I admire you, Kate,' he'd said. 'You're brilliant at what you do.'

She'd kissed him back, but he was right. It was sometimes a game or a flirtatious dance, to make an instant connection with a suspicious – even hostile – stranger. She loved it. Loved the adrenalin rush of getting to the doorstep first, ahead of the pack, ringing the bell and hearing the sounds of life inside the house, seeing the light change in the frosted glass as the person approached and then, as the door opened, going into full performance mode.

Reporters had different techniques on the doorstep; one friend she'd trained with called it his 'last puppy in the basket' look to get sympathy, another always blamed her news editor for making her knock on the door again, and one had once stuffed a pillow up her jumper to pretend she was pregnant and asked to use the loo to get in.

Not Kate's style. She had her own rules: always smile, never stand too close to the door, don't start with an apology, and try to distract from the fact that you're after a story. She'd used the bottle-of-milk thing before, but milkmen were a dying breed. She was very pleased with herself for getting through this door with such apparent ease.

In truth, she hadn't wanted to come in the first place. She needed to get to the office and finish her expenses form before her credit-card bill came through and cleaned out her bank account. But her news editor was having none of it.

'Go and knock on the widow's door – it's on your way in,' Terry Deacon shouted down the phone above the radio news headlines blaring out beside him. 'Never know. Today might be your lucky day.'

Kate had sighed. She knew immediately who Terry meant. There was only one widow everyone wanted to interview that week, but she also knew it was a well-trodden path. Three of her colleagues at the *Post* had already tried – and she was sure she must be the

last reporter in the country to knock on this particular door.
Almost.

As she reached the turning into Jean Taylor's road, she auto-matically checked for other press and immediately spotted the man from *The Times*, standing by a car. Boring tie, elbow patches and a side parting. Classic. She edged her car forward as the traffic crawled along the main road, but kept one eye on the enemy. She'd have to go round the block again and hope he'd have left by the time she got back.

'Bloody hell,' she muttered, signalling left and swinging down a side street to park up.

Fifteen minutes and a flick through the dailies later, Kate put her seatbelt back on and restarted the car. Her phone rang and she dug deep into her bag to find it. Fishing it out, she saw Bob Sparkes' name on the display and turned off the engine again.

'Hello, Bob, how are you? What's happening?'

Detective Inspector Bob Sparkes wanted something; that was obvious. He wasn't the sort of bloke to ring for a chat and she bet herself the call would last less than sixty seconds.

'Hi Kate. Good, thanks. Quite busy – you know what it's like. Got a couple of cases on the go, but nothing interesting. Look, Kate, just wondered if you were still working on the Glen Taylor case.'

'Christ, Bob, have you got me on CCTV or something? I'm just about to go and knock on Jean Taylor's door.'

Sparkes laughed. 'Don't worry, you're not on the surveillance list as far as I know.'

'Anything I should know before I see her?' Kate asked. 'Anything new since Glen Taylor died?'

'No, not really.' She could hear the disappointment in his voice. 'Wondered if you'd heard anything. Anyway, I'd appreciate a heads-up if Jean says anything.'

'I'll give you a call afterwards,' she said. 'But she'll probably slam the door in my face. That's what she's done to all the other reporters.'

'OK, speak later.'

End of. She looked at the phone and smiled. Forty-one seconds. A new record. She must tease him about it next time she saw him.

Five minutes later she'd cruised down Jean Taylor's newly media-free street and walked up the path.

Now, she needed the story.

Oh for God's sake, how can I concentrate? she thought, digging her nails into her hand to distract herself. No – no good.

'Sorry, Jean, but would it be all right to use your loo?' she said now, smiling apologetically. 'Tea goes straight through you, doesn't it? I'll make us another if you like.'

Jean nodded and rose from her seat to guide the way. 'It's through here,' she said, standing aside so Kate could edge past into the peachy haven of the downstairs loo.

Washing her hands with the perfumed guest soap, Kate glanced up and caught her expression in the mirror. She looked a bit tired, she thought, smoothing her unruly hair and tapping the bags under her eyes with her fingertips as instructed by the girl who did her occasional facials.

In the kitchen on her own, she idly read the notes and magnets on the fridge while she waited for the kettle to boil. Shopping lists and holiday souvenirs; nothing much for her here. A photo of the Taylors taken in a beach restaurant showed the couple smiling and raising their glasses to the camera. Glen Taylor, all tousled dark hair and holiday smile, and Jean, dark blonde hair done for the occasion and tucked neatly behind her ears, going-out make-up slightly smudged by the heat, and that sideways glance at her husband.

Adoring or in awe? Kate wondered.

The last couple of years had clearly taken their toll on the woman in the photo. Jean was sitting waiting for her in cargo pants, baggy T-shirt and cardigan, her hair escaping from a stubby ponytail. Steve was always teasing her about how she noticed the little things, but it was part of the job. 'I'm a trained observer,' she'd joked and delighted in pointing out tiny, telling details. She'd immediately spotted Jean's rough and cracked hands – hairdresser's hands, she'd thought to herself – and the skin around the nails, frayed from nervous chewing.

The lines around the widow's eyes told their own story.

Kate took her phone out and photographed the holiday snap. She noted that everything in the kitchen was immaculate – nothing like her own, where her teenage sons would, no doubt, have left a trail of detritus from their abandoned breakfast – stained coffee mugs, souring milk, half-eaten toast, a lidless jar of jam with a knife sticking out of it. And the obligatory filthy football kit festering on the floor.

The kettle – and thoughts of home – clicked off and she made the tea and carried the mugs through on a tray.

Jean was staring into space, her teeth working on her thumb.

'That's better,' Kate said, plonking herself down. 'Sorry about that. Now, where were we?'

She had to admit, she was beginning to worry. She'd spent nearly an hour with Jean Taylor and had a notebook full of bits and pieces about her childhood and early married life. But that was all. Every time she edged a bit closer to the story, Jean would change the subject to something safe. They'd had a long discussion at one point about the challenges of bringing up kids, and then there had been a brief interlude when Kate had finally taken one of the insistent calls from the office.

Terry was beside himself when he heard where Kate was. 'Brilliant!' he yelled down the phone. 'Well done. What's she saying? When can you file?'

Under Jean Taylor's watchful eyes, Kate muttered, 'Hang on a minute, Terry. The reception isn't very good here,' and slipped into the back garden, signalling mock irritation to Jean with a weary shake of her head.

'For God's sake, Terry, I was sitting next to her. I can't talk now,' she hissed. 'It's a bit slow, to be honest, but I think she's beginning to trust me. Let me get on with it.'

'Have you got her under contract yet?' Terry asked. 'Get her under contract and then we can take our time getting the full works.'

'I don't want to scare her off by pushing things, Terry. I'll do my level best. Speak later.'

Kate pressed the Off button on the phone with feeling and considered her next move. Maybe she just needed to mention the money straight away. She'd done the tea and sympathy and now she had to stop dancing round the edge.

After all, Jean might be hard up now her husband was dead.

He wasn't there to provide for her any more. Or to stop her talking.

Chapter 4

The Widow

She's still here, an hour later. Before today, I'd have asked her to go. I've never had a problem before telling the press people to get lost when they knock. Easy when they are so rude. 'Hello,' they say, then they're straight into their questions. Horrible, intrusive questions. Kate Waters hasn't asked anything hard. Yet.

We've talked about all sorts of things: when Glen and I bought, the price of property round here, what we've done to the house, the price of paint, the neighbourhood, where I grew up and where I went to school, that sort of thing. She chimes in with everything I say. 'Oh, I went to a school like that. I hated the teachers, didn't you?' That kind of thing. Makes me feel I'm chatting to a friend. That she's just like me. Clever really, but maybe it's what she does every time she does an interview.

She's not so bad really. I think I could quite like her. She's funny and seems kind, but maybe it's all an act. She's telling me about her husband – her 'old man' as she calls him – and how she must give him a ring later to let him know she might be late home. Not sure why she'll be late – it isn't even lunchtime yet and she only lives thirty minutes round the South Circular – but I tell her she needs to ring straight away or he'll worry. Glen would've worried. He'd have given me hell if I stayed out without telling him.

'It's not fair on me, Jeanie,' he'd have said. But I don't tell her that.

Kate is laughing and says her old man is used to it now, but will complain because he'll have to deal with the kids. She's got teenagers, she tells me, Jake and Freddie, with no manners and no respect.

'He'll have to cook dinner,' she says. 'But I bet he orders a pizza. The boys'll love that.'

The boys are driving her and the old man mad, apparently, because they won't clear up their bedrooms.

'They're living in a pigsty, Jean,' she says. 'You won't believe how many cereal bowls I found in Jake's room. Practically a dinner service. And they lose socks every week. Our house is like the Bermuda Triangle of footwear.' And she laughs again because she loves them, pigsty or not.

All I can think is: Jake and Freddie, what lovely names. I stash them away for later, for my collection, and I'm nodding like I understand how she feels. But I don't, do I? I'd have loved her problems. I'd have loved to have a teenager to nag.

Anyway, I find myself saying, 'Glen could be a bit difficult when I let the house get in a mess,' out loud. I just wanted to show her I had my own fair share of problems, that I was just like her. Stupid, really. How could I ever be just like her? Or anybody? Me.

Glen always said I was different. When we were going out, he'd show me off, telling his mates that I was special. I couldn't figure it out really. I worked in a salon called Hair Today – Lesley, the owner's, little joke – and spent all my time shampooing and making cups of coffee for menopausal women. I thought hair-dressing was going to be fun – glamorous even. Thought I'd be cutting hair and creating new styles, but at seventeen I was bottom of the ladder.

'Jean,' Lesley would call across to me, 'can you shampoo my lady and then sweep up round the chairs.' No please or thank you.

The customers were all right. They liked telling me all their news and problems because I listened and didn't try and give them advice, like Lesley. I nodded and smiled and daydreamed while they rabbited on about their grandson and his glue sniffing or the neighbour who was throwing her dog mess over the fence. Whole days would go past without me giving an opinion beyond 'That's nice' or making up holiday plans to keep the conversation going. But I stuck at it. I did the courses, learning how to cut and colour, and started getting my own clients. It wasn't very well paid but I wasn't really fit for anything else. Didn't work at school. Mum told people I was dyslexic, but the truth is I couldn't be bothered.

Then Glen showed up and I was suddenly 'special'.

Nothing much changed at work. But I didn't socialize with the three other girls because Glen never liked me going out on my own. He said the other girls were single and out for sex and booze. He was probably right if their Monday-morning stories were anything to go by, but I just made excuses and in the end they stopped asking me.

I used to enjoy my work because I could drift off in my head and there was no stress. It made me feel safe – the smells of chemicals and straightened hair, the sounds of chatter and running water, hairdryers roaring and the predictability of it all. The appointment book, marked up in blunt pencil, ruled my day.

Everything was decided, even the uniform of black trousers and white top – apart from Saturday when we all had to wear jeans. 'Demeaning on a woman of your experience. You're a stylist, not a junior, Jeanie,' Glen had said later. Anyway, it meant I didn't have to decide what to wear – or do – most days. No grief.

They all loved Glen. He'd come and pick me up on a Saturday and lean on the desk to talk to Lesley. He knew so much, my Glen. All about the business side of things. And he could make people laugh even when he was talking about serious stuff.

'He's so clever, your husband,' Lesley would say. 'And so good-looking. You're a lucky girl, Jean.'

I always understood that she couldn't believe Glen had chosen me. Sometimes, I couldn't either. He would laugh if I said it and pull me in to him. 'You are everything I want,' he'd say. He helped me see things for what they were. He helped me grow up, I suppose.

I didn't know the first thing about money and running a home when we got married, so Glen gave me housekeeping each week and a notebook to write down everything I spent. Then we'd sit and he'd balance the figures. I learned so much from him.

Kate is talking again, but I've missed the start. It's something about an 'arrangement' and she's talking about money.

'Sorry,' I say, 'I was miles away for a minute.'

She smiles patiently and leans forward again. 'I know how difficult this is, Jean. Having the press on your doorstep, night and day. But honestly, the only way to get rid of them is to do an interview. Then they'll all lose interest and leave you alone.'

I nod to show I'm listening. but she gets all excited, thinks I'm agreeing to it. 'Hang on,' I say in a bit of a panic. 'I'm not saying yes or no. I need to think it through.'

'We'd be happy to make a payment – to compensate you for your time and to help you at this difficult time,' she says quickly. Funny, isn't it, how they try and dress things up. Compensate! She means they'll pay me to spill the beans, but she doesn't want to risk offending me.

I've had lots of offers over time, the sort of money you win on the Lottery. You should see the letters that've been pushed through my letterbox by reporters. They'd make you blush, they're so false. Still, I suppose it's better than the hate mail that gets sent.

Sometimes people tear out an article from the papers about Glen and write MONSTER in block capitals with lots of underlining. Sometimes they underline it so hard their pen goes through the page.

Anyway, the reporters do the opposite. But they are just as sickening, really.

'Dear Mrs Taylor,' – or just Jean sometimes – 'I hope you won't mind me writing to you at this difficult time, blah, blah, blah. So much has been written about you, but we would like to give you the chance to tell your side of the story. Blah, blah, blah.'

Glen used to read them out in one of his funny voices and we'd laugh and I'd stick them in a drawer. But that was when he was still alive. There was no one to share this offer with.

I look back down at my tea. It's cold now and there's a bit of a skin on the top. It's that full-fat milk that Glen insists on. Insisted. I can get low-fat milk now. I smile.

Kate, who's doing her big sell on how sensitive and responsible her newspaper is and God knows what else, sees the smile as another positive signal. She's offering to take me to a hotel for a couple of nights, 'To get away from the rest of the reporters and all that pressure,' she says. 'To give you a break, Jean.'

I need a break, I think.

As if on cue, there's a ring on the front-door bell. Kate peeps through the net curtains and hisses, 'Bloody hell, Jean, there's a bloke from the local TV station outside. Keep quiet and he'll go away.'

I do as I'm told. As usual. You see, she's taking over where Glen left off. In charge. Protecting me from the press outside. Except, of course, she's the press too. Oh God, I'm in here with the enemy.

I turn to say something but the bell goes again and the letterbox flap pings up. 'Mrs Taylor?' a voice shouts into the empty hall. 'Mrs Taylor? It's Jim Wilson from Capital TV. I only want a minute of your time. Just a quick word. Are you there?'

Kate and I sit looking at each other. She's very tense. It's strange to see someone else going through what I go through two or three times a day. I want to tell her that I've learned to just stay quiet. I even hold my breath sometimes so they won't know there's a living soul in the house. But Kate can't sit still. Then she gets her mobile out.

'Are you going to phone a friend?' I ask, trying to break the tension, but of course the telly bloke hears me.

'Mrs Taylor, I know you're there. Please come to the door. I promise I'll only take a moment. I just need to speak to you. We want to give you a platform—'

Kate suddenly shouts, 'Fuck off!' and I stare at her. Glen would never have allowed a woman to say that word in his house. She looks at me and mouths, 'Sorry', and then puts her finger to her lips. And the telly man does fuck off.

'Well, that obviously works,' I say.

'Sorry, but it's the only language they understand,' she says and laughs. It is a nice laugh, sounds genuine, and I haven't heard much laughter lately. 'Now then, let's sort out this hotel before another reporter comes.'

I just nod. The last time I went to a hotel was when Glen and I went to Whitstable for a weekend, a few years ago now. 2004. For our fifteenth anniversary.

'A milestone, Jeanie,' he'd said. 'It's longer than most armed robbers get.' He liked a joke.

Anyway, Whitstable was only an hour from home, but we stayed in a lovely place on the seafront and ate posh fish and chips and went walking along the stony beach. I picked up flat stones for Glen and he skimmed them through the waves and we counted the skips together. There was the clanging of sails on the masts of the little boats and the wind whipping my hair into a mess, but I think I was truly happy. Glen didn't say much. He just wanted to walk and I was happy to get some of his attention.

You see, Glen was disappearing from my life really. He was there but not there, if you know what I mean. The computer was more of a wife than I was. In all sorts of ways, as it turned out. He had a camera thing so people could see him and he could see them when they were talking. The lighting on those things makes everyone look like they are dead. Like zombies. I just left him to it. To his nonsense.

'What do you do on there all evening?' I'd say, and he'd shrug and say, 'Just talking to friends. Nothing much.' But he could spend hours doing whatever it was. Hours.

Sometimes I'd wake up in the night and he wouldn't be there, beside me in bed. I could hear the murmur of his voice from the spare room but I knew better than to disturb him. He didn't welcome my company when he was on the computer. When I used to take him a cup of coffee I had to knock before going in. He said I made him jump if I came into the room suddenly. So I'd knock and he'd turn off the screen and take the cup off me.

'Thanks,' he'd say.

'Anything interesting on the computer?' I'd ask.

'No,' he'd answer. 'Just the usual.' End of conversation.

I never used the computer. It was very much his department.

But I think I always knew there was something going on in there. That's when I started calling it his nonsense. Meant I could talk about it out loud. He didn't like it being called that, but he couldn't really say anything, could he? It was such a harmless word. Nonsense. Something and nothing. But it wasn't nothing. It was filth. Things that no one should see, let alone pay to look at.

Glen told me it wasn't him when the police found it on his computer.

'They found stuff I didn't download – horrible stuff that just finds its way on to the hard drive when you're looking at something else,' he said. I didn't know anything about the internet or hard drives. It could've happened, couldn't it?

'Loads of blokes are being wrongly accused, Jeanie,' he said. 'It's in the papers every week. People steal credit cards and use them to buy this stuff. I didn't do it. I've told the police that.'

And when I didn't say anything, he went on, 'You don't know what it's like to be accused of something like this when you haven't done anything. It tears you apart.'

I reached out and stroked his arm and he grabbed my hand.

'Let's have a cup of tea, Jeanie,' he said. And we went into the kitchen to put the kettle on.

When I was getting the milk out of the fridge, I stood and looked at the photos on the door – us on New Year's Eve, all poshed up, us painting the ceiling in the front room, covered in spots of magnolia, us on holiday, us at the fair. Us. We were a team.

'Don't worry. You've got me, Jeanie,' he'd say when I came home after a bad day or something. 'We're a team.' And we were. There was too much at stake to split up.

And we were in too deep for me to walk away. I'd lied for him.

It wasn't the first time. It started with ringing up the bank to say he was ill when he didn't fancy going in. Then lying about losing the credit card when he said we'd got into financial trouble so the bank would write off some of the withdrawals.

'It doesn't hurt anyone, Jeanie,' he'd say. 'Go on, just this once.'

Of course it wasn't just once.

I expect that this is what Kate Waters wants to hear about.

I hear her say my name in the hall and when I get up to look, she's talking to someone on the phone, telling them to come and rescue us.

Glen used to call me his princess sometimes, but I'm sure no one is coming on a white horse to save me today.

I go and sit down again and wait to see what happens.

Chapter 5

The Detective

Bob Sparkes smiled the first time he heard Bella Elliott's name. His favourite auntie – one of his mum's flock of younger sisters – was called Bella; the joker in the pack. It was the last time he smiled for weeks.

The 999 call had come in at 15.38. The woman's voice was breathless with grief.

'She's been taken,' she said. 'She's only two. Someone has taken her—'

On the recording, played over and over again in the ensuing days, the soothing alto tones of the male operator could be heard in an agonizing duet with the shrill soprano of the caller.

'What is your little girl's name?'

'Bella – she's called Bella.'

'And who am I talking to?'

'I'm her mum. Dawn Elliott. She was in the garden, at the front. Our house. 44a Manor Road, Westland. Please help me.'

'We will, Dawn. I know this is hard, but we need to know a few more things to help us find Bella. When did you last see her? Was she on her own in the garden?'

'She was playing with the cat. On her own. After her nap. She hadn't been out there long. Just a few minutes. I went out to bring her in about three thirty and she'd gone. We've looked everywhere. Please help me find her.'

'OK. Stay with me, Dawn. Can you describe Bella? What is she wearing?'

'She's got blonde hair – in a ponytail today. She's only little. She's just a baby . . . I just can't remember what she was wearing. A T-shirt and trousers, I think. Oh God, I can't think. She had her glasses on. Little round ones with pink frames – it's because she's got a lazy eye. Please find her. Please.'

It was thirty minutes later, after two uniforms from the Hampshire force had gone to confirm Dawn Elliott's story and make an immediate search of the house, that Bella's name came to DI Sparkes' attention.

'Two-year-old gone missing, Bob,' his sergeant said as he barged into the DI's office. 'Bella Elliott. Not been seen for nearly two hours. In the front garden, playing, and then gone. It's a council estate on the edge of Southampton. Mum's in pieces – the doctor's with her now.'

Sergeant Ian Matthews laid a slim folder on his boss's desk. Bella Elliott's name was written in black marker on the cover and attached with a paper clip was a colour photo of a little girl.

Sparkes tapped the photo, taking it in before opening the file. 'What are we doing? Where are we looking? Where's the dad?'

Sergeant Matthews sat down heavily. 'The house, the loft, the garden so far. Doesn't look good. No sign of her. Dad is from the Midlands, mum thinks – a brief encounter who left before Bella was born. We're trying to trace him, but mum isn't helping. She says he doesn't need to know.'

'And what about her? What's she like? What was she doing while her two-year-old was playing outside?' Sparkes asked.

'Said she was making Bella's tea. The kitchen looks out over the back garden so she couldn't see her. There's only a low wall at the front, barely a wall at all.'

'Bit careless to leave a child that age unsupervised,' Sparkes mused, trying to remember his two kids at the same age. James was now thirty – an accountant, of all things – and Samantha twenty-six and newly engaged. Had he and Eileen ever left them in the garden as toddlers? He couldn't remember, to be honest. Probably wasn't around much at that stage, always out at work. He'd ask Eileen when he got home – if he got home tonight.

DI Sparkes reached for his coat, on a hook behind him, and fished his car keys out of a pocket. 'I'd better get out there and have a look, Matthews. Sniff the air, talk to the mum. You stay here and get things organized in case we need an incident room. I'll call you before seven.'

In the car on the way to Westland, he turned on the radio to hear the local news. Bella was top of the news bulletin, but the reporter had found nothing that Sparkes didn't already know.

Thank goodness for that, he thought. His feelings towards the local media were decidedly mixed.

The last time a child had gone missing, things had turned ugly when the reporters started their own investigation and stomped all over the evidence. Laura Simpson, a five-year-old from Gosport, had been found, dirty, scared and hidden in a cupboard at her step-uncle's place – 'It was one of those families where every Tom, Dick and Harry was a relative,' he'd told Eileen.

Unfortunately, one of the reporters had removed the family album from the mother's flat, so the police hadn't seen a photo of Uncle Jim – a registered sex offender on the patch – or realized his connection with the missing girl.

He'd tried to have sex with the child but failed, and Sparkes believed he would have killed her as the detectives ran round in circles, sometimes only yards from her prison, if another member of the extended family hadn't got drunk and rung in with his name. Laura escaped with bruising to her body and mind. He could still see her eyes as he opened the door to the cupboard. Terror – no other word for it. Terror that he was going to be like Uncle Jim. He'd called a female detective forward to hold Laura in her arms.

Safe at last. Everyone had tears in their eyes except Laura. She looked numb.

He'd always thought he'd let her down somehow. Should've found the link earlier. Should've asked different questions. Should've found her quicker. His boss and the press had treated her discovery like a triumph, but he couldn't celebrate. Not after he'd seen those eyes.

Wonder where she is now? he thought. Wonder where Uncle Jim is now?

Manor Road was filled with reporters, neighbours and police officers, all interviewing each other in a verbal orgy.

Sparkes pushed his way through the knot of people at the gate of Number 44a, nodding at the journalists he recognized.

'Bob,' a woman's voice called. 'Hi. Any news? Any leads?' Kate Waters pushed forward and smiled mock-wearily. He'd last seen her during a grisly murder in the New Forest and they had enjoyed a couple of drinks and a gossip in the weeks it took to nail the husband.

They went way back, bumping into each other every so often on different cases and picking up where they'd left off. Not really a friendship, he thought. It was definitely all about work, but Kate was all right. Last time, she'd held on to a line in the story she'd stumbled on until he was ready for the information to come out. He owed her one.

'Hello, Kate. Just got here, but maybe I'll have something to say later,' he said, ducking past the uniform guarding the house.

There was a smell of cats and cigarettes in the front room. Dawn Elliott was huddled on the sofa, her trembling fingers clutching a mobile phone and a doll. Her blonde hair was tethered off her face in a half-hearted ponytail, making her look even younger than she was. She looked up at the tall, serious-looking man in the doorway, her face collapsing.

'Have you found her?' she managed.

'Ms Elliott, I'm Detective Inspector Bob Sparkes. I'm here to help find Bella and I want you to help me.'

Dawn looked at him. 'But I've told the police everything. What's the good of asking the same questions over and over? Just find her! Find my baby!' she shouted hoarsely.

He nodded and sat down beside her. 'Come on, Dawn, let's go through it together,' he said gently. 'There may be something new you remember.'

So she told him her tale, dry sobs choking her words. Bella was Dawn Elliott's only child, the result of a doomed relationship with a married man she'd met at a nightclub; a sweet little girl who loved watching Disney videos and dancing. Dawn didn't mix much with the neighbours – 'They look down their noses at me – I'm a single mum on benefits – they think I'm a scrounger,' she told Bob Sparkes.

But as they talked, his team and scores of volunteers from the community, many still in their work clothes, were searching back gardens, dustbins, hedges, attics, basements, sheds, cars, kennels and compost heaps all over the estate. The light was beginning to fade outside and a voice suddenly cried out, 'Bella! Bella! Where are you, lovey?' Dawn Elliott jumped to her feet to look out of the window.

'Dawn, come and sit down,' Sparkes said. 'I want to ask if Bella has misbehaved today?'

She shook her head.

'Have you been cross with her about anything?' he continued. 'Little ones can be a bit of a trial, can't they? Did you have to smack her or anything?'

The intent behind the questions slowly dawned on the young woman and she shrieked her innocence.

'No, of course not. I never smack her. Well, not very often. Only when she acts up sometimes. I haven't hurt her. Someone's taken her . . .'

Sparkes patted her hand and asked the family liaison officer to make another cup of tea.

A young constable put his head round the sitting-room door and gestured to his senior officer that he needed a word.

'Someone saw a bloke wandering about the area earlier this afternoon,' he told Sparkes. 'A neighbour saw him. Didn't recognize him.'

'Description?'

'A bloke on his own, he said. Long hair, looked rough. The neighbour said he was looking in the cars.'

Sparkes fished his phone out of his pocket and called his sergeant. 'Looks like a live one,' he said. 'No sign of the child. We've got a description of a suspicious character walking down the road – details on their way. Get it out there to the team. I'm going to talk to the witness.

'And let's knock on the door of every known sex offender in the area,' he added, his gut churning at the thought of the child in the clutches of any of the twenty-two registered sex offenders living on the Westland council estate.

Hampshire Police Force had about three hundred offenders on its patch, a shifting population of flashers, voyeurs, doggers, paedophiles and rapists who disguised themselves as friendly neighbours in unsuspecting communities.

Across the road, at the window of his neat bungalow, Stan Spencer was waiting for the senior detective. Sparkes had been told he'd started an ad hoc Neighbourhood Watch a few years back when the spot in which he felt he was entitled to park his Volvo kept being taken by commuters. Retirement held few activities for him and his wife Susan, apparently, and he relished the power a clipboard and nightly patrol gave him.

Sparkes shook his hand and they sat together at the dining-room table.

The neighbour referred to his notes – 'These are contemporaneous, Inspector,' he said and Sparkes suppressed a smile. 'I was watching out for Susan coming back from the shops after lunch and I saw a man walking down our side of the road. He looked a rough sort – scruffy, you know – and I was worried he was going to break into one of the neighbours' vehicles or something.

You have to be so careful. He was walking past Peter Tredwell's van.'

Sparkes raised his eyebrows.

'Sorry, Inspector. Mr Tredwell is a plumber who lives down the road and has had his van broken into several times. I stopped the last one. So I went outside to keep watch on the man's activities, but he was quite far down the road. Unfortunately, I only saw the back of him. Long dirty hair, jeans and one of those black anorak things they wear. Then my phone rang indoors and by the time I came back out, he'd gone.'

Mr Spencer looked very pleased with himself as Sparkes noted it all down.

'Did you see Bella when you went down your path?'

Spencer hesitated, but shook his head. 'I didn't. I haven't seen her for a few days. Lovely little thing.'

Five minutes later, Sparkes perched on a chair in Dawn Elliott's hallway and scribbled a press statement before going back to her sofa.

'Have you got any news?' she asked.

'Nothing new at the moment, but I'm going to tell the media that we need their help to find her. And—'

'And what?' Dawn said.

'And that we want to trace anyone who was in the area this afternoon. People who might have been driving or walking down Manor Road. Did you see a man walking down the road this afternoon, Dawn?' he asked. 'Mr Spencer across the road says he saw a man with long hair, in a dark coat; someone he hadn't seen before. It might be nothing . . .'

She shook her head, tears sliding down her face. 'Was it him that took her?' she said. 'Was it him who took my baby?'

Chapter 6

Wednesday, 9 June 2010

The Widow

MORE FEET ON the gravel. This time Kate's phone rings twice and stops. Must be some sort of signal because she immediately opens the front door and lets in a man with a big bag over his shoulder.

'This is Mick,' she says to me. 'My photographer.'

Mick grins at me and sticks out his hand. 'Hello, Mrs Taylor,' he says. He's come to pick us up and take us to a hotel – 'Somewhere nice and quiet,' he says and I begin to protest. Everything's moving so fast.

'Wait a minute,' I say. But no one is listening.

Kate and Mick are discussing getting past the reporters who've gathered at the gate. The man from the telly must've told people I had someone in the house and they're taking turns in knocking on the door and opening the letterbox to shout to me. It's awful, like a nightmare. Like it was at the beginning.

Then they were shouting at Glen, accusing him of all sorts.

'What've you done, Mr Taylor?' one shouted.

'Have you got blood on your hands, you pervert?' the man from the *Sun* said as Glen took the bin out. Right in front of people walking by. Glen said one of them spat on the pavement.

He was shaking when he came in.

My poor Glen. But he had me to help him then – I would stroke his hand and tell him to pay no attention. But there's just me now and I don't know if I can cope on my own.

A voice is yelling horrible things through the door: 'I know you're there, Mrs Taylor. Are you being paid to talk? What do you think people will say if you take this blood money?'

I feel like I've been hit. Kate turns and strokes my hand and tells me to ignore it, that she can make it all go away.

I want to trust her but it's hard to think straight. What does making it all go away mean? Hiding has been the only way to deal with it, according to Glen.

'We have to wait it out,' he would say.

But Kate's way is to go at it head on. Stand up and say my piece to shut them up. I would like to shut them up but it means being in the spotlight. The thought is so terrifying I can't move.

'Come on, Jean,' Kate says, finally noticing me still sitting in the chair. 'We can do this together. One step at a time. It'll all be over in five minutes and then no one will be able to find you.'

Apart from her, of course.

I can't face more abuse from those animals outside, so I obediently start to get my things together. I pick up my handbag and stuff some knickers into it from the tumble drier in the kitchen. Upstairs to get my toothbrush. Where are my keys?

'Just the essentials,' Kate says. She will buy me anything I need when we get there. 'Get where?' I want to ask, but Kate has turned away again. She's busy on her mobile, talking to 'the office'.

She has a different voice when she talks to the office. Tense. A bit breathless, like she's just walked upstairs.

'OK, Terry,' she says. 'No, Jean is with us . . . I'll give you a call later.' She doesn't want to talk in front of me. I wonder what the office wants to know. How much money she's promised? What will I look like in the pictures?

I bet she wanted to say, 'She's a bit of a mess but we can make her look presentable.' I feel panicky and go to say I've changed my mind but everything's moving too fast.

She says she's going to distract 'them'. She'll go out of the front door and pretend to get her car ready for us while Mick and I slip down the garden and over the fence at the back. I can't really believe I'm doing this. I start to say 'Hang on' again, but Kate is pushing me towards the back door.

We wait while she goes out. The noise is suddenly deafening. Like a flock of birds taking off by my front door.

'Snappers,' Mick says. I guess he means photographers. Then he throws his jacket over my head, grabs my hand and pulls me along behind him out of the back door into the garden. I can't see much because of the jacket and I've got stupid shoes on. My feet are sliding out of them but I try to run. This is ridiculous. The jacket keeps slipping off. Oh God, there's Lisa next door, looking out of her top window, mouth open. I wave my hand limply. God knows why. We haven't spoken for ages.

At the back fence, Mick helps me over. It's not high, really. More for show than security. I've got trousers on but it's still a bit of a struggle. He's parked his car round the corner, he says, and we creep slowly to the end of the alley at the back of the houses, in case one of the reporters is there. I suddenly want to cry. I'm about to get into a car with people I don't know and head off to God knows where. It's probably the craziest thing I've ever done.

Glen would've had a fit. Even before all the police stuff, he liked to keep things private. We've lived in this house for years – all our married life – but, as the neighbours were only too glad to tell the press, we kept ourselves to ourselves. It's what neighbours always say, isn't it, when dead bodies or mistreated children are found next door? But in our case, it was true. One of them – it could've been Mrs Grange opposite – described Glen to a reporter as having 'evil eyes'. He had nice eyes, actually. Blue with longish lashes. Little-boy eyes. His eyes could turn me over inside.

Anyway, he used to say to me, 'Nobody's business but ours, Jeanie.' That was why it was so hard when our business became everyone else's.

Mick the photographer's van is filthy. You can't see the floor for burger boxes, crisp packets and old newspapers. There's an electric razor plugged into the lighter thing and a big bottle of coke rolling around in the foot well.

'Sorry about the mess,' he says. 'I practically live in this van.'

Anyway, I'm not getting in the front. Mick takes me round the back and opens the doors. 'In here,' he says, grasping my arm and guiding me in. He puts his hand on my head and ducks me down so I don't bang myself. 'Keep down when we drive off and I'll give you the all-clear.'

'But—' I start to say, but he's slammed the doors and I'm sitting in semi-darkness among camera gear and dustbin bags.

———

Chapter 7

Thursday, 5 October 2006

The Detective

BOB SPARKES YAWNED loudly, stretching his arms above his head and arching his aching back in his office chair. He tried not to look at the clock on the desk but it winked at him until he focused. It was 2 a.m. Day three of the hunt for Bella over and they were getting nowhere.

Dozens of calls about long-haired, scruffy men and other leads were being checked in an ever-widening circle from the locus, but it was meticulous, slow work.

He tried not to think about what was happening to Bella Elliott – or, if he was honest, what had already happened. He had to find her.

'Where are you, Bella?' he asked the photo on his desk. The child's face was everywhere he looked – the incident room had a dozen photographs of her, smiling down at the deskbound detectives like a small religious icon giving a blessing to their work. The papers were full of pictures of 'Baby Bella'.

Sparkes ran his hand over his head, registering the growing bald patch. 'Come on, think!' he told himself, leaning into the computer screen. He read once more through the statements and reports from the trawl of the local sex offenders, searching for the tiniest weakness in their individual stories, but he could see no real leads.

He scanned through the profiles one last time: pathetic creatures, most of them. Solitary blokes with body odour and bad teeth, living in a fantasy online universe and occasionally straying into the real world to try their luck.

Then there were the persistent offenders. His officers had gone to Paul Silver's house – he'd abused his kids for years and done time for it – but his wife – *his third?* he wondered. *Or is it still Diane?* – confirmed wearily that her old man was inside, doing five years for burglary. Diversifying, apparently, Bob Sparkes had said to his sergeant.

Naturally, there'd been sightings of Bella reported all over the country in the first forty-eight hours. Officers had rushed off to check and some calls had got his heart racing.

A woman from just outside Newark had rung to say a new neighbour had been playing in the garden with a child. 'She's a little blonde girl. I've never seen a child in the garden before. I thought she didn't have kids,' she said. Sparkes sent the local force round immediately and waited at his desk for the phone to ring.

'It's the neighbour's niece, visiting from Scotland,' the local DI had told him, as disappointed as he was. 'Sorry. Maybe next time.'

Maybe. His problem was that most of the calls to the incident room were always going to be from chancers and attention-seekers, desperate to be part of the drama.

The bottom line was that the last sighting of Bella by anyone other than Dawn was at the newsagent's shop down the road. The owner, a mouthy grandmother, remembered mother and child coming into the shop around eleven thirty. They were regulars. Dawn went in most days to buy cigarettes and this visit, Bella's last, was recorded in the grainy stop-start images of the shop's cheap security camera.

Here, little Bella holding her mother's hand at the counter; cut to Bella, face blurred and indistinct as if she were already disappearing, with a paper bag in her hand; cut to shop door closing behind her.

Dawn's mum had phoned the house after lunch – 2.17 according to her phone records – and told the police she'd heard her grand-daughter shouting along to 'Bob the Builder' in the background and had asked to speak to her. Dawn had called Bella but apparently she had run off to fetch a toy.

The timeline of the next sixty-eight minutes was Dawn's. It was vague, punctuated by her household chores. The detectives had got her to re-enact the cooking, washing up and folding of Bella's clothes from the tumble drier to try and get a sense of the minutes that passed after Dawn said she saw Bella wander into the garden to play, just after three o'clock.

Margaret Emerson, who lived next door, had gone to fetch something from her car at 3.25 p.m. and was sure the front garden was empty then. 'Bella always shouted "Peepo" to me. It was a bit of a game for her, poor little thing. She loved attention. Her mum wasn't always interested in what she was doing,' Mrs Emerson said carefully. 'Bella used to play on her own a lot, carting her dolly round and chasing Timmy, the cat. You know what kids get up to.'

'Did Bella cry a lot?' Sparkes had asked.

The question had given Mrs Emerson pause for thought, but then she'd shaken her head and said briskly, 'No, she was a happy little thing.'

The family doctor and health visitor agreed. 'Lovely child . . . little poppet,' they chorused. 'Mum struggled a bit on her own – it's hard bringing up a child alone, isn't it?' the doctor said and Sparkes nodded as if he understood. All of this was logged in the now bulging files of evidence and statements, proof of the effort his blokes were making, but he knew it was all surface chatter. They were making no progress.

The long-haired man was the key, he concluded, switching off his computer and carefully stacking the files on his desk before heading for the door and five hours' sleep.

'Maybe tomorrow we'll find her,' he whispered to his sleeping wife when he got home.

*

A week later, with no news, Kate Waters was on the phone.

'Hi Bob, the editor has decided to offer a reward for any information that leads to Bella being found. He's putting up twenty grand. Not too shabby.'

Sparkes groaned inwardly. 'Bloody rewards,' he cursed to Matthews later. 'The papers get all the publicity and we'll get every nutter and conman in the country on the phone.'

'That's very generous, Kate,' he said. 'But do you think this is the right moment? We're working on a number . . .'

'It's going on the front page tomorrow, Bob,' she interrupted. 'Look, I know the police usually hate the idea of a reward, but people who see or hear things and are worried about ringing the police will see twenty grand and pick up the phone.'

He sighed. 'I'll go and tell Dawn,' he said. 'I need to prepare her.'

'Right,' Kate said. 'Look, what are the chances of getting a sit-down chat with Dawn, Bob? The poor woman could barely speak at the press conference – this would be a proper chance for her to talk about Bella. I'll be very gentle with her. What do you think?'

He thought he wished he hadn't answered her call. He liked Kate – and there weren't many reporters he could say that about – but he knew she was like a terrier with a bone when she was after something. He knew she wouldn't let up until she got what she wanted, but he wasn't sure he and Dawn were ready for this sort of grilling.

Dawn was still a largely unknown quantity; she was an emotional mess, drugged against her terror and unable to focus on anything for more than thirty seconds. Bob Sparkes had spent hours with her and he felt he'd only scratched the surface. Could he really let Kate Waters loose on her?

'It might help her to talk to someone who isn't a police officer, Bob. Might help her remember something . . .'

'I'll ask her, Kate, but I'm not sure she's up to it. She's on tranquillizers and sleeping pills and is finding it hard to concentrate on anything.'

'Brilliant. Thanks Bob.' He could hear the smile in the reporter's voice.

'Hold on, it's not a done deal yet. Let me talk to her this morning and I'll give you a ring back.'

When he arrived, he found Dawn sitting in exactly the same spot as when he had first met her, on the sofa that had become her ark, among Bella's toys, crushed empty cigarette packs and pages torn from newspapers, cards from well-wishers and letters on lined notepaper from the mad and angry.

'Have you been to bed, love?' he asked her.

Sue Blackman, a young woman in uniform acting as family liaison officer, shook her head silently and raised her eyebrows.

'Can't sleep,' Dawn said. 'Need to be awake for when she comes home.'

Sparkes took PC Blackman into the hall. 'She needs some rest or she's going to end up in hospital,' he hissed.

'I know, Sir. She's dozing on the sofa during the day but she hates it when it gets dark. She says Bella is afraid of the dark.'

Chapter 8

Wednesday, 11 October 2006

The Reporter

KATE WATERS ARRIVED AT the house at lunchtime with a photographer and a bunch of ostentatious supermarket lilies. She'd parked down the road, away from the pack, so she could get out of the car without attracting attention. She rang Bob Sparkes to let him know she was there and swept past the journalists sitting outside the house in their cars, Big Macs in their fists. By the time they'd leapt from their vehicles, she was inside. She heard a couple of them swearing loudly, warning each other that they were about to be shafted, and tried not to grin.

As Bob Sparkes led the way, Kate took it all in, the shambles and stasis created by grief: in the hall, Bella's blue anorak with a fur-lined hood and teddy-bear backpack hanging on the bannister; her tiny, shiny red wellies by the door.

'Get a photo of those, Mick,' she whispered to the photographer following her as they made their way into the front room. There were toys and baby photos everywhere; the scene took Kate straight back to her own early days of motherhood, struggling against the tide of chaos. She had sat and cried the day she brought Jake home from the hospital, lost in the postnatal hormonal wash and sudden sense of responsibility. She remembered she'd asked the nurse if she could pick him up, the morning after he was born, as if he belonged to the hospital.

The mother looked up, her young face creased and made old by weeping, and Kate smiled and took her hand. She was going to shake it, but simply squeezed it instead.

'Hello, Dawn,' she said. 'Thank you so much for agreeing to talk to me. I know how hard it must be for you, but we hope it will help the police find Bella.'

Dawn nodded as if in slow motion.

Bloody hell, Bob wasn't kidding, Kate thought.

She picked up a red Teletubby doll from the sofa – 'Is this Po? My boys preferred Power Rangers,' she said.

Dawn looked at her, interested. 'Bella loves Po,' she said. 'She likes blowing bubbles, chases after them, trying to catch them.'

Kate had noticed a photo on a table of the toddler doing exactly that and got up to bring it to Dawn. 'Here she is,' she said and Dawn took the frame in her hands. 'She's beautiful,' Kate said. 'Full of mischief, I bet.'

Dawn smiled gratefully. The two women had found their common ground – motherhood – and Dawn started to talk about her baby.

First time she's been able to talk about Bella as a child, not a crime victim, Bob Sparkes thought.

'She's good, Kate. You have to give her that. She can get inside your head quicker than a lot of my coppers,' he had told his wife later. Eileen had shrugged and returned to the *Telegraph* crossword. Police work took place on a different planet, as far as she was concerned.

Kate fetched more photos and toys to keep the conversation flowing, letting Dawn tell her story about each item with barely a question needed. She used a discreet tape recorder, slipped quickly on to the cushion between them, to capture every word. Notebooks were a bad idea in a situation like this – it would be too much like a police interview. She just wanted Dawn to talk. She wanted to hear about the ordinary pleasures and everyday struggles of being a mum. Of getting Bella ready for nursery, bathtime games, the child's delight at choosing her new wellies.

'She loves animals. We went to the zoo once and she wanted to stay watching the monkeys. She laughed and laughed,' Dawn told her, taking temporary shelter in memories of a previous life.

The glimpses of Bella and Dawn would bring the reader straight into the nightmare the young mother was enduring, Kate knew, writing the intro in her head.

A pair of tiny red wellington boots stand in Dawn Elliott's hallway. Her daughter Bella chose them two weeks ago and has yet to wear them . . .

This was what the public wanted to read so they could shiver in their dressing gowns over tea and toast and say to their spouse, 'This could have been us.'

And the editor would love it. 'Perfect womb trembler,' he'd say, clearing the front page and a spread inside the paper for her story.

After twenty minutes, Dawn began to tire. The drugs were starting to wear off and the terror crept back into the room. Kate glanced at Mick and he stood up with his camera and said gently, 'Let's take a photo of you, Dawn, with that lovely picture of Bella blowing bubbles.'

She complied, like a child herself.

'I'll never forgive myself,' she whispered as Mick's shutter clicked. 'I shouldn't have let her go outside. But I was just trying to get her tea ready. She was only out of sight for a minute. I'd do anything to turn the clock back.'

And then she cried; dry sobs shook her frame as Kate held her hand tightly and the rest of the world came back into focus around the sofa.

Kate always marvelled at the power of interview. 'When you're talking to real people – people without an ego or something to sell – it can be complete exposure of one person to another, an intense intimacy that excludes everyone and everything else,' she'd told someone once. Who was it? Must've been someone she was trying to impress, but she remembered every line of every interview that touched her like this.

'You've been so brave, Dawn,' she said, squeezing her hand

again. 'Thank you very much for talking to me and giving me so much time. I'll contact Detective Inspector Sparkes to let him know when the story will appear. And I'll leave my card so you can get in touch whenever you want.'

Kate tidied up her things quickly, sliding the recorder into her bag and relinquishing her place beside Dawn to the family liaison officer.

Sparkes took her and Mick to the door.

'That was great. Thanks, Bob,' she said in his ear. 'I'll call you later when I've written it.' He nodded as she brushed past and out of the house to face her furious colleagues.

In the car, she sat for a moment, running through the quotes in her head and trying to assemble the story. The intensity of the encounter had left her drained and, if she was honest, a little shaky. She wished she still smoked, but rang Steve's number instead. It went straight to answerphone – he'd be on the wards – but she left a message. 'It went really well,' she told him. 'Poor, poor girl. She'll never get over this. I've taken a lasagne out of the freezer for tonight. Speak to you later.'

She could hear the catch in her voice as it recorded.

'For goodness' sake, pull yourself together, Kate, it's work,' she told herself as she started the engine and drove off to find a quiet car park and start writing. 'Must be getting old and feeble.'

Dawn Elliott began ringing Kate Waters the next day, the day the story appeared. She rang from her mobile, standing in the bathroom away from the ever-attentive Sue Blackman. She wasn't sure why she was making it a secret, but she needed something just for herself. Her whole life was being unpicked by the police and she wanted to have something normal. Just a chat.

Kate was thrilled – a direct line to the mother was the prize she'd allowed herself to hope for but hadn't taken for granted and she cultivated it carefully. There were to be no direct questions about the investigation, no prying, no pressing. No scaring her off. Instead, she talked to Dawn as if she were a friend, sharing details of her own life – her boys, traffic jams, new clothes and celebrity gossip. And Dawn responded as Kate knew she would eventually, confiding her fears and the latest police leads.

'They've had a call from abroad. Near Malaga? Someone on holiday there has seen a little girl in a park they think is Bella,' she told Kate. 'Do you think she could be there?'

Kate murmured reassurance while noting everything down and texting the Crime correspondent, a hard-drinking hack who'd had a couple of bad misses lately. He was grateful to be included in Kate's exclusive tips, putting a call through to a contact in the incident room and telling the news editor to book a flight to Spain, pronto.

Not Bella. But the paper got an emotional interview with holidaymakers and a perfect excuse for another spread of photographs.

'Well worth a punt,' the editor had said to the news desk, adding as he passed Kate's chair, 'Well done, Kate. You're doing a great job on this.'

She was on the inside, but she had to be careful. If Bob Sparkes found out about the secret phone calls, it would not be pretty.

She liked Sparkes. They'd helped each other out on a couple of the cases he'd run – he'd given her the odd bit of information to make her story stand out from the rest of the pack's, and she'd tipped him off when she got something new that might be of interest. It was a sort of friendship, she thought, useful for both of them. And they got on well. But there was nothing deeper. She almost blushed when she remembered she'd developed a bit of a schoolgirl crush on him when they had first met, back in the nineties. She'd been drawn to his quietness and brown eyes and had been flattered when he'd singled her out for a drink a couple of times.

The Crime man at her last paper had teased her about her cosy relationship with Sparkes, but they both knew the detective was not a swordsman like some of his colleagues. He was renowned for never straying and Kate didn't have the time or the inclination for extra-maritals.

'He's a straight-up-and-down copper,' her colleague had said. 'One of the last.'

Kate knew she risked burning Sparkes as a contact by carrying on with Dawn behind the detective's back, but having the inside edge on the story was worth it. This could be her story of a lifetime.

She rehearsed her arguments as she drove into work: 'It's a free country and Dawn can talk to whoever she wants, Bob . . . I can't stop her phoning me . . . I'm not phoning her . . . I don't ask her any questions about the investigation. She just tells me stuff.' She knew it wouldn't wash with Sparkes. He'd got her in there in the first place.

'Oh well, all's fair,' she told herself irritably, making a silent promise to tell Bob anything that might help the police. She crossed her fingers at the same time.

It didn't take long for the phone call from Sparkes to come.

Her phone rang and she picked it up and headed for the privacy of the corridor.

'Hello, Bob. How are you?'

The detective was stressed and told her so. Dawn's latest bathroom conversation with her favourite reporter had been overheard by the family liaison officer and Sparkes was disappointed in Kate. Somehow, that was worse than if he'd been furious.

'Hold on, Bob. Dawn Elliott is a grown woman – she can talk to whoever she wants. She rang me.'

'I bet. Kate, this was not the deal. I got you in there for the first interview and you've been sneaking around behind my back. It could affect the investigation – you do understand that?'

'Look, Bob, she rings me for a chat that isn't about the investigation. She needs some time, even a couple of minutes, to escape.'

'And you need stories. Don't play the social worker with me, Kate. I know you better than that.'

She felt ashamed. He did know her better than that.

'I'm sorry you're upset, Bob. Why don't I come down and meet you for a drink and we can talk things through?'

'Too busy at the moment, but maybe next week. And Kate . . .'

'Yes, yes. No doubt you've told her not to call me, but I'm not ignoring her if she does.'

'I see. You'll have to do what you have to do, Kate. I hope Dawn will see sense, then. Someone has to act like a responsible adult.'

'Bob, I'm doing my job and you're doing yours. I'm not hurting the investigation, I'm keeping it alive in the paper.'

'I hope you're right, Kate. Got to go.'

Kate leaned against the wall, having a completely different argument with Bob Sparkes in her head. In this version, she ended up on the higher moral ground and Bob was grovelling to her.

Bob would come round when he calmed down, she told herself, and texted Dawn to apologize for any trouble caused.

She got a message back immediately that ended 'Speak later.' They were still on. She grinned at the screen and decided to celebrate with a double espresso and muffin.

'To life's little triumphs,' she said as she raised the cardboard cup in the canteen. She'd drive down to Southampton tomorrow and meet Dawn for a sandwich in the shopping centre.

Chapter 9

Wednesday, 9 June 2010

The Widow

KATE GETS IN MICK'S VAN a couple of miles further on, in a super-market car park. She laughs and says 'the pack' had rushed up the path to see if I was in the house when she drove off alone. 'Idiots,' she says. 'Fancy falling for that.'

She has twisted round in the front seat so I can see her face. 'Are you all right, Jean?' she says. Her voice has changed back to caring and gentle. I'm not fooled. She doesn't care about me. She just wants the story. I nod and keep quiet.

As we drive, she and Mick chat about 'the office'. Seems her boss is a bit of a bully who shouts and swears at people.

'He uses the C word so often, they call morning news conference the Vagina Monologue,' she tells me, and they both start laughing. I don't know what a Vagina Monologue is but I don't let on.

It's like she and Mick live in another world. Kate is telling him about how the news editor – the Terry she was talking to on the phone – is very happy. Happy that she has got the widow, I suppose.

'He'll be in and out of the editor's office all day, poor sod. Still, it'll stop him bitching at the other reporters. He's a funny bloke – get him in the pub and he's the life and soul. But in the office, he

55

sits at his desk twelve hours a day, staring at his computer screen. He only looks up to give someone a bollocking. He's like one of the living dead.'

Mick laughs.

I lie down on the sleeping bag. It's a bit grubby but it doesn't smell too bad, so I doze and their voices fade into a background hum. When I wake up, we've arrived.

The hotel is big and expensive. The sort of place that has those enormous flowers that practically fill the lobby and real apples on the reception desk. I never know if those flowers are real, but the apples are. You can eat them if you want, the apples.

Kate's in charge.

'Hi, you have three rooms for us under the name of Murray,' she informs the receptionist, who smiles and looks at her screen. 'We only booked a couple of hours ago,' Kate says impatiently.

'Here you are,' the receptionist says finally. Mick must be the Murray. He gives his credit card to the lady and she looks at me.

I suddenly realize what I must look like. A sight. My hair's all over the place after having the jacket over my head and sleeping in the van, and I was hardly dressed to go to the shops, let alone a posh hotel. I stand there, in my old trousers and T-shirt, looking at my feet in my cheap flip-flops while all the form-filling goes on. They put me down as Elizabeth Turner and I look at Kate.

She just smiles and whispers, 'This way, no one will find you. They'll be looking for us.' I wonder who Elizabeth Turner really is and what she's doing this afternoon. I bet she's going through the racks at TK Maxx, not hiding from the press.

'Any bags?' the woman asks and Kate says they're in the car and we'll get them out later. In the lift, I look at her and raise my eyebrows. She smiles back. We don't speak because there's a porter with us. Daft really because there's nothing to carry, but he wants to show us our rooms. And get a tip, I suppose. Room 142 is mine, next door to Kate in 144. The porter makes a big show of opening the door and ushering me in. I stand and look. It's lovely. Huge and bright with a chandelier. There's a sofa and a coffee table and lamps and more apples. They must have some sort of deal with Sainsbury's or somewhere to have so much fruit around.

'Is this all right?' Kate asks.

'Oh yes,' I say and sit down on the sofa to look at it all again.

Our honeymoon hotel wasn't as posh as this. It was a family-run place in Spain. Still that was lovely, too. We had such a laugh. When we got there, I still had bits of confetti in my hair and the staff made a big fuss of us. There was a bottle of champagne waiting – Spanish stuff, which was a bit sickly – and the waitresses kept coming up and kissing us.

We spent our days lying by the pool, looking at each other. Loving each other. Such a long time ago.

Kate says there's a pool here. And a spa. I haven't got a swimsuit – or anything, really – but she asks my size and sets off to get me 'some things'.

'The paper will pay,' she says.

She books me a massage for while she's out.

'To relax you,' she says. 'It'll be lovely. They use essential oils – jasmine, lavender, that sort of thing – and you can go to sleep on the table. You need a bit of pampering, Jean.'

I'm not sure, but I go along with it. I haven't asked how long they're keeping me here. The subject hasn't come up and they seem to be treating it like a weekend break.

An hour later, I'm lying on the bed in a hotel dressing gown, practically floating I feel so relaxed. Glen would've said I smelled like a 'tart's boudoir' but I love it. I smell expensive. Then Kate knocks and I'm back where I started. Back to reality.

She comes through the door with loads of carrier bags.

'Here you go, Jean,' she says. 'Try these on to see if they fit.'

Funny how she keeps using my name. Like a nurse. Or a conman.

She has chosen lovely things. A pale blue cashmere jumper I could never have afforded, a smart white shirt, a floaty skirt and a pair of tailored grey trousers, knickers, shoes, a swimsuit, luxury bubble bath, and a beautiful long nightie. I unpack it all while she watches.

'I love that colour, don't you, Jean?' she says, picking up the jumper. 'Duck-egg blue.'

She knows I love it too, but I try not to show too much.

'Thank you,' I say. 'I really don't need all this. I'm only here overnight. Perhaps you can take some of it back.'

She doesn't reply, just gathers up the empty bags and smiles.

It's well past lunchtime and they decide to have something to eat in Kate's room. All I want is a sandwich but Mick orders steak and a bottle of wine. I look afterwards and the wine was thirty-two pounds. You could get eight bottles of Chardonnay for that at the supermarket. He said it was 'effing delicious'. He uses the F word a lot but Kate doesn't seem to notice. Her attention is all on me.

When the plates are put outside the door to be collected, Mick goes off to his room to sort out his cameras and Kate settles back in an armchair and starts chatting. Just normal chat, the sort of thing I would say to a client while I was shampooing her hair. But I know it can't last.

'You must have been under a terrible strain since Glen's death,' she begins.

I nod and look strained. I can't tell her I haven't. The truth is that the relief has been wonderful.

'How have you coped, Jean?'

'It's been terrible,' I say with a catch in my voice and switch back to being Jeanie, the woman I used to be when I first got married.

Jeanie saved me. She bumbled on with her life, cooking tea, washing customers' hair, sweeping the floor and making the beds. She knew that Glen was the victim of a police plot. She stood by the man she married. The man she had chosen.

At first, Jeanie only reappeared when family or the police asked questions, but as more bad stuff began to leak under the door, Jeanie moved back into the house so Glen and I could carry on our life together.

'It was a terrible shock,' I tell Kate. 'He fell under the bus right there, in front of me. I didn't even have time to call out. He was gone. Then all these people came running up and kind of took over. I was too shocked to move and they took me to hospital to make sure I was all right. Everyone was so kind.'

Until they found out who he was.

You see, the police said Glen had taken Bella.

When they said her name, when they came to our house, all I could think of was her picture, that little face, those little round glasses and the plaster over one eye. She looked like a baby pirate. So sweet, I could've eaten her. No one had been able to talk about anything else for months – in the salon, in the shops, on the bus. Little Bella. She was playing in the garden outside her house in Southampton and someone just walked in and took her.

Course, I'd never have let a child of mine play outside on her own. She was only two and a half, for goodness' sake. Her mum should've taken better care of her. Bet she was sat watching Jeremy Kyle or some rubbish like that. It's always people like that that these things happen to, Glen says. Careless people.

And they said it was Glen who took her. And killed her. I couldn't breathe when they said it – the police, I mean. They were the first. Others said it later.

We stood there in our front hall with our mouths open. Well, I say we. Glen sort of went blank. His face was blank. He didn't look like Glen any more.

The police were quiet when they came. No banging down the door or anything, like on the telly. They knocked, rat-tat-tat-a-tat-a-tat. Glen had only just come in from cleaning the car. He opened the door and I put my head out of the kitchen to see who it was. It was two blokes, asking to come in. One looked like my geography teacher at school, Mr Harris. Same tweedy jacket.

'Mr Glen Taylor?' he asked, all quiet and calm.

'Yes,' Glen said, and asked if they were selling something. I couldn't hear properly at the beginning, but then they came in. They were policemen – Detective Inspector Bob Sparkes and his sergeant, they said.

'Mr Taylor, I'd like to talk to you about the disappearance of Bella Elliott,' DI Sparkes said. And I opened my mouth to say something, to make the policeman stop saying these things, but I couldn't. And Glen's face went blank.

He never looked at me once the whole time. Never put his arm round me or touched my hand. He said later he was in shock. He and the policemen carried on talking, but I can't remember hearing what they were saying. I watched their mouths moving but I couldn't take it in. What had Glen got to do with Bella? He wouldn't harm a hair on a child's head. He loves children.

Then they left, Glen and the policemen. Glen told me later that he said goodbye and told me not to worry, it was just a stupid mix-up he'd sort out. But I don't remember that. Other policemen stayed at the house to ask me questions, to root around in our lives, but through it all, going round and round in my brain, I kept thinking about his face and how for a second I didn't know him.

He told me later someone had said he'd been making a delivery near where Bella disappeared, but that didn't mean anything. Just coincidence, he said. There must've been hundreds of people in the area that day.

He'd been nowhere near the scene of the crime – his delivery was miles away, he said. But the police were going through everyone, to check if they had seen anything.

He'd started as a delivery driver after he got laid off by the bank. They were looking for redundancies, he told people, and he fancied a change. He'd always dreamed of having the chance to start his own business, be his own boss.

The night I discovered the real reason was a Wednesday. Aerobics for me and late supper for us. He shouted at me about why I was later than usual, horrible tight words spat out, angry and dirty. Words he never used normally. Everything was wrong. He was crowding the kitchen with his accusations, his anger. His eyes were dead, as if he didn't know me. I thought he was going to hit me. I watched his fists clench and unclench at his sides, frozen at the cooker, spatula in my hand.

My kitchen, my rules, we used to joke. But not that Wednesday. Wednesday's child is full of woe.

The row ended with a slammed door as he marched off to bed – to sleep in the spare room, cut off from me. I remember standing at the foot of the stairs, numb. What was this about? What had happened? I didn't want to think about what it meant for us.

'Stop it,' I told myself. 'It'll be all right. He must've had a bad day. Let him sleep it off.'

I started tidying, picking up his scarf and jacket from where he'd hung them on the bannister and putting them on the coat hooks by the door. I felt something stiff in one pocket, a letter. A white envelope with a see-through panel, with his name and our address showing. From the bank. The words were official and as stiff as the envelope: 'inquiry . . . unprofessional behaviour . . . inappropriate . . . termination, forthwith'. I was lost in the formal language but I knew this meant disgrace. The end of our dreams. Our future. Clutching the letter in my hand, I ran up the stairs. I marched into the spare room and flicked on the light. He must've heard me coming but pretended to be asleep until I heard myself screech, 'What is this about?'

He looked at me like I was nothing. 'I've been fired,' he said and rolled back over to pretend to sleep.

The next morning, Glen came into our bedroom with tea in my favourite cup. He looked like he'd hardly slept and said he was sorry. He sat down on the bed and said he was under a lot of pressure and it was all a misunderstanding at work and that he'd never got on with the boss. He said he'd been set up and blamed for something. Some mistake, he said. He'd done nothing wrong. His boss was jealous. Glen said he had big plans for his future, but that didn't matter if I wasn't beside him.

'You are the centre of my world, Jeanie,' he said and held me close, and I hugged him back and let go of my fear.

Mike, a friend he said he met on the internet, told him about the driving job – 'just while I work out what business I want to get into, Jeanie,' he said. It was cash in hand at first and then they took him on permanently. He stopped talking about being his own boss.

He had to wear a uniform, quite smart: pale-blue shirt with the company logo on the pocket and navy trousers. Glen didn't like wearing a uniform – 'It's demeaning, Jeanie, like being back at school' – but he got used to it and seemed happy enough. He'd go out in the morning and wave as he drove off to pick up the van. Off on his travels, he'd say.

I only went with him once. A special job for the boss on a Sunday just before Christmas one year. Must've been the Christmas before he was arrested. It was only down to Canterbury and I fancied a run out. We sat in total silence on the way down. I had a root through his glove box. Just stuff. Some sweets. I helped myself and offered one to Glen to cheer him up. He didn't want it and told me to put them back.

The van was lovely and clean. Spotless. I never normally saw it. It was kept at the depot and he took his car to pick it up in the morning. 'Nice van,' I said, but he just grunted.

'What's in the back?'

'Nothing,' he said and turned up the radio.

And he was right. I had a look when he was talking to the customer. The back was as clean as a whistle. Well, almost. There was a corner torn from a sweet packet poking out from under one edge of the mat. I got it out with my fingernail. It was a bit fuzzy and dusty but I put it in my coat pocket. To be tidy.

It all seems so long ago. Us going for a drive like normal people.

'Glen Taylor?' the nurse is saying to me, startling me out of my thoughts and frowning as she writes his name on a form. Trying to remember. I wait for the inevitable.

The penny drops.

'Glen Taylor? The one accused of taking that little girl, Bella?' she says quietly to one of the paramedics and I pretend not to hear.

When she turns back to me, her face is harder. 'I see,' she says and walks away. She must've made a phone call because half an hour later the press are there, hanging around Casualty trying to look like patients. I can spot them a mile off.

I keep my head down and refuse to speak to any of them. What sort of people are they, hounding a woman who's just seen her husband die?

The police are there, too. Because of the accident. They're not the ones we usually see. They're the local police, the Met, not the Hampshire officers. Just doing routine work, taking statements from the witnesses, from me, from the bus driver. He's here, too. Apparently he got a nasty knock to the head when he braked and says he didn't even see Glen step out.

He probably didn't, it was that fast.

Then DI Bob Sparkes shows up. I knew he'd turn up eventually, like a bad penny, but he must've driven like the wind to get here from Southampton so quickly. He's all sad face and condolences for me, but he's even sadder for himself. He certainly didn't want Glen dead. Him gone means that the case will never be closed. Poor Bob. He'll be stuck with that failure all his life.

He sits down beside me on a plastic chair and reaches for my hand. I'm so embarrassed I let him. He has never touched me before like this. Like he cares for me. He holds my hand and speaks in a soft, low voice. I know what he's saying but I don't hear it, if you know what I mean. He's asking me if I know what Glen did with Bella. He's saying it nicely, telling me I can let go of the secret now. Everything can be told. I was as much a victim as Bella was.

'I don't know anything about Bella, Bob. Neither did Glen,' I say and pull my hand away, pretending I need it to wipe away a tear. Later I'm sick in the hospital toilets. I clean myself up and sit on the loo with my forehead resting on the lovely cool tiles on the wall.

Chapter 10

Thursday, 12 October 2006

The Detective

DI BOB SPARKES was standing in the incident room scanning the boards for emerging patterns and links. He took off his glasses and narrowed his eyes in case a change of focus might reveal something.

There was a maelstrom of activity all around the Elliotts' garden, but, at the epicentre, Bella remained the missing piece.

All that information but no sign of her, he thought. She's here somewhere. We're missing something.

The Forensics team had dusted and swabbed every inch of the brick garden wall and painted metal gate; the garden had been the subject of a fingertip search by a line of police officers, making religious progress on their knees, and fibres from her clothes, golden hairs from her head, dismembered toy parts and discarded sweet wrappers had been preserved in plastic bags like holy relics. But of the abductor, nothing.

'I think the bastard must have reached over the wall and lifted her straight up and into his vehicle,' Sparkes said. 'It would only have taken seconds. She was there and then she wasn't.'

The team had found a half-sucked red sweet on Bella's side of the wall. 'Maybe it fell out of her mouth when he picked her up?' Sparkes said. 'Is it a Smartie?'

'I'm not exactly an expert on Smarties, Boss, but I'll get someone to check,' Sergeant Matthews said.

When it came back from Forensics, it had been identified as a Skittle. Bella's saliva was on the sweet, matched with the comforter she sucked at night.

'She never had Skittles,' Dawn said.

He gave her one to keep her quiet, Sparkes thought. How old-fashioned. He remembered his mum telling him as a boy, 'Never take sweets from a stranger.' That and something about men with puppies.

He was reviewing the list of evidence and his energy was dipping. It didn't look good. There were no CCTV cameras watching over the street – only good old Mr Spencer – and no images collected from the nearest camera sites so far of a scruffy man.

'Maybe he was just lucky,' Sparkes said.

'Luck of the devil, then.'

'Get on the phone, Matthews, and see when we can get on *Crimewatch*. Tell them it's urgent.'

The television reconstruction seemed to take for ever to organize, although it was only eight days. A Bella lookalike had to be found from a nursery school in another town because no parent living near the Westland estate would let their child take part.

'Can't blame them, really,' Sparkes told the exasperated director. 'They don't want to see their kid as a kidnap victim. Even a pretend one.'

They were waiting at the end of Manor Road for the film crew to set up, discussing what Sparkes would say in his appeal for information.

'It'll be live in the studio, Bob,' the director said, 'so make sure you have everything sorted in your head before you speak. You'll know what questions you're going to get.'

Sparkes was too distracted to take it all in. He had just been putting Dawn Elliott in a police car to her mum's as the actress playing her arrived.

'She looks like me,' she'd whispered to him. She hadn't been able to look at the child playing Bella. She had laid out a set of her daughter's clothes, a little headband and Bella's spare glasses on the sofa, stroking each item and saying her child's name. Sparkes had helped her up and she had walked, dry-eyed and holding his arm, to the car. She got in beside Sue Blackman and didn't look back.

The street was now quiet, deserted, as it must have been that day. Sparkes watched as the re-enactment took shape, the director gently coaching 'Bella' to chase a borrowed grey cat into the garden. Her mother stood just off camera, with emergency chocolate buttons in case bribes were needed, smiling at her little girl and trying not to cry.

Mrs Emerson volunteered to play her own small role, walking stiffly down her garden path, pretending to look for her little friend next door, and then responding to Dawn's cries for help. Across the road, Mr Spencer acted out spotting the actor in a long wig strolling past his house, his mimed puzzlement filmed through the bay window by a cameraman standing on Mrs Spencer's French marigolds.

The 'abduction' took only minutes but it was three hours before the director was satisfied and everyone crowded round the monitor in the film truck to watch the end product. No one spoke as they watched 'Bella' playing in the garden and only Mr Spencer stayed to mull over the events with the crew.

Afterwards, one of the older officers took Sparkes aside. 'Have you noticed that our Mr Spencer is always hanging around the investigation team and giving interviews to the reporters? Telling them he saw the man who took her. Bit of a glory-seeker, if you ask me.'

Sparkes smiled sympathetically. 'There's always one, isn't there? He's probably lonely and bored. I'll get Matthews to keep an eye on him.'

As expected, the broadcast, twenty-three days after Bella vanished, triggered hundreds of phone calls to the studio and incident room, the film igniting public emotion and a fresh outpouring of variations on 'My heart goes out to . . .' and 'Why, oh why?' messages on the show's website.

About a dozen callers claimed to have seen Bella, many of them sure they had spotted her in a café, on a bus, in a playground. Each call was acted upon immediately, but Sparkes' optimism began to fade as he took his turn answering the phones at the back of the studio.

The following week, a sudden buzz of voices from the incident room reached Sparkes as he walked down the corridor.

'Got a flasher in a kids' playground, Sir,' the duty officer told him. 'About twenty-five minutes from the Elliott house.'

'Who is he? Is he known to us?'

Lee Chambers was a middle-aged, divorced minicab driver who'd been questioned six months earlier for exposing himself to two female passengers. He'd claimed he was just having a quick pee and they'd caught a glimpse as he zipped himself up. Completely unintentional. The women didn't want to take it further, didn't want the attention, and the police sent him on his way.

Today, he'd been in bushes beside the swings and slides at Royal Park as children played near by.

'I was just having a quick pee,' he told the police officer called by a horrified mother.

'Do you normally have an erection while peeing, Sir? That must be inconvenient,' the officer said as he led him to a waiting car.

Chambers arrived at Southampton Central police station and was put in an interview room.

Peering through the toughened glass panel in the door, Sparkes saw a skinny man in tracksuit bottoms and a Southampton FC shirt, with long greasy hair in a ponytail.

'Scruffy, long hair,' Matthews said.

Did you take Bella? Sparkes thought automatically. Have you got her somewhere?

The suspect looked up expectantly as Sparkes and Matthews entered.

'This is all a mistake,' he said.

'If I had a quid . . .' Matthews muttered. 'Why don't you tell us all about it, then?' he said as the officers dragged their chairs closer to the table.

Chambers told his lies and they listened. Just a quick pee. Didn't choose a playground deliberately. Didn't see the children. Didn't talk to the children. Completely innocent mistake.

'Tell me, Mr Chambers, where were you on Monday, October the second?' Sparkes asked.

'God, I don't know. Working, probably. Monday is one of my regular days. The cab controller would know. Why d'you ask?'

The question hung in the air for a beat and then Chambers was all eyes. Sparkes almost expected an audible *ding*.

'That's when that little girl went missing, isn't it? You don't think I had anything to do with that? Oh God, you can't think that.'

They left him to stew for a bit while they went to join their colleagues already searching his address, a bedsit in a converted Victorian house in the city's rundown red-light area near the docks.

Leafing through the extreme porn magazines beside Chambers' bed, Matthews sighed. 'This is all about hating women, not wanting sex with kids. What've you got?'

Sparkes was silent. Photos of Dawn and Bella had been cut from newspapers and slipped into a clear plastic folder on the floor of the wardrobe.

The minicab controller was a bored-looking woman in her fifties, bundled up against the cold of her unheated office in a green cable-knit cardigan and fingerless mittens.

'Lee Chambers? What's he been up to? More of his accidental flashing?' She laughed and slurped a Red Bull. 'He's a nasty little man,' she said as she flicked through the records. 'Everyone thinks so, but he knows a friend of the boss.'

She was interrupted by the fizz of static and a voice rendered robotic by the tinny speakers, and gave some incomprehensible instructions back.

'Right, where were we?

'Monday, the second of October. Here we are. Lee was in Fareham early on – hospital run for a regular customer. All quiet until lunch, then he picked up a couple from the airport at Eastleigh to go to Portsmouth. Dropped about 14.00. Last job of the day.'

She printed out the details for them and turned back to the microphone as they left without saying goodbye.

'They call this firm Rapists' Cabs in the nightclubs,' Sergeant Matthews said. 'I've told my girls never to use them.'

The team was all over Chambers' life. His ex-wife was already waiting for a chat with Sparkes and Matthews, and his colleagues and landlord were being questioned.

Donna Chambers, hard-faced with thick, homemade highlights, hated her former husband, but she didn't think he would hurt a child. 'He's just a wanker who can't keep it in his trousers,' she said.

Neither of the detectives dared catch the other's eye. 'Bit of a Romeo, then?'

The list was long – almost impressive – as she detailed how Lee Chambers had worked his way through her friends, work colleagues, even her hairdresser.

'Every time he said it would never happen again,' the wronged wife said. 'He had a high sex drive, he said. Anyway, he was very bitter when I finally left him and threatened to come after any bloke I saw, but nothing came of it. All talk. The thing is he's a born liar. He can't tell the truth.'

'What about the indecent exposure? Is that a new thing?'

Mrs Chambers shrugged. 'Well, he didn't do it when we were married. Maybe he ran out of women who fell for his lines. Sounds desperate, doesn't it? Horrible thing to do, but he is a horrible man.'

The landlord knew little about him. Chambers paid his rent on time, made no noise and put out his rubbish. Perfect tenant. But the other drivers had stories to tell. One of them told the detectives about the mags Lee Chambers sold and swapped from the boot of his car.

'He used to set up a stall at motorway service areas for lorry drivers and other blokes who like that sort of thing. You know, photos of violent sex, rape and kidnap. That kind of stuff. He said he made quite a bit of money.'

He was a horrible man, everyone was agreed, but that didn't make him a child abductor, Sparkes said miserably to his sergeant.

During their second interview with Chambers later that afternoon, he claimed he'd kept the cuttings in the folder because he fancied Dawn Elliott.

'I cut pictures of women I'm attracted to out of the papers all the time. Cheaper than the skin mags,' he offered. 'I've got a high sex drive.'

'Where did you go when you finished the job in Portsmouth, Mr Chambers?'

'Home,' he said emphatically.

'Anyone see you there?'

'No, everyone was out working and I'm on my own. I watch telly when I'm off-duty and wait for the next call-out.'

'Someone says they saw a man with long hair walking down the road where Bella Elliott was playing.'

'Not me. I was at home,' Chambers said, touching his ponytail nervously.

Sparkes felt dirty when he came out of the interview room for a short break.

'He deserves locking up just for breathing,' Matthews said, joining his boss in the corridor.

'We've spoken to the fare, and they say he helped them in with their suitcase and they offered him a cold drink but he left straight away. No witnesses to his whereabouts after that.'

As they talked, Chambers sauntered past them with an officer. 'Where are you going?' Sparkes snapped.

'To the bog. When are you letting me go?'

'Shut up and get back in the interview room.'

The two men stood for a moment in the corridor before going back in.

'Let's see if we can see him on the cameras. We also need to find his contacts for the boot sales at the services. They're all perverts travelling the motorways round here. Who are they, Matthews? They may have seen him on the second of October. Get on to Traffic and see if they've got any likely names.'

Back in the interview room, Chambers squinted at them across the table and said, 'They don't give me their names, do they? It's all very discreet.'

Sparkes waited for him to claim he was doing a public service, keeping perverts off the street, and Chambers didn't disappoint.

'Would you recognize your customers again?' he asked.

'Don't think so. Staring isn't good for business.'

The detectives began to lose heart, and in the next break, Sparkes called time.

'We'll have to watch and see, but make sure we do him for the indecent exposure. And Matthews, tell the local press to look out for him in court. He deserves a bit of publicity.'

Chambers smirked when they broke the news that the interview was over. But it was a brief moment of triumph before he was led away to be processed by the custody sergeant.

'God, one flasher. That's all we've got to show for the investigation so far,' Sparkes said.

'Early days, Boss,' Matthews murmured.

Chapter 11

Thursday, 2 November 2006

The Detective

MATTHEWS HAD STAN Spencer's notebook in his hand and looked unhappy.

'I've been looking at this again, Boss, and reading back through Mr Spencer's observations. Very thorough. Weather conditions, number and ownership of vehicles parked in the road, who went in and out of the houses. Including Dawn.'

Sparkes perked up.

'Clocked her in and out of the house most days.'

'Watching her in particular?'

'Not really. All the neighbours are mentioned. 'But there's something we need to ask him about his notes. They end halfway through a sentence on the Sunday and then switch to Monday 2 October and the stuff about the long-haired man. Looks like there may be a page missing. And he wrote the full date at the top of the page. He doesn't do that normally.'

Sparkes took the notebook and scrutinized it, his stomach sinking. 'Christ, do you think he's made it up?'

Matthews grimaced. 'Not necessarily. He may have been interrupted doing the Sunday log and not gone back to it. But . . .'

'What?'

'The notebook says it has thirty-two pages on the cover. There are only thirty now.'

Sparkes ran both hands through his hair. 'Why would he do it? Is it him, then? Is he our man? Has our Mr Spencer been hiding in plain sight?'

Stan Spencer was dressed for gardening when he answered his door, in old trousers, a woolly hat and gloves.

'Good morning, Inspector. Good morning, Sergeant Matthews. Good to see you. Any news?'

He ushered them through the house to the conservatory, where Susan was reading a paper.

'Look who's here,' he chirped. 'Get the officers a drink, dear.'

'Mr Spencer,' Sparkes tried to bring an official note to what was turning into a coffee morning, 'we want to talk to you about your notes.'

'Of course. Go ahead, please.'

'There appears to be a page missing.'

'I don't know what you mean,' he answered, reddening.

Matthews spread the relevant pages on the table in front of him. 'Sunday finishes here, in the middle of your remarks about litter outside Dawn's house, Mr Spencer. The next page is Monday and your notes about the man you say you saw.'

'I did see him,' Spencer blustered. 'I tore out the page because I made a mistake, that's all.'

There was silence round the table.

'Where is the missing page, Mr Spencer? Did you keep it?' Sparkes asked gently.

Spencer's face crumpled.

His wife emerged with a tray of tasteful mugs and a plate of home-made biscuits. 'Help yourselves,' she was saying gaily when she noticed the heavy silence round the table. 'What's the matter?' she asked.

'We'd like to talk to your husband for a moment, Mrs Spencer.'

She paused, taking in Stan's face and turned, tray still in hand.

Sparkes asked his question again.

'I shoved it in my desk drawer, I think,' Spencer said and went into the house to look.

He reappeared with a folded sheet of lined paper. The rest of Sunday's log was there, and halfway down the page, Monday's original log started.

'Weather, clement for the season,' Sparkes read out loud. 'Legal vehicles in road during day: AM: No. 44's Astra, midwife's car at No. 68. PM: Peter's van. Illegal vehicles in road: AM: usual 7 commuter cars. PM: Ditto. Leaflets on nuisance parking stuck under wipers. All quiet.'

'Did you see the long-haired man on the day Bella was taken, Mr Spencer?'

'I . . . I'm not sure.'

'Not sure?'

'I did see him but it might have been on another day, Inspector. I may have got confused.'

'And your contemporaneous notes, Mr Spencer?'

He had the grace to blush.

'I made a mistake,' he said quietly. 'There was so much going on that day. I just wanted to help. To be of assistance to Bella.'

Sparkes wanted to wring his neck, but maintained the crisp, professional tone of the interview. 'Did you think you were helping Bella by sending us off in the wrong direction, Mr Spencer?'

The older man slumped in his chair. 'I just wanted to help,' he repeated.

'The thing is that people who lie often have something to hide, Mr Spencer.'

'I haven't got anything to hide. I swear to you. I'm a decent man. I spend my time protecting the neighbourhood from crime. I've stopped thefts from vehicles along this road. Single-handedly. Ask Peter Tredwell. He'll tell you.'

He stopped. 'Will everyone know I got it wrong?' he asked, his eyes pleading with the officers.

'That's not really our main concern at the moment,' Sparkes snapped. 'We'll need to search your house.'

As members of his team began sifting through the Spencers' life, he and Matthews let themselves out of the house, leaving the couple to contemplate their new role in the spotlight.

Matthews rubbed his jaw. 'I'm going to talk to the neighbours about him, Boss.'

At the Tredwells' house, they had nothing but praise for 'Stan the Man' and his patrols.

'He chased off some hooligan who broke into my van last year. Saved my tools from being nicked. Fair play to him,' Mr Tredwell said. 'I park it in a lock-up now. Better security.'

'But your van was parked in Manor Road on the day Bella Elliott was taken. Mr Spencer noted it down.'

'No, it wasn't. I was using it for work and then put it in the lock-up. Do the same thing every day.'

Matthews quickly took the details and stood up to go.

Sparkes was still standing outside the Spencers' bungalow.

'There's a blue van in the road unaccounted for at the material time, Boss. It wasn't Mr Tredwell's.'

'For Christ's sake. What else has Spencer got wrong?' Sparkes asked. 'Get the team looking back through the witness statements and CCTV in the area. And see which of our perverts owns a blue van.'

Neither man spoke again. They didn't need to. They knew they were thinking the same thing. They'd wasted a whole month. The papers would crucify them.

Sparkes fished out his phone and rang the Press Office to try to limit the damage.

'We'll tell the reporters that we have a new piece of evidence,' he said. 'And steer them away from the long-haired man. Soft pedal on that front and focus on the hunt for the blue van. OK?'

The media, hungry for any new detail, put it on the front pages. This time, there were no quotes from their favourite source. Mr Spencer was no longer answering his door.

Chapter 12

Saturday, 7 April 2007

The Detective

IT TOOK ANOTHER five months of donkey work, tracing every blue van in the country, for a breakthrough to come.

It was Easter Saturday when the incident room took a call from a delivery firm in south London. One of their vehicles, a blue van, had been making drops on the south coast the day Bella disappeared.

An old hand answered the call and then went straight through to Sparkes. 'Think this is one for you, Sir,' he said, putting the information sheet down on the desk.

Sparkes rang Qwik Delivery back immediately to confirm the details. The manager, Alan Johnstone, started by apologizing for wasting police time but said he'd only recently joined the company and his wife had made him call in.

'She talks about the Bella case all the time. And when I talked about the cost of re-spraying the vans the other day, she said to me, "What colour were they before?" She nearly shouted the house down when I said they were originally blue. They're silver now. Anyway, she asked if they'd been checked by the police. She kept on and on at me, so I went through the paperwork and found that one was in Hampshire. Didn't go to Southampton, so that's probably why the old management didn't contact you at the time

– they probably didn't think it was worth bothering you with. Sorry, but my wife made me promise.'

'Don't you worry, Mr Johnstone. No information is a waste of our time,' Sparkes coaxed, his fingers crossed. 'We're very grateful that you took the time to call. Now, tell me about the van, the driver and the journey it took.'

'The driver was Mike Doonan, a regular of ours. Well, he's left now – wasn't due to retire for another couple of years but he had a terrible back problem and could hardly walk, let alone drive and lug parcels about. Anyway, Mike had drops in Portsmouth and Winchester on the second of October. Spare parts for a chain of garages.'

Sparkes was scribbling it all down, phone under his chin, and entering the name and details into his computer with his left hand. The driver was within a twenty-mile radius of Manor Road to make his drops and, potentially, fitted the timeframe.

'Mike left the depot just before lunchtime – it's a one-and-a-half to two-hour journey if the M25 doesn't come to a standstill,' Mr Johnstone said.

'What time did he deliver the parcel?' Sparkes asked.

'Hold on, I'll have to call you back when I've got the paperwork in front of me.'

As he hung up, Sparkes shouted, 'Matthews. In here now!' and handed over the computer search to his sergeant as his phone rang again.

'He dropped first at 2.05,' Johnstone said. 'Signed for and every-thing. The second drop time doesn't seem to figure on this sheet. Not sure why. Anyway, they didn't see him come back, according to this. The office staff clock off at five o' clock and, according to this, the van was left on the forecourt, clean and hoovered out for the next day's work.'

'OK, that's great. We'll need to talk to him, just in case. He might've seen something helpful to us. Where does he live, your driver?' Sparkes asked, fighting to quell a note of excitement in his voice. He wrote down an address in south-east London on his notepad. 'You've been very helpful, Mr Johnstone. Thanks very much for phoning in.' He ended the call.

An hour later, he and Matthews were on their way up the M3.

At first glance, the driver's profile on the police computer hadn't contained anything to make their pulses race. Mike Doonan was in his late fifties, lived alone, had been a driver for years and was reluctant to pay his parking fines. But Matthews' scan of the police database had pulled him up as 'of interest' to the boys on the Operation Gold team. 'Of interest' meant there was a possible link to child-sex-abuse websites. The Operation Gold team was working its way through a list of hundreds of men in the UK whose credit cards appeared to have been used to visit specific sites. They were concentrating on those with access to kiddies first – the teachers, social workers, care staff, scout leaders – then moving on to the rest. They hadn't reached Doonan (DOB 04/05/52; Profession: Driver; Status: Council tenant, divorced, three children) yet and at the current pace of the investigation were not due to knock on his door for another year.

'I've got a good feeling about this,' Sparkes told his sergeant. Everything was in place: Met officers had been discreetly positioned to watch the address but no one was to move until the Hampshire officers arrived.

The DI's mobile buzzed in his hand.

'We're on. He's at home,' he said when he hung up.

Mike Doonan was marking his race card in the *Daily Star* when he heard his doorbell.

Swinging his bulk forward to rise out of his armchair, he groaned. The pain shot down his left leg and he had to stand for a moment to catch his breath.

'Hang on, I'm coming,' he shouted.

When he cracked open the door on to the walkway, it was not his Good Samaritan neighbour with his Saturday shop of lager and sliced bread, but two men in suits.

'If you're Mormons, I've already got enough ex-wives,' he said and made to close the door.

'Mr Michael Doonan?' Sparkes said. 'We're police officers and we'd like to talk to you for a moment.'

'Bloody hell, it isn't about a parking ticket, is it? I thought I'd cleared them all. Come in, then.'

In the tiny sitting room of his council flat, he slowly lowered himself back into his chair. 'Back's buggered,' he said, gasping from a spasm of pain.

At the mention of Bella Elliott, he stopped wincing.

'Poor little thing. I was in Portsmouth that lunchtime on a job. Is that why you're here? I told the boss he ought to ring in when the papers said about the dark-blue van – you know I drove one that colour – but he said he didn't want coppers sniffing around his business. Not sure why – you'll have to ask him. Anyway, I was nowhere near where the little girl lived. Just did my job and came back.'

Doonan continued to be helpful to a fault, offering his thoughts on the case and what should happen to 'the bastard who took her'.

'I'd do anything to get my hands on him. Mind you, couldn't do much if I did, not in the state I'm in.'

'How long have you been in this state, Mr Doonan?' Sergeant Matthews asked.

'Years. I'll be in a wheelchair soon.'

The officers listened patiently, then broached his alleged interest in internet child pornography. He laughed when they talked about Operation Gold.

'I haven't even got a computer. Not my kind of thing. Bit of a technophobe, if I'm honest. Anyway, all these investigations are bollocks, aren't they? Clever blokes in Russia stealing credit-card numbers and selling them on to paedos, it says in the papers. Don't take my word for it. Have a look round, officers.'

Sparkes and Matthews took up his offer, pushing through clothes jammed into a wardrobe and lifting the mattress on Doonan's bed to look in the storage bags underneath. 'Lot of women's clothes, Mr Doonan,' Matthews observed.

'Yes, bit of a cross-dresser when the mood takes me,' Doonan laughed easily. Too easily, Sparkes thought. 'Nah, the clothes belonged to my latest ex-wife. Haven't got round to chucking them out.'

There was no sign of a child.

'Do you have kids, Mr Doonan?'

'Grown-ups now. Don't really see much of them. They sided with their mothers.'

'Right. We'll take a quick look in the bathroom.'

Sparkes looked across at his sergeant, digging through the laundry basket and trying not to breathe.

'Well, she's not here, but I don't like him,' Matthews hissed through his teeth. 'Over-friendly. Creepy.'

'We need to talk to the Operation Gold boys again,' Sparkes said, closing the bathroom cabinet. 'And get his van in for Forensics to go over.'

When they filed back into the sitting room, Doonan smiled. 'All done? Sorry about the washing. Expect you'll be off to see Glen Taylor now?'

'Who?' Sparkes asked.

'Taylor. One of the other drivers. He did a drop in the area the same day. Didn't you know?'

Sparkes stopped putting on his coat and moved closer to Doonan. 'No. Mr Johnstone didn't mention a second driver when he called in. Are you sure there were two of you?'

'Yeah, I was going to do both jobs but I had a doctor's appointment and had to get back to town by four thirty. Glen said he'd do the second drop. Maybe he didn't put it on the log. You should ask him.'

'We will, Mr Doonan.'

Sparkes signalled to Matthews to go and call Johnstone to confirm the new information.

As the sergeant closed the front door behind him, Sparkes

looked hard at Doonan. 'Is this other driver a friend of yours?'

Doonan sniffed. 'Not really. Bit of a mystery, if I'm honest. Clever boy. Deep, I'd say.'

Sparkes wrote it down. 'Deep, how?'

'Acted all friendly but you never knew what he was thinking. The blokes would be talking in the canteen and he'd just be listening in. Secretive, I suppose.'

Matthews knocked on the window, startling them both, and Sparkes put his notebook away and said goodbye without shaking hands.

'We'll see you again, Mr Doonan.'

The driver excused himself from getting up to let him out.

'Slam the door behind you and come back any time,' he called after him.

The officers got into the stinking lift and looked at each other as the doors closed.

'Mr Johnstone says there's nothing in the log about Glen Taylor doing any jobs that afternoon,' said Matthews. 'He's looking for the delivery receipt to see whose signature is on it. I've got Taylor's address.'

'Let's go there now,' Sparkes said, reaching for his keys. 'And check if Doonan turned up for his doctor's appointment.'

In the flat, Mike Doonan waited for an hour and then staggered to the coat hooks in the hall and fished out a padlock key from his jacket pocket. He shook two of his special painkillers from a white plastic container and swallowed them with a gulp of cold coffee. He stood while they kicked in and then shuffled out to remove the pictures and magazines from his locker in the neighbour's garage.

'Fucking police,' he grumbled as he braced himself against the lift wall. He'd burn the photos later. He'd been stupid to keep them really, but they were all that was left of his little hobby. The computer stuff had come to an end months ago when his spine had started to collapse and he couldn't get to his special internet café any more.

'Too crippled for porn,' he laughed to himself – his painkillers making him lightheaded and giddy. 'That's tragic.'

He opened the door of the grey metal cabinet and pulled the battered-looking blue folder off the top shelf. The corners of the photocopies had become dog-eared with use and the colours were beginning to fade. He'd bought them from another driver, a bloke who drove cabs down on the coast and sold his stuff from the boot of his car. Doonan knew his pictures off by heart. The faces, the poses, the domesticity of the backgrounds – living rooms, bedrooms, bathrooms.

He hoped the detectives were giving Glen Taylor a good going-over. Serve him right, jumped-up little prick.

The older one had looked interested when he said Taylor was 'deep'. He smiled.

Chapter 13

Saturday, 7 April 2007

The Detective

SPARKES' HEART WAS going like a steam hammer as he walked up the Taylors' path, all senses heightened. He'd done this walk a hundred times but his reactions never seemed blunted by repetition.

The house was a semi, painted and well cared for, with double-glazed windows and clean net curtains.

Are you here, Bella? he repeated in his head as he raised a hand to knock on the door. Softly, softly, he reminded himself. Let's not panic anyone.

And then, there he was. Glen Taylor.

He looks like the bloke next door, was Sparkes' first thought. But then monsters rarely look the part. You hope you'll be able to see the evil shining out of them – it would make police work a damned sight easier, he often said. But evil was a slippery substance, only glimpsed occasionally and all the more horrifying for that, he knew.

The detective made a quick visual sweep behind Taylor for any signs of a child, but the hall and stairs were spotless, nothing out of place.

'Normal to the point of abnormal,' he told Eileen later. 'Looked like a show house.' Eileen had taken offence, seeing the remark as a judgement on her own housekeeping skills, and hissed her discontent at him.

'Bloody hell, Eileen, what's the matter with you? No one is talking about you, about our house. I'm talking about a suspect. I thought you'd be interested.' But the damage was done. Eileen retreated to the kitchen and some loud cleaning. Another quiet week, he thought and turned the telly up.

'Mr Glen Taylor?' Sparkes asked quietly and courteously.

'Yes, that's me,' Taylor replied. 'What can I do for you? Are you selling something?'

The officer stepped closer, Ian Matthews at his heels.

'Mr Taylor, I'm Detective Inspector Bob Sparkes from the Hampshire Police Force. Can I come in?'

'Police? What is this about?' Taylor asked.

'I would like to talk to you about the case of a missing child I'm investigating. It's about the disappearance of Bella Elliott,' he said, trying to keep the emotion out of his voice. The colour drained from Glen Taylor's face and he stepped back as if recoiling from a punch.

Taylor's wife came out of the kitchen and was wiping her hands on a tea towel when the words 'Bella Elliott' were spoken. A nice, decent-looking woman, Sparkes thought. She gasped and her hands flew up to her face. Strange how people react. That gesture, to cover your face, must be hardwired into people. Is it shame? Or an unwillingness to look at something? he wondered, waiting to be shown through to the sitting room.

Odd really, he thought. He hasn't looked at his wife once the whole time. It's as if she isn't there. Poor woman, she looks like she's going to collapse.

Taylor quickly pulled himself together and answered their questions.

'We understand you were making a delivery in the area where Bella was taken, Mr Taylor.'

'Well, I think so.'

'Your friend, Mr Doonan, said you were.'

'Doonan?' Glen Taylor's mouth tightened. 'Not a friend of mine, but – hang on a minute. Yes, I think I was.'

'Try to be sure, Mr Taylor. It was the day Bella Elliott was abducted,' Sparkes insisted.

'Right, yes. Of course. I think I had one drop early afternoon and then came home. About four, as I remember.'

'Home at four, Mr Taylor? You made very good time. Are you sure it was four?'

Taylor nodded, forehead creased as if miming thinking hard. 'Yes, definitely four. Jean will bear me out.'

Jean Taylor said nothing. It was as if she hadn't heard and Sparkes had to repeat the question before she made eye contact with him and nodded.

'Yes,' she said, as if on automatic pilot.

Sparkes turned back to Glen Taylor. 'The thing is, Mr Taylor, your van matches the description of a vehicle that was noticed by a neighbour just before Bella vanished. You probably read about it – it was in all the papers – and we're checking all blue vans.'

'I thought you were looking for a man with a ponytail. I've got short hair, and anyway, I wasn't in Southampton. It was Winchester,' Taylor said.

'Yes, but are you sure you didn't take a little drive after the delivery?'

Taylor laughed off the suggestion.

'I don't do any more driving than I have to – not my idea of relaxation. Look, this is all a terrible mistake.'

Sparkes nodded to himself thoughtfully. 'I'm sure you understand how serious this matter is, Mr Taylor, and won't mind if we have a look around.'

An immediate search of the house began with the officers moving quickly through the rooms, calling Bella's name and looking in cupboards, under beds, behind sofas. There was nothing.

But there was something about the way Taylor had told his story. Something rehearsed about it. Sparkes decided to take him in for further questioning, to go over the details once more. He owed it to Bella.

Jean Taylor was left weeping on the stairs, while the officers finished their work.

Chapter 14

Thursday, 10 June 2010

The Widow

THEY LET ME REST for a bit and then we have dinner by the big windows in Kate's room, overlooking the gardens. The waiter wheels in a table with a white tablecloth and a vase of flowers in the middle. The plates have those fancy silver domes on them. Kate and Mick have ordered starters, mains and puds and they're stacked on a shelf under the table.

'Let's push the boat out,' Kate says.

'Yeah,' Mick says. 'We deserve it.'

Kate tells him to shut up but I can see they're really pleased with themselves. They've won the big prize – an interview with the widow.

I have chicken and play with it for a bit. Not hungry for it or their celebrations. They pile into the wine and order a second bottle, but I make sure I don't drink more than a glass. Must stay in control.

When I feel tired, I pretend to cry and say I need some time alone. Kate and Mick exchange a look. Obviously this isn't going to plan. But I stand and say, 'Goodnight. See you in the morning.'

They scrape their chairs back and stumble to their feet. Kate walks me to my door and makes sure I'm safely inside.

'Don't answer the phone,' she tells me. 'If I need to talk to you, I'll knock on the door.'

I nod.

It's boiling hot in my room so I lie on the enormous bed with the windows open to let out the heat of the radiators. Today is playing over and over in my head on a loop and I feel dizzy and out of control, like I'm a bit drunk.

I sit up, to stop the room spinning, and see myself reflected in the window.

It looks like someone else. Some other woman who's let herself be taken away by strangers. Strangers who, until today, were probably banging on my door and writing lies about me. I rub my face and so does the woman in the window. Because it is me.

I stare back at myself.

I can't believe I'm here.

I can't believe I let myself agree to come. After everything the press have done to us. After all the warnings Glen gave.

I want to tell him that I don't actually remember agreeing, but he'd say I must have done or I wouldn't have got into the van with them.

Well, he's not here any more to say anything. I'm on my own now.

Then I hear Kate and Mick talking on the balcony next door.

'Poor thing,' Kate says. 'She must be exhausted. We'll do it in the morning.'

Whatever 'it' is. The interview, I suppose.

I feel dizzy again. Sick inside, because I know what is coming next. There'll be no more massages and treats tomorrow. No more chat about what colour the kitchen units are. She will want to know about Glen. And Bella.

I go into the bathroom and throw up the chicken I've just eaten. I sit on the floor and think about the first interview I gave – the one to the police, while Glen was in custody. It was Easter when they came. We'd planned to walk up to Greenwich Park the next day to see the Easter egg hunt. We went every year – that and

Bonfire Night were my favourite times of the year. Funny the things you remember. I loved it. All those excited little faces looking for eggs or under their woolly hats, writing their names with sparklers. I'd stand close to them, pretend they were mine for a moment.

Instead, that Easter Sunday, I sat on my sofa while two police officers went through my things and Bob Sparkes questioned me. He wanted to know if Glen and I had a normal sex life. He called it something else, but that's what he meant.

I didn't know what to say. It was so horrible being asked that by a stranger. He was looking at me and thinking about my sex life and I couldn't stop him.

'Of course,' I said. I didn't know what he meant or why he was asking me that.

They wouldn't answer my questions, just kept asking theirs. Questions about the day Bella disappeared. Why was I at home at four, instead of at work? What time did Glen come in the door? How did I know it was four o'clock? What else happened that day? Checking everything and going over the same things again and again. They wanted me to make a mistake, but I didn't. I stuck to the story. I didn't want to make any trouble for Glen.

And I knew he'd never do anything like that. My Glen.

'Do you ever use the computer we took away from your husband's study, Mrs Taylor?' Inspector Sparkes suddenly asked.

They'd taken it the day before, after they searched upstairs.

'No,' I said. It came out as a squeak. My throat betraying me and my fear.

They'd taken me up there the day before and one of them sat down at the keyboard to try and start it. The screen lit up but then nothing happened and they asked me for the password. I told them I didn't even know there was a password. We tried my name and birthdays and Arsenal, Glen's team, but in the end they unplugged it and took it away to crack it open.

From the window, I'd watched them leave. I knew they'd find something, but I didn't know what. I tried not to imagine. In the end, I couldn't have imagined what they found. DI Sparkes told me when he came back the next day to ask more questions. Told me there were pictures. Terrible pictures of children on there. I told him Glen couldn't have put them there.

I think it must've been the police who let Glen's name out of the bag because the morning after he finally got home from the police station the press came knocking.

He'd looked so tired and dirty when he walked through the door the night before and I'd made toast and pulled my chair close to his so I could put my arms round him.

'It was awful, Jeanie. They wouldn't listen to me. Kept going on and on at me.'

I started crying. I couldn't help myself. He sounded so broken by it.

'Oh love, don't cry. It will be all right,' he said, wiping my tears with his thumb. 'We both know I wouldn't harm a hair on a child's head.'

I knew it was true, but I felt so relieved hearing him say it out loud that I hugged him again and got butter on my sleeve.

'I know you wouldn't. And I didn't let you down about coming home late, Glen,' I said. 'I told the police you were home by four.' And he looked at me sideways.

He'd asked me to tell the lie. We were sitting having our tea the night after the news came out that the police were looking for the driver of a blue van. I said maybe he ought to ring in and say he'd been in a blue van in Hampshire on the day she went missing so they could rule him out.

Glen looked at me for a long time. 'It would just be inviting trouble, Jeanie.'

'What do you mean?'

'Look, I did a little private job while I was out – a delivery I took on for a friend to make a bit of extra money – and if the boss finds out, he'll sack me.'

'But what if the boss reports that you were in the area in a blue van?'

'He won't,' Glen said. 'He's not keen on the police. But if he does, we'll just say I was home by four. Then everything will be all right. OK, love?'

I nodded. And anyway, he did ring me at about four to say he was on his way. Said his mobile was on the blink and he was ringing from a garage phone.

It was practically the same thing, wasn't it?

'Thanks, love,' he said. 'It's not a lie really – I was on my way – but we don't want the boss to know I was doing that extra work on the side. We don't need any complications or me losing my job. Do we?'

'No, course not.'

I put some more bread in the toaster, breathing in the comforting smell.

'Where did you go for your extra drop?' I said. Just asking.

'Over near Brighton,' he said. And we sat in silence for a while.

The next morning, the first reporter knocked on the door – a young bloke from the local paper. Nice lad, he looked. Full of apologies.

'So sorry to disturb you, Mrs Taylor, but please may I speak to your husband?'

Glen came out of the living room just as I was asking the lad who he was. When he said he was a reporter, Glen turned on his heel and disappeared into the kitchen. I stood there, not sure what to do. Frightened that whatever I said, it would come out wrong. In the end, Glen shouted through, 'There's nothing to say. Goodbye,' and I closed the door on him.

We got better at dealing with the press after that. We didn't answer the door. We sat quietly in the kitchen until we heard the footsteps going away. And we thought that was the end of it. Course it wasn't. They went next door, and across the road, to the paper shop and the pub. Door-knocking for bits of information.

I don't think Lisa next door said anything to the reporters at the beginning. The other neighbours didn't know much, but that didn't stop them. They loved the whole thing and two days after he was released, there we were in the papers.

'HAVE POLICE FINALLY MADE A BREAKTHROUGH IN BELLA CASE?' one headline read. In another one, there was a blurry picture of Glen from when he played for the pub football team, and a load of lies.

We sat and looked at the front pages together. Glen looked shell-shocked and I took his hand to reassure him.

In the papers, lots of it was wrong. His age, his job, even the spelling of his name,

Glen smiled at me weakly. 'That's good, Jeanie,' he said. 'Maybe people won't recognize me.' But of course they did.

His mum rang. 'What's all this about, Jean?' she said.

Glen wouldn't come to the phone. Went and had a bath. Poor Mary, she was in tears.

'Look, it's all a misunderstanding, Mary,' I told her. 'Glen has had nothing to do with this. Someone saw a blue van like his on the day Bella went missing. That's all. It's a coincidence. The police are just doing their job, checking out every lead.'

'Then why is it in the papers?' she asked.

'I don't know, Mary. The press get excited over everything to do with Bella. They've chased all over the place when people have said they've seen her. You know what they're like.'

But she didn't and neither did I, really. Not then, anyway.

'Please don't worry, Mary. We know the truth. It'll all blow over in a week. Take care of yourself and love to George.'

After I put the phone down, I stood in the hall in a daze. I was still there when Glen came down from the bathroom. He had wet hair and I could feel his damp skin when he kissed me.

'How was my mum?' he asked. 'In a state, I suppose. What did you tell her?'

I repeated the whole conversation as I made him some break-fast. He had hardly eaten for two days since he got home from the police station. He had been too tired to eat anything except toast.

'Bacon and eggs?' I asked.

'Lovely,' he said. When he sat down, I tried to talk about normal things, but it sounded so false.

In the end, Glen stopped me talking by kissing me and said, 'There are going to be some very difficult days ahead, Jeanie. People are going to say some terrible things about us and probably to us. We need to be prepared. This is a terrible mistake, but we mustn't let it ruin our lives. We need to stay strong until the truth comes out. Do you think you can do that?'

I kissed him back. 'Of course I can. We can be strong for each other. I love you, Glen.'

He smiled at me properly then. And squeezed me tight so I wouldn't see him getting emotional.

'Now, is there any more bacon?'

He was right about it ruining our lives. I had to give up work after he was questioned. I tried to keep going, telling my clients that it was all a terrible mistake, but people stopped talking when I got near them. The regulars stopped booking appointments and began going to another hairdresser down the hill. Lesley took me to one side one Saturday night and told me she liked Glen and was sure there was no truth in the press reports, but I had to leave 'for the good of the salon'.

I cried because I knew, then, it would never end and nothing would ever be the same again. I rolled up my scissors and brushes in my colouring overall and shoved them into a carrier bag and left.

I tried not to blame Glen. I knew it wasn't his fault. We were both victims of the situation, he said and tried to keep me cheerful.

'Don't worry, Jean. We'll be fine. You'll find another job when this blows over. Probably time for a change, anyway.'

Chapter 15

Saturday, 7 April 2007

The Detective

THE FIRST INTERVIEW with Glen Taylor had to wait until everyone arrived back in Southampton and took place in an airless cupboard of a room with a door painted hospital green.

Sparkes looked through the glass panel in the door. He could see Taylor, sitting up like an expectant schoolboy, his hands on his knees and his feet tapping some mystery tune.

The detective pushed open the door and walked to his mark on this tiny stage. It was all about body language, he'd read in one of the psychology books on his bedside table. Dominating by making yourself bigger than the interviewee – standing over them, filling their frame of reference. Sparkes stood for slightly longer than necessary, shuffling the papers in his hand, but finally lowered himself into a chair. Taylor wasn't waiting for the detective to make himself comfortable.

'I keep telling you, this is all a mistake. There must be thousands of blue vans out there,' he complained, banging down his hands on the coffee-stained table. 'What about Mike Doonan? He's a strange bloke. Lives on his own, did you know that?'

Sparkes took a deep, slow breath. He was in no hurry. 'Now then, Mr Taylor. Let's concentrate on you and look at your journey again on October the second. We need to be sure of the timings.'

Taylor rolled his eyes. 'There's nothing more to tell. Drove there, dropped the package, drove home. End of story.'

'Right. You say you left the depot at twelve twenty, but it isn't recorded in the worksheets. Why didn't you record the journey?'

Taylor shrugged. 'I did the job for Doonan.'

'I thought you didn't get on with him.'

'I owed him a favour. The drivers did it all the time.'

'So where did you have lunch that day?' Sparkes asked.

'Lunch?' Taylor asked and let out a bark of a laugh.

'Yes, did you stop somewhere for lunch?'

'I probably had a bar of chocolate, a Mars bar or something. I don't eat much at lunchtime – I hate supermarket sandwiches. Prefer to wait till I get home.'

'And where did you buy the Mars bar?'

'I don't know. Probably bought it at a garage.'

'On the way there or back?'

'Not sure.'

'Did you buy fuel?'

'I can't remember. This is months ago.'

'What about your mileage? Is it recorded at the beginning and end of your working day?' Sparkes asked, knowing full well the answer.

Taylor blinked. 'Yes,' he said.

'So if I did the journey you've described, my mileage should be the same as yours?' Sparkes reasoned.

Another blink. 'Yes, but . . . well, there was a bit of traffic before Winchester and I tried to find a way round it. I got a bit lost until I got back on the ring road, and had to double back on myself before I found the drop-off point,' he said.

'I see,' Sparkes said, and exaggerated the time it took him to note the response on his pad. 'Did you get a bit lost on the way back?'

'No, of course not. It was just the traffic jam.'

'You took a long time to get home though, didn't you?'

Taylor shrugged. 'Not really.'

'Why did no one see you return the van if you were back so quickly?'

'I went home first. I told you. I'd finished the job and popped in,' Taylor said.

'Why? Your worksheets show that you usually go straight to the depot,' Sparkes pressed.

'I wanted to see Jean.'

'Your wife, yes. Bit of a romantic, are you? Like to surprise your wife?'

'No, I just wanted to tell her I'd sort out supper.'

Supper. The Taylors ate supper, not dinner or tea. The bank had given Glen Taylor aspirations to a lifestyle, then, Sparkes mused.

'And you couldn't have phoned her?'

'My mobile had run out of juice and I was passing the house anyway. And I fancied a cup of tea.'

Three excuses. He's spent too long putting together this story, Sparkes thought. He'd check the mobile straight after the interview.

'I thought drivers had to stay in touch with the depot. I've got an in-car charger.'

'So have I, but I'd left it in my car when I picked up the van.'

'What time did your phone battery die?'

'I didn't notice it was dead until I got off the M25 and tried to ring Jean. Could've been five minutes or a couple of hours.'

'Do you have children?' Sparkes asked.

Taylor clearly hadn't expected the question and pressed his lips together while he gathered his thoughts.

'No, why?' he muttered. 'What's that got to do with anything?'

'Do you like children, Mr Taylor?' Sparkes pressed on.

'Course I do. Who doesn't like children?' His arms were crossed now.

'You see, Mr Taylor, there are some people who like children in a different way. Do you know what I mean?'

Taylor tightened his grip on his upper arms and closed his eyes, just for a second, but it was enough to encourage Sparkes.

'They like children in a sexual way.'

'They are animals, aren't they?' Taylor spat.

'So you don't like children in that way?'

'Don't be disgusting. Of course I don't. What kind of a man do you think I am?'

'That's what we're trying to find out, Mr Taylor,' Sparkes said, leaning forward to crowd his quarry. 'When did you start driving for a living? Strange change of career – you had a good job, didn't you, at the bank?'

Taylor did his pantomime frown. 'I fancied a change. I didn't get on with the boss and thought I would look at starting my own delivery business. I needed to get experience of every aspect so I began driving—'

'What about the business with the computers at the bank?' Sparkes interrupted him. 'We've spoken to your former manager.'

Taylor reddened.

'Weren't you sacked because of inappropriate use of the computers?'

'It was a stitch-up,' Taylor said quickly. 'The boss wanted me out. I think he felt threatened by a younger, better-educated man. Anyone could've used that computer. The security was laughable. Leaving was my decision.'

His arms were so tightly crossed over his chest it was constricting his breathing.

'Right. I see,' Sparkes countered, leaning back in his chair to give Taylor the space he needed to embellish his lie. 'And the "inappropriate use" of the computer you were accused of?' His voice was casual.

'Porn. Someone was looking at porn on an office computer in work time. Bloody idiot.' Taylor was on a roll of self-righteousness. 'I would never do something as stupid as that.'

'So where do you look at porn?' Sparkes asked.

The question stopped Taylor dead.

'I want to see a lawyer,' he said, his feet now dancing beneath the table.

'And you shall, Mr Taylor. By the way, we're looking at the computer you use at home. What do you think we'll find on it? Is there anything you want to tell us about now?'

But Taylor had closed down. He sat silently, staring at his hands and shaking his head at the offer of a drink.

Tom Payne was the duty solicitor that weekend. A middle-aged man in a dusty-looking dark suit, he strode into the room an hour later, a pad of yellow paper under one arm and his briefcase flapping open.

'I would like some time to consult with Mr Taylor,' he told Sparkes and the room was cleared.

As Sparkes left, he looked at Tom Payne, the two men sizing each other up before Payne offered his hand to his new client.

'Now, let's see what I can do to help you, Mr Taylor,' he said, clicking his pen.

Thirty minutes later, the detectives were back in the room and rootling through the details of Taylor's narrative, snouts to the scent of fakery.

'Let's go back to your dismissal from the bank, Mr Taylor. We will be talking to the bank again, so why don't you tell us all about it?' Sparkes said.

The suspect repeated his excuses, with his lawyer impassive at his side. Apparently, everyone was at fault apart from him. And then there was his alibi. The detectives stormed it from all sides, but it proved unbreachable. They had knocked on the neighbours' doors, but no one had seen him arrive home the day Bella went missing. Apart from his wife.

Two frustrating hours later, Glen Taylor was being swabbed and scraped before being taken to a cell, while the police checked his story. For a moment, when he realized he was not going home, he looked young and lost as the custody sergeant asked him to empty his pockets and take off his belt.

'Will you phone my wife, Jean, please,' he asked his lawyer, his voice cracking.

In the bleached emptiness of the police cell, he sank on

to a discoloured plastic bench along one wall and closed his eyes.

The custody sergeant squinted through the eyehole in the door. 'Looks calm enough,' he told his colleague, 'but let's keep a close eye on him. Quiet types make me nervous.'

Chapter 16

Thursday, 10 June 2010

The Widow

I USED TO LOVE Sunday lunch. Always roast chicken and all the trimmings. It used to feel like a family thing, and when we were newlyweds we had our mums and dads over to share it with us. Sitting round the table in the kitchen, they'd half-listen to the end of *Desert Island Discs* and read the Sunday papers as I put the potatoes in the oven to roast and poured us cups of tea.

It was lovely being part of this grown-up world where we could invite our parents for lunch. Some people say they felt it when they started their first job or moved into their first home, but those Sundays were when I felt like a real adult.

We loved our house. We'd painted the sitting room magnolia – Glen said it was 'classy' – and we bought a green three-piece suite on credit. We must've paid hundreds of pounds for it in the end, but it looked just right so Glen had to have it. It took longer to save up for a new kitchen, but we managed in the end and picked one with white doors. We walked round the showroom for ages, holding hands like the other couples. I liked the pine cupboards but Glen wanted something 'clean'. So we went for white. Looked a bit like an operating theatre when we first put it together, to be honest, but we bought red handles, and snazzy jars and things to liven it up. I loved my kitchen – 'my department' as Glen called it.

He never did any cooking – 'I'd only make a mess,' he'd say and we'd laugh about it. So I did the cooking.

Glen would lay the table around them, play fighting with my dad to move his elbows and teasing his mum about reading the horoscopes. 'Any tall, dark strangers this week, Mum?'

His dad, George, didn't say much, but he came. Football was the only interest they shared, really. Only they couldn't even agree on that. Glen liked to watch football on the telly. His dad went to the match. Glen didn't like all those bodies squashed together, all that sweat and swearing. 'I'm more of a purist, Jean. I like the sport, not the social life.' His dad said he was a 'poofter'.

George didn't understand Glen at all and we thought he probably felt threatened by his education. Glen did well at school – always near the top of the class – and he worked hard because he was determined not to end up a cabbie, like his dad. Funny that he did end up in the same profession. I said it as a joke once, but Glen told me there was a world of difference between being a cabbie and being a driver.

I didn't know what I wanted to be. Maybe one of the pretty girls who didn't have to try. I didn't try, anyway, and Glen always said I was pretty, so it sort of came true. I did make an effort for him, but not too much make-up. He didn't like it – 'Too tarty, Jeanie.'

On our Sunday get-togethers, Mary used to bring an apple crumble and my mum brought a bunch of flowers. She wasn't a cook. She preferred tinned veg to real ones. Funny really, but Dad said it was what she'd been brought up with and he'd got used to it.

When I did domestic science at school, I used to bring home the dishes we cooked. They weren't bad, but if we'd done something 'foreign' like lasagne or chilli con carne, Mum pushed it round her plate a bit.

So roast chicken suited everyone and I always did tinned peas for her.

There was lots of laughing, I remember that. About nothing, really. Funny things that had happened at the salon or the bank, gossip about the neighbours and *EastEnders*. The kitchen would get all steamy when I was draining the carrots and cabbage and Glen would draw with his finger on the windows. Sometimes he drew hearts and Mary would smile at me. She was desperate for grandchildren and would whisper to me when we did the washing up, asking if there was any news. At first I said, 'Plenty of time for babies, Mary. We've only just got married.' Later, I pretended not to hear as I stacked the dishwasher and she stopped asking. I think she guessed it was Glen's problem. I was closer to her than my mum at the time and she knew I'd tell her if it was me. I never told her the reason, but I suppose she guessed, and Glen blamed me. 'No one's business but ours, Jeanie.'

The Sunday lunches started to tail off because Glen and his dad couldn't bear to be in the same room.

His dad found out about our fertility problem and made a joke of it the Christmas after we were told by the specialist.

'Look at this,' he said, picking up a satsuma out of the fruit bowl. 'It's like you, Glen. Seedless.'

George was a nasty man, but even he knew he'd gone too far. No one said anything. The silence was awful. No one knew what to say, so we all looked at the telly and passed the Quality Street. Pretended it hadn't happened. Glen was white as a sheet. He just sat there and I couldn't bring myself to touch him. Seedless.

In the car home, he said he'd never forgive his dad. And he didn't. We didn't refer to it again.

I wanted a baby so badly, but he wouldn't talk about 'our problem', as I had to call it, or about adoption. He disappeared inside himself and I kept myself to myself. Two strangers in the house for a while.

At the Sunday lunches Glen stopped drawing in the steam, he opened the back door to let it out. And everyone began leaving earlier and earlier and then we all started making excuses. 'We're so busy this weekend, Mary. Do you mind if we leave it until next Sunday?' Then 'next month', and gradually family lunches were just on birthdays and at Christmas.

If we'd had kids, they'd have been grandmas and granddads. It would've been different, but the pressure to perform for our parents became too much. There were no distractions. Just us. And the scrutiny of our lives was too intense for Glen. 'They want to interfere in everything,' he said after one lunch when Mary and my mum had decided where would be best for me to buy a new cooker. 'They only want to help, love,' I'd said lightly, but I could see the dark clouds gathering over him. He'd be quiet and busy with his own thoughts for the rest of the day.

He hadn't always been like that. But he started to take offence at everything. Tiny things – something the paper-shop man said about Arsenal losing, or a kid on the bus cheeking him – would upset him for days. I'd try to laugh him out of it, but I got worn down by the effort so I stopped and let him work it out for himself.

I began to wonder if he was looking for reasons to be upset. The people he'd always liked working with at the bank began to annoy him and he'd come home moaning about them. I knew he was working himself up to something – a row, probably – and I tried to talk him out of his moods. There was a time I might've been able to – when we were younger – but things were changing.

One of my ladies at the salon said all marriages 'settle down after the "truly, madly, deeply" bit'. But was this settling down? Was this it?

I suppose it was then that he started going upstairs to his computer more. Closing himself off from me. Choosing his nonsense over me.

Chapter 17

Sunday, 8 April 2007

The Detective

TAYLOR'S DELIVERY VAN was being dismantled and scrutinized, inch by inch, by the forensic boys in Southampton, along with his uniform and shoes taken from home, fingerprints, saliva swabs, and samples from under his fingernails, his genitals and hair.

And experts were conducting their dig into the dark recesses of his computer.

They were all over him. Now Sparkes wanted to try his luck with the wife.

On Easter Sunday morning, fresh from their Premier Inn breakfast in south London, Sparkes and Matthews knocked at 8 a.m.

Jean Taylor answered the door with her coat half on. 'Oh God,' she said when she saw Sparkes. 'Has something happened to Glen? His lawyer said it would all be sorted out today and he could come home.'

'No, not quite,' Sparkes said. 'I need to have a chat with you, Mrs Taylor. We can talk here rather than at the station.'

Mention of the station made Jean Taylor's eyes widen. She stood back to let the detectives in before the neighbours spotted them and wearily shrugged off the sleeve of her coat.

'You'd better come through,' she said and led the way into the living room. Jean hovered by the arm of the sofa. She looked like she hadn't slept much. Her hair was lank with exhaustion and there was a scrape of throatiness to her voice as she asked them to sit down.

'I answered all the questions yesterday with the other officers. This is all wrong.'

She was so agitated, she got up and then sat down again, lost in her own sitting room.

'Look, I'm due at my mum and dad's. I always go on a Sunday to do Mum's hair. I can't let her down,' she explained. 'I haven't told them about Glen . . .'

'Perhaps you could phone and say you're sick, Mrs Taylor,' Sparkes said. 'We need to talk about a few things.'

Jean closed her eyes as if she was about to cry, then walked to the phone to tell her lie.

'It's just a headache, Dad, but I think I'll stay in bed for a bit. Tell Mum I'll call her later.'

'Now then, Mrs Taylor,' Sparkes said. 'Tell me about you and Glen.'

'What do you mean?'

'How long have you been married? Are you both from round here?'

Jeanie told the bus-stop story and Sparkes listened attentively as she progressed through their courtship to the fairytale wedding and blissful married life.

'He worked for the bank, didn't he?' Sparkes asked. 'That must've been a good job with prospects . . .'

'Yes, it was,' Jeanie said. 'He was very proud of his job. But he left to start a business of his own. Glen has lots of ideas and plans. He likes to think big. And he didn't get on with his boss. We think he was jealous of Glen.'

Sparkes paused. 'And there was the business with the office computer, wasn't there, Mrs Taylor?'

Jean stared at him, all eyes again. 'What do you mean?' she asked. 'What about the office computer?'

Bloody hell, she doesn't know about the porn, Sparkes thought. Christ, here we go then.

'The indecent images found on his office computer, Mrs Taylor.'

The word 'indecent' hung in the air as Jean blushed and Sparkes pressed on.

'The images found on his computer at work. And on the computer we took away yesterday. Do you ever use the computer?'

She shook her head.

'There were pornographic images involving children, Mrs Taylor, found on both computers.'

She put her hands out to stop him.

'I don't know anything about pornographic images or computers,' she said, the colour deepening to bruise her neck. 'And I'm sure Glen doesn't, either. He isn't that sort of man.'

'What sort of man is he, Mrs Taylor? How would you describe him?'

'Goodness, what sort of question is that? Normal, I suppose. Normal. Hard-working, a good husband . . .'

'In what way is he a good husband?' Sparkes asked, leaning forward. 'Would you say you were happy as a couple?'

'Yes, very happy. We hardly ever argue or fall out.'

'Have you been having any problems? Money problems? Problems in your intimate life?' He didn't know why he had shied away from using 'sex life' but the woman's distress at the questions was palpable.

'What do you mean, our intimate life?' Jean had said.

'In the bedroom, Mrs Taylor,' he'd clarified delicately.

She looked as if she'd been spat on. 'No, no problems,' she managed to get out before starting to weep.

Matthews passed a box of tissues from the nest of tables at his elbow. 'There you go,' he said. 'I'll get you a glass of water.'

'I'm not trying to upset you, Mrs Taylor,' Sparkes said, 'but these are questions I need to ask. I'm investigating a very serious matter. Do you understand?'

She shook her head. She didn't understand.

'What about children, Mrs Taylor?' The detective moved on to the next incendiary subject.

'None,' she said.

'Did you decide not to have any?'

'No, we both wanted children, but we couldn't.'

Sparkes waited a beat.

'It was a physical problem with Glen. The doctor said.' She faltered. 'We love kids. That's why I know Glen could never have had anything to do with Bella's disappearance.'

The child's name was now in the room and Sparkes asked the question he'd been waiting to put.

'Where was Glen at four o'clock on the day Bella went missing, Mrs Taylor?'

'He was here, Inspector Sparkes,' Jean answered immediately. 'Here with me. He wanted to see me.'

'Why did he want to see you?' Sparkes asked.

'Just to say hello, really,' she said. 'Nothing special. Quick cuppa and then off to the depot to get his car.'

'How long was he home?'

'About . . . about forty-five minutes,' she said a little too slowly.

Is she doing the maths in her head? Sparkes thought.

'Did he often come home before returning the van?' he asked.

'Well, sometimes.'

'When was the last time he called in like this?'

'I'm not sure – I can't remember . . .' she said, ragged blotches spreading to her chest.

'I hope she doesn't play poker,' Matthews said later. 'She has more tells than I've seen for a long time.'

'How did you know it was four o'clock, Mrs Taylor?' Sparkes asked.

'I had an afternoon off work because I'd worked Sunday morning and I heard the news at four on the radio.'

'It could've been the news at five. There's a bulletin every hour. How do you know it was four?'

'I remember them saying it. You know, 'It is four o'clock, this is the BBC News.'

She stopped to sip her water.

Sparkes asked about Glen's reaction to the news of Bella's disappearance and Jean told him he was as shocked and upset as she was when they saw it on the news.

'What did he say?' Sparkes asked.

'Poor little girl. I hope they find her,' she said, carefully putting her glass on the table beside her. 'He said he thought it was probably a couple whose child had died who took her and went abroad.'

Sparkes waited for Matthews to catch up in his notebook and turned to Jean Taylor again. 'Did you ever go in the van with Glen?'

'Once. He prefers driving on his own so he can concentrate, but I went for a ride out last Christmas. To Canterbury.'

'Mrs Taylor, we're having a good look at the van at the moment. Would you mind coming to the local station to give your finger-prints so we can rule them out?'

She wiped another tear away. 'Glen keeps his van spotless. He likes everything spotless.

'They will find her, won't they?' she added as Matthews helped her on with her coat and opened the front door.

Chapter 18

Sunday, 8 April 2007

The Detective

GLEN TAYLOR WAS PROVING to be a man with an answer for everything. He had a quick brain and, once the shock of his arrest wore off, he seemed almost to be enjoying the challenge, Sparkes told his wife.

'Arrogant little sod. Not sure I'd be so confident in his position.'

Eileen squeezed his arm as she passed him his evening glass of red wine. 'No, you'd confess everything immediately. You'd be a terrible criminal. Chops or fish tonight?'

Sparkes perched on one of the high stools Eileen had insisted on when breakfast bars were de rigueur and helped himself to shards of raw carrot from the pan on the counter. He smiled at Eileen, relishing the *entente cordiale* in the kitchen that evening. Their marriage had been through the usual peaks and troughs of a shared life, but, although neither would admit it out loud, the children leaving home had put it under unexpected strain. They had talked before about all the things they would be able to do, the places they'd see, the money they could spend on themselves, but when it happened, they found their new freedom forced them to look at each other properly for the first time in years. And, Bob suspected, Eileen found him wanting.

She'd been ambitious for him when they were first going out and then married, urging him to study for his sergeant's exams and bringing him endless cups of coffee and sandwiches to fuel his concentration.

And he carried on, bringing home his triumphs and disasters as small promotions and anniversaries passed. But he suspected she was now seeing what he'd actually achieved in the cold light of late middle age and was wondering, Is that it?

Eileen squeezed by with some frozen chops and ordered him to leave the veg alone.

'Hard day, love?' she asked

It had been an exhausting day, combing through Taylor's statements for gaps and inconsistencies.

Images of children being sexually abused found on his computer were, according to the suspect, downloaded 'by mistake – the internet's fault' or without his knowledge; use of his credit card to buy porn was done by someone who had cloned his card – 'Don't you know how rife credit-card fraud is?' he'd asked scornfully. 'Jean reported our card stolen last year. She'll tell you. There's a police report somewhere.' And there was.

'Interesting that it was around the time the papers started writing about the link between credit cards and online child sex abuse,' Sparkes mused, going over the interview transcript at his desk later. But it was circumstantial.

He can see daylight, Sparkes thought during a coffee break. He thinks his story is solid, but we haven't finished yet.

Nothing seemed to get through to Taylor until they interviewed him again and showed him a scrapbook of children's pictures, torn from magazines and newspapers, found behind the water tank in the airing cupboard at his home.

There was no pantomime this time. It was clear he'd never seen it before; his mouth fell open as he leafed through the pages of images of little cherubs in cute outfits and fancy dress.

'What is this?' he asked.

'We thought you might tell us, Glen.'

They were on first-name terms by now. Glen hadn't protested. But he called the detective 'Mr Sparkes' to preserve a distance between them.

'This isn't mine,' he'd said. 'Are you sure you found it at home?'
Sparkes nodded.

'It must belong to the previous owners,' Glen said. He crossed his arms and tapped his feet as Sparkes closed the book and pushed it to one side.

'Hardly, Glen. You've lived there how many years? Maybe it belongs to you or to Jean, Glen?'

'Well, it isn't mine.'

'So it must be Jean's. Why would she keep a book like this?'

'I don't know – ask her,' Taylor had snapped. 'She's obsessed with babies. You know we couldn't have any and she used to cry all the time about it. I had to tell her to stop it – it was ruining our lives. And anyway, we've got each other. We're lucky in a way.'

Sparkes nodded along, considering Jean Taylor's luck to have a husband like Glen.

Poor woman, he thought.

A forensic psychologist they were consulting on the case had already warned him that it was very unlikely the scrapbook belonged to a paedophile.

'This isn't a predator's book,' he said. 'There's nothing sexual in the images – it's a fantasy collection, but not made by someone who objectifies children. It is more like a wish list – the sort of thing a teenage girl might make.'

Or a childless woman, Sparkes had mused.

Jean's secret fantasy life had rattled Taylor. That much was clear. He was lost in thought, perhaps wondering what else he didn't know about his wife. It had, Sparkes and Matthews agreed afterwards, created a hairline crack in his certainty that he had her under control. Secrets were dangerous things.

But at the case review meeting with his bosses, as the thirty-six-hour deadline loomed, Sparkes felt defeated. They had crawled over everything. The van had yielded nothing and they had nothing to charge Taylor with apart from the internet stuff, and that wouldn't keep him in custody.

Two hours later, Glen Taylor was bailed and walked out of the police station, already on his mobile phone. Bob Sparkes watched him go through a window in the corridor.

'Don't get too comfortable at home. We'll be back,' he told the retreating figure.

The next day, Taylor was back at work, according to the team assigned to watch him round the clock.

Sparkes wondered what Taylor's boss was making of it all.

'Bet they let him go by the end of the month,' he said to Matthews. 'Good. It'll give him time to make some mistakes if he's hanging around the house all day. Bound to get up to mischief.'

The detectives looked at each other.

'Why don't we give Alan Johnstone a call and ask if we can come and look at his driver records again. Might give him a nudge in the right direction,' Matthews said.

Mr Johnstone welcomed them into his office, sweeping paperwork off threadbare office chairs.

'Hello, Inspector. Back again? Glen said it'd all been cleared up as far as he's concerned.'

The detectives pored over the worksheets, noting the mileage all over again, while Johnstone hovered uneasily.

'Are these yours?' Sparkes said, picking up a picture of two small boys in football shirts from the desk. 'Lovely kids.' He let that hang in the air as Johnstone took the picture back.

'See you again,' Matthews said cheerily.

Glen Taylor was asked to leave later that week. Alan Johnstone rang Sparkes to let him know.

'It was freaking out the other drivers. Most of us have children. He didn't make a fuss when I paid him off; just shrugged and emptied his locker.'

Matthews grinned. 'Let's see what he does now.'

Chapter 19

Saturday, 21 April 2007

The Widow

GLEN'S MUM AND DAD came round the weekend after he was sacked. We hadn't seen them for a while and they stood at the door while the press tried to talk to them and took their pictures. George was furious and started swearing at them and Mary was in tears when I opened the door. I hugged her in the hall and led her through to the kitchen.

George and Glen went into the living room. We sat at the table and Mary carried on crying.

'What's going on, Jean? How could anyone think my Glen could do such a thing? He couldn't have done something so wicked. He was a lovely little boy. So sweet, so clever.'

I tried to calm her down and explain, but she kept talking over me, saying 'Not my Glen' over and over. In the end, I made a cup of tea to give myself something to do and took a tray through to the men.

There was a terrible atmosphere – George was standing in front of the fireplace staring at Glen, all red in the face. Glen was sitting in his armchair, looking at his hands.

'How're you doing, George?' I asked as I passed him a tea.

'I'd be a damned sight better if this idiot hadn't got himself involved with the police. Thanks, Jean. We've had the press knocking and on the phone morning, noon and night. We've had to take the phone off the hook to get some peace. Your sister's had the same, Glen. It's a bloody nightmare.'

Glen said nothing. Perhaps everything had been said before I came in.

But I couldn't let it go. I said, 'It's a nightmare for Glen, too, George. For all of us. He's done nothing and he's lost his job. It isn't fair.'

Mary and George left soon afterwards.

'Good riddance,' Glen said afterwards, but I was never sure if he meant it. It was his mum and dad, after all.

My mum and dad came next. I told Dad on the phone to go to Lisa's next door so they wouldn't be bothered by the reporters and could come through the gate between the gardens. Poor Mum, she opened the back door and came tumbling in as if a dog was after her.

She's lovely, my mum, but she finds it hard to cope with things. Ordinary things. Like catching the right bus to the doctor's or meeting new people. Dad is very good about it, really. He doesn't fuss about her 'little panics' as they call them. He just sits her down and strokes her hand and talks to her softly until she feels better. They really love each other – always have. And they love me, but Mum needs all Dad's attention.

'Anyway, you've got Glen,' she used to say.

When she sat down in the kitchen, all pale and breathless, Dad sat with her and held her hand. 'It's all right, Evelyn,' he said.

'I just need a minute, Frank.'

'Your mother just needs a bit of reassurance, Jean,' Dad had told me when I first tried to suggest they talk to the doctor. So I reassured her as well.

'Everything's going to be fine, Mum. It'll all get sorted out, you'll see. It's a horrible mistake. Glen has told them where he was and what he was doing and the police will put it right.'

She looked at me hard, as though she was testing me. 'Are you sure, Jean?'

I was.

After that, they didn't visit. I used to go and see them.

'It's too much for your mum to come over,' Dad said on the phone. I'd do her hair every week. She used to enjoy going to the hairdresser's 'for an outing' once a month, but she went out less and less after Glen's arrest. It wasn't his fault, but some days I found it hard to even like him.

Like the day he told me he'd seen my scrapbooks. It was a couple of days after he was released on bail. He'd known when he got home, but he waited. I knew he was building up to something. I could tell.

And when he found me looking at a picture of a baby in a magazine, he exploded.

My love of babies was obsessive, he said. He was angry when he said it. It was because they'd found my books at the back of the airing cupboard where I kept them, behind the water tank. They were only pictures. What harm was there in that?

He was shouting at me. He didn't shout very often, he usually just closed down and stopped talking when he got mad. Didn't like to show his feelings, really. We'd sit and watch a film together and I'd be bawling my eyes out and he'd just sit there. I thought he was so strong at first, that it was manly, but I don't know now. Perhaps he just doesn't feel things the way other people do.

But that day, he shouted. There were three little scrapbooks, each one filled with pictures I had cut out of the magazines at work, newspapers and birthday cards. I wrote 'My Babies' on the cover of each book, because they were. So many babies. I had my favourites, of course. There was Becky, with her striped Babygro and matching headband, and Theo, a chubby toddler with a smile that made me shiver.

My babies.

I suppose I knew Glen would see it as a dig at him, at him being infertile, that's why I hid them, but I couldn't stop myself.

'You're sick!' he shouted at me.

He made me feel ashamed. Perhaps I was sick.

The thing was that he wouldn't talk to me about what he called 'our problem'.

It wasn't meant to be a problem. It's just that having a baby was all I wanted to do in my life. Lisa next door felt the same.

She moved next door with her bloke, Andy, a couple of months after us. She was nice – not too nosey, but interested in me. She was pregnant when they moved in and Glen and I were trying, so we had loads to talk about, lots of plans to make – how we'd bring up our babies, what colour to do the nurseries, names, local schools, E numbers. All those things.

She didn't look like me, Lisa. She had short black hair all spiked up with bleached white tips and three earrings in one ear. She looked like one of the models in the big photos in the salon. Beautiful, really. But Glen wasn't sure about her.

'Doesn't look like our sort of person, Jeanie. Looks a bit of a flake. Why do you keep inviting her round?'

I think he was a bit jealous of sharing me, and he and Andy had nothing in common. Andy was a scaffolder, always away some-where. He went to Italy once. Anyway he went off with a woman he met on his travels and Lisa was left on her own, struggling by on benefits while she tried to get anything out of him for the children.

Lisa was lonely and we got on like a house on fire, so I went round to hers mostly, to save disturbing Glen.

I used to tell her the stories I heard at the salon and she'd laugh her head off. She loved a good gossip and a cup of coffee. She said it was an escape from the kids. She had two by then – a boy and a girl, Kane and Daisy – while I continued to wait for my turn.

After our second wedding anniversary, I went to the doctor's on my own to talk about why I couldn't get pregnant.

'You're very young, Mrs Taylor,' Dr Williams said. 'Relax and try not to think about it. That's the best thing to do.'

I tried. But after another year without a baby, I persuaded Glen to come with me. I told him there must be something wrong with me and he agreed to come, to support me.

Dr Williams listened and nodded and smiled. 'Let's do some tests,' he said, and our treks to the hospital began.

They did me first. I was willing to do anything to get pregnant and I put up with the speculums, the examinations, the ultra-sounds, the endless prodding.

'Tubes as clean as a whistle,' the gynaecologist said at the end of the tests. 'Everything healthy.'

Glen went next. I don't think he wanted to, but I'd been through it all and he couldn't really back out. It was awful, he said. They made him feel like a piece of meat. Samples, plastic cups, old torn porn magazines. All that. I tried to make it better by saying how grateful I was, but it didn't work. Then we waited.

He had almost a zero sperm count. And that was the end of it. Poor Glen. He was devastated at first. He felt he'd be seen as a failure, less of a man, and was so blinded by that that perhaps he couldn't see what it meant for me. No babies. No one to call me Mummy, no life as a mother, no grandchildren. He tried to comfort me at the beginning when I cried, but I think he got bored with it and then hardened to it after a while. He said it was for my own good. That I had to move on.

Lisa was brilliant about it and I tried not to hate her luck because I liked her, but it was hard. And she knew how hard it was for me, so she said I could be the kids' 'other mother' – I think it was a joke but I gave her a hug and tried not to cry. I was part of their lives and they became part of mine.

I persuaded Glen to make a gate between the back gardens for them to come in and out and I bought a paddling pool one summer. Glen was nice with them, but he didn't get involved like I did, really. He'd watch them through the window sometimes and wave. He didn't try to stop them coming round and sometimes, when Lisa had a date – she went on those websites to try to find the perfect man – they stayed in the spare room, sleeping top to tail. I would do fish fingers and peas and tomato sauce for dinner and watch a Disney DVD with them.

Then when they settled down in bed, I'd sit watching them go to sleep. Drinking them in. Glen didn't like that. Said I was acting creepy. But every moment with them was special. Even changing their nappies when they were little. As they got older they called me 'geegee' because they couldn't get their tongues round 'Jean' and would fling themselves at my legs when they came round so I had to walk with one on each of my feet. 'My sweet peas', I called them. And they'd laugh.

Glen would go up to his study when our games got too wild – 'too much noise', he'd say – but I didn't mind. I preferred having them to myself.

I even thought about giving up my job and looking after them full-time so Lisa could go out to work, but Glen put his foot down.

'We need your money, Jean. And they're not our kids.'

And he stopped apologizing for being infertile and started saying, 'At least we have each other, Jean. We're lucky really.'

I tried to feel lucky, but I didn't.

I've always believed in luck. I love the fact that people can change their lives instantly. Look at *Who Wants to Be a Millionaire?* And the Lottery. One minute an ordinary woman on the street. Next, a millionaire. I buy a ticket every week and can while away a morning fantasizing about winning. I know what I'd do. I'd buy a big house at the seaside – somewhere sunny, maybe abroad – and adopt orphans. Glen doesn't really figure in my plans – he wouldn't approve and I don't want those pursed lips wrecking my daydreams. Glen stays as part of my reality.

The thing is that the two of us wasn't enough for me, but he was hurt that I needed anyone but him. That was probably why he wouldn't consider adoption – 'I'm not having someone prying into our lives. No one's business but ours, Jeanie' – let alone something as 'extreme' as artificial insemination or surrogacy. Lisa and I had discussed it one evening over a bottle of wine and it all sounded possible. I tried to introduce it casually into a conversation with Glen.

'Disgusting ideas, if you ask me,' he said. End of discussion.

So I stopped crying in front of him, but every time a friend or relative said they were pregnant it was like having my heart ripped out. My dreams were filled with babies, lost babies, endless searches for them, and sometimes I'd wake up still feeling the weight of a baby in my arms.

I began to dread sleep and was losing weight. I went back to the doctor and he gave me tablets to make me feel better. I didn't tell Glen. I didn't want him to be ashamed of me.

And I began my collection, quietly tearing out the pictures and slipping them in my handbag. Then, when there were too many, I started sticking them in my books. I'd wait until I was alone and get them out and sit on the floor, stroking each picture and saying their name. I could spend hours like that, pretending they were mine.

The police said Glen did the same thing on his computer.

He told me the day he shouted at me about the scrapbooks that I drove him to look for porn on the computer. It was a wicked thing to say, but he was so angry it just came out.

He said I'd shut him out because of my obsession with having a baby. That he'd had to look for comfort elsewhere.

'It's just porn,' he said to me when he realized he'd gone too far. When he saw my face. 'All blokes like a bit of porn, don't they, Jeanie? It doesn't do any harm to anyone. Just a bit of fun.'

I didn't know what to say. I didn't know all blokes liked porn. The subject had never come up in the salon.

When I cried, he told me it wasn't his fault. He'd been drawn into online porn by the internet – they shouldn't allow these things on the web. It was a trap for innocent men. He'd become addicted to it – 'it's a medical condition, Jeanie, an addiction' – he couldn't help himself, but he'd never looked at children. Those images just ended up on his computer – like a virus.

I didn't want to think about it any more. It was too hard to keep everything apart in my head. My Glen and this other man the police talked about. I needed to keep things straight.

I wanted to believe him. I loved Glen. He was my world. I was his, he said. We were each other's.

And the idea of me being guilty of pushing him to look at those horrible photos grew in my head, crowding out the questions about Glen. Of course, I didn't find out about his 'addiction' until after the police came knocking on our door that Easter Saturday, and then it was too late to say or do anything.

I had to keep his secrets as well as mine.

Chapter 20

Friday, 11 June 2010

The Widow

WE HAVE CROISSANTS and fruit salad for breakfast at the hotel. Big linen napkins and a cafetière of proper coffee.

Kate won't let me eat on my own. 'I'll keep you company,' she says and plonks herself down at the table. She gets a cup from the tea and coffee tray under the television and pours herself a coffee.

She's all businesslike now. 'We really need to sort out the contract today, Jean,' she says. 'The paper would like to get the formalities out of the way so we can press on with the interview. It's Friday already and they want to publish it tomorrow. I've printed a copy of the contract for you to sign. It's quite straightforward. You agree to give us an exclusive interview for an agreed fee.'

I can't really remember when I'd said yes. Maybe I hadn't. 'But—' I say. But she just passes me several sheets of paper and I start to read them because I don't know what else to do. It is all 'the first party' and 'the second party' and lots of clauses. 'I haven't got a clue what it means,' I say. Glen was the one who dealt with all the paperwork and signed everything.

She looks anxious and starts to try and explain the legal terms. 'It really is very simple,' she says. She really wants me to sign it. She must be getting grief from her boss, but I put the contract down and shake my head and she sighs.

'Would you like a lawyer to have a look at it for you?' she asks. I nod. 'Do you know one?' she says and I nod again. I call Tom Payne. Glen's lawyer. It's been a while – must be two years – but I still have his number on my mobile.

'Jean! How are you? I was sorry to hear about Glen's accident,' he says when the secretary finally puts me through.

'Thank you, Tom, that's kind of you. Look, I need your help. The *Daily Post* wants me to do an exclusive interview with them and they want me to sign a contract. Will you look at it for me?'

There is a pause and I can imagine the surprise on his face.

'An interview?' he says. 'Are you sure you're doing the right thing, Jean? Have you thought this through?'

His real questions remain unasked and I'm grateful to him for that. I tell him I've thought about it and this is the only way to get the press off my doorstep. I'm starting to sound like Kate. I don't really need the money. Glen got a quarter of a million in compensation for the trick the police pulled – dirty money we put away in a building society – and there'll be the insurance money from his death. But I might as well take the fifty thousand pounds the paper wants to pay me.

Tom sounds unconvinced, but he agrees to read the contract and Kate emails it over to him. We sit and wait and she tries to persuade me to have a facial or something. I don't want to be fiddled with again so I say no and just sit there.

Tom and I have had a special bond since the day Glen's case ended.

We stood together waiting for him to be released from the dock and Tom couldn't look at me. I think he was scared of what he'd see in my eyes.

I can see us standing there. The end of the ordeal, but not the end really. I'd been so grateful for the order that the court case had given my life. Every day planned out. Every day setting out from home at 8 a.m., dressed smartly, like I was going to work in an office. Every day, home at five thirty. My job was to be supportive and say nothing.

The court was like a sanctuary. I liked the echoing halls and the breezes wafting the notices on the boards and the canteen chatter.

Tom had taken me there before Glen was due to appear, to be committed for trial, so I could see what it was like. I'd seen the Old Bailey on the telly – on the news with a reporter standing on the pavement in front of it, talking about a murder or terrorist or something, and the inside, in police dramas. But it was still nothing like I expected. Dim, smaller than it looked on TV, dusty-smelling like a classroom, old-fashioned with lots of dark wood.

It was lovely and quiet when we went for a look round before business began for the day. Hardly anyone else there. Bit different when Glen appeared so they could set a date for his trial. It was packed. People had queued to see him. They brought sandwiches and flasks like it was the sales or something. And the reporters crammed into the press seats behind me. I sat with my head down, pretending to look for something in my handbag, until Glen was brought into the box by the prison warders. He looked small. I'd brought in his best suit for the appearance and he'd had a shave, but he still looked small. He looked over and winked. Like it was nothing. I tried to smile at him but my mouth was too dry, my lips got stuck to my teeth.

It was over so quickly I hardly had time to look at him again before he disappeared down the stairs. I was allowed to see him later. He'd changed out of his suit into his prison stuff, a sort of tracksuit, and taken off his best shoes. 'Hello, Jeanie love. Well, that was a bit of a farce, wasn't it? The whole thing is a farce, my solicitor says,' he said.

Well, he would, I wanted to say. You're paying him to say just that.

The trial was set for February, four months away, and Glen was sure it would be thrown out before then. 'It's all nonsense, Jeanie,' he said. 'You know that. The police are lying to make themselves look good. They need an arrest and I was one of the poor sods who was driving a blue van in the area that day.' He gave my hand a squeeze and I squeezed back. He was right. It was nonsense.

I went home and pretended everything was normal.

Inside the house it was. My little world stayed exactly the same – same walls, same cups, same furniture. But outside, everything had shifted. The pavement in front of the house was like a soap opera with people coming and going and sitting looking at my house. Hoping to get a glimpse of me.

I had to come out sometimes, and when I did I dressed anonymously, covering myself completely, and I steeled myself in the hall before leaving suddenly and quickly. It was impossible to avoid the cameras but I hoped they'd get tired of the same shots of me walking down the path. And I learned to hum a song in my head so I could blank out the remarks and questions.

The visits to the prison were the worst part. It meant catching a bus and the press would follow me to the stop and photograph me and the other passengers as we waited together. Everyone got upset with them and then me. It wasn't my fault, but they blamed me. For being the wife.

I tried walking to different bus stops, but I got fed up with playing their games, and in the end I just put up with it and waited for them to get bored.

I'd sit on the 380 bus to Belmarsh with a plastic carrier bag on my knee, pretending to be on a shopping trip. I'd wait to see if someone else would press the bell before the prison stop and then get off quickly. Other women would get off as well, with a tangle of crying kids and pushchairs, and I'd walk a long way behind them to the visitors' centre so people wouldn't think I was like them.

Glen was on remand so there weren't so many rules about visits, but the one I liked best was that I couldn't wear high heels, short skirts or see-through clothes. It made me laugh. The first time, I wore trousers and a jumper instead. Nice and safe.

Glen didn't like it. 'I hope you're not letting yourself go, Jean,' he said, so I put lipstick on next time.

He could have three visits a week, but we agreed I'd only come twice so I didn't have to deal with the reporters too often. Mondays and Fridays. 'It'll give my week a shape,' he said.

The room was noisy and brightly lit and it hurt my eyes and ears. We'd sit across from each other and when I'd told him my news and he'd told me his, we'd listen to the other conversations going on around us and talk about them instead.

I thought my job was to comfort him and reassure him that I was standing by him, but he seemed to have that covered already.

'We can weather this, Jeanie. We know the truth and so will everyone else soon. Don't you worry,' he'd say at least once a visit. I tried not to, but I felt like our life was slipping away.

'What if the truth doesn't come out?' I asked him once and he looked disappointed that I would even suggest it.

'It will,' he insisted. 'My lawyer says the police have screwed up royally.'

When Glen's case wasn't thrown out before the trial, he said the police 'want their day in court'. He looked smaller every time I saw him, as if he was shrinking inside himself.

'Don't worry love,' I heard myself say. 'All over soon.'

He looked grateful.

Chapter 21

Monday, 11 June 2007

The Detective

SPARKES WAS REVIEWING the situation. It had been two months since he'd first knocked on Glen Taylor's door and they were not making any progress. It wasn't that they hadn't been looking. His colleagues had been examining every detail of his life – and the lives of Mike Doonan and Lee Chambers – but they had little to show for it so far.

Doonan appeared to have led a pretty grey existence, with even his divorces failing to provide a splash of colour. The only point of interest was that the two ex-wives had become close friends and chimed in with each other when discussing Mike's faults. 'He's a bit selfish, I suppose,' Marie Doonan said. 'Yeah, selfish,' Sarah Doonan chorused. 'We're better off without him.'

Even his children were uninterested in his involvement with the police. 'Never see him,' his eldest said. 'He was gone before I realized he was there.'

Matthews dug on, dogged in his pursuit. His blood pressure flickered when he discovered that Doonan had not arrived for his doctor's appointment on the day Bella vanished, but the driver said his spine had been so painful he couldn't leave the flat. And the GP backed him up. 'He can barely stand at times,' he said. 'Poor man.'

He still couldn't be ruled out, but Sparkes was becoming impatient with Matthews, demanding that he turn his attention to Taylor.

'Doonan is crippled – he can hardly walk, so how the hell could he kidnap a child?' Sparkes asked. 'We've got nothing beyond the fact that he was driving a blue van to link him to the case, have we?'

Matthews shook his head. 'No, Boss, but there's the Operation Gold stuff.'

'Where's the evidence he looked at those images? There isn't any. Taylor has got child porn on his computer. He's the one we should be concentrating on. I need you on this, Matthews.'

The sergeant was not convinced it was time to close the book on Doonan, but he knew that his boss had made up his mind.

The real problem for Sparkes was that he couldn't let go of his first instinct that they'd already found their man and he was afraid that, unless they stopped him, he would go looking for another Bella.

Sparkes had begun to notice every child of Bella's age – in the street, in shops, in cars and cafés – and then he'd scan for predators. It was beginning to affect his appetite, but not his focus. He knew it was taking over his life, but there was nothing else he could do.

'You are obsessed with this case, Bob,' Eileen had said the other night. 'Can't we just go out for a drink without you disappearing back inside your head? You need to relax.'

He had wanted to scream, 'Do you want another child to be taken while I'm off having a glass of wine?' But didn't. It wasn't Eileen's fault. She didn't understand. He knew he couldn't protect every little girl in the city, but he couldn't stop trying.

There had been many other cases involving children during his career – little Laura Simpson; Baby W, shaken to death by his stepfather; the Voules boy, who'd drowned in a park paddling pool surrounded by other kids; traffic accidents and runaways – but he had not known them the way he knew Bella.

He remembered the feeling of helplessness when he had first

held his son James, the thought that he alone was responsible for his child's well-being and safety in a world full of danger and bad people. That's how he felt about Bella.

He'd begun dreaming about her. That was never a good sign.

He wondered if the blue van was distracting them from other lines. But then why had the man in the blue van never come forward? Everyone wanted to help find this child. If it had just been a bloke visiting a house, he would've rung in, wouldn't he?

Unless it was Glen Taylor, he thought.

The search had been thorough, fragment by fragment pored over by the team. A discarded T-shirt in a hedge, a single shoe, a blonde child spotted in a shopping centre trying to get away from an adult. The detectives were on a hair trigger as the hours, then days, then weeks passed with no results. They were all exhausted, but no one could call it over.

Every morning, the update meeting got shorter and gloomier. The T-shirt was for an eight-year-old, the shoe wasn't Bella's, and the blonde screamer was a toddler having a tantrum. Leads evaporated as soon as they were examined.

Sparkes kept his despair to himself. Once his head went down, the team would give up. Each morning he gave himself a pep talk in his office, sometimes standing in front of the mirror in the toilets, making sure no one could read failure in his increasingly pouchy eyes. Then he'd stride in, energy high, and galvanize his men and women.

'Let's go back to basics,' he said that morning. And they did, following him from photos to maps to names to lists. 'What are we missing?' he challenged them. Tired faces. 'Who would take a child? What do we know from other cases?'

'A paedophile.'

'A paedophile ring.'

'Kidnapper for money.'

'Or revenge.'

'A woman who's lost a baby.'

'Or can't have a baby.'

'A fantasist who needs a child to fulfil a scenario.'

Sparkes nodded. 'Let's split into two-man – sorry, person – teams and look at our witnesses and persons of interest again, to see if any fit those categories.'

The room began to buzz and he left Ian Matthews to it.

He wondered how quickly Jean Taylor's name would come up and wanted time to think it through himself. Jean was an odd one. He remembered the first time he'd seen her, the shock on her face, the tricky interviews, the unshakable answers. He felt certain she was covering for Glen and had put this down to blind loyalty, but was it because she was involved somehow?

Women who killed children were rare, and those who did almost exclusively killed their own, according to the stats. But they did steal children occasionally.

He knew infertility could be a powerfully motivating force. It burned within some women, sending them mad with grief and longing. The neighbour and colleagues at the salon had said Jean was devastated when she couldn't have a baby. Used to cry in the back room if a customer talked about being pregnant. But nobody had placed Jean in Southampton on the day Bella was taken.

Sparkes doodled as he thought, drawing spiders on the pad in front of him.

If Jean loved children so much, why would she stay with a man who looks at child abuse on the computer? Why would she be loyal to a man like that? He was certain Eileen would be out of the door instantly. And he wouldn't blame her. So what was Glen's hold over his wife?

'Perhaps we've been looking at it from the wrong angle,' he told his reflection as he washed his hands in the Gents'. 'Maybe it's her hold over Glen? Perhaps Jean put him up to it?'

Sure enough, Jean's name was scrawled on the whiteboard in the incident room when he returned. The officers looking at 'women who can't have babies' were discussing previous cases. 'Thing is, Sir,' one of the team said, 'it's usually a woman acting on her own who takes a child and they don't go for toddlers. Some pretend to their partners or family that they are pregnant, wearing maternity clothes and padding, and then take babies from maternity units or prams outside shops to fulfil the pretence. Taking a toddler is high risk. Little kids can put up quite a fight if they are frightened and a crying child attracts attention.'

Dan Fry, one of the force's new graduate recruits, raised his hand and Matthews nodded at him to add his piece. He was young, barely out of the Student Union bar, and stood to speak to the group, unaware that the culture was to stay seated and address the desktop.

Fry cleared his throat. 'Then there's keeping an older child out of sight. It's a lot harder to explain the sudden appearance of a two-year-old to friends and family. If you were snatching a child of that age to bring up as your own, you'd have to disappear too. And the Taylors haven't budged.'

'Quite right, um, Fry, is it?' Sparkes said, waving him to sit down.

The other teams had ruled out kidnap for cash or revenge. Dawn Elliott didn't have any money of her own and they'd trawled back through her teenage years for previous boyfriends and evidence of drugs or prostitution, in case there was an organized-crime connection. But there was nothing. She was a small-town girl who'd worked in an office until she'd fallen for a married man and become pregnant.

They still hadn't found Bella's father – the name he had given Dawn seemed to be false and the mobile phone number was a pay-as-you-go that no longer rang.

'He's a chancer, Boss,' Matthews said. 'Just out for a bit of extra-marital and then disappears. The life of a thousand reps. A shag in every town.'

'Paedophiles' was all that was left on the board.

The energy leached out of the room. 'Meanwhile, back at Glen Taylor,' Sparkes said.

'And Mike Doonan,' Matthews muttered. 'What about Operation Gold?'

But his superior officer appeared not to hear him. He was listening to his own fears.

Sparkes was certain that Glen Taylor was already thinking about his next victim. Fuelling his thoughts with internet porn. Looking at those images became an addiction – as hard to kick as a drug, according to psychologists.

Sparkes had been told the reasons why blokes became dependent on internet porn – depression, anxiety, money troubles, work problems – and some of the theories about the 'chemical payoff' – the thrill produced by adrenalin, dopamine and serotonin. One report he read as homework compared viewing porn to 'the rush of first-time sex' for some men, leading them to chase a repetition of the same high with more and more extreme images. 'A bit like how cocaine addicts describe their experience,' it had added.

Surfing on the net was a safe fantasy world full of excitement, a way of creating a private space in which to offend.

'Interestingly,' Sparkes told Matthews later, as they sat in the canteen, 'not all porn addicts get erections.'

Ian Matthews raised an eyebrow as he rested his sausage sandwich on the Formica table. 'Do you mind, Boss? I'm eating. What are you reading there? Sounds like complete bollocks.'

'Thank you, professor,' he snapped. 'I'm trying to get inside Glen Taylor's murky little world. We're not getting in there through interviews, but he won't be able to break his habit and I'll be waiting for him. We'll find him and catch him.'

The sergeant sat back heavily and resumed chewing on his lunch. 'Go on then, tell me how.'

'Fry, one of the clever kids they've sent us to knock into shape, came to see me yesterday. He says we've missed a potential trick. Chat rooms. That's where porn addicts and sexual predators look for friends and lose their inhibitions.'

DC Fry had paid a visit to his senior officer's office, pulling up a chair without being invited and treating the conversation like a university tutorial.

'The problem, as I see it, is we need disclosure from Glen Taylor.'

No shit, Sherlock, Sparkes thought. 'Go on, Fry.'

'Well, perhaps we need to enter his world and catch him at his most vulnerable.'

'I'm sorry, Fry, can we cut to the chase? What are you on about – "his world"?'

'I bet he's on the prowl in chat rooms – probably looking for new prospects – and he could disclose some key evidence to us if we pose as punters. We could put in a CHIS.'

Sparkes raised an eyebrow. 'Sorry?'

'A Covert Human Intelligence Source, Sir, to watch him at work. We covered it at college and I think it's well worth a try,' he finished, uncrossing his long legs and leaning on Sparkes' desk.

Sparkes had automatically leaned back – physically and mentally. It wasn't that Fry was cleverer than him. It was the confidence the younger man had that he was right that needled him. That's what university does for you, he thought.

Bloody university education, he could hear his dad say. *Waste of bloody time. It's for people with money and nothing to do.*

Not you, was the message to the seventeen-year-old with an application form in his hand.

There'd been no further discussion on the subject. His dad was a clerk at the district council and preferred his world small and known. 'Security' was his watchword and he urged his son to have the same lower-middle-class mindset.

'Get your A levels and get a nice office job, Robert. Job for life.'

Bob had kept his application to the police secret from both his parents – funny, he always thought of them as one person, mumanddad – and presented it as a fait accompli when he was accepted. He didn't use the words 'fait accompli'. His mumanddad didn't hold with foreign stuff.

He'd done well with the police but his rise had not been meteoric. That wasn't how things were done in his day; it was words like 'committed', 'insightful' and 'methodical' that had punctuated his appraisals and recommendations.

The new breed of graduates on fast-track entry would cringe

if they were described in the same way, Sparkes thought.

'Tell me about chat rooms,' Sparkes said, and Fry, who looked like he barely shaved, let alone went looking for sex on the internet, told him he had written a dissertation on the subject.

'My Psychology tutor is researching the effects of pornography on personality. I'm sure she'd help us,' he'd said.

By the end of the week, Sparkes, Matthews and Fry were on their way to the young officer's alma mater in the Midlands. Dr Fleur Jones greeted the men at the lift door and looked so young Sparkes thought she must be a student.

'We're here to talk to Dr Jones,' Matthews said and Fleur laughed, used to – and secretly enjoying – the confusion created by her dyed red hair, pierced nose and short skirt.

'That's me. You must be DI Sparkes and Sergeant Matthews. Nice to meet you. Hello, Dan.'

The three men squeezed their joint bulk into the utilitarian booth that served as Fleur Jones's workspace and Sparkes and Matthews began scrutinizing the walls out of habit. The message board was covered in childish drawings, but when they focused in on the detail, they realized they were looking at pornographic images.

'Good grief,' Bob Sparkes said. 'Who the hell did these? Not your usual kindergarten artworks.'

Dr Jones smiled patiently and Fry smirked. 'Part of my research,' she said. 'Getting habitual pornography users to draw what they witness online can reveal personality traits and lets them see things differently, perhaps enabling them to see the human beings behind the sexual objects they seek out.'

'Right,' said Sparkes, wondering what the sex offenders on his patch would produce given crayons. 'Well, Dr Jones, we don't want to take too much of your valuable time, so shall we get down to the reason we're here?'

The psychologist crossed her bare legs and nodded intently, eye contact unwavering. Sparkes tried to mirror her body language but he couldn't cross his legs without kicking Matthews and he started to feel a bit hot.

Dr Jones rose and opened her window. 'Getting a bit stuffy in here – sorry, it's a small room.'

Sparkes cleared his throat and began: 'We're investigating the disappearance of Bella Elliott, as DC Fry has told you. We have a suspect, but we're looking for new approaches to find out if he took the child. He has an extensive interest in sexual images of children and adults dressed as children. There are images on his computer. He says he didn't download them intentionally.'

Dr Jones allowed herself a twitch of a smile of recognition.

'He's very manipulative and is turning our interviews into a masterclass in evasion.'

'Addicts are brilliant liars, Inspector. They lie to themselves and then to everyone else. They're in denial about their problem and they are experts at finding excuses and other people to blame,' Dr Jones said. 'Dan tells me you are interested in trying to interact with the suspect in sex chat rooms?'

She can't be more than thirty, Sparkes thought.

The psychologist clocked the pause and smiled knowingly.

'Er, yes, yes, that's right. But we need to understand much more about these chat rooms and how to approach our man,' he said quickly.

There followed a lecture on finding sexual partners online, with the older detectives following with difficulty. It wasn't that they were computer illiterates, it was that the close proximity of Dr Jones and her restless legs was far too distracting to allow full concentration. In the end, Dan Fry took over, using the psychologist's computer to take his bosses into a cyber-fantasy world.

'As I'm sure you know, it's basically instant messaging, Sir,' he explained. 'You sign into a chat room that advertises itself as for singles, say, or teenagers, use a nickname to hide your real identity, and you can communicate with everyone else in that 'room' or just one person. You just start chatting by writing texts.

'They can't see each other so they can be anyone. That's the attraction for predators. They can assume a new identity, or gender, or age group. Wolf in sheep's clothing,' Fry said.

Once contact was established with a likely individual – a young teen, perhaps – the predator might persuade her to give her email address so grooming could go on in private.

'Once they have one-to-one contact, anything is possible. For consenting adults, that isn't a problem, but some youngsters have been tricked or manipulated into posing for explicit photographs, using a webcam. The predator can then blackmail them into other acts. Young lives ruined,' Fry added.

Recap over, Sparkes had a go in an over-eighteens chat room. Matthews had suggested Superstud as his nickname and snorted when his boss opted instead for Mr Darcy – Eileen's favourite. But Mr Darcy was greeted by a flurry of flirty messages from would-be Elizabeth Bennets that quickly escalated into direct sexual propositions.

'Bloody hell,' he said as the explicit messages scrolled up the screen. 'A bit in-your-face for Jane Austen, isn't it?'

Dr Jones laughed from behind him. He signed himself out and turned to face her.

'But how do we find Glen Taylor?' he asked. 'There must be hundreds of these chat rooms.'

Fry had his plan ready.

'Yes, but we've got his computer so we know where he's been. Taylor's clever and when Operation Gold started to bite he probably deleted files and data, but it's all still there on the hard drive, invisible to him but very visible to the blokes in the forensic lab. They've dug out all sorts of information and we know where he hangs out.'

Sparkes found himself nodding, seduced by the mental picture of Taylor's face when he arrested him. He could almost smell the fox-like stench of Taylor's guilt. He tried to focus on the practicalities.

'" We" being who, exactly?' he asked.

'Fleur and I would work out a character, a back story and a script with some trigger words to use,' DC Fry said, pink with excitement at the prospect of real detective work, and Dr Jones murmured her assent.

'It could be very valuable for my research.'

It felt signed and sealed, but Matthews piped up with the question no one had asked. 'Is it legal?'

The others in the room looked at him.

'Will it stand up as evidence in court, Sir? It could be seen as entrapment,' he pressed.

Sparkes wondered if Matthews was reacting to the new boy's clever-dickery. He didn't know the answers, but Fry gave him a possible way out.

'We don't have a case to destroy, from what I've seen, Sir. Why don't we see how far we get first? Then we can revisit this question,' he said.

Matthews looked unhappy, but Sparkes nodded his agreement.

Chapter 22

Tuesday, 12 June 2007

The Widow

FUNNY THINGS, BIRTHDAYS. Everyone seems to love them, but I dread them – the build-up, the pressure to be happy, to have a good time, the disappointment when I don't. I'm thirty-seven today and Glen is downstairs doing a tray of breakfast. It's still early and I'm not hungry yet so the food will be like sawdust in my mouth, but I'll have to tell him I love it. Love him. I do. I do. He's my world, but every birthday, I wonder if maybe this year there'll be a miracle and we'll have a baby.

I try not to think about it, but birthdays are difficult. It's that moment when you realize another year's gone past, isn't it? I know there's everything else going on, but I can't help it.

We could adopt from abroad. I've seen all these articles about babies from China, but I can't say anything to Glen without upsetting him.

Here he comes. I can hear the cups and plates rattling on the tray. He's all smiles and there's a red rose in a vase beside the boiled egg. He sings 'Happy Birthday' as he comes round to my side of the bed, putting on a funny voice to make me laugh. 'Happy birthday, dear Jeanie, happy birthday to you,' he croons and kisses me on the forehead, nose and mouth.

It makes me cry and he shifts the tray off my lap and sits so he can put both arms round me.

'Sorry, love. Don't know what's wrong with me,' I say, trying to smile. He shushes me and goes to get his card and present from the wardrobe.

It's a nightie. White broderie anglaise with pink bows. Like a little girl's. 'It's lovely,' I say and give him a kiss. 'Thank you, darling.'

'Try it on,' he says.

'Later. Need the loo.' I don't want to put it on. I go to the bathroom and take a Jeanie pill. I hate birthdays.

Just before Bella's birthday, in April, the first since she went missing, I went to Smith's to buy a card for her. I spent ages looking at the pictures and messages and I picked one with Teletubbies and a badge – 'I am 3' – because I read in the papers that she liked them best.

I didn't know what to write so I went and sat on a bench in the park to think about her. I don't feel sad because I know she's alive. Her mother and I believe she's alive. So does Glen. We think a couple whose child died took her and went abroad. I wonder if the police have thought of that. I expect Glen's told them his theory.

So I write 'Dearest Bella. Happy Birthday. I hope you are home soon' and some kisses. I address it to her, Miss Bella Elliott. I don't know the number of her house but I expect the postman will know. The mother says she gets dozens of letters every day. She said on *Woman's Hour* that some of them are nasty letters from 'mad' people, telling her she deserved to lose Bella. One of those must be mine.

I wrote at the beginning, when I was so angry with her for leaving Bella on her own when I couldn't even have a baby. I wanted her to know how wrong she'd been. I didn't sign that one either.

I put a stamp on the birthday card, all bumpy with the badge inside, and walked home the postbox way.

On the day, 28 April, Dawn was on breakfast television with a little cake with three candles. She was wearing the birthday badge

I sent next to her Find Bella badge. She thanked everyone for the lovely cards and presents and said she wasn't unwrapping them until Bella comes home. The woman doing the interview got all choked up.

I unwrapped the present I bought for her – a baby doll with golden hair and a white and pink dress – and put her on my bed.

I could do it because Glen wasn't here. He'd gone out for a drive. He wouldn't be back for ages and until then I could spend time with Bella.

I have photos of her from the papers and nice colour ones from magazines. I decided not to put her in the scrapbooks because she's real and special and I hope to meet her one day. When she comes home.

I plan it. How we'll meet in a park and she'll know it's me and come running over, laughing and nearly tripping over she's running so fast. Her little arms will wrap round my legs and I'll bend down and pick her up and swing her round.

It's my favourite daydream, but it's beginning to take over my day. Sometimes I find myself sitting at the kitchen table and the clock shows I've been there for more than an hour and I don't remember the time passing. Sometimes I find I'm crying but I don't know why, exactly. I went to the doctor to talk to him. I didn't mention Bella but he knew all about Glen's 'circumstances', as he put it, and I came away with a new prescription.

'You need some peace of mind, Mrs Taylor,' he said, tearing it off his pad. 'Have you thought about taking a break from what's happening?' He meant well but there is no break to be taken. I can't stop the thoughts by catching a plane somewhere. I don't control them – or anything – any more. I'm a passenger, not the driver, I want to tell him. Anyway, the pills should let me carry on being Jeanie when I need to be.

Bella's mum is on the telly all the time. She's being interviewed on every talk show, spewing out the same old stuff about 'her angel' and how she cries herself to sleep every night. She never misses an opportunity. I wonder if she's getting paid.

139

I raise the question on a radio phone-in late at night. Chris from Catford comes straight on the line to back me up. 'What kind of mother is she?' he screeches. I'm glad other people see through her too.

Since 'retiring', as Glen calls it, I spend my days watching day-time telly and doing word searches in puzzle books and taking part in radio phone-ins. Funny, I used to think that the radio was for brainy people – all that talking. But I started to put the local commercial station on for company and I got pulled in. There is a sort of gang of people who phone in – the same voices, week in, week out. The old bloke who wants all immigrants thrown out, the woman who can't say her Rs who thinks politicians should be put in pwison, the young lad who blames women for the rise in sex crime. They start at angry and their voices get higher and louder as they work themselves up. It doesn't matter what the subject is, they can always be outraged, and I got addicted to it.

I finally picked up the phone one day when they were discussing whether paedophiles could be cured. I said my name was Joy and told the presenter that paedophiles should be strung up. It went down well because there were loads of calls agreeing. And that was it. I was one of them. I changed my name every week or so. Ann, Kerry, Sue, Joy, Jenny, Liz. It was brilliant being someone else, even for ninety seconds, and having someone listen to you without knowing who you're married to and judging you.

I found I had lots of opinions. I could be Mrs Angry or a 'bleeding heart liberal' as Glen puts it. I could be anyone I wanted.

And it stopped me being lonely. Of course, Lisa had disappeared with the rest of my life. At first, she kept calling round and inviting me in. She wanted to know all about it and was so sweet to me. She said she didn't believe a word of it. But the kids didn't come round any more. There was always an excuse: Kane had a cold, Daisy was practising her ballet for an exam, Lisa's sister was coming to stay. Then she nailed the gate shut. Just one nail, high up.

'I was worried about break-ins,' she said. 'You understand, Jeanie?' And I tried to.

Chapter 23

Monday, 18 June 2007

The Detective

OVER THE WEEKEND, Dan Fry and Fleur Jones had picked the name Jodie Smith. Jodie because they thought it had a childlike ring to it and Smith for anonymity. Jodie was a twenty-seven-year-old woman from Manchester, a junior secretary in a local authority office who'd been abused as a child by her father and who got a sexual thrill from dressing up as a child for sex.

'It's hardly subtle,' Sparkes had commented when presented with the first draft of the lurid back story. 'He'll see straight through this. Couldn't we tone things down a bit? Anyway, why would a woman who's been sexually abused want to relive that as an adult?'

Fry sighed. He was impatient to get going, finally get his teeth into some real police work instead of acting as the incident room gopher, but he could sense the mood was changing in the room; the DI was in retreat. 'That's a good question, Sir,' he said, using his favourite positive-reinforcement technique.

Sparkes thought Fry was a patronizing little twat but decided to hear him out.

The younger officer pointed out that Jodie was modelled on an actual case study and there followed a detailed psychological analysis of motives, Post Traumatic Stress Disorder, acting out and the darker side of human sexuality. Sparkes looked impressed and interested, his misgivings pushed back into a recess for the time being.

'What does Dr Jones say? Has she signed off on this?' he asked.

'Yes, well almost, Sir,' Fry said. 'I read the final draft to her on the phone this morning and she seemed happy with it, and I'll email it in a minute for her comments.'

'OK. Once we have her approval we'll present the strategy to the DCI,' Sparkes said.

DCI Brakespeare loved new ideas. Innovation was his byword, along with a clutch of other management clichés – and, crucially, he was as determined as Sparkes to nail Taylor. 'This could make our names,' he said, rubbing his hands together as he heard them out. 'Let's take it to the Chief Super.'

It was decided to put the whole team before Chief Superintendent Parker. The meeting was a classic. Dr Jones arrived wearing what looked like pyjamas, a diamond glinting in one nostril, and Parker sat behind his Master of the Universe desk in full uniform and Brylcreem.

He listened in silence as DCI Brakespeare outlined the plan and the risk assessment, and quoted the necessary legislation to go undercover, then blew his nose and said, 'Where's the evidence that this will work? Has anyone else tried it? Sounds like entrapment to me.'

Brakespeare, Sparkes and Fry took turns in offering answers and Dr Jones interjected with scientific data and charm. Finally, CS Parker put up his hands and pronounced judgement.

'Let's give it a punt. If we don't get the evidence here, it sounds like we're unlikely to ever manage to put it in front of a jury. Let's make sure we have clean hands – no prompting or leading. Everything done by the book. We'll get the evidence and then see if the judge allows it. Let's face it, if Taylor takes us to a body, it won't matter how we got it.'

He called Sparkes back in after the others had left to ask him about Fleur Jones.

'Is she flakey, Bob? She looked like she got dressed in the dark and we are trusting her as our expert. How will she stand up to cross-examination?'

Sparkes sat down again. 'Very well, Sir. She knows her stuff – has degrees and research papers coming out of her ears.'

Parker looked dubious.

'She's an expert in sexual deviancy and frequently works with criminals,' Sparkes ploughed on. 'And that's just the university staff.' The joke fell to the ground, writhing.

'Right,' the Chief Super said. 'OK, she's qualified, but why her and not our own people?'

'Because she's got an excellent working relationship with Fry already – he trusts her. And she'll look good in front of a jury.'

'This is on your head, Bob. Let's see how she gets on, but make sure you are there every step of the way.'

Sparkes closed the door quietly.

He joined Fleur Jones and the others in the forensic lab for a tour of Glen Taylor's virtual playground. It was not an edifying experience, but Dr Jones seemed the least affected. They stood behind the technician as he scrolled through the websites and chat rooms they had found on Taylor's hard drive during their first search, spotting his favourites, the times when he visited, length of stay and other helpful habits. LolitaXXX seemed to be top of his list of porn sites and he hung out in Teen Fun and Girls Lounge chat rooms, using five different identities, including Whosthedaddy and BigBear. Matthews smirked. 'Not Mr Darcy, then, Boss.'

Taylor's public chats were fairly innocuous, flirtatious and jokey – the sort of small talk you'd hear at a teenage party. The more explicit stuff happened away from the chat rooms. The inbox of an email address used only for his 'sexcursions', as Taylor called them in his mails, offered up a far more sinister glimpse into his secret world. Here, he persuaded others to join him. From the photos sent to him, some were teens, others adults, but they all looked like kids.

Sparkes asked for a printout of all the chat-room conversations and private emails and Fry took them away to confer with Dr Jones.

'Is he up to this?' Matthews asked. 'He's only just got here and he's got no operational experience.'

'I know, but he's got the knowledge . . . and we'll be there every step of the way. Let's give him a chance,' Sparkes answered.

'You're going to call yourself Goldilocks? Are you sure?' Matthews laughed when Fry and his tutor reappeared in Sparkes' office.

Fry nodded. 'We think it will appeal to his interest in children and fantasy,' he explained.

'Bloody hell. Bet he doesn't fall for that one.'

But he did. Goldilocks met BigBear and flirted discreetly for a week. Fry and Matthews sat for hours in front of a computer screen, their working life compressed into a tiny room in the Forensics department lit by a buzzing fluorescent tube, with Jodie's life story pasted up on a wall beside them. Fry had found a photo of a girl he'd admired at college on Facebook and had an enlargement of her face stuck just above the screen.

'Hi Goldie.'

'How's things?'

'How are you feeling tonight?'

Sparkes, occasionally watching over his shoulder, felt a mixture of excitement and nausea as the nightly tango with Glen Taylor continued. Fleur Jones had given Dan Fry extensive coaching and she was on the end of a phone if they needed her, but even with Matthews in the room, Sparkes worried that his newest recruit must feel very alone.

He'd gone out on a limb and he realized it was all about pushing himself up the ladder. But he knew it could also finish him if it went wrong.

'It'll work,' Fry kept saying when spirits dipped.

Occasionally, another member of the team would put their head round the door. 'Shagged him yet?' one asked Fry. 'Has he asked what colour your eyes are?' said another. Matthews had laughed – joined in the joke – but Sparkes realized the young detective had become a sideshow. He caught a glimpse of Fry one night reflected in the window behind the desk. He'd pushed himself back from the keyboard and was sprawled, legs splayed and spine curled back into the chair. Perhaps realizing that he was probably the mirror image of his quarry, Fry straightened up instinctively.

Fry was also having to engage with other blokes in the chat rooms so that Taylor didn't feel singled out, and the puerile humour and endless innuendo was beginning to wear him down. He could picture them, he said. Heavy-metal T-shirts and bald spots.

Sparkes began to worry that being the bait would prove too much for him.

He couldn't fault the younger man for his commitment – he found Fry leafing through women's magazines to get in character and starting to talk about PMT, much to Matthews' disgust.

And it was all taking so long. After fifteen nights in the chat room, Matthews was getting restless and told his boss it was a waste of time.

'What do you say, Daniel?' Sparkes asked. It was the first time he'd used the junior officer's first name and Fry realized he was being put in the driving seat.

'We're building a relationship with him because we don't want it to be a quick sex session. We want him to talk. Why don't we give it another week?'

Sparkes agreed and Fry, glowing with a new sense of power, rang his former tutor to urge her to up the ante. She was doubtful at first, but they agreed that Jodie should play hard to get and disappear for a couple of days, and then hit Glen hard.

'Where've you been?' BigBear asked when Goldilocks reappeared. 'Thought I'd lost you in the woods.'

'My dad said I was on the computer too much,' Goldilocks said.

'He punished me.' They both knew that she was twenty-seven, but the game was on.

'How?'

'Don't want to say. I might get into trouble again.'

'Go on.'

And so she did. BB, as she now called him, was hooked.

'Why don't we meet up, somewhere online where your dad will never find us?' he suggested.

Chapter 24

Tuesday, 10 July 2007

The Detective

GLEN TAYLOR SAID he was tapping the keys softly, telling his new friend that everyone in the house was asleep apart from him.

Goldie, as he now called her, had finally sent a photo of herself, in baby-doll pyjamas, and he was trying to persuade her to take them off.

DI Sparkes had asked Fleur Jones to be present during all the private email sessions with Taylor and they sat behind Dan Fry, barely lit by the glow of the screen.

'You are so sweet, Goldie. My lovely girl.'

'Your bad baby girl. You know I'll do what you want.'

'That's right. My bad baby girl.'

There followed a series of instructions from BB that Goldie told him she was obeying and enjoying. When it was over, Dan Fry took the next step. It wasn't what Dr Jones had scripted but he was clearly growing impatient.

'Have you ever had a bad baby girl before?' Fry asked. Reflected in the window, Sparkes could see Fleur raise a hand to urge caution.

'Yes.'

'Was it a real baby girl, or like me?'

'I like both, Goldie.'

Dr Jones signalled for him to get back on the agreed track. They were going too fast, but it felt like Taylor was ready to open up.

'Tell me about the other bad baby girls. What did you do with them?'

And Glen Taylor told her. He told her about his nightly adventures online, his encounters, his disappointments and triumphs.

'But you've never done it for real? In real life?' Dan asked and all three of them held their breath.

'Would you like that, Goldie?'

Sparkes went to put up his hand, but Fry was already typing.

'Yes. I'd like that very much.'

He had, he said. He had found a real baby girl once. Sparkes wavered. It was happening too fast to think straight. He looked at Fleur Jones and she got out of her chair and stood behind her protégé.

Fry could barely type, he was shaking so hard.

'I'm really turned on. Tell me about the real baby girl.'

'Her name began with B, like me,' he said. 'Can you guess?'

'No. You tell me.'

The silence suffocated them as the seconds ticked by and they waited for the final piece of the confession.

'Sorry, Goldie, got to go. Someone knocking on my door. Speak later . . .'

'*Shit*,' Fry said and put his head on the desk.

'I think we've still got him,' Sparkes said, looking at Dr Jones, and she nodded firmly.

'He's said enough for me.'

'Let's put it in front of the grown-ups,' Sparkes said and got up. 'Excellent work, Fry. Really excellent.'

Eight hours later, the three of them were sitting in the DCI's office putting the case for arresting and charging Glen Taylor.

DCI Brakespeare listened carefully, read the transcripts and made some notes, before sitting back to give his judgement.

'He never used the name Bella,' he said.

'No, he didn't—' Sparkes began.

'Did Fry go too far in his prompts?'

'We're talking to the legal team but, at first glance, they're comfortable with it. It's always a fine balance, isn't it?'

'But,' Brakespeare talked over him, 'we have him talking about taking a real baby girl beginning with B. Let's get him back in and put it to him. Say we have a witness statement from Goldilocks.'

They all nodded.

'We've got very good reasons to have pursued this line: we've got him in the area on the day, the blue van, the child porn on his computer, his predatory nature shown in his chat-room outings, a shaky alibi from his wife. And, key, is the risk of further offences.'

Everyone nodded again.

'Do you believe he's our man, Bob?' Brakespeare asked finally.

'Yes, I do,' Sparkes croaked, his mouth dry with anticipation.

'So do I. But we need more to nail it. Fine toothcomb, Bob. Do it all again while we've got him in. There must be something linking him to the scene.'

The team were sent back up the M3 to the south London suburb to start afresh. 'Bring everything he has ever worn,' Sparkes said. 'Everything. Just empty the cupboards.'

It was pure chance that they picked up Jean Taylor's black puffa jacket. It was wedged between her husband's winter coat and a dress shirt and was bagged and tagged like everything else.

The technician who received the bags stacked them according to type and started the tests on the outerwear, as it would have been likely to come into contact with the crime victim first.

The jacket pockets were emptied and contents bagged again. There was only one item. A scrap of red paper, about as big as the technician's thumbnail. In the hush of the laboratory, he went through the process of examining it for fingerprints and fibres, lifting any evidence with sticky tape and cataloguing it meticulously.

No prints, but dirt particles and what looked like an animal hair. Finer than a human hair, but he'd need to look at it under the microscope to get more details of colour and species.

He took off his gloves and walked to the phone on the wall.

'DI Sparkes, please.'

Sparkes jumped down the stairs two at a time. The technician had told him not to bother coming – 'It's too early to be sure of anything, Sir' – but Sparkes just wanted to see the piece of paper. To reassure himself it was real and wasn't going to disappear in a puff of smoke.

'We're comparing the dirt particles with those taken from Glen Taylor's van in the original sweep,' the technician told him calmly. 'If there's a match, we can place the paper in the van. And we can tell you what sort of paper it is, Sir.'

'I'll bet it's a bit of a Skittles packet,' Sparkes said. 'Look at the colour. Get on with it, man. Do you know what sort of animal the hair comes from? Could it be a cat?'

The technician put up a hand. 'I can tell you if it's a cat quite quickly. I'll get it under the microscope. But we can't say if it came from a specific animal. It's not like humans. Even if we have hairs to compare it with, we can't say definitively that it came from that specific animal. Furthest we can go – if we're lucky – is that it came from the same breed.'

Sparkes ran both hands through his hair. 'Get samples from Timmy Elliott pronto and let's see.'

He hovered and the technician waved him out of the door. 'Give us some time. I'll ring you as soon as we have results.'

Back in his office, he and Matthews drew a Venn diagram, putting all the potential new evidence in interconnecting circles to see where they were.

'If the paper is from a Skittles packet and the hair is from a cat the same breed as Timmy, it could place Jean Taylor at the scene,' Matthews said. 'It's her coat. Must be. It's too small for Glen.'

'I'll go and get her,' Sparkes said.

Chapter 25

Thursday, 12 July 2007

The Widow

OF COURSE, THE POLICE don't give up. They've got their teeth into Glen with his van, his pretend child porn and his 'misconduct'. They'll never let him go. They'll try and prosecute him for those pictures if nothing else, his solicitor says.

The visits and phone calls from DI Sparkes have become part of our lives. The police are building a case and we watch from the sidelines.

I say to Glen that he should just tell the police about the 'private job' and where he was that day, but he insists it would make things worse. 'They'll say we've lied to them about everything, Jeanie.'

I'm terrified I'll do something to make things worse, say the wrong thing. But in the end, it was Glen who let the side down, not me.

The police came to get him for further questioning today. They took him back to Southampton. When they left, he kissed me on the cheek and told me not to worry. 'You know, it'll be all right,' he said to me and I nodded. And I waited.

The police collected more of Glen's things. All the clothes and shoes they hadn't taken before. They took things he'd only just bought. I tried to tell them, but they said they were taking everything. They even took my jacket by mistake. I'd hung it in his space in the wardrobe because my side was full.

The next day, Bob Sparkes came and asked me to go with him down to Southampton for questioning. He wouldn't say anything in the car, just that he wanted me to help with the inquiry.

But when we got to the police station, he sat me in an interview room and read me my rights. Then he asked me if I had taken Bella. Had I helped Glen take Bella?

I couldn't believe he would ask me that. I kept saying 'No, of course not. And Glen didn't take her,' but he wasn't listening properly. He was moving on to the next thing.

He pulled out this plastic bag like a conjuror and I couldn't see anything in it at first, but at the bottom was a scrap of red paper.

'We found this in your coat pocket, Mrs Taylor. It's from a Skittles packet. Do you eat many Skittles?'

I didn't know what he was talking about for a moment, but I remembered then. It must've been the bit of sweet packet I'd got from under the mat in the van.

He must've seen my face change and kept pushing me. Kept saying Bella's name. I said I couldn't remember, but he knew I could.

I told him in the end, to stop him asking me. I told him it might be a bit of paper I'd found in the van. Just a bit of rubbish, all fuzzy and dirty. I'd put it in my pocket to throw away later, but never did.

I said it was just a sweet paper, but Mr Sparkes said they'd found a cat hair stuck to it. A grey cat hair. Like from the cat in Bella's garden. I said that didn't prove anything. The hair could have come from anywhere. But I had to make a statement.

I hoped they wouldn't say anything to Glen before I got a chance to explain. I'd tell him when we both got home that they had made me tell them. That it didn't matter. But I didn't get the opportunity. Glen didn't come home.

Seems he went on looking for porn on the internet. I couldn't believe he'd be so stupid, when Tom Payne, Glen's lawyer, told me. He was always the clever one in the family.

The police had taken his computer, of course, but he bought himself a cheap little laptop and a Wi-Fi router – 'for work, Jeanie' – and sat in the spare room while he went into sex chat rooms or whatever they're called.

It was all very clever – they got some police officer to pretend to be a young woman on the internet and chat him up. She called herself Goldilocks. Who would fall for that? Well, Glen, apparently.

It wasn't just chatting up, either. Tom wanted to prepare me for what might be in the papers, so he told me that eventually Goldilocks had cybersex with Glen. It's sex without touching, Glen said when he tried to explain when I visited him the first time. 'It's just words, Jeanie. Written-down words. We didn't speak or even see each other. It was like it was happening in my head. Just a fantasy. You do see, don't you? I'm under such a lot of stress with all these accusations. I can't help myself.'

I try to see. I really do. It's an addiction, I keep saying to myself. Not his fault. I focus on the real villains here. Glen and I are very angry about what the police did.

I couldn't believe someone would do that as part of their job. Like a prostitute. That's what Glen said, too. Before he found out Goldilocks was a man. That was hard for him to accept – he thought the police were just saying it to make him look like he was gay or something. I said nothing – I couldn't get my head round cybersex, let alone worry about who he was doing it with. Anyway, it was hardly his biggest problem.

He'd said too much to Goldilocks. Glen told me he'd told 'her' he knew something about a famous police case to impress her. 'She' practically told him to say it.

This time, Bob Sparkes charged Glen with Bella's kidnap. They said he'd taken her and killed her. But they didn't charge him with murder. Tom Payne said they were waiting until they had a body. I hated him talking about Bella like that, but I didn't say anything.

I went home alone and then the press came back.

I'm not a big newspaper reader, really. I prefer magazines. I like the real-life stories – you know, the woman who fostered one hundred kids, the woman who refused cancer treatment to save her baby, the woman who had a baby for her sister. The papers have always been more Glen's department. He likes the *Mail* – he can do the crossword on the back page and it's the sort of paper his former boss at the bank read. 'Gives us something in common, Jeanie,' he said once.

But now the papers and the telly – and even the radio – are about us. Glen is big news and the reporters have started knocking on the door again. I found out they call it 'doorstepping' and some of them actually sleep in their cars outside all night to try and catch a word with me.

I sit upstairs in our bedroom at the front, peeking out from behind the curtain, watching them. They all do the same thing. It's quite funny, really. They drive past first, checking out the house and who's already outside. Then they park and stroll back to the gate, a notebook in their hand. The others jump out of their cars to cut the new one off before he or she can get to the door. Like a pack of animals, sniffing round the new arrival.

After a few days, they're all friends – sending one to get coffees and bacon sandwiches from the café at the bottom of the hill. 'Sugar? Who wants sauce on their sarnie?' The café must be making a fortune. I notice the reporters keep to one group and the photographers to another. Wonder why they don't mix. You can tell them apart because the photographers dress differently – trendier, in scruffy jackets and baseball caps. Most of them look like they haven't shaved for days – the men, I mean. The women photographers dress like men, too. In chinos and baggy shirts. And the photographers are so loud. I feel a bit sorry for the neighbours at first, having to listen to them laughing and carrying on. But then they start bringing out trays of drinks, standing and chatting to them and letting them use their loos. It's a bit of a street party for them, I think.

The reporters are quieter. They spend most of their time on their phones or sitting listening to the radio news in their cars. Lots are young blokes in their first suits.

But after a few days, when I won't talk, the press send the big guns. Big beery men and women with sharp faces and smart coats. They roll up in their expensive, shiny cars and step out like royalty. Even the photographers stop messing about for some of them. One man who looks like he's stepped out of a shop window parts the crowd and walks up the path. He bangs on the door and calls out, 'Mrs Taylor, what is it like to have a child murderer as a husband?' I sit there on the bed, burning with shame. It feels like everyone can see me even though they can't. Exposed.

Anyway, he isn't the first to ask me that. One reporter shouted it at me after Glen was rearrested, as I was walking down to the shops. He just appeared, must've followed me away from the other journalists. He was trying to make me angry, to get me to say something, anything, so he'd have 'an interview' with the wife, but I wasn't falling for that. Glen and I'd discussed it.

'Jeanie, just stay quiet,' he said when he rang me from the police station. 'Don't let them get to you. Don't let anything show. You don't have to talk to them. They are scum. They can't write about nothing.' But of course they did. The stuff that came out was awful.

Other women said they'd had cybersex with him on the internet and were queuing up to sell their stories. I couldn't believe any of it was true. Apparently, he was called BigBear and other ridiculous names in the chat rooms. I would look at him sometimes on my prison visits and try to imagine calling him BigBear. It made me feel sick.

And there was more stuff about his 'hobby' – the pictures he bought on the net. According to 'informed sources' in one of the papers, he'd used a credit card to buy them, and when the police did a big swoop on paedophiles, tracking them through their card details, he panicked. I expect that's why he got me to report his card missing, but how do papers get information like that? I thought about asking one of the reporters, but I can't without saying more than I should.

When I asked Glen about it at our next visit, he denied it all. 'They're just making it up, love. The press make it all up. You know they do,' he said, holding my hand. 'I love you,' he said. I didn't say anything.

I didn't say anything to the press either. I went to different supermarkets so they couldn't find me and started wearing hats that hid my face a bit so other people wouldn't recognize me. Like Madonna, Lisa would've said if she was still my friend. But she wasn't. No one wanted to know us now. They just wanted to know about us.

Chapter 26

The Detective

THE INCIDENT ROOM had been packed up four months before the trial; walls and whiteboards stripped and the mosaic of photos and maps dismantled and packed into cardboard box files for the prosecution.

When the last box had been taken out, Sparkes stood and looked at the faint rectangles left on some of the walls. 'Barely a trace that the investigation ever took place,' he mused. This moment in any case was a bit like post-coital tristesse, he'd once told Eileen. 'Post what?' she'd asked. 'You know, that sad feeling after sex, that it's all over,' he'd explained, adding sheepishly, 'I read about it in a magazine.'

'Must be a man thing,' she'd said.

The final interviews with Taylor had been long but, ultimately, frustrating. He'd disputed the sweet-paper evidence, sweeping it aside as coincidence.

'How do you know Jean didn't get it wrong? She could've picked it up in the street or in a café.'

'She says she found it in your van, Glen. Why would she say that if it wasn't true?'

Taylor's mouth had hardened. 'She's under a lot of pressure.'

'And the cat hair on the paper? Hair from exactly the same type of cat that Bella was playing with that day?'

'For God's sake. How many grey cats are there in this country? This is ridiculous.'

Taylor turned to his lawyer. 'That hair could've been floating around anywhere . . . Couldn't it, Tom?'

Sparkes paused, savouring the rare note of panic in Taylor's voice. Then he moved on to what he anticipated would be the *coup de grâce*. The moment when Taylor realized he'd been seen and played by the police.

'So, *BigBear* then, Mr Taylor,' Sparkes said.

Taylor's mouth had fallen open, then snapped shut. 'Don't know what you're talking about.'

'You've been down in the woods, looking for friends. Finding friends, haven't you? But we've met Goldilocks too.'

Taylor's feet started tapping and he stared at his lap. His default position.

At his side, Tom Payne looked mystified by the turn in the questions and interrupted, 'I'd like a few moments with my client, please.'

Five minutes later, the pair had their story straight.

'It was a private fantasy between two consenting adults,' Glen Taylor said. 'I was under a lot of stress.'

'Who was the baby girl beginning with B, Glen?'

'It was a private fantasy between two consenting adults.'

'Was it Bella?'

'It was a private fantasy . . .'

'What have you done with Bella?'

'It was a private fantasy . . .'

When they charged him, he stopped mumbling about his private fantasy and looked the detective in the eye. 'You're making a terrible mistake, Mr Sparkes.'

It was the last thing he said before he was locked up to await trial.

A winter on remand did not persuade him to cooperate and on 11 February 2008, Glen Taylor stood in the Old Bailey to deliver his plea of Not Guilty to abduction in a loud and steady voice.

He sat down, barely acknowledging the prison officers on either side as he fixed his gaze on the detective inspector, making his way to the witness box.

Sparkes felt the power of Taylor's stare boring into the back of his head and tried to collect himself before he took the oath. There was the slightest of tremors in his voice as he spoke the words on the card, but he went on to give his evidence in chief competently, keeping his answers short, clear and humble.

The months of foot-slogging, chasing, heavy lifting, checking, questioning and stacking up the evidence were condensed into a short performance before a small and select audience and a battery of critics.

Chief among them was Glen Taylor's barrister, a patrician war-horse in ancient, fraying wig and gown, who stood up to cross-examine him.

The jury of eight men and four women, winnowed by the defence to ensure male sensibilities and sympathies were in the majority, turned their heads like a patch of sunflowers to focus on him.

The barrister, Charles Sanderson QC, stood with one hand in his pocket, his notes in the other. He exuded confidence as he began his attempt to undermine some of the nuggets of evidence and plant doubt in the jury's collective consciousness.

'When did the witness, Mr Spencer, make a note about the blue van? Was it before he fabricated the long-haired man sighting?'

'Mr Spencer was mistaken about the sighting. He has admitted that,' Sparkes said, keeping his voice level.

'Yes, I see.'

'His evidence will be that he wrote down that he saw what he thought was Peter Tredwell's blue van when he made his notes on the afternoon of 2 October.'

'And he is sure he didn't fabricate – sorry, make a mistake about seeing – a blue van?'

'Yes, he is sure. He will tell you himself when he gives evidence.'

'I see.'

'Now how far away was the witness when he saw the blue panel van?

'And does Mr Spencer wear glasses?'

'I see.'

'And how many blue panel vans are there on the road in the UK, inspector?'

'I see.'

It was the 'I see's that did the damage, 'I see' meaning 'Oh dear, another point to us.'

Chip, chip, chip. Sparkes parried the blows patiently. He'd faced a number of Sandersons over the years – 'Old Boy' show-offs – and knew this sort of grandstanding didn't always play well with a jury.

They reached the sweet-paper discovery and Sanderson took the expected line about the chances of contamination of evidence.

'Detective Inspector, how long was the sweet paper in Jean Taylor's coat pocket?'

Sparkes kept his voice steady, making sure he looked across at the jurors to emphasize the point.

'Seven months, we believe. She said in her statement that she found it in the van on 17 December. It was the only time she was allowed to go on a delivery with her husband so she remembers it well.'

'Seven months? That's a long time to gather other fluff and hair, isn't it?'

'Hair from a grey Burmese cross, like the Elliott family's cat? We will bring expert testimony to say that is statistically extremely unlikely. And the likelihood of a coincidence drops still further when that cat hair evidence is found on a Skittles packet. Both a Burmese-cross cat and a Skittle sweet were present at the scene when Bella Elliott was abducted.'

Sparkes saw that the jurors were writing notes and Sanderson moved swiftly on. Sparkes took a gulp of water from the glass at his elbow. He knew his adversary was building up to his grand finale: the Goldilocks conversations.

160

Sparkes had prepared with the lawyers to make sure he was ready. He knew every nuance of the Regulation of Investigatory Powers Act 2000, every step of the authorization procedure, the careful preparation of the CHIS and the preservation and chain of evidence.

The team had spent a significant amount of time prepping him to emphasize Taylor's use of chat rooms and his porn habit.

'The jury won't be interested in sub-clause 101 or who gave permission for what – we need to tell them about the risk of Taylor feeding his appetite for baby girls,' the CPS team leader had urged, and Sparkes knew he was right.

He felt ready when the barrister marched into the minefield of pornography addiction, challenging the police action every step of the way. Sanderson's goal was to force him to concede that Taylor could have inadvertently downloaded some of the 'more extreme' images found on his computer.

'The images of children being sexually abused?' Sparkes had answered. 'We believe he deliberately downloaded them – that he couldn't have done it accidentally – and experts will testify on that matter.'

'We also have experts who will say that it could have been accidental, Inspector.'

Sparkes knew the defence was helped by the fact that Taylor looked nothing like the perverts who normally stood in the dock. The prosecution team told him that Sanderson had shown a photo of his client to the juniors and solicitors in his chambers and the phrase most often used to describe him in his impromptu focus groups was 'clean-cut'.

With the images filed away, Sanderson challenged the detective head on about Bella Elliott's disappearance.

'Detective Inspector Sparkes, isn't it right that Bella Elliott has never been found?'

'Yes, that is correct.'

'And that your team has failed to find any leads to her whereabouts?'

'No, that isn't right. Our investigation led us to the accused.'

'Your case is based on suspicions, supposition and circum-stantial evidence, not facts, Inspector, isn't it?'

'We've clear evidence to link the accused to the disappearance of Bella Elliott.'

'Ah, the evidence. Forensic guesswork and unreliable witnesses. All a bit flimsy because, I suggest, you were always after the wrong man. You were so desperate you resorted to leading my client into a fictitious and mendacious relationship.'

The jurors didn't look as if they knew what a fictitious and mendacious relationship was, but they looked interested in the spectacle. Four stars and 'compelling performances' was how the *Telegraph* might review it the next day, Sparkes thought as he finally stepped down from the witness box at lunchtime and returned to his seat in the audience.

But the star turn came that afternoon. Dulled by an institutional lunch, the jurors filed back in and slumped in their seats. They did not stay there long.

The mother entered the witness box, dressed in simple black with a red Find Bella badge blooming on her breast.

Sparkes smiled encouragingly at her, but he was unhappy she'd chosen to wear the badge and concerned about the questions it would raise.

The prosecutor, a reed of a woman alongside the bulk of her opponent, led Dawn Elliott through her evidence in chief, letting the young woman tell her story simply and effectively.

When Dawn broke down as she described the moment when she realized her child had gone, the jurors were transfixed and some seemed close to tears themselves. The judge asked her if she'd like a glass of water and the usher obliged as the barristers rustled their papers, ready to resume.

It was Sanderson's turn. 'Miss Elliott, did Bella often go outside to play? Out at the front, where you couldn't see her?'

'Sometimes, but only for a few minutes.'

'Minutes pass very quickly, don't you find? So many things to do as a mum?'

The mother smiled at this bit of sympathy. 'It can get busy, but I know she was only out of my sight for minutes.'

'How do you know?'

'I was just cooking some pasta, like I said before. That doesn't take long.'

'Anything else?'

'Well, I did the washing up as I went along. And I folded some of Bella's clothes from the tumble drier so I wouldn't have to iron them.'

'Sounds like a busy afternoon for you. And there were a couple of calls to your mobile as well. Easy to forget that Bella was outside.'

Dawn began sobbing again, but Sanderson did not falter. 'I know this is hard for you, Miss Elliott, but I just want to establish the timeframe when Bella disappeared. You understand how important this is, don't you?'

She nodded and blew her nose.

'And we're relying on you to pinpoint this because the last time anyone else saw Bella was at the newsagent's at 11.35. Wasn't it, Miss Elliott?'

'We bought some sweets.'

'Yes, Smarties, according to the till receipt. But that means the window for Bella's disappearance is actually from 11.35 to 15.30. That's almost four hours. Because no one else laid eyes on her during that time.'

Voice dropping, Dawn gripped the rail of the witness box. 'No, we didn't go out again. But my mum heard Bella when she rang in the afternoon. She told me to give her a kiss.'

'Miss Elliott, please could you keep your voice up so the learned judge and jury can hear your evidence.'

Dawn cleared her throat and mouthed 'Sorry' to the judge.

'Your mother heard a child's voice in the background, but that could've been on the television, Miss Elliott, couldn't it? Your mother told the police she didn't speak to Bella.'

'Bella wouldn't come to the phone, she ran off to get something.'

'I see. And then she went outside an hour or so later later.'

'She was only out of my sight for a few minutes.'

'Yes, thank you, Miss Elliott.'

Dawn made to step down from the box, but Sanderson halted her. 'Not quite finished, Miss Elliott. I see you are wearing a Find Bella badge.'

Dawn touched the badge instinctively.

'You believe that Bella is still alive, don't you?' the barrister asked.

Dawn Elliott nodded, uncertain where the question was going.

'Indeed, you have sold interviews to newspapers and magazines saying exactly that.'

The accusation that she was making money out of her missing child made the press benches vibrate and pens pause for the response.

Dawn was defensive and suddenly loud. 'Yes, I do hope she's alive. But she's been taken, and that man took her.'

She pointed at Taylor, who looked down and began writing on his legal pad.

'And the money is for the Find Bella fund,' she added quietly.

'I see,' the barrister said and sat down.

It was another week of neighbours, police experts, sick jurors and legal argument before DC Dan Fry entered the witness box to give his evidence.

It was Fry's big moment and he stood with trembling legs, despite the frequent rehearsals with his bosses.

The prosecutor painted the picture of a young, dedicated officer, backed by his superiors and the legal process and determined to prevent another child being taken. She lingered over the words used by Glen Taylor, looking at the jurors to underline the import of the evidence, and they began to glance over at the accused. It was going well.

When Sanderson rose to take his turn, there were no hands in pockets, no lazy vowels; this was his moment. The young officer was taken through the conversations he'd had as Goldilocks, line by ghastly line. He'd been prepared by the prosecution for the pressure he'd be put under, but it was much worse than anyone could have foreseen.

He was asked to read out his replies to BigBear's obscene banter and in the cold light of the courtroom the words took on a surreal, sniggerish air.

'What're you wearing tonight?' the barrister, his face drink-mottled and his shoulders dusted with dandruff, asked. Straight-faced, six-foot-three Fry read, 'Baby-doll pyjamas. My blue ones with the lace.' There was a suppressed bark of laughter from the press box, but Fry kept his nerve and read on, 'I'm a bit hot. I might have to take them off.'

'Yes, take them off,' the barrister intoned in a bored voice. 'Then touch yourself.

'It's all a bit adolescent, isn't it?' he added. 'I assume you were not wearing blue baby-doll pyjamas, Detective Constable Fry?'

The laughter from the public gallery bruised him but he took a deep breath and said, 'No.'

Order was quickly restored, but the damage was done. Fry's crucial evidence was in danger of being reduced to a dirty joke.

The barrister basked in the moment before entering the most dangerous area of the cross-examination: the last email conversation with Glen Taylor. He addressed it head on.

'Detective Constable Fry, did Glen Taylor, aka BigBear, say he'd kidnapped Bella Elliott?'

'He said he'd had a real baby girl before.'

'That's not what I asked you. And was this after you, as Goldilocks, asked him to tell you that?'

'No, Sir.'

'He asked you, "Would you like that, Goldie?" and you told him you'd like that very much. You said it was a turn-on.'

'He could've said no at any stage,' Fry said. 'But he didn't. He said he'd found a baby girl once and her name began with B.'

'Did he ever use the name Bella in your conversations?'

'No.'

'This was a fantasy conversation between two consenting adults, DC Fry. This was not a confession.'

'He said he'd found a baby girl. Her name began with B,' Fry insisted, the emotion beginning to break through. 'How many baby girls with names beginning with B have been taken recently?'

The barrister ignored the question and scanned his notes.

Bob Sparkes looked at Jean Taylor perched on the edge of a bench, below her fantasizing, consenting-adult husband, and saw the numbness. It must be the first time she's heard the whole story, he thought.

He wondered who felt worse – him with the case falling apart in front of him or her with the case piling up in front of her.

Fry was beginning to stutter now and Sparkes silently willed him to pull himself together. But Sanderson continued his attack. 'You coerced Glen Taylor into making these remarks, didn't you, Constable Fry? You acted as an agent provocateur by pretending to be a woman who wanted to have sex with him. You were determined to get him to make damning statements. You would do anything. Even have internet sex with him. Is this really police work? Where was the caution or the right to a solicitor?'

Sanderson, who was well into his stride, looked almost regretful when his victim finally stepped down from the witness box, diminished and exhausted.

The defence immediately called for an adjournment and, with the jurors safely tucked away in the jury room, made the case that the trial should be halted.

'This whole case rests on circumstantial evidence and an entrapment. It cannot continue,' Sanderson said. 'The Goldilocks evidence must be ruled as inadmissible.'

The judge tapped her pencil impatiently as she listened to the prosecution's response.

'The police acted entirely properly in every respect. They followed procedure to the letter. They believed they had proper cause. That this was the only way to get the final piece of evidence,' the prosecutor said and sat down.

The judge put down her pencil and looked at her notes in silence. 'I will retire,' she said finally and the court rose as she walked back to her chambers.

Twenty minutes later, the clerk called 'All rise' and the judge delivered her verdict. She ruled out the Goldilocks evidence, criticizing Fry's encouragement and prompting and the exposure of such a junior officer. 'The evidence is unsafe and cannot be relied upon,' she said.

Sparkes knew it was simply a formality for the prosecution team to throw in the towel and offer no further evidence and began packing his briefcase.

In the dock, Taylor listened to the judge carefully, the reality slowly dawning on him that he was about to be freed. Below him, Jean Taylor looked stunned. 'I wonder what she's thinking,' Sparkes muttered to Matthews. 'She's got to go home with a porn addict who has cybersex with strangers dressed as children. And a child-killer.'

Suddenly it was over. The judge ordered the jury to return a formal verdict of not guilty and Taylor was taken down to the cells to prepare for freedom. In the courtroom, a press free-for-all began, with Jean Taylor the main prize.

She half stood, surrounded by reporters, white-faced and silent as Tom Payne tried to extricate her from the pew in the well of the court. Finally, the press parted and she struggled sideways like a fleeing crab, her legs knocking against the bench in front and her bag strap catching on edges.

Chapter 27

Monday, 11 February 2008

The Widow

SHE GIVES EVIDENCE, of course. Her five minutes in the spotlight. She wears a black dress and a Find Bella badge. I try to avoid her stare but she's determined and in the end our eyes meet. I feel hot and the flush rises up my face, so I look away. It doesn't happen again. She keeps staring at Glen, but he's wise to her game and looks straight ahead.

I find my attention wandering as she tells the story I've read and heard a hundred times since she lost her baby – a nap, then play-time while she cooks tea, Bella laughing as she chases Timmy the cat out of the front door into the garden. Then realizing she can't hear her any more. The silence.

The court goes completely quiet, too. We can all hear that silence. The moment when Bella vanished.

Then she sobs and has to sit down with a glass of water. Very effective. The jury look worried and one or two of the older women look like they might cry as well. It's all going wrong. They must see this is all her fault. That's what Glen and I think. She let her baby out of her sight. She didn't care enough.

Glen sits quietly and lets it all wash over him, like it's happening to someone else. When the mum is ready, the judge lets her stay sitting down to finish her evidence and Glen cocks his head to listen to her story of running to neighbours, ringing the police and waiting for news as the hunt went on.

The prosecutor uses this special tone of voice with her, treating her like she's made of glass. 'Thank you very much, Miss Elliott. You've been very brave.'

I want to shout, 'You've been a very bad mother.' But I know I can't, not here.

Our barrister, a scary old bloke who had shaken my hand firmly at each meeting but gave no other sign that he knew who I was, finally gets his turn.

The mother begins sobbing when the questions get hard, but our barrister doesn't put on the understanding voice.

Dawn Elliott keeps saying her little girl was only out of her sight for a few minutes. But we all know now she wasn't.

The jury is beginning to look at her a bit harder now. About time.

'You believe that Bella is still alive, don't you?' the barrister asks.

There is a rustle in the court and the mum starts sniffling again. He points out that she's been selling her story to the press and she looks really angry and says the money is for her campaign.

One of the reporters gets up and goes out quickly, clutching his notebook. 'He's going to file that line to his news desk,' Tom whispers and winks.

It's a goal for us, he means.

When it's all over, when the police have been told off for tricking Glen and he's been freed, I feel completely numb. My turn to feel like this is happening to someone else.

Tom Payne finally lets go of my arm when we get into one of the witness rooms and we stand, catching our breath. Neither of us speaks for a moment. 'Can he come home now?' I ask him, my voice sounding strange and flat after all that noise in the courtroom. Tom nods and busies himself with his briefcase. Then he takes me downstairs to the cells to see Glen. My Glen.

'I always said the truth would come out,' he says triumphantly when he spots me. 'We've done it, Jean. We've bloody well done it.'

I hug him when I get to him. It's been a long time since I've held him and it means I don't have to say anything because I don't know what to say to him. He's so happy – like a little boy. Pink and laughing. A bit out of control. All I keep thinking is that I've got to go home with him. Be on my own with him. What will it be like when we shut the door? I know too much about this other man I'm married to for it to be like before.

He tries to pick me up and whirl me round like he used to when we were younger, but there are too many people in the room: the lawyers, the barristers, the prison officers. They're all around me and I can't breathe. Tom notices and takes me out into a cool hall and sits me down with a glass of water.

'It's a lot to take in, Jean,' he says kindly. 'All a bit sudden, but it's what we all hoped would happen, isn't it? You've waited a long time for this moment.'

I raise my head, but he doesn't look me in the eye. We don't speak again.

I keep thinking about that poor young officer, pretending to be a woman to try and get to the truth. I'd thought he'd acted like a prostitute when Tom told us about the evidence, but when I watched him in the witness box with everyone laughing at his act, I felt sorry for him. He would've done anything to find Bella.

When Glen comes out, Tom goes to him and shakes his hand again. Then we leave. On the pavement, Dawn Elliott is weeping for the cameras. 'She'll have to be careful what she says,' Tom says as we hover by the doors at the back of the mob. She's bathed in light from the TV cameras and the reporters are tripping over power cables, trying to get near her. She's saying she'll never give up looking for her little girl, that she's out there somewhere and she'll find out the truth about what happened to her. When she finishes, she's led away by friends to a waiting car and is gone.

Then it's our turn. Glen's decided to let Tom read his statement. Well, Tom advised it. He wrote it. We step into the spotlight and there's a noise that physically shakes me. The noise of a hundred voices shouting at once, firing questions without waiting for answers, demanding attention. 'Over here, Jean,' a voice near me hollers. I turn to find out who it is and the flash goes off in my face. 'Give him a hug,' another says. I recognize some of them from the pavement in front of the house. I go to smile, then realize they're not friends. They're something else. They're the press.

Tom is all serious and quietens everything down. 'I'm going to read Mr Taylor's statement. He's not going to be answering any questions.' A forest of tape recorders rises above heads.

'I am an innocent man who has been hounded by police and deprived of my liberty for a crime I never committed. I'm very grateful to the court for their decision. But today, I'm not celebrating my acquittal. Bella Elliott is still missing and the person who took her is still out there. I hope the police will now get back to finding the guilty person. I would like to thank my family for standing by me and I would like to pay a special tribute to my wonderful wife, Jeanie. Thank you for listening. I would ask you to respect our privacy now as we try to rebuild our lives.'

I look at my shoes throughout, filling in the gaps in my head. *Wonderful wife*. This is my role now. The Wonderful Wife who stood by her husband.

There's a single silent beat, then the noise deafens again. 'Who do you think took Bella?', 'What do you think of the police tactics, Glen?' Then a passer-by shouts, 'Well done, mate!' and Glen grins in response. It is the picture everyone uses the next day.

An arm snakes through the cameramen and hands me a card. It has 'Congratulations' on it and a picture of a bottle of champagne with a cork popping. I try to see who the arm belongs to but it's been swallowed up, so I slide the card in my bag and am guided forward with Glen and Tom and some of the security people. The press come too. It's like a swarm of bees moving in a cartoon.

That journey home is a taste of what is to come. The reporters and photographers block the way to the taxi Tom has got waiting for us and we can't move forward. People are pushing each other and us, shouting their stupid questions into our faces, shoving their cameras everywhere. Glen has my hand and he suddenly makes a break for it, dragging me behind him. Tom has the door of the taxi open and we throw ourselves on to the back seat.

Cameras are slammed against the windows, flashing and banging, metal on glass. And we just sit there, like fish in an aquarium. The driver is sweating but you can see he's enjoying it. 'Bloody hell,' he says. 'What a circus!'

The journalists are still shouting: 'What does it feel like to be a free man, Glen?', 'What do you want to say to Bella's mother?', 'Do you blame the police?'

Of course he does blame them. He stews over it, the humiliation and the baby-doll pyjamas. Funny how he can think about that when he's been accused of killing a little girl, but getting even with the police becomes his new addiction.

Chapter 28

Wednesday, 2 April 2008

The Widow

I've ALWAYS WONDERED what it would feel like if I let out the secret. Sometimes I daydream about it and can hear myself saying, 'My husband saw Bella the day she was taken.' And I feel the physical release, like a rush to the head.

But I can't, can I? I'm as guilty as he is. It's a strange feeling, owning a secret. It's like a stone in my stomach, crushing my insides and making me feel sick every time I think of it. My friend Lisa used to talk about being pregnant like that – the baby pushing everything out of its way. Overwhelming her body. My secret does that. When it gets too much, I switch to being Jeanie for a while and pretend the secret belongs to someone else.

But that didn't help when Bob Sparkes questioned me during the investigation. I felt heat rising through my body, my face reddened and my scalp pinpricked with sweat.

Bob Sparkes was trespassing in my lies. The first time was when he asked, 'So what did you say you did on the day Bella disappeared?'

My breathing became shallow and I tried to catch and control it. But my voice betrayed me. It became a breathless squeak, a deafening dry gulp as I swallowed mid-sentence. I'm lying, my treacherous body was saying.

'Oh, in the morning, work, you know. I had a couple of high-lights to do,' I said, hoping the truths in my lie would convince. I was at work, after all. Justify, justify, deny, deny. It ought to get easier, but it doesn't as each lie feels sourer and tighter, like an unripe apple. Unyielding and mouth-drying.

The simple lies are the hardest, funnily enough. The big ones seem to just fall off the tongue: 'Glen? Oh, he left the bank because he has other ambitions. He wants to start his own transport company. Wants to be his own boss.' Easy.

But the little ones – 'I can't come out for a coffee because I've got to go to my mum's' – stick and stutter, making me flush. Lisa didn't seem to notice in the beginning, or if she did, she hid it well. We were all living in my lie now.

I was never a liar as a child. My mum and dad would've been able to tell immediately and I didn't have a brother or sister to share a secret with. With Glen, it turned out, it was easy. We were a team, he'd say, after the police came round.

Funny that. I hadn't thought of us as a team for a long time before that. We each had our departments. But Bella's disappear-ance brought us together. Made us a real couple. I always said we needed a child.

Ironic really. You see, I was going to leave him. After he was released by the court. After I knew all about his online stuff. His 'sexcursions', as he called them, in the chat rooms. The stuff that he was going to put behind him.

You see, Glen likes to put things behind him. When he says it, it means we'll never talk about it again. He can do that, just cut off a part of his life and let it drift away. 'We need to be thinking of the future, Jeanie, not the past,' he'd explain patiently, drawing me closer, kissing my head.

It made sense when he said it like that and I learned never to go back to the things we'd put behind us. It didn't mean I didn't think about them, but it was understood that I wouldn't mention them again to him.

Not Being Able to Have a Baby was one of the things. And Losing

His Job. And then the Chat Rooms and all the awful things with the police. 'Let's put it behind us, love,' he said the day after the court case ended. We were lying in bed; it was so early the street lights were still on, shining through a gap in the curtains. Neither of us had slept much – 'Too much excitement,' Glen said.

He'd made some plans, he said. He'd decided to get back to a normal life – to our life – as quickly as possible, to make things like they were before.

It sounded so simple when he said it and I tried to put all the things I'd heard out of my mind, but they wouldn't go. They kept hiding in corners and leering at me. I stewed for a few weeks before I made a decision. In the end, it was the pictures of children that made me pack a bag.

I'd stood by him from the day he was accused of Bella's murder because I believed in him. I knew my Glen couldn't do something so awful. But that was over now, thank God. He'd been found Not Guilty.

Now I had to look at the other stuff that he did do.

He denied it all when I said I couldn't live with a man who looked at pictures like that.

'It's not real, Jeanie. Our experts said in court that they're not really kids in those pictures. They're women who look really young and dress up as kids for a living. Some of them are really in their thirties.'

'But they looked like children,' I shouted. 'They do it for people who want to see children and men doing those things.'

He started to cry. 'You can't leave me, Jeanie,' he said. 'I need you.'

I shook my head and went and got my bag. I was shaking because I'd never seen Glen like this before. He was the one who was always in control. The strong one.

And when I came downstairs, he was waiting to trap me with his confession.

You see, he told me he'd done something for me. He said he loved me. He knew I wanted a child so badly it was killing me, and that was killing him, and when he saw her, he knew he could make me happy. It was for me.

He said it was like a dream. He stopped to eat his lunch and look at his paper in a side street and saw her at a garden gate, looking at him. She was alone. He couldn't help himself. When he told me, he put his arms round me and I couldn't move.

'I wanted to bring her home for you. She was standing there and I smiled at her and she put her arms up to me. She wanted me to pick her up. I got out of the van, but I don't remember anything else. Next thing I was driving the van home to you.

'I didn't hurt her, Jeanie,' he said. 'It was like a dream. Do you think it was a dream, Jeanie?'

His story is so shocking, I'm choking on its details.

We're standing in our hallway and I can see our reflection in the mirror. It's like seeing it happening in a film. Glen is bending down so our heads touch, sobbing on my shoulder, with me deathly pale. I'm patting his hair and shushing him. But I don't want him to stop crying. I'm afraid of the silence that will follow. There is so much I want to ask, but so much I don't want to know.

Glen stops after a while and we sit on the sofa together.

'Shouldn't we tell the police? Tell them you saw her that day?' I ask. I have to say it out loud or my head will burst. He stiffens beside me. 'They'll say I took her and killed her, Jeanie. And you know I didn't. Even seeing her will make me the guilty man, the man they put in prison. We can't say anything. To anyone.'

I sit, unable to speak. He is right, though. Seeing Bella would be as good as taking her as far as Bob Sparkes is concerned.

I just keep thinking Glen can't have taken her.

He just saw her. That's it. He just saw her. He didn't do anything wrong.

He's still gulping from the sobs and his face is red and wet. 'I keep thinking maybe I did dream it. It didn't feel real and you know I wouldn't hurt a child,' he says and I nod. I think I know, but really I don't know anything about this man that I've lived with all these years. He's a stranger, but we're bound together tighter than we've ever been. He knows me. He knows my weakness.

He knows that I would've wanted him to take her and bring her home.

I know that I caused all this trouble with my obsession.

Afterwards, when I'm in the kitchen making him a cup of tea, I realize he didn't use Bella's name, as though she isn't real to him. I take my bag back upstairs and unpack my things while Glen lies on the sofa watching football on the telly. Like normal. Like nothing has happened.

We don't talk about Bella again. Glen is very nice to me, telling me he loves me all the time, checking up to make sure I'm all right. Checking on me. 'What are you up to, Jeanie?' he says when he rings my mobile. And so we carry on.

But Bella is with us all the time. We don't talk about her, don't mention her name. We carry on as my secret starts to grow inside me, kicking at my heart and stomach, making me throw up in the downstairs toilet when I wake up and remember.

He was drawn to Bella because of me. He wanted to find a baby for me. And I wonder what I would've done if he had brought her home to me. I would've loved her. That's what I would've done. Just loved her. She would've been mine to love.

She was almost mine.

Glen and I still shared a bed afterwards. My mum couldn't believe it. 'How can you bear to have him near you, Jean? After all the things he did with those women – and that man?'

Mum and I never talked about sex, normally. It was my best friend at school who'd told me how babies were made and about periods. Mum wasn't very easy talking about things like that. It was as if it was dirty, somehow. I suppose Glen's sex life being in the papers made it easier for her to say it out loud. After all, everyone else in the country knew about it. It was like talking about someone she didn't really know.

'It wasn't real, Mum. It was all make-believe,' I told her, not catching her eye. 'It's something all men do in their heads, the psychologist said.'

'Your father doesn't,' she said.

'Anyway, we've decided to put it all behind us and look to the future, Mum.'

She looked at me as though she was going to say something important, but then stopped.

'It's your life, Jean. You must do what you think best.'

'*Our* life, Mum. Mine and Glen's.'

Glen said I should start looking for a little job. Outside the area.

I told him I was nervous about facing strangers, but we agreed I needed something to keep me busy. And out of the house.

Glen said he'd go back to the idea of starting his own business. But not driving this time. Something on the internet. Some kind of service.

'Everyone's doing it, Jeanie. Easy money and I've got the skills.'

I wanted to say so many things, but it seemed best to keep quiet.

Our attempt at looking to the future lasted just over a month. I'd begun working Fridays and Saturdays at a big salon in town. Big enough to be anonymous with lots of walk-ins and not too many prying questions. Classier than Hair Today, and the hair products were very expensive. You could tell they cost a fortune because they smelled of almonds. On my work days, I caught the tube up to Bond Street and walked the rest. It felt OK, better than I thought.

Glen stayed at home in front of his screen, 'building his empire', as he called it. He was buying and selling stuff on eBay. Car stuff. There were always parcels being delivered and clogging up the hall, but it kept him busy. I helped a bit, wrapping things up and going to the post office for him. We got into a routine.

But neither of us could put the case behind us. I couldn't stop thinking about Bella. My almost little girl. I find myself thinking it should've been us. She should be here with us. Our baby. Sometimes I find myself wishing he had picked her up that day.

But Glen isn't thinking about Bella. He can't put the entrapment behind him. It weighs on his mind. I can see him brooding, working himself up, and every time there's something on the telly about the police, he sits there fuming, saying how they've ruined his life. I've tried to persuade him to let it go, to look to the future, but he doesn't seem to hear me.

He must've made a phone call, because Tom Payne came to see us one Thursday morning to explain about suing the Hampshire Police Force. We'd get compensation for what they'd put Glen through, he said.

'So they should. I was locked up for months because of their tricks,' Glen said and I went to make some tea.

When I came back, they were working out figures on Tom's big yellow pad. He was always good at numbers, Glen. So clever. When they did the last calculation, Tom said, 'I reckon you should get about a quarter of a million,' and Glen whooped like we'd won the Lottery. I wanted to say that we didn't need the money – that I didn't want this dirty money. But I just smiled and went over and held Glen's hand.

It's a long process but it gives Glen a new focus. The eBay parcels stop arriving and instead he sits at the kitchen table with his paper-work, reading reports and crossing stuff out, highlighting other bits with new coloured pens, punching holes in documents and filing them in his different folders. Sometimes he reads a bit out to me, to see what I think.

'The effect of the case and the stigma attached to it means that Mr Taylor now suffers frequent panic attacks when he leaves the house.'

'Do you?' I ask. I hadn't noticed. Not like my mum's panic attacks, anyway.

'Well, I feel churned up inside,' he says. 'Do you think they'll want a doctor's note?'

We don't go out much anyway. Just to the shops and once to the pictures. We tend to go very early and shop in big, anonymous supermarkets where you don't have to talk to anyone, but he's nearly always recognized. Not surprising really. His picture was in the papers every day when the trial was on and the girls on the tills know it's him. I've said I'll go on my own but he won't hear of it. He won't let me face it alone. He holds my hand and braves it out and I learn to give anyone who dares say a word a look, to shut them up.

It's more difficult when I meet people I know. When they see me, some cross the road, pretend they haven't noticed me. Others want to know everything. I find myself saying the same thing over and over: 'We're fine. We knew the truth would come out – that Glen is innocent. The police have got a lot to answer for.'

Mostly, people seem glad for us, but not all. One of my old clients from the salon said, 'Hmm. But none of us are completely innocent, are we?'

I told her it had been lovely to see her but I had to get back to help Glen.

'It'll mean going back to court,' I work myself up to say to him one day. 'Having everything dug up again and gone through. I'm not sure—'

Glen stands and holds me. 'I know it's hard for you, love, but this will be my vindication. This will make sure people know what I went through. What we went through.'

I see the sense in that and try to be more helpful, remembering dates and terrible encounters with people in public to put in his evidence. 'Remember that bloke at the cinema? He said he wouldn't sit in the same room as a paedophile. Shouted it and pointed at you.'

Of course Glen remembers. We had to be escorted out of Screen 2 by Security 'for our own safety', the manager said. The bloke kept shouting, 'What about Bella?' and the woman with him was trying to make him sit down.

I wanted to say something – that my husband was innocent – but Glen gripped my arm and said, 'Don't, Jean. It'll make it worse. He's just some nutter.'

He doesn't like remembering this but he writes it down in his statement. 'Thanks, love,' he says.

The police resist the compensation claim – Tom says they have to because it is taxpayers' money they will have to pay out – until the very last minute. I'm getting dressed in my court outfit when Glen, already in his good suit and shoes, gets a call from Tom.

'It's over, Jeanie,' he shouts up the stairs. 'They've paid up. Quarter of a million.'

The papers and Dawn Elliott call it blood money, made on the back of her little girl. The reporters write horrible things about Glen again and they are back outside. I want to say 'I told you so,' but what good would that do?

Glen goes quiet again and I pack in the job before they can let me go.

Back to where we started.

Chapter 29

Monday, 21 July 2008

The Detective

After the trial collapsed, there was a different kind of sadness for Bob Sparkes. And anger. Mostly directed at himself. He'd allowed himself to be seduced into this disastrous strategy.

What had he been thinking? He'd heard one of the senior officers describe him as a 'glory hunter' as he passed an open door on the top floor and he'd cringed. He thought he'd been thinking of Bella, but perhaps it was all about him.

'Anyway, it's not glory I'm covered in,' he told himself.

The report that finally emerged, five months after the end of the trial, was written in the sanitized language of such documents, concluding that the decision to use an undercover officer to obtain evidence against the suspect was 'taken on the basis of expert opinion and extensive consultation with senior officers, but the strategy was ultimately flawed due to the lack of proper supervision of an inexperienced officer'.

'We screwed up' was the bottom line, Sparkes told Eileen on the phone after a terse meeting with his chief constable.

The next day, he was named and shamed along with his bosses in the papers as one of the 'Top Cops' who had 'wrecked' the Bella case. There were calls from politicians and punters for 'heads to roll'; Sparkes kept his head down as the clichés were trotted out and tried to prepare himself for life after coppering.

Eileen seemed almost pleased at the thought of him leaving the force; she suggested security work, something corporate. She means something clean, he thought. His kids were brilliant, ringing most days to urge him on and make him smile with bits of their news, but he couldn't look much beyond the end of each day.

He started running again, remembering the release it had given him as a young father, letting the rhythm of his pounding feet fill his mind for at least an hour. But he returned home grey-faced and sweating, his fifty-year-old knees killing him. Eileen said he had to stop; it was making him ill. That and everything else.

In the end, his disciplinary hearing was a civilized affair with questions posed politely but firmly. They already knew all the answers, but procedures had to be followed. He was put on gardening leave while he waited for the outcome and was still in his pyjamas when he took the call from his union representative; the force had decided to place the blame higher up and he would have a reprimand on his record but he wouldn't be sacked. He didn't know whether to laugh or cry.

Eileen cried and hugged him hard. 'Oh Bob, it's all over,' she said. 'Thank God they saw sense.'

The next day he went back to work, assigned different duties.

'A fresh start for us all,' DCI Chloe Wellington, newly promoted to fill the disgraced Brakespeare's chair, told him as part of some sort of re-education interview. 'I know it is tempting, but leave Glen Taylor to someone else. You can't go back to it, not after all this publicity. It would look like victimization and any new lines would be tainted by that.'

And Sparkes nodded, talking convincingly about the new cases on his desk, budgets, rosters and a bit of office gossip. But as he walked back to his office, Glen Taylor was top of his list; he was the only name on his list.

Matthews was waiting for him and they closed the door to talk tactics.

'They'll be watching us, Boss, to make sure we don't go any-where near him. They've brought in a senior detective from Basingstoke to review and plan the next steps for the Bella Elliott case – a woman, but a good bloke. Jude Downing. Do you know her?'

DI Jude Downing tapped on Sparkes' door that afternoon and suggested a coffee. Slim and red-haired, she sat opposite him in a café down the road – 'Canteen is a bit of a bear pit,' she said. 'Let's get a latte' – and waited.

'He's still out there, Jude,' Sparkes said finally.

'What about Bella?'

'I don't know, Jude. I'm haunted by her.'

'Does that mean she's dead?' she asked and he didn't know how to answer. When he was thinking like a copper, he knew she was dead. But he could not let her go.

Dawn was still interviewed on slow news days, her childlike face staring accusingly out of the pages. He had continued to ring her every week or so. 'No news, Dawn, just checking in,' he would say. 'How are things?' and she would tell him. She had met a man she liked through the Find Bella campaign and was managing to get through the days.

'There are three of us in this marriage,' Eileen said once and laughed that dry, fake laugh she reserved for punishing him. He hadn't risen to it, but he stopped mentioning the case at home and promised to finish painting their bedroom.

Jude Downing told him she was looking at every piece of evidence to see if anything had been missed. 'We've all been there, Bob. You can get so close to a case like this, you can't see clearly any more. It's not a criticism, just how it is.'

Sparkes stared into the froth on his coffee. They had dusted a chocolate heart on it. 'You're right, Jude. Fresh eyes needed, but I can help you.'

'Best if you step back for the moment, Bob. No offence, but we need to start from the beginning again and follow our own leads.'

'OK. Thanks for the coffee. Better get back.'

Eileen listened patiently later as she poured him a beer and he vented his rage. 'Let her get on with it, love. You are giving yourself an ulcer. Do the breathing exercises the doctor gave you.' He sipped his beer and practised the feeling of letting things go, but it just felt like letting things slip away from him.

He tried to immerse himself in his new cases but it was surface activity. A month later, Ian Matthews announced his move to another force. 'Needed a change, Bob,' he said. 'We all do.'

Ian Matthews' farewell bash was a classic. Speeches from the grown-ups, then a drink-fuelled orgy of hideous anecdotes and maudlin reminiscences about crimes solved. 'End of an era, Ian,' Sparkes told him as he released himself from the sergeant's beery hug. 'You've been brilliant.'

He was the last man standing, he told himself. Apart from Glen Taylor.

His new sergeant arrived, a thirty-five-year-old, frighteningly clever girl – 'Woman, Bob,' Eileen had corrected him. 'Girls have pigtails.'

She didn't have pigtails. She wore her glossy brown hair up in a tight bun, the tension on the fine hairs at her temples causing her skin to pucker. She was a sturdy young woman with a degree and a career path apparently tattooed on the inside of her eyelids.

DS Zara Salmond – *Mum must have a thing about royalty*, he'd thought – had transferred from Vice and was there to make his life easier, she said, and began.

Cases ebbed and flowed through his door – a teenage drug death, a run of high-end robberies, a nightclub stabbing – and he waded through them, but nothing could wrest his attention from the man who shared his office.

Glen Taylor, grinning like a monkey outside the Old Bailey, glimmered on the periphery of his day. 'He's here somewhere,' became his mantra as he quietly pored over every police report from the day Bella disappeared, wearing away the letters on his keyboard.

Sparkes heard on the canteen grapevine when they hauled Lee

Chambers back in to have another look at him. He'd done his three months for the indecent exposure, lost his job and had to move, but, apparently, had lost none of his front.

Chambers apparently wriggled in his chair, protesting his innocence, but told them more about his trade in porn, including his opening hours and regular haunts, in return for immunity from further prosecution.

'One to watch' was the verdict from the new team, but they didn't believe he was their bloke. They spat him back out, but his information gave the service-station search a new focus and the CCTV finally yielded some of Chambers' customers. Sparkes waited to hear if Glen Taylor was among them. 'No sign, Sir,' Salmond told him. 'But they're still looking.'

And on they went.

It was fascinating, like watching a dramatization of his investigation with actors playing the detectives. 'Like sitting in the stalls,' he told Kate when she called.

'Who's playing you? Robert de Niro? Oh, no, I forgot, Helen Mirren.' She laughed.

But perching on the edge of his seat as a member of the audience instead of being in the bubble of the investigation gave him a view he'd never had before. He could survey the hunt, God-like, and that was when he began to notice the cracks and false starts.

'We focused on Taylor too quickly,' he told DS Salmond. It had cost him a lot to admit it to himself, but it had to be done. 'Let's look at the day Bella disappeared again. Quietly.'

Secretly, they started to rebuild 2 October 2006 from the moment the child woke, using the inside surfaces of a hastily emptied metal cabinet in the corner of Sparkes' office to paste up their montage. 'Looks like an art project,' Salmond joked. 'Just need a bit of sticky-backed plastic and we'll get a *Blue Peter* badge.'

She'd wanted to do the timeline on the computer, but Sparkes was worried it would be clocked. 'This way, we can get rid of it and leave no trace, if we have to.'

He hadn't been sure when Salmond asked to help him. She didn't tease him like Matthews did – he missed it, the intimacy and release of a shared joke, but it felt inappropriate with a woman. Flirtatious rather than comradely. Anyway, he didn't miss Matthews' disgusting ketchup-slathered sausage sandwiches and the glimpses of his belly as his shirt came adrift.

DS Salmond was very bright, but Sparkes didn't really know her or whether he could trust her. He'd have to. He needed her unemotional clear-sightedness to stop him veering off into the undergrowth again.

Bella woke at 7.15, according to Dawn. A bit later than usual, but she was late to bed the night before. 'Why late to bed?' Salmond asked. They scrolled through Dawn's statements.

'They went to McDonald's and had to wait for the bus home,' Sparkes said.

'Why? Was it a treat?' asked Salmond. 'Not her birthday – that's in April. I thought Dawn was permanently short of money? About five hundred quid owing on her credit card and the neighbour said she rarely went out.'

'We didn't ask, according to this paperwork,' Sparkes said. It went on Salmond's list. She's a girl who likes a list, Sparkes thought. Woman. Sorry.

'And then sweets at the newsagent's. More treats. Wonder what was happening in their lives?'

Salmond wrote SMARTIES on a new piece of paper and pasted it up in the cabinet.

They sat on opposite sides of his desk with Salmond in the boss's chair. Between them was a printout of the master file, acquired by Matthews as a parting gift. Sparkes began to feel he was under interrogation, but his new sergeant was teasing out the missed questions and he focused.

'Did she have a new bloke in her life? What about this Matt that got her pregnant? Did we ever talk to him?'

The holes in the investigation began to gape at Sparkes accusingly.

'Let's do that now,' Salmond said quickly, seeing the gloom descending on her boss.

Bella's birth certificate had no father's name – as an unmarried mother, Dawn had no right to record a father unless he was present at the registration – but she'd told the police his name was Matt White and he lived in the Birmingham area and said he worked for a drugs company. 'He could get his hands on Viagra whenever he wanted,' she told Sparkes.

An initial search had failed to find a Matthew White in Birmingham who fitted the bill and then Taylor had entered the picture and everyone else was shoved into a drawer.

'Matt might be a nickname. And I wonder if he gave her a false name? Married men often do – stops the new girlfriend getting in touch unexpectedly, especially after it's over,' Salmond mused.

She fitted in her new inquiries around her other work with a calm efficiency that left Sparkes feeling soothed and slightly inadequate. She had a way of swishing into and out of his office in minutes with the right document, question answered and action agreed, barely rippling the surface of his concentration.

He began to believe they would find a new lead. But this new feeling of hope distracted him, made him reckless and relaxed his guard. Discovery of his parallel investigation was probably inevitable.

He'd left the door of the cabinet propped open while he made a call when DI Downing put her head round his door without knocking. Her invitation to share a sandwich never came. She found herself confronted with the alternative Bella Elliott case, pasted up like something from a serial killer's lair.

'Jude, it's just something left over from the original case,' he said, seeing the hardening of his colleague's eyes. It sounded feeble even to him and there was nothing to be done to head off the disaster.

There was sympathy rather than a tirade and that was worse somehow.

*

188

'You need some time off, Bob,' Chief Superintendent Parker told him firmly at their formal interview the following day. 'And some help. We would recommend counselling. We've some excellent people.'

Sparkes tried not to laugh. He took the printed sheet of names and two weeks' leave, calling Salmond from his car to tell her.

'Don't go near the case again, Salmond. They know you're not going barmy and won't be so gentle next time. We have to leave it with the new team.'

'Understood,' she said curtly.

She was obviously in with someone senior, he thought. 'Call me when you can talk,' he said.

Chapter 30

Tuesday, 16 September 2008

The Mother

DAWN HAD MADE an effort. She'd bought an expensive jacket and put on a pair of heels with new tights and a skirt. The editor made a huge fuss of her, meeting her at the lift and walking her through the newsroom in front of all the reporters. They smiled and nodded from behind their computer terminals and the man who had sat in court every day put down his phone and came over to shake her hand.

The editor's secretary, an impossibly elegant woman with magazine-standard hair and make-up, followed them into the inner sanctum and asked if she wanted a tea or coffee. 'Tea, please. No sugar.'

A tray arrived and the small talk ended. The editor was a busy man.

'Now then, Dawn, let's talk about our campaign to bring Taylor to justice. We'll need a big interview with you to launch it. And a new angle.'

Dawn Elliott knew exactly what the editor wanted. Almost two years of media exposure had toughened her up. A new angle meant more space on the front page, follow-ups in all the other papers, Breakfast TV interviews, Radio 5 Live, *Woman's Hour*, magazines. Like night follows day. It was exhausting, but she had to keep going because most days she knew, really knew, deep inside her, that her baby was still alive. And on the other days, she hoped.

But sitting on a sky-blue foam cube – a corporate decorator's attempt to humanize the space – becalmed in the air-conditioned office, she also knew that this newspaper wanted her to say for the first time that Bella had been murdered. It would be the 'belter of a story' the editor required to go after Glen Taylor.

'I'm not saying Bella is dead, Mark,' she said. 'Because she isn't.'

Mark Perry nodded, his faux sympathy stiffening his face, and pressed on. 'Look, I completely understand, but it's difficult to accuse someone of murder, Dawn, if we're saying that his victim is still alive. I know how hard this must be, but the police believe Bella is dead, don't they?'

'Bob Sparkes doesn't,' she replied.

'He does, Dawn. Everybody does.'

In the silence that followed, Dawn struggled with her options: please the papers or go it alone. She'd talked to the PR advising the campaign on pro bono terms earlier that morning and he'd warned she'd face 'Sophie's Choice'. 'Once you say that Bella is dead, there's no going back and the danger is that the search for her will stop.'

That couldn't happen.

'I think we should keep the question open,' Dawn said. 'Why don't we stick with accusing him of the kidnap, because when I find her, you won't want to be the paper that said she was dead, will you? Everyone will say that you stopped people looking for her.'

Perry walked to his desk and came back with one of the A3 sheets of paper covering it. He shifted the tray to another cube and laid the sheet on the table. It was the mock-up of a front page – one of several drawn to sell the *Herald*'s exclusive. There were no stories cluttering the page, just seven words screaming: 'THIS IS THE MAN WHO STOLE BELLA' and a photograph of Glen Taylor.

Perry had favoured the headline 'KILLER!' but that would have its day when they had nailed the bastard.

191

'What about this?' he asked and Dawn picked it up and scrutinized it like a pro.

In the beginning, she could hardly bear to look at Taylor's face, seeing it beside the face of her baby in every paper, but she'd forced herself. She looked at his eyes, searching for guilt; looked at his mouth, searching for weakness or lust. But there was nothing there. He looked like a man she might sit next to on a bus or stand behind in a supermarket queue and she wondered if she ever had. Was that why he'd picked her child?

It was the question that reverberated through every waking minute. Her dreams were full of Bella: glimpses of her just out of reach; being unable to move or make any progress towards her child, no matter how hard she ran, and, on waking, realizing as if for the first time that she was gone.

At first, she had been unable to take part in any sort of life, she was so overwhelmed by failure and helplessness. But when, eventually, she'd surfaced from the sedatives, her mum had persuaded her to fill her days with practical things. 'You need to get up, get dressed every day and do something, Dawn. Even some-thing small.'

It was the same advice she'd given when Bella was born, when Dawn had struggled to cope with the sleep deprivation and the colicky screaming of her new baby.

And she'd got up and got dressed. She'd walked down the path to the gate. She'd stood in the garden like Bella had and looked out at the world passing by.

The Find Bella campaign had begun on Dawn's Facebook page with her posting something about Bella or how she was feeling most days. The response was like a tidal wave, swamping her and then buoying her up. She gathered thousands, then hundreds of thousands, of Friends and Likes as mothers and fathers all over the world reached out to her. It had given her something to focus on, and when people with money contacted her to offer cash to help find her little girl, she'd said yes.

Bob Sparkes had admitted he had reservations about some of

the directions taken by the Find Bella campaign, but said it was OK as long as his officers weren't being diverted from the task in hand. 'Still, you never know,' he'd told her. 'The campaign might shame someone into coming forward.'

'Kate will go mad when she sees I've gone with the *Herald* – "The Enemy",' she'd told herself when first approached. 'But her lot didn't match the offer on the table. She'll see the sense.'

In truth, she wished it was going to be Kate and Terry handling the story, but the *Daily Post* had passed on the opportunity.

It was hard because she'd got close to Kate over the months. They'd talked most weeks and met up every so often for lunch and a gossip. Sometimes the paper would send a car to bring Dawn to London for the day. And in return, Dawn told Kate everything first.

But the *Post*'s coverage had petered out recently. 'Is the paper bored with me?' she'd asked Kate at their last meeting, when an interview had failed to appear.

'Don't be daft,' the reporter had said. 'There's just quite a lot of other stuff happening at the moment.' But Kate hadn't been able to meet her eye.

Dawn was no longer the lost girl on the sofa. She understood.

And when the *Herald* called her to propose a campaign to bring Taylor to justice and a generous donation to the Find Bella fund, she'd accepted it.

She'd rung Kate to let her know her decision – she owed her that. The call sent the reporter into a blind panic. 'Christ, Dawn, are you serious? Have you signed anything?'

'No, I'm going to see them this afternoon.'

'OK. Give me twenty minutes.'

'Well . . .'

'Please, Dawn.'

When the reporter rang back, Dawn knew immediately that Kate was empty-handed.

'I'm sorry, Dawn. They won't do it. They think it's too risky to accuse Taylor. And they're right. It's a stunt, Dawn, and could blow up in your face. Don't do it.'

Dawn sighed. 'I'm sorry, too, Kate. You know it's not personal – you've been brilliant – but I can't stop now just because one paper has lost interest. Better go or I'll be late. Let's speak soon.'

And here she was, looking through the contract and re-checking the sub-clauses for loopholes. Her lawyer had already read it but had advised her to take another look 'in case they slip something new in'.

Mark Perry watched her, nodding encouragingly whenever she spoke and smiling broadly when she signed and dated the document.

'OK, let's get started,' he said, standing and propelling her out of the office to the waiting feature writer who would do 'The Big Interview'.

The paper had thousands of words already written, prepared for the expected guilty verdict. Before Glen Taylor's trial, they'd interviewed his former colleagues from the bank and delivery firm, collected the sordid tales of the chat-room women and had the child porn nailed from an off-the-record briefing by a detective on the team. They'd also bought up a neighbour of the Taylors' and her exclusive photos of Taylor with her kids – one of them a little blonde girl.

The neighbour had told her story about him watching the children from a window and how she'd nailed up the gate between their houses.

None of it would go to waste now.

'She won't go for the Killer headline but we've got a great first day,' he told his deputy, slipping his jacket on the back of a chair on the back bench and rolling up his sleeves. 'Let's work on the editorial. And get the lawyers up here. Don't fancy Wormwood Scrubs just yet.'

The *Herald* splashed the story over the first nine pages, pledging to bring Glen Taylor to justice and demanding that the Home Secretary order a retrial.

It was journalism at its most powerful, hammering home the message with a mallet, inciting reaction, and the readers responded.

The comment sections on the website were filled with unthinking, screaming vitriol, foul-mouthed opinion and calls for the death penalty to be reinstated. 'The usual nutters,' the news editor summed up in morning conference. 'But lots of them.'

'Let's show a bit of respect for our readers,' the editor said. And they all laughed. 'Now, what have we got for today?'

Chapter 31

The Reporter

KATE WATERS WAS fuming over her desk breakfast. 'We could've had this,' she told anyone who would listen as she turned the pages of the *Herald*. Across the newsroom, Terry Deacon heard, but carried on typing his news list. She abandoned her brown toast and honey and walked over. 'We could have had this,' she repeated, standing over him.

'Of course we could, Kate, but she wanted too much money and we've already had three big interviews with her.'

He pushed back his chair, looking pained. 'Honestly, what is new here? Wouldn't have minded the picture with the kid next door, but the internet slags and the child porn have been everywhere.'

'That's not the point, Terry. The *Herald* is now the official Bella Elliott paper. If Taylor is retried and found guilty, they'll be able to say they brought Bella's kidnapper to justice. Where will we be? Standing on the steps with our dicks in our hands.'

'Find a better story then, Kate,' the editor said as he suddenly appeared behind them. 'Don't waste time on this old rehash. Off to a marketing meeting, but let's talk later.'

'OK, Simon,' she said to his retreating back.

'Bloody hell, you've been summoned to the headmaster's study,' Terry laughed once his boss was out of earshot.

Kate returned to her seat and cold toast and began searching for the elusive better story.

In normal circumstances, she'd just ring Dawn Elliott or Bob Sparkes, but her options were vanishing fast. Dawn had decamped and Bob had mysteriously disappeared off the radar – she hadn't heard from him for weeks. She'd heard from the Crime man that there'd been a bit of trouble over interference in the Bella review and Sparkes' phone seemed to be permanently off.

She gave it another try and gave a silent cheer when it rang. 'Hello, Bob,' she said when Sparkes finally answered. 'How are you? Are you back at work yet? Guess you've seen the *Herald*?'

'Hi, Kate. Yes. Quite a bold step for them, given the verdict. Hope they've got good lawyers. Anyway, good to hear from you. I'm fine. Had a bit of a break, but back at work. I'm in town, working with the Met. Tidying up some loose ends. Up near you, actually.'

'Well, what are you doing for lunch today?'

He was sitting in the expensive, tiny French restaurant when she walked in, dark suit and black mood stark against the white tablecloths.

'Bob, you look well,' she lied. 'Sorry if I'm late. Traffic.'

He rose and offered his hand across the table. 'Just got here myself.'

The small talk stopped and started as a waiter brought menus, offered suggestions and water, hovered for the order and poured the wine. But finally, with matching plates of *magret de canard* in front of them, she began in earnest.

'I want to help, Bob,' she said, picking up her fork. 'There must be some line of inquiry we can look at again.'

He didn't speak but sawed at the rosy meat in front of him. She waited.

'Look, Kate, we made a mistake and can't unmake it. Let's see what the *Herald*'s campaign produces. Do you think he'll sue?'

'It's a dangerous game, suing for libel,' she said. 'I've been there.

197

If he does, he's got to go in the witness box and give evidence. Will he really want to do that?'

'He's a clever man, Kate. Slippery.' He was rolling bread into beads of dough between his fingers. 'I don't know any more.'

'For goodness' sake, Bob. You're a fantastic copper – why are you giving up?'

He raised his head and looked at her.

'Sorry, didn't mean to nag. I just hate seeing you like this,' she said.

In the lull, while both sipped their wine, Kate cursed her haste. Leave the poor man alone, she thought.

But she couldn't. It was not in her nature.

'So what've you been doing with the Met today?'

'Loose ends, like I said. Sorting through some stuff from a couple of joint investigations – car thefts, that sort of thing. Actually, there were also some bits and pieces left over from the Bella case. Early stuff, when we first picked up Glen Taylor.'

'Anything interesting?' she asked.

'No, not really. The Met went to make sure the other Qwik Delivery driver was at home while we drove up from Southampton.'

'What other driver?'

'There were two drivers in Hampshire that day – you know that.'

She didn't, or she hadn't remembered.

'The other one was a bloke called Mike Doonan. He was the one we went to see first. Perhaps his name didn't come out at the time. Anyway, he's crippled with a crumbling spine – could hardly walk – and we never found anything to pursue.'

'Did you question him?'

'Yes. He was the one that told us Taylor was also making a delivery in the area that day. Not sure we'd have found that out without him. Taylor did the drop as a favour, so there's no official record of it. The case-review team went to see him, too. Nothing added, apparently.'

Kate excused herself from the table and went to the Ladies', where she scribbled down the name and put a quick call through to a colleague to find an address for Doonan. For later.

When she got back to the table, the detective was putting his credit card back in his wallet.

'Bob, I invited you,' she said.

He waved away her protest and smiled. 'My pleasure. It's been good to see you, Kate. Thanks for your pep talk.'

She deserved that, she thought as they walked out in single file. On the pavement, he shook her hand again and they both headed back to work.

Kate's phone began vibrating as she hailed a taxi and she waved away the cab to take the call.

'There's a Michael Doonan in Peckham, according to the electoral roll – I'll SMS the address and the names of the neighbours,' the Crime man said.

'You're a star, thanks,' she said, raising her hand for another taxi. Her phone rang again almost immediately.

'Kate, where the hell are you? We've got a buy-up with the ex-wife of that footballer. It's up near Leeds, so get on the next train and I'll email you the background. Ring when you're at the station.'

Chapter 32

Wednesday, 17 September 2008

The Widow

SOMEONE PUT THE *Herald* through the door today – they've accused Glen all over again and he put it straight in the bin. I got it out and hid it away behind the bleach under the sink for later. We knew what was coming because the *Herald* were banging on the door yesterday, shouting questions and pushing notes through the letterbox. They said they were campaigning for a retrial so that Bella would get justice. 'What about justice for me?' Glen said.

It's a blow, but Tom phoned to say the paper will have to have deep pockets to pay the costs and, most importantly, they have no evidence. He said to 'batten down the hatches', whatever that means. 'The *Herald* are coming at us with all guns blazing, but it is all just sensationalism and tittle tattle,' he told Glen, who repeated it line by line to me.

'He talks like it is a war,' I say and then shut up. The wait will be worse than the reality, Tom predicts, and I hope he's right.

'We've got to keep quiet, Jeanie,' Glen explains. 'Tom will start legal proceedings against the paper, but he thinks we should go on a bit of a holiday – "remove ourselves from the picture" – until this all blows over. I'll go online and book something this morning.'

He hasn't asked where I want to go and to be honest, I don't care. My little helpers are beginning to have less effect and I feel so tired I could cry.

In the end he picks somewhere in France. In my other life, I would've been thrilled, but I'm not sure what I feel when he tells me he's found a cottage in the countryside that's miles from anywhere. 'Our flight leaves at 7 a.m. tomorrow morning so we need to leave here at four, Jeanie. Let's get packed up ready and we'll take our car. Don't want a taxi driver tipping off the press.'

He knows so much, my Glen. Thank God I've got him to look after me.

At the airport, we keep our heads down and sunglasses on and we wait until the queue is almost down to the last person before we head to the desk. The woman checking us in barely looks at us and sends our suitcase on to the conveyor belt before she's managed to say, 'Did you pack this bag yourself?' let alone waited to hear the answer.

I'd forgotten how much queuing there is in airports and we're so stressed by the time we get to the gate that I'm ready to go home to the press pack. 'Come on, love,' Glen says, holding my hand as we walk to the plane. 'Nearly there.'

At Bergerac, he goes to get the hire car while I wait for the bag, mesmerized by the passing luggage. I miss our case – it is so long since we used it, I've forgotten what colour it is and have to wait until everyone else has lugged theirs off. I finally go out into the bright sunshine and spot Glen in a tiny red car. 'Didn't think it would be worth getting anything bigger,' he says. 'We're not going to do much driving, are we?'

Funny, but being on our own in France is different from being on our own at home. Without a routine, we don't know what to say to each other. So we say nothing. The silence should have been a rest from the constant noise and banging on our door at home, but it isn't. It's worse, somehow. I take to going for long walks in the lanes and woods around the cottage while Glen sits on a sun lounger and reads detective novels. I could've screamed when I saw what he'd packed. As if we haven't had enough of police investigations.

I decide to leave him with his perfect murders and sit on the other side of the patio with some magazines. I find myself looking at Glen, watching him and thinking about him. If he looks up and catches me, I pretend I'm looking at something behind him. I am, I suppose.

I don't really know what I'm looking for. Some sign of something – his innocence, the toll taken by the ordeal, the real man, perhaps. I can't really say.

The only time we leave the place is to drive to the nearest supermarket to get food and loo rolls. I can't be bothered to shop for real meals. Finding the stuff to go into a spag bol is beyond me so we eat bread and ham and cheese at lunchtime and a cold roast chicken and coleslaw or more ham in the evenings. We're not really hungry anyway. It's just something to push round our plates.

We've been here four days when I think I see someone walking along the lane at the bottom of the property. First person I've seen near the property. A car is an event.

I don't think much of it, but the next morning there is a man walking up the drive.

'Glen,' I shout to him in the house. 'There's a bloke coming up.'

'Get in here, Jean,' he hisses and I hurry past him as he closes the door and begins drawing the curtains. We wait for the knock.

The *Herald* has found us. Found us and photographed us: 'The kidnapper and his wife sunning themselves outside their exclusive hideaway in the Dordogne' while Dawn Elliott 'desperately continues her search for her child'. Tom reads us the headlines the next day over the phone. 'We're only here because we're being hounded, Tom,' I say. 'And Glen has been cleared by the courts.'

'I know, Jean, but the papers have convened their own court. It won't be long before they'll be on to the next thing – they're like children, easily distracted.'

He says the *Herald* must have traced Glen's credit card to find us.

'Are they allowed to do that?' I ask.

'No. But that doesn't stop them.'

I put down the phone and begin packing. The villains again.

When we get home, they are waiting and Glen rings Tom to talk about how to stop them saying these things.

'It's libel, Jeanie. Tom says we have to sue them – or threaten to sue them – or they'll keep going, digging into our lives and putting us on the front page.'

I want it to stop so I agree. Glen knows best.

It takes a while for the solicitors to write their letter. They have to say why the stories are all wrong and that takes a bit of time. Glen and I go up to Holborn again, taking the same train I used to take when he was on trial. 'Groundhog day,' he says to me. He tries to keep my spirits up and I love him for it.

The barrister isn't a Charles Sanderson, he's a real smooth character. I bet his wig isn't falling apart. He looks rich, as if he drives a sports car and has a country house, and his office is all shiny metal and glass. Libel is obviously the money-making end of the business. Wonder if Mr Sanderson knows.

This one is all business. He's as bad as the prosecutor, asking all the questions again and again. I squeeze Glen's hand to show him I'm on his side and he squeezes back.

The smoothie pushes and pushes on every detail.

'I have to test our case, Mr Taylor, because this is basically a re-run of the Bella Elliott prosecution. That case was thrown out because of the police actions, but the *Herald* maintain you kidnapped the child. We say that is wrong and defamatory. However, the *Herald* will throw everything at you – from the case itself, and they can also use evidence they gathered that was not admissible in the criminal trial. Do you see?'

We must have looked a bit blank because Tom began to explain it in simple language while the smoothie looked out at the view.

'They'll have a lot of dirt, Glen. And they'll throw all of it at you to get the libel jury on their side. We need to show that you're innocent, Glen, to get the jury to find against the *Herald*.'

'I am,' he says, all fired up.

'We know. But we need to show it and we need to be sure there are no surprises. Just saying, Glen. You need to go into this with your eyes open, because it's a very expensive action to bring. It will cost thousands of pounds.'

Glen looks at me and I try to look brave, but inside I'm running for the door. I suppose we've got the dirty money we can use.

'No surprises, Mr Taylor?' the smoothie repeats.

'None,' my Glen says. I look at my lap.

The letter goes out the next day and the *Herald* shouts about it all over its pages and on the radio and television.

'TAYLOR TRIES TO GAG *HERALD*' is the headline. I hate the word 'gag'.

Chapter 33

Friday, 26 September 2008

The Mother

THE PHOTOGRAPHS OF the Taylors in France made Dawn furious. 'Is furious' she wrote as her Facebook status, with a link to the main picture of Glen Taylor in shorts and bare-chested, lying on a lounger reading a thriller called *The Book of the Dead*.

The crassness of it made her want to go round and shake the truth out of him. The idea stewed in her head all morning; she played the scene over and over of her bringing Taylor to his knees and him crying and begging for forgiveness. She was so sure it would work, she rang Mark Perry at the *Herald* and demanded a confrontation between her and the kidnapper.

'I could go to his house. I could look him in the eye. He might confess,' she said, high on the fear and excitement of meeting her child's abductor.

Perry hesitated. Not from any compunction about accusing Taylor – he was writing the headline in his head as he listened – but he wanted the dramatic confrontation to be exclusive and the doorstep was far too public.

'He might not open the door, Dawn,' he said. 'And then we'll be left standing there. We need to do it where he can't hide. In the street when he's not expecting us. We'll find out when he's next meeting with the lawyers and catch him as he goes in. Just us, Dawn.'

She understood and told no one. She knew her mum would try to dissuade her – 'He's scum, Dawn. He's not going to confess in the street. It'll just upset you and bring you down again. Let the courts get it out of him.' But Dawn didn't want to listen to sense, she didn't want advice. She wanted to act. To do something for Bella.

She didn't have to wait long. 'You won't believe this, Dawn. He's got an early-morning appointment next Thursday – on the anniversary of Bella's disappearance,' Perry said on the phone. 'It'll be perfect.'

Dawn couldn't speak for a moment. There was nothing perfect about the anniversary. It had been looming over the horizon and the terrible dreams had increased. She found herself re-enacting the days leading up to October the second: shopping trips, walking to nursery, watching Bella's DVDs. Two years without her little girl seemed like a lifetime.

Perry was still talking on the phone and she tuned back in, trying to reach back to her anger. 'Taylor likes to go when no one else is around, apparently, so we'll have him to ourselves.

'Come in, Dawn, and we'll plan our MO.'

'What's an MO?'

'It's Latin for how we're going to get Glen Taylor.'

Every eventuality was covered during the conference in the editor's office. Arrival by taxi, check. Arrival by public transport, check. Back entrances, check. Timings, check. Dawn's hiding place, check.

Dawn sat and received her orders. She was to sit in a black cab down the street from the barrister's chambers and jump out at a signal from the reporter. Two rings on his mobile, then out.

'You'll probably only have time for two questions, Dawn,' Tim the chief reporter advised. 'So make them short and to the point.'

'I just want to ask "Where's my daughter?" That's all.'

The editor and assembled journalists exchanged glances. This was going to be fantastic.

On the day, Dawn was not dressed too smartly, as instructed. 'You don't want to look like a TV reporter in the photos,' Tim had said. 'You want to look like a grieving mother.' He added quickly, 'Like you, Dawn.'

She was collected by the office driver and delivered to the meeting point, a café in High Holborn. Tim, two other reporters, two photographers and a video journalist were already round a Formica table, smeared plates stacked in the middle.

'All ready?' Tim said, trying not to show too much excitement.

'Yes, Tim. I'm ready.'

Sitting in the car with him later, her nerve began to fail, but he kept her talking about the campaign, keeping her anger ticking over. His mobile rang twice. 'We're on, Dawn,' he said, picking up the copy of the *Herald* she would thrust in Taylor's face and cracking open the door. She could see them coming down the street, Glen Taylor and Jean, his simpering wife, and she stepped clear of the cab, her legs shaking.

The street was quiet; the office staff who would eventually fill the buildings were still jammed together on the underground. Dawn stood in the middle of the pavement and watched them get nearer, her stomach knotted, but the couple failed to notice her until they were only a hundred yards away. Jean Taylor was fussing over her husband's briefcase, trying to stuff documents back in, when she looked up and stopped dead. 'Glen,' she said loudly. 'It's her, Bella's mother.'

Glen Taylor focused on the woman in the street. 'Christ, Jean. It's an ambush. You say nothing, no matter what she says,' he hissed and took hold of her arm to propel her to the doorway.

But it was too late to escape.

'Where is my daughter? Where's Bella?' Dawn screamed into his face, spittle landing near his mouth.

Taylor looked Dawn in the face for a fraction of a second and then was gone behind dead eyes.

'Where is she, Glen?' she repeated, trying to catch his arm and shake him. The cameramen had appeared and were capturing every second, circling the trio to get the best shots while the reporters barked questions, separating Jean Taylor from her husband and leaving her stranded like a stray sheep.

Dawn suddenly wheeled on her. 'What has he done with my baby, Mrs Taylor? What has your husband done with her?'

'He's done nothing. He's innocent. The court said so,' Jean screamed back, shocked into a response by the violence of the attack.

'Where's my child?' Dawn shouted again, unable to ask anything else.

'We don't know,' Jean yelled back. 'Why did you leave your little girl alone so someone could take her? That's what people should be asking.'

'That's enough, Jean,' Taylor said and pushed past the cameras, pulling her along in his wake as Tim comforted Dawn.

'She said it was my fault,' she breathed, her face ashen.

'She's a nasty bitch, Dawn. Only she and the nutters think it's your fault. Come on, let's get you back to the paper for the interview.'

This is going to look great, he thought as they travelled through the traffic to west London.

Dawn stood beside one of the pillars to watch as the photographs were laid out along the whole length of the back bench so the newsroom could look and admire. 'Fucking brilliant shots of Glen Taylor. That look he gave Dawn is chilling,' the picture editor said as he hawked his wares.

'We'll put it on the front,' Perry said. 'Page three, Dawn in tears and Jean Taylor shouting at her like a fishwife. Not the mousy little woman, after all. Look at the fury in that face. Now, where are the words?'

THE KIDNAPPER AND THE MOTHER blared out of the front page the next morning on trains, buses and at Britain's breakfast tables.

Tim, the chief reporter, rang to congratulate her. 'Great job, Dawn. Would love to be a fly on the wall at the Taylors' this morning. Everyone's happy here.' What he didn't say was that the *Herald's* sales were up – as was the editor's annual bonus.

Chapter 34

Thursday, 2 October 2008

The Widow

I WAS SHAKING when we got into the lawyer's. Not sure if it was anger or nerves – a bit of both, probably, and even Mr Smoothie put his arm round me. 'Bloody stunt merchants,' he said to Tom Payne. 'We should Press Council them or something.'

I kept replaying it in my head, from the moment I realized it was her. I should've recognized her straight away, I've seen her enough times on the telly and in court. But it's different when you see someone in the street where you're not expecting them. You don't really look at people's faces, I think, just their outlines. Of course, as soon as I really looked at her I knew it was her. Dawn Elliott. The mother. Standing there with the idiots from the *Herald*, egging her on, and accusing my Glen when he's been found Not Guilty. It's not right. It's not fair.

I suppose it was the shock that made me shout at her like that.

Glen was angry that I told her what I thought. 'It'll just keep everyone going, Jean. She'll feel she has to defend herself and keep giving interviews. I told you to keep quiet.'

I said I was sorry, but I wasn't. I meant every word. I'll do a phone-in tonight and say it again. It felt good to say it out loud, in public. People should know it's all her fault. She was responsible for our little girl and she let her get taken.

They sat me down with a hot drink in the clerks' room while they got on with the meeting. I wasn't in the mood for legal stuff anyway, so I sat quietly in a corner, replaying the row in the street in my head and sort of listening to the secretaries' chatter. Invisible again.

It took ages for the meeting to end and then we had to discuss how we were going to get out without the press seeing us. In the end, we went out the back, down an alleyway where they put the bins and bikes. 'They won't be hanging around now, but there's no point taking chances,' Tom said. 'It'll be on their website by now and all over the paper tomorrow. It'll put up the damages – just keep thinking about the money.'

Glen shook his hand and I just sort of waved. I don't want the money. I want it to stop.

He was extra nice to me when we got in, taking my coat off and making me sit with my feet up while he put the kettle on.

It's the anniversary today. I'd marked it in my diary with a dot. A little dot that could be a slip of the pen so no one else would know if they looked.

Two years since she was taken. They'll never find her now – the people who took her must have persuaded everyone by now that she is theirs and she must think they are her mum and dad. She's little and she probably hardly remembers her real mother. I hope she's happy and they love her as much as I would if she was here with me.

For a moment, I can see her sitting on our stairs, bumping down on her bottom and laughing. Calling for me to come and watch her. She could've been here if Glen had brought her home to me.

Glen hasn't said much since we got back. He's got his computer on his knee and closes it quickly when I go to sit next to him. 'What were you looking at, love?' I ask.

'Just flicking through the sports pages,' he says and then goes to put petrol in the car.

I pick up the computer and open it. It says it's locked and I sit and stare at the screen, at the photo of me Glen has put on it. There I am, locked like the computer.

When he comes home, I try to talk to him about the future. 'Why don't we move, Glen? Have the fresh start we keep talking about? We're never going to escape this unless we do.'

'We're not moving, Jean,' he snaps at me. 'This is our home and I won't be driven out of it. We're going to weather this. Together. The press will forget about us in the end and move on to some other poor sod.'

'They won't,' I want to say. Every anniversary of Bella's disappearance, every time a child goes missing, every time there is a quiet news day, they'll come back. And we'll just be sitting here, waiting.

'There are so many nice places to live, Glen. We've talked about living by the sea one day. We could do that now. We could even move abroad.'

'Abroad? What the hell are you talking about? I don't want to live somewhere I can't speak the language. I'm staying put.'

So we do. We might as well have moved to a desert island in the end as we are completely isolated in our little house. Just the sharks circling occasionally. We keep each other company, doing the crossword together in the kitchen – him reading out the clues and writing the answers in while I'm still guessing, watching films together in the living room, me learning to knit, him chewing his nails. Like an old retired couple. I'm not even forty yet.

'I think the Mannings' poodle must've died. It's been weeks since any dog shit has been left on the doorstep,' Glen says conversationally. 'It was very old.'

The graffiti persists. That paint is terrible to get off and neither of us want to stand there in full view, scrubbing at it, so it stays. 'SCUM' and 'PEEDOFILE' in big red letters on the garden wall. 'Kids,' Glen says. 'From the local comprehensive, if the spelling's anything to go by.'

There are letters from the 'green biro brigade' most weeks, but we've started putting them straight in the bin. You can tell them a mile off. I never see those tiny envelopes or the green pens they use for sale – the poisonous people must have their own source of them and the rough, lined notepaper they prefer. I suppose it must be cheap.

I used to look at the handwriting to try and guess what sort of person had sent it. Some are all loops and swirls – the sort of writing on a wedding invitation – and I think they must be written by old people. No one else writes like that any more.

They're not all anonymous. Some write their address in spidery writing on the top – lovely names like 'Rose Cottage' or 'The Willows' – and then spew out their bile underneath. I'm so tempted to write back and tell them what I think of them – give them a dose of their own medicine. I write the replies in my head when I'm pretending to watch the television, but I don't take it any further. It would cause trouble.

'They're just sick, Jeanie,' Glen says each time one plops through the letterbox. 'We should feel sorry for them, really.'

Sometimes I wonder who they are and then I think they are probably people like me and Glen. Lonely people. People on the edge of things. Prisoners in their own homes.

I buy a big jigsaw at the local charity shop. It's a picture of a beach with cliffs and seagulls. It'll give me something to do in the afternoons. It's going to be a long winter.

Chapter 35

Friday, 18 December 2009

The Reporter

IT HAD BEEN a quietish week – Christmas, fast approaching, had filled the paper with festive nonsense and warming stories of adversity overcome. Kate flicked through her notebook, more from habit than hope, but there was nothing to pick at. The paper was already full of Saturday reads – long features, shrieking columnists, pages of cheffy Christmas fare and post-festivity diets. Terry looked happy, anyway.

Unlike the Crime man, who, passing her desk on his way to the Gents', paused to vent his anger. 'My Christmas anniversary piece has been chucked out,' he said.

'Poor you. Which one?' Kate asked. He was notorious for recycling stories – 'The green bin of news,' he called it cheerfully.

'Bella. It's Dawn's third one without her. How about a drink at lunchtime?'

'Bella. Oh my God, I forgot you,' she told the child's picture stuck on her filing cabinet. 'I'm so sorry.'

The *Herald's* campaign had gone quiet once the threat of a libel action had become a reality, and both camps had drawn back behind their battlelines.

Kate heard on the grapevine that the legal director of the *Herald* had had a stand-up row with the editor over the initial coverage, and she persuaded Tim, her oppo on the *Herald* and an old friend, to tell her all about it over a glass or three of wine. He'd been cautious about the details at first, but the story was too good not to tell properly. He propped up the bar in a pub opposite the High Court and told her how the house lawyer had accused Mark Perry of ignoring his advice and using 'lurid comments' and allegations in the copy.

'I expect "Taylor's killer eyes" was one of them,' Kate laughed. 'I thought you were on pretty shaky ground there.'

'Yes, one of Perry's choicer phrases. Anyway, the lawyer said Mark was ramping up the potential damages every time he pulled a stunt like that.'

'And Taylor's got money to fund a case. All that compensation from the police,' Kate said.

'The editor's agreed to pull back from the direct accusations and harassment. Soft-pedal while the libel case is pending.'

'But he's not going to give up the campaign, is he?' Kate asked. 'He'll definitely have to pay up if he does that. It's tantamount to admitting he's in the wrong.'

Tim grimaced into his Merlot. 'He's not happy. He hit his monitor with his fist, then crashed back into the newsroom to tell everyone they were "fucking amateurs". He likes to spread the pain. Calls it inclusivity.'

Kate had patted his arm sympathetically and headed for home.

As Tim had predicted, the *Herald* had quietened down and the libel action appeared to have stalled in the chambers of both sides.

But Kate was ready to have another go. She needed to find her notebook from a year ago. There, scribbled on the cover, was an address in Peckham for one Mike Doonan.

'Slipping out to knock a door on a tip,' she told Terry. 'On my mobile if you need me.'

It took an age to cross Westminster Bridge and crawl down the Old Kent Road, but the cabbie finally pulled up in the shadow of a grim relic of 1960s cutting-edge architecture. A grey concrete box, studded with filthy windows and satellite dishes.

Kate went to the door and pressed the bell. She knew what she was going to say – she'd had plenty of time in the taxi to plan – but there was no answer. The flat echoed with the bell ringing, but it was the only sound.

'He's out,' a voice called from next door. A woman's voice.

'Bugger, I hoped I'd catch him in. I thought he was housebound,' she replied.

A head appeared out of the door. Ancient, tight perm and a pinny.

'He's down at the bookies'. Doesn't go out much now, with his back, poor Mike. But he tries to get out once a day. Was he expecting you?'

Kate smiled at the neighbour. 'Not really. It was on the off-chance. I'm doing a story about a man he used to work with when he was a driver. Glen Taylor. The Bella case.'

The neighbour opened her door wider. 'The Bella case? Did he work with that bloke? He never said. Do you want to come in and wait?'

Within the first five minutes, Mrs Meaden had told Kate about Doonan's medical condition – 'degenerative osteoarthritis, getting steadily worse' – his betting habit, ex-wives, kids and diet – 'beans on toast practically every night, can't be good for him.

'I do a bit of shopping for him every week and the kids on the estate run errands.'

'That's kind of you – he's lucky to have a neighbour like you.'

Mrs Meaden looked pleased. 'It's what any Christian would do,' she said. 'Tea?'

Kate balanced the flowered cup and saucer on the arm of her chair and took a shop-bought mince pie out of the tin.

'Funny he never mentioned he knew this Glen Taylor man, isn't it?' Mrs Meaden said, brushing crumbs off her lap.

'They worked together. At Qwik Delivery,' Kate prompted.

'He drove for years. Says that's what did it for his back. He

216

doesn't really have friends. Not what I call friends – people who come and see him. He used to go to a computer place round here – said it was sort of a club. Used to go regularly before he retired. Funny thing for a man of his age to be doing, I always thought. Still, he's on his own so he must get bored.'

'I didn't know there was a computer club round here. Do you know what it's called?'

'It's in Princess Street, I think. Shabby-looking place with blacked-out windows. Oh, there's Mike now.'

They could hear the heavy sound of dragging feet and the stabbing of a stick on the concrete walkway.

'Hello, Mike,' Mrs Meaden called as she opened her door. 'Got a lady from the press here for you.'

Doonan pulled a face as Kate emerged. 'Sorry, love. My back is killing me. Can you come back another time?'

Kate moved closer to him and took his arm. 'Let me at least help you in,' she said. And did.

The smell in Doonan's flat was nothing like the cabbage and Dettol permeating next door. It smelled of men. Sweat, old beer, old fags, feet.

'What do you want to talk to me for? I told the police all I knew,' Doonan said as Kate perched on a hard chair opposite him.

'Glen Taylor,' she said simply.

'Oh, him.'

'You used to work together.'

Doonan nodded.

'I'm writing a profile on him. Trying to get a better picture of who he really is.'

'Then you've come to the wrong person. He was no friend of mine. I've told the police. Stuck-up little prick, if you want to know.'

I do, she thought.

'Always thought he was better than us. Slumming it until some-thing better came along.'

She had found his sore spot and scratched it. 'Heard he was a bit arrogant.'

'Arrogant? That's an understatement. Lorded it over us in the canteen with his stories of when he ran a bank. And then he dropped me in it over my back problem. Told the boss I was having them on about how bad it was. Said I was faking.'

'That must've caused trouble.'

Doonan smiled bitterly. 'Joke of it is that I helped him get the job at Qwik Delivery.'

Kate pounced. 'Really? So you knew him before. Where'd you come across him?'

'On the net. On a forum or something.' Doonan sounded less sure of himself.

'And at the club in Princess Street?'

Doonan flashed a look at Kate. 'What club?' he said. 'Look, I need to take my pills. You'll have to go.'

She put her business card down beside him and shook his hand. 'Thanks for talking to me, Mike. I really appreciate it. I'll let myself out.'

She headed straight for Princess Street.

The sign for Internet Inc. was small and amateurish, the shop window painted black on the inside and there was a CCTV camera positioned over the door. Looks like a sex shop, Kate thought.

The door was locked and there were no opening times posted. She walked back to the greengrocer's at the top of the street and waited until an assistant in a Santa hat came out to serve her from the stall on the pavement.

'Hi, I want to use the internet but the place down the street is closed. Do you know when it opens?' she said.

The young man laughed. 'You don't want to go in there, love. It's for blokes.'

'How do you mean?'

'Porn place, innit. They don't let the public in. It's a sort of club thing for dirty old men.'

'Oh, right. Who runs it then?'

'Dunno really. Manager is a bloke called Lenny, but it's open at night mainly so we don't see him much.'

'Thanks. I'll have four of those apples.'

She'd come back later.

Internet Inc. looked even less savoury in the dark. Kate had spent two and a half hours in a grimy pub, sipping a succession of warm fruit juices and listening to Perry Como work his magic on 'Frosty the Snowman'. She was not in the mood for a brush-off.

When she tried the door it was still locked, but knocking on the blackened glass produced a voice from within.

'Hello. Who is it?'

'I need to speak to Lenny,' Kate said, looking up at the camera with her most winning smile.

Silence.

The door opened and a tall, muscular man in training vest and jeans appeared. 'Do I know you?' he asked.

'Hi, you must be Lenny. I'm Kate. I wondered if I could have a quick word.'

'What about?'

'About a story I'm writing.'

'You're a reporter?' Lenny slid backwards into the shop. 'We've got a licence. It's all legit. There's no story here.'

'No, it's not about you. It's about Bella Elliott.'

The name was like a magic talisman. It transfixed people. Drew them in.

'Bella Elliott? Little Bella?' he said. 'Look, come on through to my office.'

She entered a narrow, darkened room, lit only by the LED glow of a dozen computer screens. Each was in a booth with a chair. There was no other furniture, but, in a nod to the season, a piece of tinsel hung limply from the central light.

'No customers yet. They usually come a bit later,' Lenny explained as he led her to his cupboard of an office, the walls lined with stacks of DVDs and magazines. 'Ignore those,' he advised as he caught her looking at the titles.

'Right,' she said and sat.

'You've come about Glen Taylor, haven't you?'

Kate couldn't speak for a moment. He'd cut to the chase before she'd had a chance to ask her first question.

'Yes.'

'I wondered when someone would finally knock on my door. Thought it'd be the police. But it's you.'

'Did he come here? Was Glen Taylor a member of your club?'

Lenny considered the questions. 'Look, I never talk about members – no one would come if I did. But I've got kids . . .'

Kate nodded. 'I understand, but I'm not interested in anyone else. Just him. Will you help me? Please.'

The manager's struggle between the omertà of his sex shop and doing the right thing played out in the seconds of silence. He gnawed at a fingernail and Kate let him stew.

Finally he looked up and said, 'Yes, he came here occasionally. Started two or three years ago. I looked up his card when I saw his face in the paper. We don't use real names here – members prefer it that way. But I knew the face. It was 2006 he started coming. Another member brought him.'

'Mike Doonan?'

'You said you wouldn't ask about anyone else. Anyway, as I said, no real names, but I think they worked together.'

Kate smiled at him. 'That's so helpful, thanks. Can you remember the last time he came – are there any records?'

'Hang on,' Lenny said and unlocked an ancient filing cabinet. ''007, he registered as. Very smooth. No visits registered after 6 September 2006 until August this year.'

'This year? He's come back?'

'Yeah, just a few sessions, now and then.'

'What was he doing here? Do you know, Lenny?'

'That's enough questions. It's all confidential. But you don't need to be a genius to guess. We don't monitor sites visited – best not to, we decided. But basically, our members come to view adult sites.'

'Sorry to be blunt, but you mean porn?'

He nodded.

'Weren't you tempted to look to see after you realized it was him?'

'It was months after he stopped coming in that I realized it was him, and he'd used different computers. It would've been a big job and we're busy.'

'Why didn't you call the police about Glen Taylor?'

Lenny looked away for a moment.

'I thought about it, but would you invite the police in here? People come because it's private. It would've closed the business. Anyway, they arrested him so I didn't need to.'

A loud knock on the shop door ended the conversation. 'You've got to go. Got a customer.'

'OK, thanks for telling me all this. Here's my card, in case you think of anything else. Can I use your loo quickly before I go?'

Lenny pointed at a door in the corner of the room. 'It's pretty grim, but help yourself.'

He left her to it and as soon as he'd gone she pulled out her phone and photographed the membership card still sitting on the desk, before pulling open the toilet door, holding her breath and flushing the toilet.

Lenny was waiting for her. He opened the door and stood to shield the cowering customer from Kate's inquiring look.

In the street, she phoned Bob Sparkes.

'Bob, it's Kate. I think he's at it again.'

Chapter 36

Friday, 18 December 2009

The Detective

Sparkes listened in silence as Kate told her story, casually noting the address and names but unable to comment or question. Beside him, his new boss worked on, crunching numbers of street-robbery victims by gender, age and race.

'OK,' he said when Kate drew a breath. 'Bit busy at the moment. Can you send me the document you mentioned? Perhaps we could meet tomorrow?'

Kate understood the professional code. 'Ten a.m. outside the pub at the end of the road, Bob. I'm emailing you the photo I took now.'

He returned to his computer screen, miming regret for the interruption to his colleague, and waited until they had finished their work to look at his phone.

Sparkes felt sick as he looked at the membership card. Taylor's last visit was only three weeks earlier.

He called Zara Salmond as he walked to the tube station.

'Sir? How are you doing?'

'Fine, Salmond. We need to go back to the case.' He didn't need to say which. 'We've got to look at every detail again to find a way to nail him.'

'Right. OK. Can you tell me why?'

He could imagine the look on his sergeant's face.

'Difficult at the moment, Salmond, but I've had information that he's back on the porn trail again. Can't say more than that, but I'll be in touch when I've got more.'

Salmond sighed. He could hear her thought bubble *Not again*, and couldn't blame her.

'I'm off for Christmas, Sir. On leave. But back in on 2 January. Can it wait until then?'

'Yes. Sorry to ring out of the blue, Salmond. And Happy Christmas.'

He put his phone in his overcoat pocket and trudged down the steps, his stomach knotted.

The force had scaled back the Bella Elliott case, after Downing's lengthy review found no new leads, no van and no further suspects. DI Jude Downing had tidied her desk and gone back to her real job, and the Hampshire Police Force put out a press release saying that the investigation would continue. In reality, this meant leaving it to tick over with a team of two to check out the now occasional calls about possible sightings and pass them on. Nobody was saying it in public, but the trail had gone dead.

Even the appetite for Dawn Elliott's emotional campaign was beginning to wane. There were only so many ways you could say, 'I want my daughter back,' Sparkes supposed. And the *Herald* had gone very quiet on the subject after its initial firestorm of publicity.

And when Sparkes went, it had removed the daily impetus for their hunt. DCI Wellington had also made sure Salmond was too busy with other work to take it up on her own initiative. She'd heard when Sparkes was brought back from sick leave, but he'd still not set foot in the office. His call before Christmas had stirred up all sorts of feelings.

She missed Sparkes' dry humour and determination more than she'd admit to her colleagues – 'Can't get sentimental if I'm to get anywhere in the police,' she'd told him.

The day she went back to work, she pulled up her own Bella case file, filled with all the loose ends, and made a list while she waited for his call.

Leafing through, she found the query on Matt White. Unfinished business. She'd put it under 'Priorities' originally, but had been sidetracked by Sparkes' latest idea. Not this time. She would chase it down. She went online to search the electoral register for the name. Dozens of Matthew Whites, but none matching Dawn's information about age, marital status and area.

She needed to find Mr White's true identity and went back to the basic information about Dawn's relationship with him. It had taken place largely in the Tropicana nightclub and, once, in a hotel room.

'Where would he have had to use his real name, Zara?' she said out loud. 'When he used his credit card,' she finally answered. 'I bet he paid by card at the hotel where he took Dawn.'

The hotel was part of a chain and Salmond mentally crossed her fingers as she dialled its number to ask if they still had records for the dates when Dawn was seeing Matt White.

Five days later, Salmond had another list. The hotel manager was a woman in the same efficient mould as the detective and had emailed the relevant data.

'Matt White is here, Sir,' she said confidently to Sparkes in a brief phone call and didn't speak to anyone for the rest of the day.

Sparkes put down his phone and allowed himself a moment to examine the possibilities. His new boss was an impatient man and he'd a paper to finish on the impact of ethnicity and gender on community policing efficiency. Whatever that meant.

The last five months had been surreal.

As instructed by his superior officer and advised by his union rep, he'd contacted one of the counsellors on the list and spent sixty gruelling minutes with an overweight and under-qualified woman who was all about tackling demons. 'They are sitting on your shoulder, Bob. Can you feel them?' she said earnestly, sounding more like a psychic on Blackpool Pier than a professional. He listened to her politely but decided she had more demons than he did and never went back. Eileen would have to do.

His leave was extended piecemeal and as he waited to be recalled to duty, he toyed with the idea of signing up for an Open University course in Psychology; he printed out the reading list and began his studies quietly in his dining room.

When the recall finally came, he was to be sent zigzagging across a series of short-term assignments to other forces, plugging gaps and writing reports, while Hampshire worked out what to do with him. He was still seen as damaged goods as far as the Murder Investigation Unit was concerned, but he wasn't ready to retire on a pension as they had hoped. He couldn't leave yet. Things still to do.

It took Salmond a week to work through the dates and names, listing and relisting as she checked the electoral register, police computer records and social media to track down the guests. She loved this sort of work – the chase through data, knowing that if the information was there, she would find it and experience the moment of triumph when the name emerged.

It was a Thursday afternoon when she found him. Mr Matthew Evans, a married man living with his wife Shan in Walsall, and in Southampton on Dawn's dates. Right age, right job.

She immediately went back to the helpful hotel manager to ask her to put the name back through their system to see if he'd been in the city on the day Bella went missing. 'No, no Matthew Evans since July 2003. He stayed one night in a deluxe double and had room service,' the manager reported.

'Brilliant, thanks,' she said, already texting Sparkes with the news. She took a breath and walked up the stairs to DCI Wellington's office to tell her about the new lead. She'd barely registered Zara before, except as part of the Bob Sparkes problem, but that was about to change. Zara Salmond would be on the map.

But if she'd expected a ticker-tape parade, she was mistaken.

Wellington listened carefully, muttered, 'Good work, Sergeant. Write your report and get it to me immediately. And let's send West Midlands round to see this Evans.'

Salmond walked back to her office, her disappointed feet heavy on the stairs.

Chapter 37

Saturday, 16 January 2010

The Detective

MATTHEW EVANS WAS not a happy man. The police had come knocking on his door without warning and his wife, baby on hip and toddler at her side, had opened the door to them.

Bob Sparkes smiled politely with Salmond standing nervously at his side. The young officer had agreed to go with her old boss to knock on the door but knew she was putting herself on the line. She would have the book thrown at her if her superiors found out, but he'd persuaded her that they were doing the right thing.

'I know I'm not on the case now.'

'You were removed, Sir.'

'Right, thank you for reminding me, Salmond. But I need to be there. I know the case inside out and I'll be able to spot the lies,' he'd said.

She knew he was right and called West Midlands police to let them know she'd be on their patch, but as soon as she put the phone down, she felt pressurized and sick.

Salmond drove, but Sparkes took the train north to avoid being seen by his former colleagues. When he spotted Salmond waiting for him outside the railway station, she looked grim and stressed.

'Come on Salmond, it'll be fine,' he said quietly. 'No one will know I was here. The invisible man, I promise.'

She'd given him a brave smile and the pair had trudged off to meet Matt Evans.

'Matt, there's two police officers here to see you,' his wife had called to him. 'What's this about?' she asked the officers on the doorstep, but Sparkes and Salmond waited until they had her husband in front of them before saying anything further. Fair's fair, Sparkes thought.

Evans had a good idea why the police were there. The first time he saw Dawn and Bella on the television and did the maths, he knew the cops would appear one day. But as the weeks, months and then years passed, he had begun to hope.

'She might not be mine,' he'd told himself at the start. 'Bet Dawn was sleeping with other blokes.' But in his stomach – a much more reliable organ than his heart – he knew Bella was his. She looked so much like his 'real' daughter he was amazed people hadn't seen it and rung into *Crimewatch*.

But they hadn't and he'd continued his life, adding to his family and picking up new Dawns along the way. He never had sex without a condom again, though.

The senior officer suggested a quiet chat and he gratefully took them into the dining room they never used.

'Mr Evans, do you know a Dawn Elliott?' Salmond said.

Evans had considered lying – he was very good at it – but knew Dawn would identify him if it came to it. 'Yes. We had a bit of a romance a few years ago, when I was repping down on the south coast. You know what it's like when you're working long hours, you need a bit of fun, a bit of relaxation . . .'

Salmond looked at him coolly, registering the floppy fringe, big brown eyes and cheeky, persuasive smile, and moved on.

'And did you know that Dawn had a baby after your romance? Did she contact you?'

Evans swallowed hard. 'No, I knew nothing about the baby.

Look, I changed my mobile number because she was getting a bit clingy and—'

'You didn't want your wife to find out,' Sparkes finished for him.

Matt looked grateful and turned on the man-to-man stuff. 'Yeah. Look, Shan, my wife, doesn't need to know about this, does she?' The last time Shan Evans had been contacted by one of her husband's conquests, she'd said there would be no more chances and demanded that they have another baby, their third. 'It'll bring us closer, Matt.'

It hadn't. The sleepless nights and post-natal sex moratorium had sent him out looking for fun and relaxation again. There was a secretary in London at the moment. He couldn't help himself.

'That's up to you, Sir,' Sparkes said. 'Has there ever been any contact between you since you changed your mobile?'

'No, I steered well clear. Dangerous to go back – they think you have come back to marry them.'

Heartless bastard, Zara Salmond thought, writing HB in the margin of her notebook. Then amending it to FHB. She'd had her own teenage encounters with married men on the prowl.

Evans was fidgeting in his hard chair.

'Actually, funny thing, I did spot her once in a chat room on the internet. I was just browsing through, like you do, and there she was. Seem to remember she was Little Miss Sunshine, like the children's book – my eldest's got that one – but she was using her own photo. Not the brightest spark, Dawn.'

'Did you make yourself known to Little Miss Sunshine?'

'Course not. The whole point of chat rooms is everyone is sup-posed to be anonymous. More fun that way.'

DS Salmond wrote it all down, asking him to spell out the names of the chat rooms he favoured and his own online identities. After twenty-five minutes, Evans began to rise to show them out, but Sparkes had not finished.

'We need you to give some samples, Mr Evans.'

'What for? I'm pretty sure Bella was mine – she looks just like my other kids.'

'Well, that's good to know. But we need to be sure and we need to be able to rule you out of our investigation.'

Evans looked aghast. 'Investigation? I haven't had anything to do with the disappearance of that little girl.'

'*Your* little girl.'

'Well, yes, OK, but why would I kidnap a child? I've got three of my own. Some days I'd pay someone to kidnap them.'

'I'm sure,' Sparkes said. 'But we need to be thorough so we can rule you out. Why don't you get your jacket and tell your wife you need to go out?'

The officers waited outside.

Salmond looked as if she might burst, she was so pleased with herself. 'He saw Dawn in an over-eighteens chat room. She was a player – an amateur, but a player.'

Sparkes tried to remain calm, but the adrenalin was pumping through him too.

'This could be the link, Salmond. The link between her and Glen Taylor.' Sparkes laughed, despite himself.

Neither of them heard the exchange between husband and wife, but Salmond sensed there was unfinished business when Evans got into the car with them.

'Let's get this over with,' he said and shut up.

At the local police station, Evans gave DNA samples, attempting laddish banter with the younger officers, but no one was charmed. Tougher audience than the pissed girls on the dance floor, Sparkes thought, as Salmond applied a little more force than was strictly necessary on Evans' fingers in the ink.

'Sorry, Sir, you have to press hard to get a good impression.'

Zara Salmond told Sparkes she was driving back to her HQ to tell her new boss the news, face to face. She needed time to put together her story without dropping Sparkes – and herself – in it.

'I'll say West Midlands didn't have the manpower so I popped up here and found him, Bella Elliott's father. He's a serial shagger from Brum, like we thought – one Matthew Evans. Company rep, married with three children. What do you think, Sir?'

He'd smiled encouragement, adding, 'And he may provide the link between Glen and Bella.'

Cue champagne corks, Sparkes thought, more in hope than in expectation.

In the end, she told him later, the significance of the breakthrough swept aside any questions about why she had taken it upon herself to visit Evans on her own.

'We'll talk about that later, Salmond,' DCI Wellington said as she picked up the phone to Chief Superintendent Parker to claim her part of the glory.

Sparkes' recall to the Hampshire squad came four days later. CS Parker was short and to the point. 'We've got a fresh lead on the Bella case, Bob. No doubt you've heard. We want you to take it on. I've talked to the Met to clear it. How quickly can you come back?'

'On my way, Sir.'

His return was typically low key. 'Hello, Salmond. Let's see where we are with Matthew Evans,' he said as he took his coat off.

And he slipped back in, as if he'd just stepped out for a few minutes.

Salmond and the IT Forensics team did not have encouraging news. They had gone steaming back through the data downloaded from Taylor's original computer to hook out Little Miss Sunshine as soon as they got the information. But she wasn't there.

'No chats, no emails, Sir. We've looked under all the permutations but she doesn't seem to figure.'

Sparkes, Salmond and DC Dan Fry, who had been brought back to the team, stood in a ragged semi-circle behind the techie's chair and stared at the screen as names rolled up, willing her to appear.

It was the fourth time through the list and the mood in the room was bleak.

Sparkes went back to his office and picked up the phone. 'Hello, Dawn, it's Bob Sparkes. No, no news exactly, but I have a couple of questions. I need to talk to you, Dawn. Can I come now?'

She deserved to be handled carefully after all she'd been through, but this had to be addressed head on.

Chapter 38

Thursday, 13 July 2006

The Mother

Dawn Elliott liked going out. She loved the ritual of a deep, perfumed bath, conditioning her hair and blow-drying it in front of the mirror. Putting on thick mascara with party music playing loudly. The final look in the full-length mirror on the wardrobe door and then clip-clopping to the taxi in high heels, the fizz of excitement rising in her chest. Going out felt like being seventeen for ever.

Bella had stopped all that for a while. It had been bloody stupid getting pregnant, but it was her own fault. Too eager to please. He was so sexy – dancing to be close to her that first time they set eyes on each other. He'd taken her hand and twirled her round until she was dizzy and laughing. They'd taken their drinks outside with the smokers, to get some air. His name was Matt and he was already taken, but she didn't care. He only visited Southampton once a month for work, but he phoned and texted every day in the beginning, when his wife thought he was fetching something from the car or taking the dog for a walk.

It had lasted six months; until he told her his office had moved him from the south coast to the north-east. Their last encounter had been so intense, she felt drunk on the experience afterwards. He'd begged her to have sex without a condom – 'It'll be more special, Dawn.' And it was, she supposed, but he didn't hang around to hear the result. 'Married men don't,' her mother had told her, despairing of her naivety. 'They've got wives and children, Dawn. They just want sex with stupid girls like you. What are you going to do about the baby?'

She didn't know at first, putting off any decision in case Matt reappeared like a knight on a white horse to whisk her away to a new life. And when he didn't, she read glossy baby magazines and sleepwalked into motherhood.

She didn't regret going ahead with the pregnancy – well, not often – only when Bella woke up every hour from 3 a.m. or was teething and screaming, or filling a nappy. The baby years turned out not to be as advertised in the magazines, but they had survived them together and things got better as Bella became a person and a bit of company for Dawn.

She'd tell her daughter all her secrets and thoughts, safe in the knowledge that Bella wouldn't judge her. The little girl laughed along with her when she was happy and cuddled into her lap when Dawn cried.

But hours spent watching CBeebies and playing video games on her phone didn't fill her life. Dawn was lonely. She was only twenty-six. She shouldn't be on her own, but who would be interested in a single mum?

She was attracted to married men – she'd read somewhere that the older man represented a father figure and the excitement of forbidden fruit. She hadn't got the biblical allusion but understood the mixture of danger and safety all too well. She wanted to find another Matt, but couldn't afford babysitters and her mum disapproved of her going out until late.

'What are you doing? Nightclubs? For goodness' sake, Dawn, look where that got you last time. You are a mother now. Why don't you go out for a meal with one of your friends?'

So she did. Sharing a Hawaiian pizza with Carole, an old school friend, was nice, but she didn't return home buzzing with music and vodka shots.

She found the chat room through a magazine in the doctor's waiting room. Bella had a temperature and a rash and Dawn knew that Dr John, as he liked to be known, would chat to her, give her some attention – *fancies me a bit*, she told herself, deciding to put on make-up at the last minute. She needed to be fancied. Every woman did.

Flipping through the pages of a teen mag, grimy from dozens of fingers and thumbs, she had read about the new dating scene online. She was so engrossed she missed her number being called. The receptionist had to shout her name and she got up quickly, grabbing Bella from the Lego pit and stuffing the magazine in her bag for later.

Her laptop was old and battered, not helped by the fact that she kept it on top of the wardrobe, away from Bella's sticky fingers. A bloke at work had given it to her when he got a new one. She'd used it at first, but when the charger stopped working and she didn't have the money to get another one, she'd lost interest.

On the way home from the doctor's, she used her emergency credit card to buy a new charger.

The chat room was brilliant. She basked in the attention of her new friends: the men who wanted to know all about her, who asked about her life and her dreams, and wanted her photo, who weren't put off by her having a child. Some even wanted to know about her little girl.

She didn't tell anyone else. No one outside the laptop. This was her thing.

Chapter 39

Thursday, 21 January 2010

The Detective

THE HOUSE IN Manor Road looked cleaner and tidier. Bella's toys were stacked in a box by the television and the front room had been turned into the Find Bella campaign headquarters. Volunteers were sitting at a table going through the post – 'We get a hundred letters on a good day,' Dawn said proudly – and sorting them into three piles: possible sightings, well-wishers and nutters. The nutters pile looked a lot bigger than the others, but Sparkes didn't comment.

'Lots of people are sending money to help us look for Bella,' Dawn said. The fund was putting adverts in newspapers all over the world and paying for the occasional private investigator to check out a lead.

'Let's go somewhere quiet, Dawn,' he said and guided her by her elbow to the kitchen, closing the door behind them.

At the mention of Matt, she burst into tears. 'How did you find him? What did he say about me? About Bella?'

'He said he thought he was her father. We're waiting for the DNA results.'

'Has he got other children?'

'Yes, Dawn.'

'Do they look like her?'

'Yes.'

She cried harder.

'Come on, Dawn, we need to talk about something else Matt Evans told us. About seeing you in an online chat room.'

That stopped the tears. 'Matt saw me in a chat room? I didn't see him.'

'But you went in chat rooms?'

'Yes, but not like the places you talked about in the trial. It wasn't nasty or about sex.'

Sparkes paused. 'Why didn't you say you had used chat rooms?'

Dawn reddened. 'I was embarrassed. I never told anyone when I was doing it because I thought people would think I used them to find sex. I didn't, Inspector Sparkes. I was just lonely. It was just chatting. Stuff about what happened on *EastEnders* or *I'm a Celebrity* . . . I never met anyone in real life. I honestly didn't think it was worth mentioning.'

Sparkes leaned forward to pat her hand on the kitchen table. 'Did you talk about Bella in the chat rooms, Dawn?'

She looked at him and struggled to speak. 'No. Well, yes, a bit. To other girls. But just, you know, stuff like if Bella had kept me up or funny things she'd done. We were just talking.'

'But other people can hear you, can't they?'

Dawn looked like she might faint and Sparkes moved round to her side of the table, easing her chair back and gently pushing her head down into her lap for a moment. She was still deathly pale when she sat back up.

'Him, you mean?' she said. 'Did he hear me talk about Bella? Is that how he found her?'

There was no need for names, they both knew who 'him' was.

'We can't be sure, Dawn, but we need you to think back, to try to remember who you talked to online. We'll look on your laptop, too.'

A volunteer came in to ask Dawn a question and, seeing her tearful face, immediately started to back out.

237

'No, please stay,' Sparkes said. 'Can you look after Dawn for a minute? She's had a shock and could probably do with a cup of tea.'

He went outside and phoned Salmond.

He bagged Dawn's battered computer and brought it back to HQ while his sergeant took a statement from the devastated mother. Sparkes wanted to be in on the hunt through the sites. He wanted to be there when BigBear, or whatever sick nursery allusion Taylor had used, popped up.

The atmosphere in the lab was fetid, a mixture of locker room and abandoned pizzas, and the technicians looked weary as they took away the computer for cataloguing and mining. They were grateful there was only a fraction of the activity to plough through this time, but it would still take time to produce a list of chat-room sites and contacts.

The list, when it came, was the familiar jumble of fantasy and lurid names and Sparkes ran through them quickly to rule out the known Taylor avatars. 'He must have used another name,' he told Fry.

'We got all the identities he used from his laptop, Sir.'

'Are we sure he only had one laptop?'

'No sign of any others, but he was definitely using at least one internet café. Maybe others on his travels.'

The technician sighed. 'We'll have to rule out all the ones we can and then narrow the field a bit.'

Sparkes picked up the list and drove back to Dawn Elliott's kitchen.

She was still crying. Salmond was holding her hand and talking in a low voice. 'Let's carry on, Dawn. You're doing brilliantly.'

'She's doing brilliantly, Sir.'

Dawn looked up at him standing in the doorway like he had on the day Bella had gone. The sense of déjà vu was uncanny.

'I've got a list of the people you encountered here. Let's look at it together to see if you remember anything.'

The rest of the house was silent. The volunteers had long gone, chased out by the sense of doom and Dawn's distress.

She ran her finger down the names, page after page. 'I didn't know I talked to so many people,' she said.

'You probably didn't, Dawn. People can just join a chat room and say hello and then listen.'

She paused several times, making Sparkes' pulse jump, telling Salmond some small remembered detail – 'Seagull – she lived in Brighton and wanted to know about house prices here . . . BillieJean was a big Michael Jackson fan – was always telling us about him . . . Redhead100 was looking for love. Wonder if she found it' – but most of the chat had been so mundane, Dawn had little recollection.

When she reached TallDarkStranger she stopped. 'I do remember him. It made me laugh when I saw his name. Such a cliché. I think we emailed once or twice outside the chat room. There was nothing romantic. He was nice to talk to when I felt low once, but we didn't stay in touch.'

Sparkes went out of the room and phoned Fry. 'Look for TallDarkStranger. Could be him. They emailed outside the chat room. Text if you find anything.'

It took a while, but finally his phone beeped. 'Found him' was the message.

One of the Forensics team was waiting to see Sparkes when he arrived. 'We've found the email contact between Dawn Elliott and TallDarkStranger – just three emails, but there is mention of Bella in them.' Sparkes wasn't a punching-the-air kind of man, but at that moment he came close. 'Next step is linking the email address to Taylor, Sir.'

They were also all over Dawn's Facebook site. There were hundreds of photos of Bella on it, but Dan Fry was helping search for the images available before the kidnap and working his way through the friends for signs of their man.

It's the new version of footslogging, Sparkes thought as he watched the team at work.

A weary-looking techie came to see him later that day. 'Problem, Sir. Dawn Elliott didn't put any security on her Facebook page until after the little girl went missing, so anyone could have looked at her info and photos without becoming a friend.'

'Christ. Have we looked anyway?'

'Of course. Neither Glen Taylor nor any of the identities we know about appear. The odd thing is that Jean Taylor is there. She's a friend of the Find Bella campaign.'

'Jean? Are you sure it is her?'

'Yes, security was put on the page by then. She not only "liked" the page, she posted a couple of messages.'

'Messages?'

'Yes, she told Dawn she was praying for Bella's safe return, and later sent a message on Bella's fourth birthday.'

Sparkes was mystified. Why would Jean Taylor befriend Dawn Elliott? 'Are we sure it's her, not someone posing as her?'

'The email address is one she uses, and the IP address matches her area of London. We can't be rock solid, but it certainly points that way.'

Sparkes considered the possibilities. It could be her husband posing as her, but it was after the kidnap. Maybe he was just making sure he heard all the info about the hunt.

'Great work. Let's keep digging,' he told the technician and closed his office door to get some thinking space.

He needed to talk to Glen and Jean. Separately.

Chapter 40

Friday, 22 January 2010

The Widow

I WAS DOING some hand-washing in the sink when Bob Sparkes knocked. I stuck my hands under the tap to rinse off the soap and then shook them dry as I walked to the door. I wasn't expecting anyone, but Glen had put in a little camera so we could see who was on the doorstep on a video screen. 'Saves us wasting our time opening the door to the press, Jeanie,' he said, putting the last screw in the bracket.

I didn't like it. It made everyone look like criminals, all distorted like in the back of a spoon, even his mum. But he insisted. I looked and saw DI Sparkes, his nose filling the screen. I pressed the intercom and asked, 'Who is it?' No point making it easy for him. He sort of smiled. He knew it was a game and said, 'It's DI Bob Sparkes, Mrs Taylor. Can we have a quick word?'

I opened the door and he was there, his face restored to normal proportions – a nice face, really. 'I didn't think I'd see you again, after the compensation settlement and everything else,' I said.

'Well, here I am. It's been a while. How are you both?' he said, bold as brass.

'Fine, no thanks to you, but I'm afraid Glen isn't here, Inspector. Maybe you should call ahead next time, if you want to come back.'

241

'No, that's fine. I just want to ask you a couple of questions.'

'Me? What can you possibly have to ask me? The case against Glen is closed.'

'I know, I know, but there is something I need to ask you, Jean.'

The intimacy of using my first name threw me off guard and I told him to wipe his feet.

When he came in, he went straight into the living room – like he was family. He sat down in his usual place and I stood in the door. I wasn't going to get comfortable with him. He shouldn't have come. It wasn't right.

He didn't look sorry for coming, harassing us after the courts had said it was all over. I suddenly felt frightened. Having him here was like it starting all over again. The questions starting again. And I was afraid. Afraid he'd found something new to hound us with.

'Jean, I want to ask you why you became Dawn Elliott's friend on Facebook.'

I hadn't expected that. I didn't know what to say. I'd started using the internet after Glen was charged and taken away. I wanted to understand how it worked – put myself in Glen's shoes, maybe – so I bought a little laptop and the man in the shop helped me set it up with an email address and Facebook. It took a while to get the hang of it, but I bought an idiot's guide to help me and I had lots of time to spend figuring it out. It whiled away my evenings and was a change from the telly. I didn't tell Glen while he was in Belmarsh. I was worried he'd think I was doing it to try and catch him out. He might think I was being disloyal.

I didn't use it much, anyway, and when he came out he was surprised, but not in an angry way. I suppose there was too much going on for anything I did to matter much.

But he certainly didn't know that I was a Facebook friend of Dawn's, and now Bob Sparkes was here to make trouble about it. It was stupid of me – 'reckless', Glen would say if he knew. I did it one night after I saw Dawn on the news. I just wanted to be part of the campaign to find Bella, to do something to help, because I believed she was alive.

I didn't think the police would see me in the middle of all those hundreds of names, but of course they see everything. 'You never think, Jean,' Glen would say if he was here now. I shouldn't have done it, though, because it's going to make the police look at us all over again. It's going to cause Glen problems. DI Sparkes is looking at me, but I think I should say nothing and look stupid and let him blunder on.

And on he goes. 'Did you sign up to the campaign, Jean, or did someone use your identity?'

I suppose he means Glen.

'How would I know, Inspector Sparkes?' Need to keep my distance. No first names. Where's Glen? He said he'd only be ten minutes. Finally, I hear his key in the lock.

'We're in here, Glen,' I call. 'DI Sparkes is here.'

Glen looks in, his coat still on, and nods to the inspector. Bob Sparkes stands and goes into the hall to talk to him on his own. I sit, petrified that Glen will explode about the Facebook thing, but there are no raised voices and then I hear the door click.

'He's gone,' Glen says from the hall. 'He shouldn't have come. I told him it's police harassment and he left. What did he say to you?'

'Nothing. He wanted to know when you'd be back.' Well, he did.

I go upstairs to put my rinsed tights on the airer over the bath, then get my laptop out to see if I can delete myself from Bella's Facebook page. Bit pointless really as the police have already seen it, but Glen hasn't. I don't think Inspector Sparkes said anything to him. That was good of him.

I expect he'll be back, though.

Glen is rummaging in the fridge for something to put in a sandwich when I come downstairs and I jokily push him aside so I can do it for him. 'What do you fancy? Cheese or tuna?'

'Tuna, please. Have we got any crisps to go with it?'

I fix up a plate of food with a bit of lettuce and tomato. He needs to eat more fresh veg. He's looking pasty and putting on weight with all this sitting around indoors.

'Where did you go?' I say as I put the plate in front of him. 'Just now?'

Glen puts on that face, the one when I'm irritating him. 'Down to the paper shop, Jean. Stop checking up on me.'

'I'm just interested, that's all. How's your sandwich? Can I have a look at the paper?'

'I forgot to buy one. Now let me eat in peace.'

I go off into the other room and try not to worry, but I think it's all starting again. His nonsense. He has begun doing his disappearing act again. Not in the house – I'd know. But he sometimes goes out for an hour or two and comes back unable to say what he's been doing and gets cross if I ask too many questions.

I don't really want to know, but I need to. If I'm honest, I thought that was why Bob Sparkes came today. I thought Glen had been caught doing something on a computer again.

I try so hard not to doubt him, but some days, like today, I struggle. I start imagining what could happen. No point thinking the worst, my dad says to my mum when she gets in a state, but it's hard not to. Hard when the worst is just out there. Just outside the door.

I should do something to stop it. If I don't, we'll both be lost.

Chapter 41

Friday, 11 June 2010

The Widow

Tom Payne calls me back at the hotel and says the contract looks OK but he's worried about what they'll write. It's hard to talk with Kate in the room, so I go in the bathroom for a bit of privacy. 'The press are not your friends, Jean,' he says. 'They'll get the story they want to write. There is no copy control in the contract, so you've got no comeback if they twist things round. I'm concerned that you are doing this alone. Do you want me to come over?'

I don't want Tom there. He'll want me to change my mind, but I know what I'm doing. I'm ready.

'I'm fine, Tom, thanks. I'll let you know how I get on.'

Kate's back in my room, clutching the contract again. 'Come on, Jean,' she says. 'Let's get this signed and get on with the interview.'

She's determined and I want to go home so I reach for the piece of paper and sign my name on the dotted line. Kate smiles and her shoulders relax and she sits herself down in one of the armchairs.

'That's the formalities out of the way, Jean,' she says and pulls a battered tape recorder out of the bottom of her handbag. 'You don't mind if I tape the interview?' she says, putting the machine in front of me. 'Just in case my shorthand blows up,' she adds, smiling.

I nod dumbly and try to sort out how to start, but I needn't have bothered. Kate's in charge.

'When did you first hear about Bella Elliott going missing, Jean?'

I'm all right on this. I think back to the day in October 2006 when the story came over the radio as I stood in the kitchen.

'I'd been working that morning,' I tell Kate. 'But I'd had the afternoon off for working the Sunday-morning shift. I'd just been pottering around, tidying, peeling potatoes for supper. Glen came home for a quick cuppa and I got ready for my class at the sports centre. I'd just got back and was putting the oven on when the news came on the radio. They said there was a massive police search for a little girl who'd gone missing in Southampton. A little girl who'd disappeared out of her garden. I felt really cold and shivery, a little girl like that, still a baby really. Didn't bear thinking about.'

I feel cold again now. It was a shock to be confronted with that little face, the plaster and the curls. Kate is looking anxious so I start talking again.

'The papers the next day were full of it. Lots of pictures and some quotes from her grandma about how sweet she was. Heartbreaking, really. We all talked about it in the salon. Everyone was upset and interested – you know how people are.'

'And Glen?' Kate asks. 'What was his reaction?'

'He was shocked about it. He'd been making a delivery in Hampshire that day – of course, you know that – and he couldn't get over it. We both loved children. We were upset.'

The truth is we didn't have much of a conversation about the disappearance beyond what a coincidence it was that he'd been in Hampshire. We had our tea on our laps, while he watched the news on the telly, and then he went back upstairs to his computer. I remember I said, 'I hope they find that little girl, Bella.' And I can't remember him saying much else. I didn't think it was odd at the time – it was just Glen being Glen.

'And then the police came,' Kate says, leaning forward over her notebook and looking at me intently. 'That must've been terrible.'

I give her the story about me being too shocked to speak and still being stood in the hall an hour after the police left, like a statue.

'Did you have any doubts about him being involved, Jean?' she asks.

I swallow another mouthful of coffee and shake my head. I've been waiting for her to ask this – it's what the police have asked me over and over again – and I've prepared my answer. 'How could I believe he would be involved in something as awful as that?' I say. 'He loved children. We both did.'

But not in the same way, it turned out.

Kate is looking at me and I suppose I've gone quiet again. 'Jean,' she says, 'what are you thinking?'

I want to say I'm thinking about when Glen told me he had seen Bella, but I can't tell her that. That's too big to say.

'Just about things,' I say. And then I add, 'About Glen and whether I knew him at all.'

'How do you mean, Jean?' she asks and I tell her about Glen's face that day he was arrested. 'His face went blank,' I say. 'I didn't recognize him for a few seconds. It frightened me.'

She writes it down, glancing up to nod and look me in the eye. She lets me talk as the stuff about the porn spills out. She sits, writing quickly in her notebook but never taking her eyes off me. Nodding, egging me on with her eyes, all sympathy and under-standing. For years, I accepted the blame for what Glen did, telling myself it was my sick obsession with having a baby that made him do terrible things, but today he's not here to give me that look. I can be angry and hurt by what he did in our spare room. While I was lying in bed just across the way, he invited that filth into our house.

'What kind of man looks at pictures like that, Kate?' I ask her.

She shrugs helplessly. Her old man doesn't look at toddlers being abused. Lucky her.

'He told me it wasn't real. That it was women dressed up as children, but it wasn't. Not all of it, anyway. The police said it was

247

real. Glen said it was an addiction. He couldn't help himself. It started with "normal porn", he said. I'm not sure what normal is. Are you?'

She shakes her head again. 'No, Jean, I'm not sure. Naked women, I suppose.'

I nod; that's what I thought. The sort of stuff you get in magazines in the newsagent's or in eighteen-rated films.

'But this wasn't normal. He said he kept on finding new things to look at, he couldn't help himself. He said he found stuff by accident, but that isn't possible, is it?'

She shrugs, then shakes her head.

'You have to pay,' I tell her. 'You have to put your credit-card number in, your name and address. Everything. You can't just stumble on to one of these websites. It's a deliberate act which takes time and concentration – that's what the police witness said at his trial. And that my Glen did it night after night, searching for worse and worse things. New pictures and videos, hundreds of them, the police said. Hundreds! You wouldn't think there were that many to look at. He told me he hated looking at them but something in him made him look for more. He said it was a sickness. He couldn't help himself. And he blamed me.'

Kate looks at me, willing me to go on, and I can't stop now. 'He said I drove him to it. But he betrayed me. He pretended to be a normal man, going to work, having a beer with his mates and helping with the washing up, but he turned into a monster in our spare room each night. He wasn't Glen any more. He was sick, not me. If he could do that, I believe he was capable of anything.'

I stop, shocked by the sound of my own voice. And she looks at me. She stops writing, leans forward and puts one hand on mine. It is warm and dry and I turn my hand over to hold it.

'I know how hard this must be, Jean,' she says and looks like she means it. I want to stop, but she squeezes my hand again. 'It's such a relief to be able to say these things,' I say and tears start. She produces a tissue and I blow my nose hard. I keep talking as I sob. 'I didn't know he was doing it, I really didn't know. I would've walked out if I had. I wouldn't stay with a monster like that.'

'But you stayed when you found out, Jean.'

'I had to. He explained it all so I couldn't see what was right any more. He made me feel guilty for thinking that he'd done these things. Everything was concocted by the police or the bank or the internet companies. And then he blamed me. He made me see it was my fault. He was so convincing when he told me things. He made me believe him,' I say. And he did. But he's not here any more to make me.

'And Bella?' Kate asks, as I knew she would. 'What about Bella? Did he take her, Jean?'

I have gone too far to stop now. 'Yes,' I say. 'I think he did.'

The room goes quiet and I close my eyes.

'Did he tell you he had taken her? What do you think he did with her, Jean?' she asks. 'Where did he put her?'

Her questions are battering me, coming so fast. I can't think. I mustn't say anything else or I will lose everything.

'I don't know, Kate,' I say. The effort of stopping myself from saying any more makes me feel shaky and cold so I wrap my arms around myself. Kate gets out of her seat and sits on the arm of my chair and puts her arm round me. It is lovely to be held and I feel like I did when my mum used to gather me up when I was upset. 'Don't cry, chick,' she'd say and hold me so I felt safe. Nothing could touch me. Course it's different now. Kate Waters can't protect me from what's to come, but I sit there with my head resting on her for a while.

She starts again, quietly. 'Did Glen tell you anything about Bella, Jean? Before he died?'

'No,' I breathe.

Then there's a knock at the door. The secret signal. It must be Mick. She mutters under her breath and I can feel she's struggling to decide whether to shout 'Fuck off!' or let him in. She eases her arm out and raises her eyebrows to indicate 'Bloody photographers' and goes to the door. The conversation between them is in fierce whispers. I catch the words 'Not now,' but Mick isn't going away.

He says that he's got to get some photos 'in the can' because the picture editor is 'doing his nut'. I get to my feet and go into the bathroom to pull myself together before he comes in.

In the mirror I see my face, red, with my eyes swollen and puffy.

'Whatever do I look like?' I say out loud. It's something I often say – pretty much every time I look in the mirror, lately. I look dreadful and nothing is going to help, so I run a bath. I can't hear what's happening in the other room until I turn off the taps. Kate is shouting, Mick is shouting. 'Where is she?' he yells. 'In the bloody bathroom, where do you think? You fuckwit, we were just getting going and you had to barge in.'

I lie in the hotel bubbles, swishing the water around me, and think. I decide I've said as much as I'm going to. I'll sit and have my picture taken because I promised I would, but I'm going home straight afterwards. There, a decision all on my own. There, Glen. Fuck off! And I smile.

Fifteen minutes later I come out, all pink from the heat of the bath and hair frizzy from the steam. Kate and Mick are sitting there, not looking at each other and not speaking. 'Jean,' Kate says, getting up quickly, 'are you OK? I was worried. Didn't you hear me calling you through the door?' I feel quite sorry for her, really. I must be driving her mad, but I must think of myself.

Mick attempts a friendly smile. 'Jean, you look great,' he lies. 'Would you mind if I took some pics while the light is right?'

I nod and look for my hairbrush. Kate comes over to help me and whispers, 'Sorry. But it's got to be done. Promise it won't be too painful.' And she squeezes my arm.

We have to go outside because Mick says it will look more natural. 'More natural than what?' I want to ask, but don't bother. Let's get it over with and then I can go home.

He has me walking in the garden of the hotel, up and down, towards him and away from him. 'Look into the distance, Jean,' he calls and I do. 'Can you put on something else? I'm going to need some different shots.' I dumbly obey, returning to the room to put on my new blue jumper and borrowing a necklace from Kate and coming back down the stairs. The receptionist must think I'm famous or something. I suppose I'm just about to be. Famous.

When even Mick gets bored with snapping me leaning on a tree, sitting on a bench, perching on a fence, strolling down a lane – 'Don't smile, Jean!' – we all go back inside.

Kate has to start writing, she says and Mick needs to put his photos on the computer. We stand in the corridor outside the rooms and Kate tells me to relax for a couple of hours and charge anything I want to the room. When she disappears into her room, I go back to mine and start packing everything into a carrier bag. I'm not sure if I can keep the clothes the paper bought for me, but I'm wearing most of them and I can't be bothered to change. Then I sit down again. For a moment I'm no longer sure if I can leave. This is ridiculous. I'm a woman of almost forty. I can do what I want. I pick up my stuff and walk down the stairs. The receptionist is all smiles, still thinking I'm a celebrity, I suppose. I ask her to ring for a taxi to take me to the nearest station and I sit on one of the armchairs in front of a bowl of apples. I pick one up and take a big bite out of it.

Chapter 42

Friday, 11 June 2010

The Reporter

KATE PLONKED HERSELF down at the reproduction Regency desk and pushed the reproduction leather blotter aside. Her much-loved and abused laptop was on the bed, where she'd left it that morning after typing up her notes with the first cup of coffee of the day. Its cable snaked across the expanse of white sheets to a plug behind the bedside table. She untangled and re-connected, took off her jacket and powered up. Her head rang with Jean Taylor's voice and the story was already taking shape in her head.

She was a plunger, not a planner, when it came to writing. When it came to her life, really. Some of her colleagues sat with their notebooks, marking quotes with an asterix and underlining important points. Some even numbered paragraphs, as if frightened their notes might disappear or that they'd break some sort of spell by starting to write.

Others – the real talent, she acknowledged to herself – wrote the whole thing in their heads over a coffee or a beer and then threw it down on the page in one beautiful, flowing draft. She did a bit of both, depending on how much was going on around her: wrote a bit in her head as she left the interview and then plunged into the story on her computer, getting a flow going and editing and re-jigging as she went.

It was funny; even though they all wrote on computers, the journalists of her generation still talked as if they were scribbling on bits of scrap paper and filing stories to heartless copytakers – 'Is there much more of this?' – from piss-stained telephone boxes. She'd come in at the very tail end of the Fleet Street years, but had loved the raw edges of journalism then. The newsroom had rung with the sounds of newsmen and women at work. Now, her newsroom was open plan, hushed and planed smooth by designers. It felt more like an insurance office than a national newspaper and, exposed by the silence, bad behaviour and colourful office characters had faded. It was a grey world now.

She ought to ring the news editor, but she didn't want to hear his take on her interview just yet. He was bound to get in on the act, telling her how to write it even though he only knew a couple of quotes. Then he'd stride into the editor's office and tell him he'd got the scoop. It was his reward – seldom paid out – for all the shit he had to take. She understood, but wanted to savour the moment; she'd got a confession from Jean about Glen and Bella. It wasn't the full Monty, but Jean had said she thought Glen had taken the child. Good enough. The first words from the widow. Kate began typing.

From time to time, she looked up to rethink a phrase and caught sight of a woman's face in the huge mirror over the desk. She looked like a stranger – serious, focused on something in the distance, and somehow younger. She didn't look like a mother or wife. She looked like a journalist.

Her phone rang as she finished the section of killer quotes and she answered immediately. 'Hi Terry. Just got out of the interview. I've got a brilliant line from her.'

Fifteen minutes later, he rang back. The paper had cleared three pages inside and planned a second day. All Kate had to do was finish writing it. 'Two thousand, five hundred words for the inside, Kate. Let's do the background on their marriage and all that for Day Two. Give it a kick up the arse for the front, OK?'

The serious woman in the mirror was nodding.

She wondered what Jean Taylor was doing next door while she was writing about her. 'This is a weird job,' she told herself as she started to perform surgery on the body of the story, cutting all the good quotes on the Taylors' marriage and pasting them into the follow-up story.

Despite what most people thought, the ordinary men and women facing tragedy or drama who crossed Kate's path were largely grateful for her attention and the stories she wrote. The celebs, the infamous and other critics claimed everyone hated the press because they did, but many of Kate's interviewees stayed in touch for years. She was part of their lives, part of an event that changed everything for most of them.

'It's really intense and intimate during the time we're together,' she told Steve in the early days of their relationship. 'Even if it's only a few hours. It's like when you meet someone on a long train journey and you tell them everything. Because you can, because it's a moment in time.' Steve had laughed at her seriousness.

They'd met through friends at a disastrous Murder Mystery dinner party in north London and clicked when they laughed at the wrong moment, mortally offending their hosts.

In a shared taxi home afterwards, he'd perched on the fold-down seat opposite so he could look at her and they had talked drunkenly about themselves.

Steve was a final-year medical student, working with cancer patients, and thought journalism was superficial, fluffy even, and she understood. It was a common misconception and she tried to explain why journalism was important to her. Then she waited to see if their love affair would take, and when it did, Steve came to see things differently.

He witnessed the early-morning calls from the distressed, the late nights she spent reading court documents or driving up the motorway to track down a key piece of evidence for a story. It was serious stuff, and the proof was her annual haul of Christmas cards that hung alongside those from Dr Steve's grateful patients. Hers were festive greetings from parents of the murdered, rape victims, survivors of plane crashes, rescued kidnap victims and winners of court cases. They all took their place on the ribbon streamers festooning their house from early December. Reminders of happy days.

Two hours later, Kate was polishing: reading, re-reading, searching for repeated adjectives, changing a word here and there, trying to look at the intro with fresh eyes. She had about five minutes before Terry would start screaming for copy and should be pushing the Send button, but she didn't want to let go of the story. She was fannying around when she suddenly realized she hadn't discussed Day Two with Mick and lifted her phone to check with him.

He sounded very laid back when he picked up – probably was laid back on his bed, watching an adult movie on the paid channel. 'Mick, sorry, but the desk says they are running the story over two days. Just wanted to check you're happy with what you've got.'

He wasn't. 'Let's get Jean to do another set of pictures,' he suggested. Kate rang her room, preparing a bright 'Just need another couple of photos, Jean. Won't take a minute,' but the phone rang out. Kate could hear it trilling through the wall of her room.

'Come on, Jean, pick up,' she muttered. She slipped her feet into her shoes and padded next door to knock. 'Jean!' she said to the door, her mouth almost touching the surface. Mick emerged from his room with a camera in his hand. 'She's not answering. What the hell is she doing?' Kate said, banging on the door again.

'Calm down. Maybe she's in the spa? She loved that massage,' Mick said.

Kate almost ran to the lift, then turned back and raced down the corridor to her room. She had to send the story first. 'That'll keep the grown-ups busy while we find her,' she shouted back to Mick.

The beautician in the ylang-ylang-scented spa could not help. She bobbed her tightly bunned head apologetically as she ran her finger over the screen in front of her, mouthing the names. No booking.

The journalists retreated and regrouped. Mick took the grounds and Kate kept trying Jean's mobile phone, the sense of panic curdling in her stomach as she catastrophized; another paper must have found her and squirrelled her away right under Kate's nose. What would she tell the desk? How would she tell them?

Twenty minutes later, the pair were standing in the hotel lobby, gazing out of the glass doors, desperately planning their next move, when the second receptionist returned from her coffee break and piped up from behind her desk, 'Are you looking for your friend?'

'Yes,' Kate croaked. 'Have you seen her?'

'She checked out a couple of hours ago – nearer three hours, really. I called a taxi for her to go to the station.'

Kate's phone rang. 'It's the desk,' she said to Mick.

Mick made a face and decided to go outside for a cigarette.

'Hello, Terry,' she said, sounding manic as she over-compensated. 'No, everything's fine . . . Well, sort of. Look, we've got a slight problem. Jean's gone walkabouts. She left while I was writing. Pretty sure she has gone home but we're on our way . . . I know . . . I know . . . I'm sorry. Call you as soon as I know more . . . How's the copy?'

Chapter 43

Friday, 11 June 2010

The Widow

WHEN I GET HOME, the place feels small and dingy after all those deep carpets and chandeliers. I walk through it in silence, opening the doors and switching on the lights. I tell myself I'm going to sell this house as soon as I can. Glen is everywhere, like a faint smell. I don't go in the spare room. It's empty – we threw away what the police hadn't taken. 'Fresh start,' Glen said.

When I come back to the hall I can hear a buzzing noise and I can't work out what it is for a minute. It's my mobile. I must've put it on Silent earlier and I rummage in my bag for it. The bloody thing is right at the bottom and I have to tip everything out on the carpet to find it. I've got dozens of missed calls. All from Kate. I wait for the buzzing to stop, then I take a breath and call back. Kate answers almost before it can ring.

'Jean, where are you?' she says. She sounds terrible. Her voice is all squeaky and tight.

'At home, Kate,' I say. 'I got a train and came home. I thought you'd finished with me and I wanted to get back. Sorry. Shouldn't I have come home?'

'I'm on my way over. Don't go out of the house. We'll be there in about forty minutes. Just stay put until I get there,' she tells me. 'Please,' she adds as an afterthought.

I put the kettle on and make a cup of tea while I wait. What can she possibly want from me now? We've talked for two days and I've had hundreds of photos taken. She's got her story. The widow has spoken.

This is taking for ever and I'm getting a bit fed up, waiting. I want to go to the shops and get some food for the week. We're out of almost everything. I'm out of almost everything.

When I finally hear a knock at the door, I jump up and open it. It isn't Kate. It's the man from the telly. 'Oh, Mrs Taylor, I'm so glad to catch you in,' he says, all excited. I wonder who tipped him off that I'm home. I look across to Mrs Grange and see a movement at the window.

'Can I talk to you for a moment?' the telly man says and makes as if he's going to come in. Then I see Kate coming up the path, storming up to us all red in the face, and I say nothing, just wait for the row.

'Hello, Jean,' she says, pushing past Mr Telly and taking me indoors with her. Poor bloke doesn't know what's hit him. 'Mrs Taylor! Jean!' he tries as the door closes. Kate and I stand in the hall and look at each other. I start to explain that I thought it was her at the door, but she interrupts, talks right over me.

'Jean, you signed a contract with us. You agreed to cooperate fully and you're putting the whole deal at risk by your behaviour. What were you thinking of, sneaking off like that?'

I can't believe she's talking to me like this. How dare she tell me off like some kid, in my own home? Something gives inside me and I can feel myself going red – can't help myself. Could never be a poker player, Glen used to say.

'If you're going to get nasty, you can go right now,' I say, a bit too loudly. It bounces off the walls and I bet Mr Telly can hear. 'I'll come and go as I like and no one is going to tell me any different. I've given you your bloody interview, done all Mick's pictures. I've done everything you asked. It's all done. You don't own me just because I signed a bit of paper.'

Kate looks at me like I've slapped her. Little Jeanie has stood up for herself. Bit of a shock, clearly.

'Jean, I'm sorry if I was a bit heavy with you, but I was so worried when you disappeared like that. Look, come back to the hotel for one more night, until the story's in the paper. You're going to have the world and his wife on the doorstep when it comes out.'

'You told me giving you the interview would stop that happening,' I say. 'I'm staying here.' And I turn and go back into the kitchen.

She follows me, all quiet now. Thinking. 'OK,' she says. 'I'll stay here with you.'

It's the last thing I need, but she looks so miserable I agree. 'Just tonight and then you can go. I need time on my own,' I say.

I go and sit in the loo while she makes phone calls to Mick and her boss. I can hear every word. 'No one else's got her. No, she hasn't spoken to anyone else, but she won't come back to the hotel, Terry,' she says. 'I *have* tried. For God's sake, of course I've tried to persuade her, but she won't. She doesn't want another massage, Terry. She wants to be at home. Short of kidnapping her, I'm completely stuck. No, that's not an option. Look, it'll be OK. I'll make sure nobody gets to her.'

There is a pause and I imagine Terry raging down the phone to her. She says she's not afraid of him – says he's a bit of a pussycat really, but I don't believe her. I see her put her fist against the knot in her stomach when he's carrying on at her on the phone, rocking slightly. That tight smile says it all. 'How's the copy?' she says to change the subject. She means the story. I'm beginning to learn the language. I go upstairs for a bit of peace.

Later, she comes and taps on my bedroom door. 'Jean, I'm making a cup of tea. Do you want one?'

We're back to square one. Funny how things go in circles. I tell her there's no milk and she offers to get some shopping brought round. 'Shall we make a list?' she says through the door, and I go and sit in the living room with her while she writes down what we need.

'What do you fancy for dinner tonight?' she asks and I want to laugh.

How can we be discussing whether to have fish fingers or chicken curry, as though this is a normal home? 'I don't mind, you choose,' I say. 'I'm not really hungry.' She says OK and puts bread and butter and tea and coffee and washing-up liquid and a bottle of wine on the list.

'I'll send Mick to get it and bring it round the back,' she says and reaches for her phone.

She reads it out to him and he seems to be taking it down really slowly so she has to repeat everything twice. She's getting twitchy by the end and breathes deeply when she puts the phone down. 'Men!' she says and forces a laugh. 'Why are they so bloody hopeless?'

I tell her that Glen never went shopping on his own, not even with a list. 'He hated it and he always bought the wrong things. He couldn't be bothered to read the labels so he'd come home with diabetic jam or decaf coffee by mistake. He'd only buy half the ingredients for a recipe and then get bored. He'd forget the tins of tomatoes for a spag bol or the meat for a casserole. Maybe he did it on purpose so I wouldn't ask him again.'

'My old man's the same. It's just a chore,' Kate adds, kicking off her shoes and wriggling her toes as if she lives here. 'Ironic that Glen was shopping when the accident happened.' She calls him Glen now. It was always 'your husband' at the beginning, but she feels she knows him now. Knows him enough to talk about him like this. She doesn't.

'It was unusual for him to come shopping with me,' I say. 'He never came with me before all this happened – he used to do football training with the pub team while I did the big shop. After he was arrested he went with me for a bit so I wouldn't have to face people on my own. He did it to protect me, he said.'

But after a while he stopped coming with me because people stopped saying things. I don't think they stopped thinking 'Child Murderer', but accusing us lost its novelty and excitement, I suppose.

'The day he died, he insisted on coming. Strange, really.'

'Why did he?' Kate asks.

'I think he might have wanted to keep an eye on me,' I say.

'Why? Were you planning to do a disappearing act in Sainsbury's?'

I shrug. 'Things were a bit tense that week,' I say.

Tense doesn't really do it justice. The air felt thick with it and I couldn't breathe properly. I sat outside the kitchen door on a stool to try and find some relief, but nothing helped. I was suffocating in my thoughts. All the time I was fighting them back. Closing my eyes so I wouldn't see them. Turning up the radio so I wouldn't hear them, but they were there, just out of reach, waiting for me to weaken.

The Monday before he died, he brought me a cup of tea in bed. He did that sometimes. He sat on the bed and looked at me. I was still half asleep, sorting out the pillows behind me and trying to get comfortable to have my tea.

'Jean,' he said and his voice sounded flat. Dead. 'I'm not well.'

'What's wrong?' I asked. 'Is it one of those headaches? I've got those really strong painkillers in the cupboard in the bathroom.'

He shakes his head. 'No, not headaches. I just feel so tired. I can't sleep.'

I know. I've felt him tossing and turning beside me and heard him getting up in the middle of the night.

He looks tired. Old, really. His skin looks greyish and there are dark shadows under his eyes. Poor Glen.

'Perhaps you should go to the doctor's,' I suggest, but he shakes his head again and turns away to look at the door.

'I keep seeing her when I shut my eyes,' he says.

'Who?' I say, but I know full well who he means. Bella.

Chapter 44

Monday, 1 February 2010

The Detective

WHILE FRY AND his team worked the data, Sparkes went back to the van. Taylor had regular routes to the south coast and Sparkes started to match other dates and times on the delivery firm's records with Taylor's statements, traffic reports and motorway cameras. It was the second time through and should have been tedious, but he had new energy now.

He'd made official requests to the Met, Surrey, Sussex and Kent forces, which controlled the patchwork of motorways and roads potentially used by his suspect, and each had promised to look again for Taylor's number plate on the dates around the kidnap. Now he had to wait.

But when the first call came, it was not about Taylor.

It was from one of his own force's motorway patrol cars. 'DI Sparkes? Sorry to disturb you, but we've picked up a Michael Doonan and a Lee Chambers at Fleet Services. Both names are flagged up as being of interest to the Bella Elliott case. Are they known to you?'

Sparkes swallowed hard. 'Both. Bloody hell, we might have expected Chambers to resurface somewhere. But Mike Doonan? Are you sure? We understood he was too disabled to leave his flat.'

'Well, he's managed to get to the Services to buy some revolting pictures, Sir. We've arrested five men for dealing in illegal pornographic images.'

'Where are you taking them?'

'Your gaff. We'll be there in about thirty minutes.'

Sparkes sat at his desk, trying to process the information and its implications. Doonan, not Taylor? Stricken by the sickening thought that he had been chasing the wrong man for more than three years, he replayed the interview at Doonan's flat, re-evaluating every word the driver had uttered. What had he missed?

Had he missed Bella?

The minutes ticked by on the wall clock as he wrestled with the fear of knowing and the burning need to know, until a voice outside his door brought him out of his paralysis. He jumped up and ran down the stairs to the Forensics lab.

'Salmond, Fry, we've got Mike Doonan being brought in on extreme pornography charges. He was buying from Lee Chambers' car boot sale at Fleet Services.'

The two officers gaped at him.

'What? The driver crippled with a bad back?' Salmond said.

'Not as immobilized as he says, apparently,' Sparkes said, all business now. 'Let's pull up the CCTV from Fleet Services on the day Bella was taken.'

Everyone looked grave as the technicians began the online search, and the mounting tension chased Sparkes into the corridor. He was looking for Ian Matthews' number when Salmond put her head round the door. 'You'd better come and look, Sir.'

Sparkes sat in front of the grainy image on the screen.

'It's him. He's there at the boot of Chambers' car, picking through the magazines. Bending over. Back obviously feeling a lot better,' Salmond said.

'Date, Salmond? Was he there on the day Bella went?'

Zara Salmond paused. 'Yes, it's the day she was taken.' Sparkes almost rose out of his chair, but his sergeant put up a warning hand. 'But it rules him out of our investigation.'

'What do you mean? We've got Doonan in the area of the abduction, lying to us about his movements and the extent of his disability and buying extreme pornography on the route home.'

'Yes, but he was recorded on film doing a deal with Chambers while Bella was being snatched. 15.02. The times don't add up – he can't have taken her.'

Sparkes closed his eyes, hoping the relief didn't show on his face.

'OK, good work to pin it down. On we go,' he said without raising his eyelids.

Back in the privacy of his office, he slammed his fist down on his desk, then went for a walk outside to clear his head.

When he returned, he went back to Day One and his gut feelings about the case. They – he – had always treated Bella's abduction as an opportunistic crime. The kidnapper saw the child and lifted her. Nothing else had made sense. No link had been found between Dawn and Taylor and, once Stan Spencer's invented long-haired man had been discounted, there had been no reports of anyone hanging around the street or acting suspiciously in the area before Bella vanished. No flashers or sexual crimes reported.

And there had been no real pattern of behaviour for a predator to follow. The child went to and from nursery with Dawn, but not every day, and she only played outside occasionally. If someone had planned to take her, they would've gone in at night when they knew where she was at a given time. No one would have sat in a residential street on the off-chance that she might come out to play. He would've been spotted.

The police case was that the child had been taken in a twenty-five-minute, random window of opportunity. At the time, on the evidence in front of them, they'd been right to discount a planned kidnap.

But, in the cold light of day, three and a half years later, Sparkes thought that maybe they'd been too quick to rule it out and he suddenly wanted to revisit that possibility.

'I'm going down to the control room,' he told Salmond. 'To pull in a favour.'

Russell Lynes, his closest friend in the force – a bloke he'd joined up with – was on duty.

'Hello, Russ, fancy a coffee?'

They sat in the canteen, stirring the brown liquid in front of them with little intention of drinking it.

'How are you holding up, Bob?'

'All right. Being back to some real work makes a big difference. And this new lead's giving me something to concentrate on.'

'Hmm. It made you ill last time, Bob. Just be careful.'

'I will. I wasn't ill, Russ. Just tired. Look, I want to look at one thing I may have missed first time.'

'You're the boss. Anyway, why're you down here pulling favours? Get someone from the team to look at it.'

'They've got enough to do and they might not get to it for weeks. If you give me a quiet hand, I can rule it in or out in a couple of days.'

'OK, what sort of quiet hand?' Russell Lynes asked, pushing the coffee away, slopping it on to the table.

'Thanks, mate. I knew I could count on you.'

The two men went and sat in Sparkes' office with the spreadsheet of Taylor's deliveries and plotted his visits to Southampton and the surrounding towns. 'We looked at every frame of CCTV footage in the area round Dawn Elliott's address on the day of the snatch,' Sparkes said. 'But the only time we saw Taylor's van was at the delivery address in Winchester and at the junction of the M3 and M25. I wore my eyes out looking, but there was nothing to place his van at the scene.'

He could recall vividly the sense of expectation every time they loaded a new piece of footage, and the bitter disappointment when it ended without a glimpse of a blue van.

'I want to look at other dates,' he said. 'The dates Taylor had other deliveries in Hampshire. Remind me, where are the cameras in the Manor Road area?'

Lynes highlighted the locations on the maps in neon green – a petrol station a couple of streets away had one on the forecourt for absconders; a camera to catch jumpers at the traffic lights on the big junction; and some of the shops, including the newsagents, had installed cheap, tinny versions to discourage shoplifters.

'And Bella's nursery school has got a camera outside, but she wasn't at nursery that day. We looked at footage from all of these cameras but there was nothing of interest.'

'Well, let's have a look again. We must have missed something.'

Four days later, Sparkes' phone rang and he knew as soon as he heard Lynes' voice that he'd found that something. 'I'm on my way,' he said.

'There it is,' Lynes said, pointing at the vehicle crossing the frame. Sparkes squinted at the screen, trying to retune his eyes to the film's grainy resolution.

It was there. The van was there. The two men looked at each other triumphantly and then back at the screen to enjoy the moment again.

'Are we sure it's him?' Sparkes asked.

'It matches the date and time of a delivery to Fareham on his work sheets and Forensics have got a partial number plate that includes three letters that match Taylor's vehicle.'

Lynes pushed the Play button. 'Now watch.'

The van stopped just within the camera's range, pointing away from the nursery school. As if on cue, Dawn and Bella appeared at the school gate at the back of the throng of children and parents, the mother fussing with her daughter's coat zip and the child clutching a huge piece of paper. The pair walked past the van and round the corner, safe in their routine. Within seconds, the van moved off in the same direction.

Sparkes knew he was watching the moment Glen Taylor had made his decision and his eyes filled with tears. He muttered that he was going to get a notepad and went to his office for a moment's privacy. 'We're so close,' he told himself. 'Now don't mess it up. No rushing; get everything in order.'

He looked at Taylor grinning at him from the wall and grinned back. 'I hope you haven't booked a holiday, Glen.'

Back in the lab, Lynes was writing on a whiteboard. 'This film was taken on Thursday, 28 September, four days before Bella was taken,' he said.

Sparkes closed his eyes before trusting himself to speak. 'He planned it, Russ. This wasn't some chance snatch. He was watching. Any other sightings of the van that day?'

'At the services at Hook, filling up on the way home. Timeline fits.'

'Let's get the work done on the images and get as much detail as we can. Then I'm going to knock on Glen Taylor's door,' Sparkes said.

The two men sat back down at the monitor as a technician wheeled back and forth over the van images, zooming in on the windscreen.

'It's blurred to buggery but we're pretty confident it is a white male with short dark hair, no glasses and no facial hair,' the technician told them.

The face at the windscreen hovered into sight. A white oval with dark patches for eyes.

Chapter 45

Monday, 2 October 2006

The Husband

GLEN TAYLOR HAD first caught sight of Bella Elliott on Facebook after meeting Dawn (aka Little Miss Sunshine) in a chat room that summer. She was telling a group of strangers about her daughter and a trip to the zoo.

One of her new friends asked if there was a picture of Bella from the trip – one with the monkeys she had loved. Glen had eavesdropped idly on the conversation and when Dawn had referred everyone to her Facebook page, he'd looked. There was no security on the page and he flicked through Dawn's photos.

When the image of Bella appeared, he looked at that small, confident face and committed it to memory, to be retrieved at will in his dark fantasies. Bella joined his gallery, but she wouldn't stay there like the others. He found himself looking for her whenever he saw a blonde child in the street or in the parks where he sometimes ate his lunch when he was on the road.

It was the first time his fantasies had moved off the screen into real life and it frightened and thrilled him in equal measure. He wanted to do something. He wasn't sure what at first, but during the hours at the wheel of his van, he started to plan a way to meet Bella.

Little Miss Sunshine was the key and he adopted a new avatar especially for encounters with her. Operation Gold had taught him that there must be no trail, so he'd stop at the internet café near the depot on his way back from jobs to enter Dawn's world. He'd draw her into his.

He called himself TallDarkStranger and approached Little Miss Sunshine quietly, joining group chats when he knew she was in the room and saying little. He did not want to draw the wrong kind of attention to himself so he asked occasional insightful questions, flattering her, and gradually he became one of her regulars. Little Miss Sunshine sent her first private Instant Message to TallDarkStranger within two weeks.

Little Miss Sunshine: Hi, How you?
TallDarkStranger: Good. You? Doing much?
Little Miss Sunshine: Stuck at home today with my little girl.
TallDarkStranger: Could be worse. She sounds lovely.
Little Miss Sunshine: She is. Lucky really.

He wasn't there every day. He couldn't be, what with Jean and his job, but he managed to keep in contact for a while, using a quiet internet place Mike Doonan had taken him to once, when they were still speaking. Still visiting the same chat rooms and forums. Before Glen told the boss about the disability scam Doonan was pulling. He'd seen him jump out of his van outside Internet Inc. like a man half his age and felt it was his duty to expose his lie. It was what any right-minded person would do, he'd told Jean. And she'd agreed.

It was in the club that he built up the details of Dawn's life. He had known her real name and Bella's birthday from her Facebook page, and found out they lived somewhere in Southampton from a chat about child-friendly restaurants. Dawn favoured McDonald's because 'no one tuts when your kid cries – and it's cheap' and made special mention of her local one.

He called in the next time he was making a delivery down there. Just looking, he told himself, as he unwrapped a burger and watched the families around him.

269

When he left, he had a drive round. Just looking.

It took a while, but Dawn finally let slip the name of Bella's nursery school as she chatted to another mother in the careless way she had developed online. Dawn treated every exchange like a private conversation – like the people on buses who talk on their mobile phones about the break-up of their marriage or genital warts. Glen mouthed a silent *Yes* and hugged the information to himself.

Later, sitting across from Jean over a chicken casserole, he asked about her day.

'Lesley said I did a lovely job on Eve's hair today. She wanted a Keira Knightley bob with red flashes. I knew it wouldn't suit her – she looks nothing like Keira Knightley with that great round face – but she loved it.'

'Well done, love.'

'I wonder what her husband said when she got home. Do you want this last piece of chicken? Go on or it'll go to waste.'

'OK. Don't know why I'm so hungry – I had a great big sandwich at lunchtime – but this is delicious. What's on the box tonight? Isn't it *Top Gear*? Let's get the washing-up done quickly and go and have a look.'

'Go on, you go. I'll see to the dishes.'

He kissed the top of her head as he squeezed past her at the sink. While it filled with hot water, she put the kettle on.

Only when he was sitting in front of the television did he let himself take out the new information and examine it minutely. He knew where to find Dawn and Bella. He could go and wait outside the nursery and follow them. But what then? What was he thinking of? He didn't want to think about it here, in his sitting room with his wife curled up on the sofa.

He'd think about it when he was on his own. Figure something out. He just wanted to see them.

Just wanted a look.

He wouldn't speak to Dawn. He'd been careful to make sure she didn't know what he looked like, but he couldn't risk speaking to her. He had to keep her at arm's length. Keep her behind the screen.

He had to wait weeks for his next south-coast delivery. It was exhausting, fretting and worrying at the details of his fantasy while keeping up his role of devoted husband at home. But he had to maintain boundaries. No slippage.

On his and Jean's seventeenth wedding anniversary, he'd made a big fuss of her with flowers and a meal out. But he hadn't really been there at the table in their favourite Italian. Jean hadn't seemed to notice. He hoped she hadn't.

He felt sick with anticipation as he drove down the motorway. He'd looked up the nursery school in the internet club and had an address. He'd sit down the road and watch.

Glen arrived as the children were beginning to trickle out of the building, clutching pictures nubbled with painted pasta with one hand, their mums with the other. He worried he might have arrived too late, but parked so he could watch in his rear-view mirror and no one would be able to see his face.

He almost missed them. Dawn looked older and scruffier than in her Facebook photos, with her hair tied back and an old jumper swamping her. It was Bella he recognized first. Skipping along the pavement. Glen followed them in the mirror until they passed his van and he got his first direct sight. Close enough to see the smudged make-up under Dawn's eyes and the golden glint of Bella's hair.

They went round the corner and he started the engine. 'Just want to see where they live,' he told himself. 'That's all. Where's the harm in that? They won't even know I've been here.'

Driving home the back way, he pulled over and edged up a farm track, turned off his phone and masturbated. He tried to think about Dawn, but she kept sliding out of the picture. He sat afterwards, shocked by the intensity of the experience and afraid of the man he'd turned out to be. He told himself it would never happen again. He would stop going online, he'd stop looking at porn. It was a sickness and he'd get better.

But on 2 October he was given a delivery in Winchester and he knew that he would drive down Bella's street again.

He turned on the radio as he made his way, to distract himself, but all he could think of was that golden glint. 'I'll just look to see if they are there,' he told himself. But when he stopped for fuel on the motorway, he bought a sleeping bag from the bargain basket and sweets.

He was so wrapped up in his fantasy that he missed his turning and had to double back to the garage. It felt dreamlike as he acted the delivery man for the customer, joking and asking after business, holding his secret close. He was on his way to Manor Road and nothing could stop him.

The danger was part of the reason he was doing it. Glen Taylor, former bank executive and devoted husband, could see the shame, the disgrace he risked by his actions, but TallDarkStranger wanted to stand close to it, to touch it, be singed by it.

'See you soon, Glen,' one of the blokes in the Parts Department called.

'Yeah. Bye,' he replied. He walked to the van and climbed in. There was still time to turn back, to go home and be himself again. But he knew what he would do and indicated to pull out.

Manor Road was deserted. Everyone was at work or indoors. He drove slowly, as if looking for an address, playing the part. Then he saw her, standing behind a low wall, looking at a grey cat rolling in the dust on the pavement. Time slowed and he found he'd stopped the van. The sound of the engine had distracted the child and she was looking at him and smiling.

He was jolted back to reality when a front door slammed shut behind the van, and in the wing mirror he saw an elderly man standing on the doorstep. Glen pulled away, turning left into a side street almost immediately, and drove around the block. Had the old boy seen him? Seen his face? And if he had, so what? He'd done nothing wrong. Just parked up.

But he knew he had to go back. The little girl was waiting for him.

The van pulled forward to turn back into Manor Road and Glen could see there was no one there. The only living things were the cat and the child, standing inside her garden, waving to him.

He didn't remember getting out or walking over to her. He remembered picking her up and holding her and getting back in the van, strapping her into the passenger seat. It took less than a minute and she didn't make any fuss. She took the sweetie and sat quietly as he took her away from Manor Road.

Chapter 46

Friday, 11 June 2010

The Widow

DAWN HAS ALWAYS been on the telly. She likes to tell everyone that Bella is alive. That someone took her because they couldn't have children and wanted a child so badly. Someone who's looking after her, loving her and giving her a good life. Dawn has got married now – one of the volunteers from her campaign, an older man who always seems to be touching her. She's got another little girl. Where's the justice in that? She holds her new baby tight when she's on the breakfast show, to show what a good mother she is, but she doesn't fool me.

Before he died, if Glen was in the room, he'd turn the telly off, casually, to pretend he didn't care, and then go out. But if he wasn't there, I'd watch. And buy the papers and magazines when they wrote about Bella. I loved seeing the pictures and videos of her. Playing, laughing, opening her Christmas presents, singing in her baby way, words muddled up, pushing her little pram. I've got quite a collection now from the magazines and newspapers Dawn has talked to. She has always loved the publicity. Her five minutes of fame.

And now, I am about to have mine.

When Mick finally turns up he's carrying bags of shopping and a Chinese takeaway. 'Couldn't be bothered to cook,' Kate says with a laugh. 'Thought we could have a treat instead.'

Mick's clearly staying, too, and I try to remember where I put the sheets and duvet for the sofa bed.

'Don't mind me, Jean,' he says with his teenager grin. 'I can sleep on the floor. I'm not fussy.'

I shrug. I'm too fed up with the whole thing to care any more. Once, I would've run round making up beds, putting clean towels out, changing the soap for a new bar. But now I can't be bothered. I sit with a plate of noodles and shiny red chicken on my knee and wonder if I have the energy to lift my fork.

Kate and Mick sit on the sofa facing me. They are eating the noodles without any enthusiasm. 'This is horrible,' Mick says eventually and gives up.

'You chose it,' Kate says and looks at my full plate. 'Sorry, Jean. Shall I get you something else?'

I shake my head. 'Just a cup of tea,' I say. Mick asks if I've got any tins in the cupboard and goes off to make beans on toast for himself. I get up to go to bed, but Kate turns on the news and I sit back down. They are saying something about soldiers and Iraq and I lean back in my seat.

The next item is me. I can't believe what I'm seeing. My face in one of the pictures Mick took. 'Mick, quick, your stuff's on the television,' Kate shouts through to the kitchen and he races in and drops heavily on to the sofa.

'Fame at last,' he says with a grin as the presenter rattles on about the exclusive interview I've given to the *Daily Post* and my 'revelation' that Glen was responsible for taking Bella. I start to say something but the programme cuts to Dawn, who's been crying, all swollen eyes, and she's asked what she thinks about the interview. 'She's an evil monster,' she says and it takes me a minute to realize she means me. Me. 'She must've known all along,' she wails. 'She must've known what her husband did to my poor baby.'

I stand up and turn on Kate. 'What have you written?' I demand. 'What have you said to make me the evil monster? I trusted you, I told you everything.'

She has difficulty looking me in the eye, but Kate tells me Dawn has 'got it all wrong'.

'That isn't what the story says,' she insists. 'It says you're another of Glen's victims, that you only realized much later that he could've taken her.'

Mick is nodding dumbly, backing her up, but I don't believe them. I'm so angry I go out of the room. I can't bear their betrayal. Then I go back in. 'Leave now,' I say. 'Get out or I'll call the police and have you removed.'

There's silence while Kate wonders if she can talk me round again. 'But the money, Jean . . .' she starts to say as I usher her and Mick into the hall, and I cut her off. 'Keep it,' I say and open the front door. Mr Telly's still standing at the end of the path with his crew.

As she reaches the gate, he says something to her, but she's already on the phone to Terry, explaining how it's all gone 'pear-shaped'. I beckon the film crew in. I've something I want to say.

Chapter 47

The Detective

Days and then weeks had ticked by without a decision being made to re-arrest Taylor. The new bosses clearly didn't want to stumble down the same disastrous path as their predecessors and defended their inaction strenuously.

'Where's the evidence to link Taylor with this new CCTV? Or the internet club?' DCI Wellington had asked after watching the images. 'We've got a partial number plate and the dodgy word of a porn merchant. There's no further identification of the suspect – apart from your gut feeling, Bob.'

Sparkes had been ready to resign, but he couldn't abandon Bella.

They were so close. The Forensics team were working on the number plate of the van in the CCTV to try to tease out one more digit or letter, and experts were trying to match phrasing in the emails from TallDarkStranger and BigBear. He almost had his hand on Glen Taylor's arm.

So when he heard that Glen Taylor was dead, he felt it like a physical blow.

'Dead?'

An officer he knew from the Met had called as soon as the news came through to the operations room. 'Thought you'd want to know immediately, Bob. Sorry.'

It was the 'sorry' that did it. He hung up and put his head in his hands. They both knew there would be no confession now, no moment of triumph. Bella would never be found.

His head suddenly shot up. Jean. She was free of him now – she could speak out, tell the truth about that day.

Sparkes shouted for Salmond and when she put her head round the door he croaked, 'Glen Taylor is dead. Knocked over by a bus. We're going to Greenwich.'

Salmond looked as if she might cry, but checked herself and went into Superwoman mode, organizing and chivvying.

In the car, Sparkes filled in the details for her. She knew as much about the case as he did but he needed to say everything out loud, to walk himself through it all.

'I always thought that Jean was covering for Glen. She was a decent woman but she was completely dominated by him. They married young – he was the bright one, the one who did well at school and had a good job, and she was his pretty little wife.'

Salmond glanced at her boss. 'Pretty little wife?'

He had the grace to laugh. 'What I mean is that Jean was so young when they met, he swept her off her feet with his suit and prospects. She never had a chance to be her own person.'

'I think my mum was a bit like that,' Salmond said, indicating to turn off the motorway.

Not you, though, Sparkes thought. He'd met her husband. Nice solid bloke who didn't try to outshine her or put her down.

'Sounds like it could be a *folie à deux*, Sir,' Salmond said thoughtfully. 'Like Brady and Hindley, or Fred and Rose West. I looked at their cases for a paper I wrote at college. A couple share a psychosis or a delusion because one is so dominant. They end up believing the same thing – their right to do something, for example. They share a value system that is not accepted by anyone outside their partnership or relationship. Not sure I'm explaining it properly. Sorry.'

Bob Sparkes was silent for a bit, turning the theory over in his head. 'But if it was a *folie à deux*, then Jean knew and approved when Glen took Bella.'

'It's happened before. Like I said,' Salmond continued without taking her eyes off the road. 'Then when you separate the couple, the one who's been dominated can quite quickly stop sharing the delusion. They kind of come to their senses. Do you see what I mean?'

But Jean Taylor had not let the mask slip when Glen had gone inside. Was it possible that he had kept control of her from behind bars?

'I wondered about cognitive dissonance or selective amnesia,' Sparkes ventured, a little nervous about trying out his homework reading in Forensic Psychology. 'Maybe she was too frightened of losing everything to admit the truth? I read that trauma can make the mind delete things that are too painful or stressful. So she deleted any details that challenged her belief that Glen was innocent.'

'But can you really do that? Make yourself believe that black is white?' Salmond asked.

The human mind is a powerful thing, Sparkes thought, but it sounded too trite to say out loud.

'I'm not an expert, Zara. Just been doing some reading at home. We'd have to talk to someone who's done the research.'

It was the first time he'd called her Zara and he felt a prickle of embarrassment. Inappropriate, he told himself – he'd always called Ian Matthews by his surname at work. He risked a quick glance at his sergeant. She showed no sign of offence or even of having registered his unprofessional slip.

'Who would we approach, Sir?'

'I know an academic who might be able to give us a steer. Dr Fleur Jones helped us before.'

He was grateful that Salmond didn't react to the name. It hadn't been Fleur Jones's fault that everything had gone bad.

'Why don't you call her?' she said. 'Before we get there. We need to know the best way to approach Jean Taylor.'

Salmond pulled over at the next service station and began to dial.

An hour later, Sparkes walked through the Accident and Emergency department doors.

'Hello, Jean,' he said and sat down beside her on an orange moulded-plastic chair. She barely moved to acknowledge him. She looked so pale and her eyes were blackened by grief.

'Jean,' he said again and took her hand. He'd never touched her before, beyond guiding her into a police car, but he couldn't help himself. She looked so vulnerable.

Jean Taylor's hand was frigid in his hot hands, but he wouldn't let go. He kept talking, low and urgent, taking his chance.

'You can tell me now, Jean. You can tell me what Glen did with Bella, where he put her. There's no need for secrets now. It was Glen's secret, not yours. You were his victim, Jean. You and Bella.'

The widow turned her head away from him and seemed to shudder.

'Please tell me, Jean. Let it go now and you'll have some peace.'

'I don't know anything about Bella, Bob,' she said slowly, as if explaining to a child. Then she slipped her hand out of his grasp and started to cry. No sound, just tears running down off her chin on to her lap.

Sparkes sat on, unable to leave. Jean Taylor stood and walked away towards the Ladies'.

When she came out fifteen minutes later, she was holding a tissue to her mouth. She headed straight for the glass doors of A&E and was gone.

Disappointment paralysed Sparkes. 'I've screwed up our last chance,' he muttered to Salmond, who was now sitting in Jean's chair. 'Royally screwed it up.'

'She's in shock, Sir. She doesn't know which way is up at the moment. Let her settle and think things through. We should go to the house in a couple of days.'

'Tomorrow, we'll go tomorrow,' Sparkes said, rising.

They were at the door twenty-four hours later. Jean Taylor was in black, looking ten years older, and was ready for them.

'How are you doing, Jean?' Sparkes asked.

'Good and bad. Glen's mum stayed with me last night,' she answered. 'Come through.'

Sparkes sat beside her on the sofa, angling himself so he had her full attention, and began a gentler courtship. Zara Salmond and Dr Jones had rethought the situation and both suggested using a bit of flattery as an opener, to make Jean feel important and in charge of her decisions.

'You've been such a rock for Glen, Jean. Always there to support him.'

She blinked at the compliment. 'I was his wife and he relied on me.'

'That must've been hard for you at times, Jean. A lot of pressure to take on your shoulders.'

'I was happy to do it. I knew he hadn't done it,' she said, the constant repetition of her stock reply leaving it hollow.

DS Salmond got up and started looking round the room. 'No cards yet?' she asked.

'Not expecting any – just the usual hate mail,' Jean said.

'Where will you hold the funeral, Jean?' Sparkes asked.

Glen Taylor's mother appeared at the door, clearly having been eavesdropping in the hall. 'At the crematorium. We're just having a simple, private service to say goodbye, aren't we, Jean?'

Jean nodded, deep in thought. 'Do you think the press will come?' she asked. 'I don't think I could bear that.'

Mary Taylor sat on the arm of the sofa beside her daughter-in-law and stroked her hair. 'We'll weather it, Jeanie. We have so far. Perhaps they'll leave you alone now.'

The remark was aimed at the two detectives cluttering up the sitting room as much as the press waiting outside.

'They've been knocking since 8 a.m. I've told them Jean is too upset to talk but they keep on coming. I think she should come back with me for a bit, but she wants to stay at home.'

'Glen is here,' Jean said, and Sparkes rose to leave.

Chapter 48

Thursday, 27 May 2010

The Widow

THE FUNERAL HAS come round so quickly I've let Mary choose the hymns and readings. I couldn't think straight and wouldn't have known what to pick. She's gone for the safe options: 'Amazing Grace' and 'The Lord Is My Shepherd' because everyone knows the tunes – which is lucky as there are only fifteen of us singing in the crematorium chapel.

We went to see Glen in the Chapel of Rest, all smart in his three-piece bank suit and the navy and gold tie he liked. I'd washed and ironed his best shirt and it looked perfect. Glen would've been pleased. Of course, it wasn't really Glen in the coffin. He wasn't there, if you know what I mean. He looked like a waxwork Glen. His mum wept and I stood back, letting her have a moment with her little boy. I kept looking at his hands with their perfect pink buffed-up nails; innocent hands.

Mary and I went from the funeral home to John Lewis to buy hats.

'You'll find the range over there,' the assistant pointed, and we stood in front of thirty black hats, trying to imagine ourselves at Glen's funeral. I picked a sort of pillbox one with a little net veil to hide my eyes and Mary went for one with a brim. They cost a fortune, but neither of us could summon the energy to mind. We came out into the street with our carrier bags and stood, lost for a moment.

'Come on, Jeanie, let's go home and have a cup of tea,' Mary said. So we did.

Today we put on the new hats in front of the mirror in the hall before getting into the taxi to the crematorium. Mary and I hold hands loosely, just touching. Glen's dad stares out of the window at the drizzle.

'Always rains at funerals,' he says. 'What a bloody awful day.'

Funny things, funerals. So much like weddings, I think. Gatherings with people you never see at any other time, catching up over a buffet, people laughing and crying. Even here at Glen's funeral I hear one of the old uncles laughing quietly with someone. When we arrive, we are guided into the waiting area, me with my mum and dad, his mum and dad and a small crowd of Taylors. I'm grateful anyone has come, really.

No one from the bank or the salon. We're not part of that world any more.

Then Bob Sparkes turns up, all respectful in black suit and tie, looking like an undertaker. He stands apart from us, on the edge of the Garden of Remembrance, pretending to read the names of the dead on the plaques. He hasn't sent flowers, but we told people not to. 'Family flowers only' the undertaker advised, so there's just my wreath of lilies and laurels – 'Classic and classy' the young florist said, almost chirpily – and Mary ordered Glen's name in white chrysanthemums. He'd have hated it. 'How common,' I can hear him say, but Mary loves it and that's what matters.

I keep looking to see where Bob Sparkes is.

'Who invited him?' Mary says, all cross.

'Don't worry about him, love,' George pats her shoulder. 'Not important today.'

The vicar from Mary's church does the service, talking about Glen like he was a real person, not the man in the papers. He keeps looking at me as if he is talking just to me. I hide behind the veil on my hat when he goes on about Glen, as if he knew him. He talks about his football and his cleverness at school and his wonderfully supportive wife during difficult times. There's a murmur from the congregation and I rest my head on my dad's shoulder and close my eyes while his coffin slides forward and the curtains close behind him. All gone.

Outside, I look for Bob Sparkes but he's gone as well. Everyone wants to kiss and hug me and tell me how fantastic I've been. I manage a smile and hug people back and then it's over. We thought about putting on a tea but we didn't know if anyone would come, and then if there was a tea we would have to talk about Glen and someone might mention Bella.

We keep it simple. The five of us go home to my house and have a cup of tea and some ham sandwiches Mary made and put in the fridge. I put my hat in its tissue paper and John Lewis bag and slide it on top of the wardrobe. Later, the house is quiet for the first time since Glen died and I put on my dressing gown and wander through all the rooms. It isn't a big house but Glen is in every corner of it and I keep expecting to hear him shout to me – 'Jeanie, where've you put the paper? . . . Off to work, love, see you later.'

In the end, I make a drink and take it up to bed with the handful of cards and letters from the family. I burned the nasty ones on the gas hob.

The bed feels bigger without him. He wasn't always in it – sometimes he slept on the sofa downstairs when he was restless. 'Don't want to keep you awake, Jean,' he'd say and pick up his pillow. He didn't want to go in the spare room any more so we got a sofa that pulls out into a bed and he'd crawl into it in the middle of the night. We kept a duvet behind it during the day. I don't know if anyone noticed.

Chapter 49

Saturday, 12 June 2010

The Detective

AFTER THE FUNERAL, Bob Sparkes had read the coverage and looked at the photographs of Jean at the crematorium and a close-up of the word 'Glen', spelled out in flowers. 'How will we find you now, Bella?' the papers had said, taunting him.

He tried to concentrate on the job but found himself staring into space, lost and unable to move forward. He decided to take some leave and get his head together. 'Let's pack up the car and drive to Devon. Find a place to stay when we get there,' he said to Eileen on the Saturday morning.

She went to talk to their neighbour about feeding the cat and he sat at the table with the post.

Eileen crashed in through the back door, her hands full of pea pods. 'I picked them quickly otherwise they'll be over by the time we get back. Shame to waste them.'

Eileen was clearly determined that life would go on in their house, even if it was stuck on pause in her husband's head. He'd always been a thinker – it was what she'd loved about him. Deep, her friends had said. She liked that. His deepness. But now it was just blackness.

'Come on, Bob, finish shelling these peas while I pack a bag. How long are we going for?'

'A week? What do you think? I just need a bit of clean air and some long walks.'

'Sounds lovely.'

Sparkes did his chore mechanically, sliding a nail along each pod and pushing the peas into a colander as he struggled with his feelings. He'd let it get personal, he knew. No other case had touched him like this, had reduced him to tears, had threatened his career. Maybe he ought to go back to the barmy counsellor? He laughed, just a short bark of a laugh, but Eileen heard it and rushed downstairs to see what had happened.

The journey was painless: a warm summer's day before the school holidays with little traffic on the motorway, which Sparkes took to put distance between him and the case as quickly as possible. Eileen sat close to him, occasionally patting his knee or squeezing his hand. They both felt young and slightly giddy at their spontaneity.

Eileen chatted to him about the children, filling him in on his family, as if he were emerging from a coma. 'Sam says she and Pete will get married next summer. She wants to do it on a beach.'

'A beach? Suppose it won't be Margate. Well, whatever she wants. She seems happy with Pete, doesn't she?'

'Very happy, Bob. It's James I'm worried about. He's working too hard.'

'Wonder where he gets that from,' he said, and glanced at his wife to see her reaction. They smiled at each other and Sparkes' stomach began to unclench for the first time in weeks. Months, really.

It was wonderful to be talking about his own life instead of other people's.

They decided to stop at Exmouth for crab sandwiches. They had brought the kids here for a summer holiday when they were little and it held happy memories. It was all still there when they pulled up – the blue pompoms of the hydrangeas, the flags fluttering around the Jubilee clock tower, the screeching seagulls, the pastel shades of the beach huts. It was as if they had stepped back into the 1990s, and they walked along the promenade to stretch their legs and look at the sea.

'Come on, love. Let's get going. I've phoned the pub to book a room for tonight,' he said, then pulled her to him and kissed her.

In another hour or so they'd be at Dartmouth, and then on to Slapton Sands for a fish supper.

They drove with the windows down and the wind blowing their hair into mad shapes. 'Blowing the badness out,' Eileen said, as he knew she would. It was what she always said. It made him think of Glen Taylor, but he didn't say anything.

At the pub, they sprawled on the benches outside, soaking up the last warmth of the sun and planning their morning swim. 'Let's get up early and go,' he suggested.

'Let's not. Let's give ourselves a lie-in and then meander down. We've got all week, Bob,' Eileen said, and laughed at the thought of a whole week to themselves.

They went up to their room late and, from habit, Sparkes clicked on the television to catch the late news while Eileen had a quick shower. The video clip of Jean Taylor sitting in her living room, being interviewed, made his stomach contract into its familiar knot and he was back in role.

'Eileen, love, I've got to go back,' he called through to her. 'It's Jean Taylor. She says Glen took Bella.'

Eileen came out of the bathroom, wrapped in a towel, with another pulled round her wet hair in a turban. 'What? What did you say?' Then she saw the faces on the television and sank down on the bed. 'Christ, Bob. Is there no end to this?'

'No, Eileen. I'm so sorry, but there isn't until I know what happened to that little girl. Jean knows and I've got to ask her again. Can you be ready to leave in fifteen minutes?'

She nodded, loosening the towel on her head and rubbing her hair dry.

The journey back was quiet. Eileen slept as Sparkes drove on deserted roads, flicking on the radio every hour, on the hour to see if there were any updates.

He had to shake his wife awake when they reached home and they fell into bed with barely a word exchanged.

Chapter 50

Sunday, 13 June 2010

The Reporter

'HERE SHE IS, our star reporter!' the editor shouted across the news-room when Kate walked in the next morning. 'Brilliant exclusive, Kate. Well done!' There was a smattering of applause from her colleagues and calls of 'Great stuff, Kate!' and she felt herself blushing and tried to smile without looking smug.

'Thanks, Simon,' she said when she finally reached her desk and could shrug off her handbag and jacket.

The news editor, Terry Deacon, had already sidled over to bask in any glory being handed out by his boss. 'What have we got for Day Two then, Kate? Another scoop?' the editor bawled, yellow teeth bared in triumph.

Kate knew he knew because she had filed the story overnight, but Simon Pearson wanted to put on a bit of a show in front of his people. He hadn't had much of a chance lately – 'Bloody boring politics. Where are the exclusives?' was his mantra – and today he was going to make the most of it.

'We've got the story of the childless marriage,' said Terry. '"Is This What Turned Mr Normal into a Monster?"'

Simon smiled widely. Kate winced. The headline was crass, turning her probing and sensitive interview into a screaming cinema poster, but she should have been used to it. 'Sell the story' was another of Simon's mantras. He was a man for mantras. Brute force and rote learning were his preferred MO with his executives, with none of your poncey creative thinking and questioning. 'Simon says,' the execs joked.

The editor knew a good headline when he wrote one and believed it was always worth using a good one more than once. Every week sometimes, when it particularly took his fancy, to be promptly discarded when even he realized it was becoming the source of derision in journalist drinking holes. The question in the headline – 'Is This the Most Evil Man in Britain?' – was a classic. It hedged bets. Just asking, not saying.

'I've got some good quotes from the widow,' Kate said, starting up her computer.

'Killer quotes,' Terry added, upping the ante. 'Everyone was scrambling to catch up last night and we've had the magazines and foreign press on already for the pictures. Talk of the street.'

'You're showing your age, Terry,' Simon said. 'There's no street any more. Didn't you know, it's a global village?'

The news editor grinned at his boss's rebuke, determined to see it as a bit of banter. Nothing was going to spoil today – he'd brought in the story of the year and was going to go in and get the pay rise he richly deserved and then take his wife – or maybe his mistress – for dinner at the Ritz.

Kate was already looking at her emails, leaving the men to their dick-swinging.

'What's she like, Kate? Jean Taylor?'

Kate looked at her editor and saw the genuine curiosity behind the bluster. He had one of the most powerful jobs in the newspaper industry, but what he really wanted was to be a reporter again, elbow-deep in the story, asking the questions, standing on the doorstep, and sending his golden words to the desk, not just hearing about it later.

'She's smarter than she makes out. Puts on the little housewifely act – you know, standing by her man – but there's all sorts going

291

on in her head. It's difficult for her because I think she believed he was innocent at one stage, but something changed. Something changed in their relationship.'

Kate knew she should've got more; she should've got the whole thing. She blamed Mick for interrupting, but she'd seen the shutters come down in Jean's eyes. Control of the interview had switched back and forth between the two women, but there was no question who'd been in charge at the end. Kate wasn't about to admit that to this audience.

The other reporters were listening now, wheeling their chairs back to catch the conversation.

'Did he do it, Kate? And did she know?' the Crime man asked. 'That's what everyone wants to know.'

'Yes and yes,' she said. 'Question is, *when* did she know? At the time, or later? I think the trouble is that she's been stuck between what she knows and what she wants to believe.'

Everyone looked at her for more and, as if on cue, Kate's phone began ringing and Bob Sparkes' name flashed up. 'Sorry, got to take this, Simon. It's the copper in charge of the case. Might be a Day Three.'

'Keep me posted, Kate,' he said as he marched off to his office, and she moved through the swing doors to the lifts to get a bit of privacy.

'Hello, Bob. Thought I'd hear from you this morning.'

Sparkes was already standing outside the newspaper office, sheltering from summer rain in the grand portico of the building. 'Come and have a coffee with me, Kate. We need to talk.'

The Italian café round the corner in a grubby side street was crowded and the windows were running with steam from the coffee machine. They sat down at a table away from the counter and looked at each other for a minute.

'Congratulations, Kate. You got her to say more than I ever managed to.'

The reporter held his gaze. His generosity disarmed her, made her want to tell him the truth. He was good, she had to admit.

'I should've got more, Bob. There was more to get, but she stopped when she chose. Incredible self-control. Frightening, really. One minute she was holding my hand and literally crying on my shoulder about the monster she married, and the next, she was back in the driving seat. Clammed up and wouldn't budge.' She stirred her coffee. 'She knows what happened, doesn't she?'

Sparkes nodded. 'I think she does. But she can't let it out and I don't know why. After all, he's dead. What has she got to lose?'

Kate shook her head in sympathy. 'Something, obviously.'

'I've often wondered if she was involved in the crime,' Sparkes said, mainly to himself. 'Maybe the planning? Maybe it was about getting a child for them both and something went wrong? Perhaps she put him up to it?'

Kate's eyes were glittering with the possibilities. 'Bloody hell, Bob. How're you going to get her to confess?'

How indeed? he thought.

'What is her weak point?' Kate asked, playing with her spoon.

'Glen,' he answered. 'But he's not here any more.'

'It's kids, Bob. That's her weak point. She's obsessed with them. Everything came back to kids when we were talking. She wanted to know everything about my boys.'

'I know. You should see her scrapbooks full of babies.'

'Scrapbooks?'

'That's off the record, Kate.'

She tucked it away for later and automatically put her head on one side. Submission. You can trust me.

He wasn't fooled. 'I mean it. It could be part of a future investigation.'

'OK, OK,' she conceded irritably. 'What do you think she'll do now?'

'If she knew anything, she might go back to the child,' Sparkes said.

'Back to Bella,' Kate echoed. 'Wherever she is.'

Jean had nothing else to think about now. She'd make a move, he was sure.

'Will you call me if you hear anything?' he asked Kate.

'I might,' she teased automatically. He flushed and, despite herself, she was pleased to see him respond to her flirty tone. Sparkes felt out of his depth suddenly.

'Kate, we're not playing games here,' he said, trying to get back on a professional footing. 'Let's stay in touch.'

They parted in the street and he tried to shake her hand, but she leaned forward to kiss him on the cheek.

Chapter 51

Friday, 11 June 2010

The Widow

WHEN THE CREW has gone, I sit quietly and wait for the late evening news. Mr Telly has said it'll be the top item and it is. 'Widow in Bella Case Speaks Out for First Time' flashes up on the screen and music rolls over it and into my front room. And there I am, on the telly. It doesn't last very long really, but I say I knew nothing about Bella's disappearance but suspected that Glen was involved. I said very clearly that I didn't know for certain, that he had not confessed to me, that journalists had twisted what I said.

I answered their questions calmly, sitting on my sofa. I admitted I was offered payment but had turned it down when I found out what the paper was printing. There was a curt statement from the *Post* and a shot of Kate and Mick leaving my house. And that was it.

I wait for the phone to ring. First is Glen's mum, Mary. 'How could you say those things, Jeanie?' she says.

'You know as well as I do, Mary,' I say. 'Please don't pretend you didn't suspect him of it, because I know you did.'

She goes quiet and says she will talk to me tomorrow.

Then Kate calls. She's businesslike, saying that the paper is including my statement from the TV interview in their article so I can 'give my side of the story'.

I laugh at the cheek of her. 'You were supposed to be writing my side of the story,' I say. 'Do you always lie to your victims?'

She ignores the question and says I can ring her any time on her mobile and I hang up without saying goodbye.

The paper comes through the letterbox the next morning. I don't have deliveries. I wonder if Kate posted it. Or a neighbour. The headline screams 'WIDOW CONFESSES BELLA KILLER'S GUILT' and I'm shaking too much to open the paper. My picture is on the front, gazing into the distance like Mick told me to. I put it down on the kitchen table and wait.

The phone rings all morning. The papers, the telly, the radio, the family. My mum calls, sobbing about the shame I have brought on them, and my dad is shouting in the background about how he warned me not to marry Glen. He didn't, but I suppose he wishes he had done now.

I try and comfort Mum, telling her I have been misquoted and the paper has twisted everything, but it's no good and in the end she rings off.

I feel exhausted so I take the phone off the hook and lie down on my bed. I think about Bella and Glen. And those last few days before he died.

He'd started asking me what I was going to do. 'Are you going to leave me, Jeanie?' he'd say. I'd say 'I'm going to make a cup of tea' and leave him standing there. Too much to think about. Betrayal. Decisions. Plans.

And I didn't speak to him again except when it was essential. 'It's your mum on the phone'. Just the bare minimum.

He was like a ghost, haunting me everywhere in the house. I'd catch him looking at me from behind the paper. I had him now. He didn't know what his Jeanie would do and it scared him to death.

Glen didn't let me out on my own that week. Everywhere I went, he came too. Perhaps he thought I would go straight to Bob Sparkes. That's because he didn't understand a thing about me. I wasn't going to tell anyone anything. Not to protect him – don't make me laugh.

That Saturday, he was on my heels as we came out of Sainsbury's and I saw him look at a little girl in a trolley. It was just a glance, but I saw something in his eyes. Something dead. And I pushed him away from the child. Such a little push, and he tripped on the kerb and stumbled into the road. The bus appeared at the same moment. It was all so quick and I remember looking at him lying there in a small pool of blood and thinking, 'Oh well. That's the end of his nonsense.'

Does it make me a murderer now? I look at myself in the mirror, try to see if it shows in my eyes, but I don't think so. Glen got off lightly really. He could have gone on suffering for years, wondering when he'd be exposed. People like Glen can't help themselves, I've heard, so really, I helped him out.

I'm going to sell the house as soon as I can. I've got to get through the inquest first, but Tom Payne says it'll be open and shut. I just have to tell the coroner about Glen stumbling over his feet and it'll all be over. I can make my own fresh start.

I rang an estate agent yesterday to find out what the house will fetch. I gave my name but she didn't seem to notice – she will eventually, but I told her I wanted a quick sale and she's coming tomorrow morning. I wonder if Glen's connection will push the price up or down. Some ghoul might pay a bit extra. You never know.

I'm still deciding where to go, but I'm definitely moving out of London. I'm going to go online to find places, maybe abroad or maybe down towards Hampshire. To be near my baby girl.

Chapter 52

Thursday, 1 July 2010

The Reporter

THE CORONER WAS well known to the press. A small, neat solicitor who favoured highly coloured silk bow ties and kept a meticulously trimmed silver moustache, Hugh Holden liked to think of himself as a Character, an occasional thorn in the side of the authorities, unafraid to reach controversial verdicts.

Normally, Kate enjoyed his inquests and his quirky line in questioning and verbal flourishes, but she wasn't in the mood today. She feared this was likely to be Jean Taylor's last public appearance. There'd be no need for her to show her face again and she could disappear behind her front door for ever.

Outside the court, Mick was milling around with the other photographers waiting for the arrival shots. 'Hi, Kate,' he called over the heads. 'See you after.'

She filed in with the rest of the reporters and the curious, managing to get one of the last press seats at the front, facing the witness box. Her thoughts were all on Jean and she watched the door for her entrance. She missed Zara Salmond slipping into the back of the court with some of the Met officers who'd be called to give evidence. Sparkes had sent her in his place. 'You go, Salmond. I need your eyes and analysis on her performance. I can't see anything straight at the moment.'

She'd only just arrived in time when the grind of the door hinges announced the arrival of the widow. Jean Taylor looked dignified and in control, in the same dress she'd worn for Glen's funeral.

She walked slowly through the court with her lawyer to her seat in the front row. That weasel, Tom Payne, Kate thought, nodding affably to him and mouthing, 'Good morning, Tom.' He raised his hand in greeting and Jean looked to see who he was waving to. Their eyes met and Kate thought for a moment that she was going to acknowledge her. She tried a small smile but Jean turned away, uninterested.

The other witnesses took their time to settle, shaking hands and hugging each other in the aisles, but finally everyone took their places and stood to attention as the coroner entered.

The coroner's officer stepped up to tell the court that the deceased's father had identified the body as that of Glen George Taylor, and then the pathologist gave his evidence of the post-mortem examination. Kate kept her eyes on Jean, registering her reaction to the details of the dissection of her husband. He'd had a good last breakfast, anyway, Kate thought as the pathologist ran through the contents of his stomach in a desultory fashion. No sign of disease. Contusions and lacerations to arms and thighs consistent with the fall and collision with the vehicle. The fatal injury was to the head. Skull fracture caused by impact with bus and road surface, traumatic brain injury. Death pretty much instantaneous.

Jean pulled her handbag on to her knee and undid a small packet of tissues ostentatiously, unfolding one to wipe an eye. She's not crying, Kate thought. She's faking.

The bus driver was next. His tears were real as he told of the flash of a man falling in front of his cab window. 'I never saw him so there was nothing I could do. It all happened so quickly. I braked, but it was too late.'

He was helped from the box by an usher, and then Jean was called.

Her performance was polished – too polished. To Kate's ear, every word sounded as if it had been practised in front of the mirror. The shopping trip was walked through, step by step: around the aisles, out of the automatic doors and into the High Street. The discussion about cereal and Glen Taylor's stumble into the path of the bus. All told in a low, serious voice.

Kate wrote it all down and glanced up to capture the expressions and any emotions.

'Mrs Taylor, can you tell us why your husband stumbled? The police examined the pavement and could find nothing to make him lose his footing,' the coroner asked kindly.

'I don't know, Sir. He fell under the bus right there, in front of me. I didn't even have time to call out. He was gone,' she answered.

She's got this off pat now, Kate thought. She's using identical phrases.

'Was he holding your hand or your arm? I know I do with my partner when we're out together,' the coroner persisted.

'No. Well, perhaps. I can't remember,' she said, less sure of herself now.

'Was your husband distracted that day? Was he himself?'

'Distracted? What do you mean?'

'Not concentrating on what he was doing, Mrs Taylor.'

'He'd a lot on his mind,' Jean Taylor said and looked at the press benches. 'But I'm sure you know that.'

'Quite,' the coroner said, pleased with himself for winkling out some new information. 'So, what was his mood that morning?'

'His mood?'

This was not going the way Jean had planned, Kate thought. Repeating questions back to the questioner was a sure sign of stress. You did it to buy time. The reporter leaned forward to make sure she didn't miss a word.

'Yes, his mood, Mrs Taylor?'

Jean Taylor closed her eyes and seemed to sway in the witness box. Tom Payne and the coroner's officer leapt up to catch her and lower her into a chair as the court hummed with concern.

'It's a line, I suppose,' the reporter behind Kate muttered to a colleague. "Widow of Bella suspect collapses." Better than nothing.'

'It's not over yet,' she hissed over her shoulder.

Jean gripped a glass of water and stared at the coroner.

'Better now, Mrs Taylor?' he asked.

'Yes, thank you. Sorry about that. I didn't eat anything this morning and . . .'

'That's perfectly all right. No need to explain. Now shall we get back to my question?'

Jean took a deep breath. 'He hadn't been sleeping properly, not for ages, and he'd been getting bad headaches.'

'And had he been treated for his insomnia and headaches?'

She shook her head. 'He said he wasn't well but he wouldn't go to the doctor's. He didn't want to talk about it, I think.'

'I see. Why not, Mrs Taylor?'

She looked at her lap for a moment, then raised her head. 'Because he said he kept dreaming about Bella Elliott.'

Hugh Holden held her gaze and the room stilled as he nodded to her to continue.

'She was there when he closed his eyes, he said. It was making him ill. And he wanted to be with me all the time. Following me around the house. I didn't know what to do. He wasn't well.'

The coroner noted it all down carefully as the reporters scribbled furiously to his left.

'Given his state of mind, Mrs Taylor, is there a possibility that your husband stepped in front of the bus on purpose?' the coroner asked.

Tom Payne rose to challenge the question, but Jean waved him away.

'I don't know, Sir. He never said anything about taking his own life. But he wasn't well.'

The coroner thanked her for her evidence, gave her his condolences and recorded a verdict of Accidental Death.

'I'll be on the news tonight,' he told the court usher gleefully as the press filed out.

Chapter 53

Thursday, 1 July 2010

The Detective

GLEN TAYLOR'S DREAMS of Bella led the news bulletins on the radio all afternoon and came a respectable third on the evening television news. In the dog days of summer – the media's 'silly season' when politicians are on holiday, schools close and the country gently grinds to a halt – anything with a hint of a news angle plays well.

Sparkes had heard it all from Salmond straight after the inquest but he read it in the papers anyway, scanning every word. 'Jean's beginning to unravel, Bob,' Salmond had said, puffing slightly as she marched back to her car. 'I tried to talk to her afterwards. All the reporters were there – your Kate Waters was there – but Jean wouldn't say another word. She's still holding it together, but only just.'

The collapse in court must have been a sign that with Glen gone, the secret was becoming too much for her, Sparkes felt. 'She's letting it seep out in a controlled fashion, like when they used to bleed a patient in medieval times. Getting rid of the bad thing a bit at a time,' he'd suggested to Salmond. He looked over at her; she was now sitting at his computer looking at the news reports. 'We're going to wait her out. Literally.'

*

They were in position at 5 a.m. the next morning, parked out of sight, half a mile from Jean Taylor's house, waiting for the surveillance team's call. 'I know this is a long shot, but we've got to try it. She will do something,' Sparkes had told Salmond.

'Feel it in your waters, Sir?' she said.

'Not sure where my waters are, but yes. I do.'

Twelve hours later, the air in the car was thick with their breath and fast food.

At 10 p.m., they had exhausted their life stories, criminals they'd lifted, holiday disasters, TV programmes from their childhoods, favourite meals, best action films and who was sleeping with whom in the office. Sparkes felt he could go on *Mastermind* and answer questions on Zara Salmond without passing, and both were quietly relieved when the surveillance team finally rang to say all the lights in the house had been turned off.

Sparkes called it a day. They would stay in the cheap hotel down the hill to grab some sleep before resuming their vigil. Another team would keep watch overnight.

His phone went at 4 a.m. 'Lights are on, Sir.'

He pulled on his clothes and rang Salmond at the same time, dropping his phone down a trouser leg.

'Sir, is that you?'

'Yes, yes. She's up. Downstairs in five.'

Zara Salmond looked less than perfect for the first time; bed-hair and bare-faced, she was waiting for him at the front door. 'And to think I told my mum I wanted to be an air hostess,' she said.

'Come on, then. Seats for take-off,' he replied with the ghost of a smile.

Jean came out of the front door quickly, triggering her own security light, and stood in the spotlight, looking up and down the street for signs of life. She pressed the key fob to open the car and the electronic beep echoed off the facades of the houses opposite as she pulled the door open and slid in behind the wheel. She was wearing her funeral dress again.

Two streets away, Zara Salmond started their car and waited for instructions from the team. Sparkes was deep in thought beside her, maps on his lap. 'She's just turned on to the A2 headed in the direction of the M25, Sir,' the officer in the unmarked van barked down the phone. And they pulled away to start their pursuit.

'Bet she's going down to Hampshire,' Salmond said as she sped down the dual carriageway.

'Let's not try to second-guess her,' Sparkes said. He could not bear to hope too much as he followed their route on the map with his finger.

The rising sun was beginning to lighten the sky but the GPS had still not switched from night colours when they took the turning for the M3 and Southampton. The convoy was evenly spaced over three miles of the motorway, with Sparkes and Salmond holding back to avoid being recognized. 'She's signalling to pull into the services, Sir,' the men in the van informed them. 'Where are your officers, now? We'll need to change over or she's going to spot us.'

'On it. We've got another vehicle waiting at the next junction. Stick with her until she leaves the services and we'll take her from there,' Sparkes replied.

The van crawled into the parking area and slid into a bay two cars back from the target. One of the police team got out, scratching his head and stretching, and headed after Jean Taylor. She went into the Ladies' and the officer stood in a queue for a burger. He pretended to compare the qualities of the meals advertised in nuclear-fall-out colours above the counter while he waited for her to emerge. She didn't take long, shaking the last drops of water from her hands as she walked. The officer munched into his double cheeseburger as she went into the shop and carefully picked through the plastic buckets of flowers, selecting a bouquet of pink rosebuds and white lilies wrapped in pink tissue paper and cellophane. She held them up to her face to catch the perfume from the powdery stamens as she walked over to the sweet counter and picked up a brightly coloured packet. Skittles, the officer noted from the other side of the deserted shop. Then she queued to pay.

'She's got flowers and sweets, Sir. She's on her way to the car. We'll follow her out on to the motorway and hand over,' he reported back.

Sparkes and Salmond looked at each other. 'She's going to a grave,' Sparkes said, his mouth dry. 'Get our boys ready.'

Five minutes later, two other vehicles were on her tail, overtaking each other, taking turns to be three cars back. Jean maintained a steady 65 mph. A careful driver. She's probably not used to driving on motorways on her own, Sparkes thought. I wonder if this is the first time she's made this journey.

He and Salmond had not spoken since they pulled out of the services; they were concentrating on the chatter on the police channels. But at Winchester, when they heard that Jean Taylor's car had exited the motorway and was heading east, he told her to put her foot down.

They were picking up a bit more traffic, but Jean's car was now only a mile ahead of them, with another police vehicle sandwiched between them.

'She's stopping,' the officer messaged. 'Trees on right, track, no gate. I'll have to go on or she'll spot me. Will double-back straight away. She's all yours.'

'Steady, Salmond,' Sparkes said. 'Nice and steady.'

They almost missed her car, tucked down the muddy track, but Sparkes spotted the glint of metal in the trees at the last minute. 'She's here,' he said and Salmond slowed and swung their car round. 'Park across the road. We'll need access for the other vehicles,' he said.

As they got out, a light rain started to patter down on the trees and they pulled their coats from the boot. 'She's probably heard the car,' Sparkes whispered. 'I don't know how far back these trees go. I'll go ahead and you wait for the team. I'll call you when I need you.'

Salmond nodded, looking suddenly tearful.

Sparkes crossed the road quickly, turning and waving before disappearing into the trees.

There was not enough daylight yet to penetrate the wood and he felt his way carefully. He couldn't hear anything apart from his breathing and the crows cawing above him, disturbed by his presence.

He suddenly saw a movement ahead. A flash of something white in the gloom. He stopped and waited a moment until he was ready. He needed to steady himself and was glad Salmond wasn't there to see him trembling like a diver on a high board. He took three deep breaths and then moved forward cautiously. He was worried he might stumble over her. He didn't want to frighten her.

Then he saw her, on the ground under a tree. She was sitting on a coat, her legs tucked sideways, for all the world as if she was at a picnic. Beside her, the flowers lay in their tissue paper.

'Is that you, Bob?'

He froze at the sound of her voice.

'Yes, Jean.'

'I thought I heard a car. I knew it would be you.'

'Why are you here, Jean?'

'Jeanie. I prefer you to call me Jeanie,' she said, still not looking at him.

'Why are you here, Jeanie?'

'I've come to see our baby girl.'

Sparkes crouched down beside her, then took off his coat and sat on it so he could be close to her. 'Who is your baby girl, Jeanie?'

'Bella, of course. She's here. Glen put her here.'

Chapter 54

Saturday, 3 July 2010

The Widow

I COULDN'T STOP myself. I had to go to her. The interview and the inquest started something in me, started me thinking all the time, and even the pills couldn't do anything about it. I thought that with Glen gone there would be some peace, but there wasn't. I was still thinking all the time. I couldn't eat or sleep. I knew I had to go to her. Nothing else mattered.

It wasn't the first visit. Glen had taken me to Bella's grave on the Monday before he died. After he sat on my bed and told me he couldn't sleep any more. He started talking about the day Bella went missing, curled up on his side of the bed, with his back to me so I couldn't see his face. I didn't move once while he told me. I was scared I'd break the spell and he'd stop. So I listened without speaking.

He said he'd picked Bella up because she wanted him to. He hadn't dreamed it. He knew that he'd left Bella on her own on the edge of a small wood on his way home to me and he knew he'd done something terrible. She'd fallen asleep in the back of the van. He had a sleeping bag in the van. He just lifted her out, still asleep, from the back of the van and put her under a tree to be found. He'd left some sweets for her to eat. Skittles. He'd meant to ring the police but he was in a panic.

Then he got up and went out of the room before I could speak. I lay still as if I could stop time there, but my mind was racing away from me. All I could think was, Why did he have a sleeping bag in his van? Where did he get it from? I couldn't let myself think about what had happened in the van. What my husband had done.

I wanted to blot it out and stood under the shower, letting the water drum on my head and fill my ears. But nothing could stop me thinking.

I went down to him in the kitchen and told him we were going to find her. Glen looked at me blankly and said, 'Jeanie, I left her nearly four years ago.' But I wasn't taking no for an answer.

'We have to,' I said.

We get in our car and go looking for Bella. I make sure we're not being watched as we come out, but the press don't live in our street any more. I've already decided that if we see one of the neighbours, we'll say we're going shopping at Bluewater.

The traffic is heavy and we don't speak as we follow the signs for the M25.

We follow the route Glen must have taken that day from Winchester to Southampton and then on. The country roads he took with Bella in the back of his van. I imagine her sitting happily on the floor of the van with a fistful of sweeties and I hold on to that image for grim death. I know it wasn't like that, really, but I can't think about that yet.

Glen is pale and sweaty at the wheel.

'This is bloody stupid, Jean,' he says. But I know he wants to go back to that day. To what happened. And I'm letting him do this because I want Bella.

About two hours after we've left home, he says, 'It was here.' It doesn't look any different from dozens of clumps of trees we've passed, but he pulls over.

'How can you be sure?' I ask.

'I made a mark on the fence,' he says. And there it is. A faded smear of car oil on a fence post.

He meant to come back, I think, then push the thought aside.

Glen drives the car off the road so it can't be seen. He must've done the same thing that day. Then we sit in silence. It's me who makes the first move.

'Come on,' I say. And he undoes his seat belt. His face has gone blank again, like it did that day in the hall. He doesn't look like Glen now, but I'm not frightened. He's shaking, but I don't touch him. When we get out, he leads me to a tree near the edge and points at the ground.

'Here,' he says. 'This is where I put her.'

'Liar,' I say and he looks startled. 'Where?' I demand, my voice sounding like a shriek, scaring us both.

He leads me deeper into the trees and then stops. I can see nothing to show anyone was here before, but I think he's telling the truth this time. 'I put her down here,' he says and stumbles to his knees. I squat down beside him under the tree and make him tell me all over again.

'She put her arms up to me. She was beautiful, Jeanie, and I just leaned over the wall and took her and put her in the van. When we stopped, I held her really close and stroked her hair. She liked it at first. Laughed. And I kissed her cheek. I gave her a sweet and she loved it. Then she went to sleep.'

'She was dead, Glen. Not asleep. Bella was dead,' I say and he starts to sob.

'I don't know why she died,' he says. 'I didn't kill her. I would know if I had, wouldn't I?'

'Yes, you would,' I say. 'You do.'

All I can hear is his sobbing, but I think he's crying for himself, not the child he murdered.

He says, 'Perhaps I held her too tight. I didn't mean to. It was like a dream, Jeanie. Then I covered her up with the sleeping bag and branches and things to keep her safe.'

I can see a shred of faded blue material, caught in the roots of the tree. We're kneeling beside Bella's grave and I stroke the ground, soothing her, letting her know she's safe now.

'It's all right, my baby,' I say, and for a second, Glen thinks I mean him.

I get up and walk back to the car and leave him to make his own way. He's left it unlocked, and when I get in I fiddle with the GPS and make this place Home. I'm not sure why, but it feels right. Glen appears and we drive back without speaking. I look out of the window at the countryside changing into suburbs and plan for my future.

Glen had done something terrible but I could care for Bella, look after her and love her. I could be her forever mummy.

And, last night, I decided that I'd get up early and go. It'd be dark still, so no one would see me leave. I didn't sleep while I waited to go. I was scared – scared of driving on the motorway – Glen always drove when we went on long journeys. His department. But I made myself do it. For her.

I stopped at the services because I wanted to buy some flowers to take with me. Some little pink rosebuds for her. She would like those. Small and pink and pretty like her. And some lilies for her grave. I wasn't sure if I was going to leave them there. Perhaps I'd bring them home again so I could look at them with her. I bought some sweets for Bella, too. I chose Skittles and then I realized in the car that that was what Glen had chosen. I threw them out of the window.

The GPS took me straight there. 'You've reached your destination,' it said. And I had. Home, it said on the screen. I slowed down a bit to let the car behind overtake me and then turned into the track. It was getting light by then but was still early so no one else was around. I walked into the trees and looked for Bella. I'd left the yellow cloth Glen used to clean the windscreen wedged beside the blue material under the tree root where he'd left her and I hoped it would still be there. The wood wasn't very big and I'd brought a little torch in case. It didn't take very long to find it. The cloth was there, a bit soggy from the rain.

I'd planned what I'd do in my head. I'd say a prayer and then talk to Bella, but in the end I just wanted to sit and be near her. I spread my coat out and sat down beside her and showed her the flowers. I don't know how long I'd been there when I heard him. I knew it would be him who found me. Destiny, my mum would say.

He was so gentle when he spoke to me. When he asked me why I was there. We both knew, of course, but he needed me to say it. Needed it so badly. So I told him. 'I've come to see our baby girl.' He thought I meant Glen's and my baby girl, but Bella is Bob's and mine, really. He loves her as much as I do. Glen never loved her. He just wanted her and took her.

We sat for a bit, not talking, then Bob told me the real story. The story Glen couldn't tell me. He told me how Glen had found Bella online and hunted her down. How the police had watched a film of him following her and Dawn from nursery four days before he kidnapped her. How he had planned the whole thing.

'He said he did it for me,' I said.

'He did it for himself, Jean.'

'He said I made him do it because I needed a baby so much. It was my fault. He did it because he loved me.'

Bob looked at me hard and said slowly, 'Glen took her for himself, Jean. No one else was to blame. Not Dawn, not you.'

I felt like I was underwater and couldn't hear or see anything clearly. I felt like I was drowning. It felt like we had been there for hours when Bob helped me up and put my coat round my shoulders and took my hand to lead me away. I turned back and whispered, 'Goodbye, darling,' then we walked towards the blue lights flashing through the trees.

I saw the funeral pictures on the television. A little white coffin with pink rosebuds on the lid. Hundreds of people went from all over the country, but I couldn't. Dawn got an injunction to stop me. We made an application to the court, but the judge agreed with the psychiatrist that it would be too much for me.

I was still there, though.

Bella knew I was there, and that's all that matters.

Acknowledgements

Sister Ursula IBVM, for turning on the light.

And those who helped replace the bulb: my parents, David and Jeanne Thurlow; my sister, Jo West; and Rachael Bletchly, Carol Maloney, Jennifer Sherwood, Wendy Turner, Rick Lee and Jane McGuinn.

The experts: former DCI Colin Sutton, for putting me right on police matters, and John Carr, the fount of all knowledge on online child safety.

My wonderful agent, Madeleine Milburn; editors Danielle Perez and Frankie Gray, and all at Transworld and NAL/Penguin Random House for their encouragement, patience and determination to put *The Widow* on the page.

Fiona Barton trains and works with journalists all over the world. Previously, she was a senior writer at the *Daily Mail*, news editor at the *Daily Telegraph*, and chief reporter at the *Mail on Sunday*, where she won Reporter of the Year at the British Press Awards. *The Widow* is her first novel. Born in Cambridge, she currently lives in south-west France.

#thewidow
@figbarton

Loved the book?

Join thousands of other readers online at

AUSTRALIAN READERS:

randomhouse.com.au/talk

NEW ZEALAND READERS:

randomhouse.co.nz/talk

THE CONTROL OF THE CAMPUS

A CARNEGIE FOUNDATION ESSAY

THE
CONTROL

A REPORT ON THE GOVERNANCE

OF THE

OF HIGHER EDUCATION

CAMPUS

THE CARNEGIE FOUNDATION FOR THE
ADVANCEMENT OF TEACHING

1785 Massachusetts Avenue, N.W.
Washington, D.C. 20036

LIBRARY OF CONGRESS CATALOGING IN PUBLICATION DATA
Main entry under title:
The Control of the campus.

  (A Carnegie Foundation essay)
  Includes bibliographical references.
  1. University autonomy—United States—History.
2. Higher education and state—United States—History.
I. Carnegie Foundation for the Advancement of Teaching.
II. Series.
LB2331.4.C66   1982   379.73   82-19772
ISBN 0-931050-21-9

ISBN 0-931050-21-9

LC 82-18772

Copies are available from the
PRINCETON UNIVERSITY PRESS
3175 Princeton Pike
Lawrenceville, N.J. 08648

CONTENTS

PREFACE

I N THIS REPORT, we take a comprehensive look at the governance of American higher education. We trace its roots, review how decision-making arrangements have been affected by current conditions, and suggest a governance framework for the future.

In the development of this study, our staff reviewed relevant literature and consulted with many authorities. We also conducted a national survey of decision making in higher education. Through it, we have been able to determine where the effective level of decision making occurs in different types of institutions in the separate states.

Our concern throughout has been with both public and private education. Independent institutions have been deeply touched in recent years by government at both state and federal levels. Such colleges also have governance connections with constituencies in the public sector. However, the emphasis of this report is heaviest on the public sector because it is there that linkages between higher education and state government are, by definition, more intense.

To generalize about American higher education—especially in matters of governance—is risky. There are, after all, over 3,000 colleges and universities in the United States, each with its own unique practices and traditions, and circumstances vary greatly from one region to another. Therefore, we acknowledge that there are marked exceptions to our conclusions about governance conditions that seem to apply to most higher learning institutions.

A word about the organization of this report may be helpful. First, we define what we call the essential core of the academic enterprise and trace its roots. We then look at the tradition of self-regulation in American higher education, beginning with the governing board and continuing to voluntary accreditation. In Section Three, we examine governance connections beyond the campus—the state, the federal government, and the courts—that have significantly altered the mission and the governance of higher education. The last section of our report summarizes major conclusions of the preceding chapters and pulls together key recommendations in what we call *A Governance Framework For Higher Education*.

This report has no single author. With the assistance of his staff, it was prepared by the president of the Foundation, who assumes responsibility for the final statement. Special credit, however, should be given to Dr. James Herbert, project director, and Ms. Carol Herrnstadt Shulman, associate director, for their excellent work in gathering data, shaping issues and drafting materials for review. We have consulted widely with educators and government officials. We wish to thank all of them for their assistance and counsel.

We particularly thank our National Panel on Government and Higher Education (see page viii), and members of the Board of Trustees who have reviewed the text and shared their reactions. While the national panel significantly helped to shape the conclusions found in the report, and while there was wide consensus on most issues, we underscore the point that members of the panel are not individually or collectively responsible for the conclusions set forth.

We submit this essay at a critical moment in American higher education. We hope that it will stimulate discussion about academic governance and, in the process, strengthen the integrity of the nation's colleges and universities and improve their accountability to the public.

ERNEST L. BOYER
President
The Carnegie Foundation for the
Advancement of Teaching

PART ONE

THE ROOTS OF INDEPENDENCE

I

THE ESSENTIAL MISSION

WHEN WE BEGAN this study almost 24 months ago, there were widespread complaints about federal instrusion into the administration of colleges and universities. Higher education, it was feared, was fast becoming just another Washington-regulated industry. Every college president, it seemed, had his or her own favorite story about paper work and bureaucratic harassment.

As our work progressed, however, the debate over control of the campus took a new turn. Colleges became more concerned about budget cutbacks than federal control, and we heard fewer complaints about Washington interference. At the same time, intervention by state governments continued to increase, and we also discovered in the course of our study that higher education, through specialized accrediting agencies, was being threatened from within.

Thus, while the debate over academic governance may have shifted, the fundamental issues have not changed. There remains, in the control of higher education, an inherent tension. Colleges and universities are expected to respond to the needs of the society of which they are a part— while also being free to carry on, without undue interference, their essential work.

Ideally, the twin obligations of institutional integrity and public accountability can be kept in balance. In practice, pressures seem continuously to push the campus in one direction, then another. At times, excessive demands of society chip away at the integrity of the university. At other times, the academy seems unresponsive to public needs. Therefore, the central issue of our report is this: How can colleges and universities that are increasingly in the nation's service sustain their traditions of self-control while being accountable to the various constituencies they serve?

In recent years, demands for accountability by agencies beyond the campus have caused confusion about where authority is lodged and have worn down the traditional governance structures of higher education. Leadership in the academy has been weakened. We conclude that if the correct balance between integrity and accountability is to be maintained, the academy must assume more responsibility for regulating itself.

We do not suggest that colleges and universities can carry on their work in isolation. There is, in the strictest sense, no such thing as autonomy on campus. Both public and private institutions are socially engaged. They are answerable to the people who support them and cannot be excused from explaining, and perhaps defending, what they do.

However, maintaining the integrity of higher learning is absolutely crucial if society is to be well served. The university is a unique institution, a repository of our cultural heritage and a source of the nation's future intellectual and economic growth. Therefore, the academy must be free to direct, without outside interference, those functions that may, from time to time, challenge, but ultimately will enrich, the culture they sustain.

But how is the essential mission of the university to be defined? Where is the line to be drawn between the campus and the state? In 1957, in *Sweezy* v. *New Hampshire,* the United States Supreme Court considered the rights of a professor who refused to testify about the contents of a lecture given on a college campus. In a concurring opinion, justices Frankfurter and Harlan affirmed "the four essential freedoms of a university: to determine for itself on academic grounds who may teach, what may be taught, how it shall be taught, and who may be admitted to study." [1]

This formulation is rooted in a long tradition. The first universities were places where scholars assembled to teach and learn. In twelfth-century Bologna, guilds of students, patronized by wealthy families, came together to manage their accommodations in the city and to monitor the performance of their instructors. In Paris, masters formed an association in the guild tradition to control the training and certification of their fellow teachers.

The Parisian masters and students received special status within the church that freed them from municipal control. And in 1215, after a conflict between local religious authorities and the university, Pope Innocent III reaffirmed the authority of the masters to grant the coveted license to teach.[2] The freedom of the masters to determine who would teach and what would be taught was vigorously defended, and in 1229, the masters at Paris suspended lectures in a dispute over their corporate jurisdiction.

Oxford, following largely in the Paris tradition, was also organized by teachers. Indeed, during the great suspension of 1229, many Parisian masters migrated to Oxford at the invitation of the English king.[3] Frequent disputes between the campus and the town arose over such matters as rents and the prices of bread and ale. The university, however, appealed directly to the king, who gave the institution considerable independence from the town.

In 1303, King Edward I asked Pope Benedict XI to recognize Oxford's right to grant the *ius ubique docendi*, the license to teach anywhere. King Edward II renewed the request in 1317, this time directing it to Pope John XXII. Although neither pope ever explicitly honored these requests, medieval lawyers reasoned that since Oxford was already operating as a university it must, therefore, possess the corporate authority needed to carry on its work.[4]

Here then is the essential point: The great medieval universities emerged as independent institutions with power and prestige. The universities' authority over who should teach and what students should be taught was firmly established and reinforced by corporate independence. Although institutional autonomy was often challenged by church and state, and although the freedom of individual teachers was often internally restricted by petty regulations, the corporate authority of the university protected scholars from outside control.

In a book on academic freedom, Richard Hofstadter describes how universities created special conditions conducive to scholarship:

In return for their loyalty, teachers were surrounded by an

institutional framework that supported their pride and security as men of learning and offered them a vigorous defense against interference. Indeed, in great crises the positions even of such heretics as Wyclif and Huss were for a time strengthened by powerful support given them within their universities.[5]

If the integrity of higher education is to be preserved, the academy must have full authority over those essential functions that relate to teaching and research. These include the selection of faculty, the content of courses, the processes of instruction, the establishment of academic standards, and the assessment of performance. Academic integrity also requires that the university have control over the conduct of campus-based research and the dissemination of results. These functions constitute, we believe, the essential core of academic life. It is here that the integrity of the campus must be uncompromisingly defended.

A related point is that the free pursuit of knowledge goes beyond the rights of individual scholars and their students. The violation of academic freedom can occur not only within a university; it can happen *to* a university as well.

University of Wisconsin President Robert M. O'Neil, writing on the issue of autonomy in American higher education, has noted that "all of the academic freedom decisions to date have involved *individual* rights and liberties—to engage in political activity, to teach freely, to join lawfully in controversial groups and the like."[6] O'Neil then proceeds to make this cogent point:

> Individuals within the academic community cannot be free to teach and study if the *institution* is not free. . . . If governmental regulation should seriously invade or disrupt these supportive activities, even without directly abridging the liberty of individual professors or students, a cogent constitutional case could be made for institutional standing to assert its autonomy.[7]

Discovering the precise point at which academic integrity battles should be waged is never easy. All activities on campus ultimately intersect, and the line between the so-called academic and nonacademic frequently is blurred. Still, some functions are more truly vital than others. The work of scholars and their students is at the essential core, and it is here—where "academic freedom" issues are involved— that the defense of the academy should take place.

There are times, of course, when the essential core of the university collides, or appears to collide, with other values of equal or, perhaps, transcendent merit to society at large. These dilemmas must be candidly confronted and, we hope, resolved. A discussion of the governance of higher education must begin, however, with the recognition that the university is a unique institution with a unique mission. At the heart of the enterprise are those who teach and those who learn. Since human curiosity and potential cannot and should not be constrained, scholars and students must have the freedom required to carry on their essential work.

In this report, then, we examine the governance of higher education. We define governance to include not only the formal decision arrangements by which colleges and universities carry on their work, but also the informal procedures by which standards are maintained. We also include in our definition those forces beyond the campus that shape the policies of higher education and to which the academy must ultimately respond. While we acknowledge that the nation's colleges are fully accountable to their public or private constituents, as the case may be, we accept—as a basic tenet of this report—that the task of governance is to sustain and strengthen the essential academic core.

II

TRUSTEES: THE AMERICAN TRADITION

A DISCUSSION OF the control of higher education in America must begin with the governing board, where, by law, authority is lodged. In 1637, the Massachusetts legislature created a Board of Overseers for Harvard College with a balanced membership of ministers and government officials. Thirteen years later, the legislature chartered Harvard as a separate "Corporation consisting of seven persons (to wit) a President, five Fellows, and a Treasurer or Bursar." [1] Immediate governance of the college was delegated to this second board, subject to the consent of the overseers.

In Virginia, the College of William and Mary was chartered by the English crown in 1693. Again, a board of trustees was created with fourteen of the original eighteen appointments filled by government officials. However, the William and Mary charter also provided that "the President and Masters or Professors, of the said College, shall be a Body politic and incorporate, in Deed and Name." [2] Thus in Virginia, as in Massachusetts, there was an external governing board *and* a college corporation comprised of those teaching in the college.

Yale, even more than Harvard and William and Mary, became the governance prototype for the nation. In 1701, the Connecticut legislature established Yale as a "collegiate school." The 10 ministers who organized the institution arranged to hold full control in their own hands. A charter granted to Yale by the Connecticut legislature in 1745 recognized president Thomas Clap and the trustees who were

8

the original organizers of the college as a legal corporation—"The President and Fellows of Yale College in New Haven."[3] The distinction was crucial. The college was to be governed by a *single* board of external trustees. Princeton, founded in 1746, and virtually all other colonial colleges, adopted the Yale College corporation model.

In the historic Dartmouth College decision of 1819, the Supreme Court not only vigorously affirmed the independence of that college from the state, but also clearly recognized its board of governors as the corporate body that held college property and exercised ultimate control. No other single action holds greater significance for the governance of American higher education.

Dartmouth was founded in 1769 under a royal charter that granted the founder, Eleazar Wheelock, and his fellow trustees the right to govern the college and hold its property in trust for the original benefactors. When Wheelock died, his son became president. The more liberal John Wheelock, who often found himself in religious and political conflict with the Dartmouth board, ultimately was dismissed.

John Wheelock turned to the New Hampshire state government for help, and got it. The legislature reorganized Dartmouth into a state university, altering its board of trustees, and restoring Wheelock as president. But, in 1819, after four years of dispute and litigation, the United States Supreme Court held that the college charter could not be altered by the state.

Daniel Webster, who represented Dartmouth in its suit, argued that independence was essential to the integrity of the institution. If independence were lost, declared Webster:

> Benefactors will have no certainty of effecting the object of their bounty; and learned men will be deterred from devoting themselves to the service of such institutions. . . . Colleges and halls will be deserted by all better spirits, and become a theatre for the contention of politics. Party and faction will be cherished in the places consecrated to piety and learning.[4]

The Dartmouth ruling strengthened the independence of higher education in America. It also slowed a push to transform colonial colleges into state-controlled institutions, a movement fostered even by progressive thinkers of the Enlightenment. Thomas Jefferson, for example, writing to the governor of New Hampshire during the Dartmouth controversy, supported the state's position:

> The idea that institutions established for the use of the nation cannot be touched or modified, even to make them answer their end, because of rights gratuitously supposed in those employed to manage them in trust for the public, may, perhaps, be a salutary provision against the abuse of a monarch, but it is most absurd against the nation itself.[5]

The Dartmouth College decision rooted American higher education in very different ground. Control of the college was firmly fixed in the hands of its board of trustees chartered as an independent corporation. The *privilege* of the sovereign to delegate functions was transformed into the *right* of trustees to carry on their work without legislative interference.

The principle of institutional independence spread from private to public colleges and universities as well. When state higher learning institutions were established, their boards of trustees were given corporate power, and some were given constitutional autonomy as well. The goal, ideally viewed perhaps, was to preserve academic freedom by keeping a respectful distance between teaching and research and the short-term political interests of the state.

In 1840, for example, a select committee of the Michigan legislature investigated the disappointing progress of the University of Michigan. In a harshly worded condemnation of constant legislative meddling, the committee stated:

> It is not surprising that state universities have hitherto, almost without exception, failed to accomplish, in proportion to their means, the amount of good that was expected from them. . . . The argument by which legislatures have hitherto convinced themselves that it was their duty to legislate universities to death is this: 'It is a state institution, and we are the direct representatives of the people, and therefore it is expected of us; it is our right . . .' As if, because a university belongs to the people, that were reason

why it should be dosed to death for fear it would be sick if left to be nursed . . . by its immediate guardians.[6]

In order to keep its higher learning institution from being "dosed to death" the state of Michigan, in 1850, established its university as an independent, constitutionally protected corporation. And in 1896, the Michigan Supreme Court made explicit the autonomy of the regents:

> The board of regents and the legislature derive their power from the same supreme authority, namely, the Constitution. Insofar as the powers of each are defined by that instrument, limitations are imposed, and a direct power conferred upon one necessarily excludes its existence in the other. . . . They are separate and distinct constitutional bodies, with the powers of the regents defined. By no rule of construction can it be held that either can encroach upon or exercise the powers conferred upon the other.[7]

The full implications of establishing state colleges and universities as public corporations are found in a decision of the Illinois Supreme Court in 1943. In this ruling the court declared:

> As long as the present statute is in force, the State has committed to the corporate entity the absolute power to do everything necessary in the management, operation, and administration of the university. . . . The University is a public corporation. . . . As such, it may exercise all corporate powers necessary to perform the functions for which it was created. . . .[8]

Thus, the governmental structure for both public and private higher education in America was set. A corporate board, the courts ruled, *was* the university. It was to that body that the state had delegated power to perform the functions for which it was created. To be sure, this principle was often neglected. The integrity of the public university has been challenged many times by legislative interference, and that of the private college by donors or church officials. Still, a unique structure was in place. Reflecting a tradition rooted in Oxford, Paris, and Bologna, the independence of American higher education had been governmentally and judicially affirmed.

11

PART TWO

THE ACADEMY REGULATES ITSELF

III

GOVERNANCE ON THE CAMPUS

F ROM THE COLONIAL ERA to the mid-nineteenth century,
America's colleges, by today's standards, were easily managed. They were small, with uncomplicated organizations.
In 1850, the University of Michigan was among the largest institutions in the nation, yet it had only twenty faculty members. Historian
Laurence Veysey wrote that "early in the nineteenth century it had
been possible to speak of the officers of an entire college—its president, its faculty, and its trustees—as being of one and the same mind."[1]

Theoretically, trustees were at the center of institutional authority.
In practice, the mind of an early American college was preeminently
the mind of its president. Selected for an unlimited term by the board
of trustees, the president ordinarily served as their executive agent.
At the same time, he was the principal teacher of the college. Because
many college tutors were recent graduates on their way to a different
permanent occupation, "only the president could stand before the
governing body as a mature man of learning."[2]

Teachers in America's first colleges were a far cry from the
specialized and sophisticated professors of today. They were young.
They taught all subjects, and, for the most part, stayed with a single
class for four years. Their principal governance role was to assist the
president in regulating student behavior. At the fifty-one meetings of
the Dartmouth faculty in 1828-29, the main items of business were
student pranks and disorders.[3]

Gradually, however, campuses became larger, more complex. In

15

1870, colleges had an average of about ten faculty members and ninety students. By 1910, these averages had quadrupled and some institutions—Michigan and Harvard, for example—enrolled more than five thousand students.[4] Administrative duties were delegated and assignments made more formal. First, librarians were appointed, and then registrars. Deans became common in the 1890s and, at about the same time, a few of the larger universities appointed their first vice presidents.

Arthur Twining Hadley, president of Yale from 1899 to 1921, observed a shift in the presidential role. Hadley said that when he visited Noah Porter, president of Yale from 1871 to 1886, he would find him reading Kant in his "study." Much later, Hadley found Porter's successor, President Timothy Dwight, examining balance sheets in his "office."[5]

The shift noted by Hadley reflected the transformation of the American university between 1876 and 1910. Beginning at Johns Hopkins, influences from continental universities brought research and professionalism to the campus. Within forty years, the new university had displaced the old.

Universities also became home for a new kind of faculty. Ambitious, research-trained holders of the Ph.D. settled on campus, determined to make permanent careers of their academic disciplines. Curricula expanded, and the growth of intellectual specialization brought new power to the faculty. Only trained, sophisticated professionals could conduct the intellectual work of the American college and university.

Daniel Coit Gilman, president of Johns Hopkins University from 1875 to 1901 foresaw that: "The power of the University will depend upon the character of its resident staff of permanent professors."[6] Professor William Rainey Harper's 1902 description of governance at the University of Chicago spelled out this new faculty role in more detail:

> All questions involving financial expenditure fall within the province of the Trustees and are to be considered by them. . . . all appointments to office in the university are made directly by the Trustees upon recommendation of the President . . . on questions of fundamental policy, involving

the establishing of new Faculties and the change of statutes as established by the Trustees, final action is reserved for the Trustees themselves. *But it is a firmly established policy of the Trustees that the responsibility for the settlement of educational questions rests with the Faculties.*[7]

The growing numbers and specialization of faculty members led to the establishment of academic divisions and departments. By 1891, Harvard had reorganized into twelve divisions, each of which included at least one department. In 1893, Chicago had twenty-six departments and other leading universities followed the same trend.[8] Since 1900, the academic department has been the principal arrangement by which faculties participate in the governance of higher education.

Academic senates and other campuswide arrangements for faculty decision-making spread rapidly with the expansion of higher education following the Civil War. But, even with the growth of faculty influence on campus, presidents continued to have the dominant institutional voice. As late as 1912, a national poll showed that 85 percent of the American professors surveyed still felt limited in their authority and sought a greater degree of participation in campus affairs.[9]

In 1915, the newly founded American Association of University Professors (AAUP) adopted the historic General Declaration of Principles. The declaration argued that the professor must be free from any financial pressure "to hold, or to express, any conclusion which is not the genuine and uncolored product of his own study or that of fellow-specialists." [10] Like federal judges, the professor's tenure in office should be unconditional, and departures from the "scientific spirit and method" should be judged only by faculty peers. However:

> If this profession should prove itself unwilling to purge its ranks of the incompetent and the unworthy, or to prevent the freedom which it claims in the name of science from being used as a shelter for inefficiency, for superficiality, or for uncritical and intemperate partisanship, it is certain that the task will be performed by others. . . .[11]

Thus, faculty self-regulation was called upon to maintain independence of intellectual inquiry, the very core of an academic institution.

In 1966, a *Statement on Government of Colleges and Universities* was issued by the AAUP, the American Council on Education (ACE), and the Association of Governing Boards of Universities and Colleges (AGB). Describing the faculty role, the statement said:

> The faculty has primary responsibility for such fundamental areas as curriculum, subject matter and methods of instruction, research, faculty status, and those aspects of student life which relate to the educational process. On these matters the power of review or final decision lodged in the governing board or delegated by it to the president should be exercised adversely only in exceptional circumstances, and for reasons communicated to the faculty.[12]

The 1966 statement insisted on the importance of a campuswide perspective to faculty participation in campus governance. In order for the faculty to carry out its role:

> Agencies for faculty participation in the government of the college or university should be established at each level where faculty responsibility is present. An agency should exist for the presentation of the views of the whole faculty.[13]

With this statement, higher education's formal understanding of the place of faculty in governance moved beyond individual and departmental roles to affirm a campuswide responsibility.

In 1965, the role of faculty in the governance of American higher education took another significant turn. In that year the state of Michigan amended its laws to permit public employees to organize and bargain collectively. Two years later, New York's Taylor Law permitted, for the first time, public employees in that state—including teachers and college faculty members—to organize. New Jersey's Public Employment Relations Act followed in 1968. In 1970, the National Labor Relations Board (NLRB) changed its longstanding policy of excluding employees in private colleges and universities from coverage by the National Labor Relations Act.

To date, nearly thirty states permit public employees to unionize.[14] And, as of July 1981, faculty on 737 campuses were represented by an elected bargaining agent. Eighty-seven percent of all unionized colleges are public. Collective bargaining has been most successful in the community colleges and least successful at the major research universities.

One of the reasons collective bargaining has been resisted by some faculties is the fear that key policy decisions will shift from the campus and be politically controlled, either by central union officials or officers of the state. In our survey, we found that the governor's office handled collective bargaining negotiations in two of the responding states, New York and Pennsylvania; another executive branch office handles it in two others.

The faculty's ability to organize and bargain collectively at private institutions was challenged at Fordham University, C. W. Post Center (Long Island University), and Adelphi University. In each case, the National Labor Relations Board ruled that faculty were not "managerial employees" (who are exempt from the bargaining law) despite their role in academic governance.

However, in 1978, the United States Court of Appeals agreed with the administration of Yeshiva University that its faculty were "managerial employees" and thus the university was not required to negotiate with its own "management." The United States Supreme Court affirmed this opinion in February 1980, citing the "pervasive" influence of Yeshiva's faculty in virtually all areas of institutional policymaking, and stressing that the administration had implemented nearly all recommendations made by the faculty.[15]

The impact of the Supreme Court's decision was immediate and far reaching. At approximately forty private four-year colleges, administrators either refused to recognize an elected faculty union or to bargain with a union already recognized. Several college administrations filed challenges to the faculty union with the NLRB. Some unions were decertified, others were not. Unionization of faculty in the private sector nearly ceased.

Defining faculty as managers is in sharp contrast to the days when presidents ran the institution and faculty were kept busy controlling unruly students. Ironically, the court ruling recognizing the managerial role of faculty comes at the very time debate about governance and faculty participation appears to have declined and when college teachers on many campuses are not actively involved in key campuswide decisions.

In 1979, college presidents reported that although the academic senate had a high level of influence over curriculum and degree requirements and some influence in long-range planning, in all other areas of institutional policy the influence of the senate was rated low.[16]

Further, our data show that campus administrators continue to exercise a dominant influence in the formulation of education policies at a time when the Yeshiva decision encourages a broader, more communal view of academic governance.

At a 1981 AAUP conference on faculty governance Henry Mason, a noted scholar of the topic, observed that "faculty 'incivism' has increased." [17] Columbia University provides an example where a faculty member reported in the summer of 1977 "certain disillusionment concerning the Senate. . . ." This was supported by the fact that:

> . . . early Senate elections were hard fought contests between a substantial number of nominees but in the last few years there have never been more faculty nominees than vacancies (at least in the Arts and Sciences). Last year, despite an enormous amount of arm-twisting, the graduate school was unable to produce a sufficient number of nominees to fill the vacancies.[18]

Legally, the rights and responsibilities of faculty are still evolving. We are concerned, however, that a decline of faculty participation in campus governance is occurring when many campuses face cutbacks and retrenchment. Difficult choices must be made in the days ahead, and if campus integrity is to be preserved, all members of the academic community—administrators, faculty, and students—must responsibly engage in the governance of higher education.

IV

REGIONAL AND
NATIONAL ASSOCIATIONS

U NTIL THE MID-NINETEENTH CENTURY, each college in
America was, in academic matters, answerable largely to
itself. Educational practices spread informally from one
campus to another, and weak colleges borrowed from the more prestigious ones. Still, there were no formally agreed-upon national or
regional educational standards to be met.

However, as higher education expanded, pressures to establish
standards expanded, too. Between 1860 and 1890 more than 200
new collegiate institutions were freely chartered by the states.[1] Many
of the new colleges were born of religious fervor and local pride.
They were started almost overnight, with few questions asked by
government officials and with no significant oversight arrangements
within the academy itself. Thoughtful leaders recognized that if the
integrity of higher education was to be preserved, the nation's colleges
would have to find ways to regulate themselves.

Thus, a new dimension was added to the governance of higher
education. Self-regulation moved beyond the campus as educators
voluntarily came together to form associations, to set standards, and,
in time, to monitor the performance of their members. These new
oversight arrangements added greatly to the academic quality of
individual campuses and strengthened the integrity of higher education.

In 1905, Andrew Carnegie established a pension fund for college faculty members. To administer this program, the new Carnegie

Foundation for the Advancement of Teaching had to decide which institutions of higher learning were eligible to participate. The task was not easy. Henry Pritchett, president of the new Foundation, observed that "the terms *college* and *university* have, as yet, no fixed meaning on this continent." [2]

The Foundation's trustees, led by President Charles W. Eliot of Harvard, decided that, to be eligible, a college would have to meet four standards: first, an admission requirement of four years of preparatory or secondary school study; second, a minimum of six full-time professors; third, a four-year course in the arts and sciences; and fourth, a productive endowment of at least $200,000.[3] Crude as it was, a yardstick to measure colleges was in place.

The push for standards also cropped up on another front. In the late nineteenth century, college admissions requirements were in disarray. Preparatory schools had to provide a different course of study for every collegiate institution. In 1885, the principal of Phillips Academy at Andover, Massachusetts, complained that "out of over forty boys preparing for college next year, we have over twenty senior classes." [4]

In response to this confusion, the New England Association of Colleges and Secondary Schools and the Association of the Colleges and Secondary Schools of the Middle Atlantic States and Maryland came together in 1900 to standardize college admissions. Their deliberations led to creation of The College Entrance Examination Board. Within the next decade, twenty-five eastern colleges and universities adopted the new "College Board" examinations.

The protection of academic standards in higher education was also encouraged from abroad. In 1905, the newly minted Association of American Universities (AAU) received a letter from the philosophy faculty of the University of Berlin. Confused by the proliferation of colleges in America and uncertain as to which degrees should be accepted, the German professors had concluded that only those degrees awarded by members of the AAU would be recognized for advanced studies at the University of Berlin. The AAU was reluctant, however, to become the certifying agency for all of American higher education.

Meanwhile, United States government officials moved to fill

the void. In 1910, Kendric Babcock, the "specialist in higher educa-tion" in the Federal Bureau of Education, developed a list of American colleges and universities, classifying them on the basis of the success of their graduates in advanced study at AAU universities. The list had four categories, ranging from most to least successful. Only 17 percent of the American colleges were ranked in the first category.

When a prepublication copy of Babcock's proposal was circulated, educators—except, perhaps, those from the top 17 percent—were dismayed. The outcry was so intense that President William Howard Taft forbade its publication. Taft's successor, Woodrow Wilson, a former university president, refused to reverse the order. Samuel P. Capen, one of Babcock's successors, wryly observed, "The bureau learned that there are no second and third and fourth class colleges; that it was an outrage and an infamy so to designate institutions whose sons reflected honor on the state and the nation." [5]

The federal bureaucracy had learned its lesson well. Between 1917 and 1952, the Office of Education confined itself to publishing a list entitled *Accredited Higher Education Institutions.* This list merely reported the colleges and universities accredited by *other* agencies.[6] Government officials refused to do the job themselves.

After Babcock's defeat in this skirmish, the Association of American Universities reluctantly agreed to take a more active role in ranking colleges. In 1914, using, ironically, Babcock's yardstick of graduate success, the AAU produced a list of 119 accredited institutions. The association's own twenty-one members were included, plus all of the colleges approved by the Carnegie Foundation and institutions the Foundation would have approved had it not excluded sectarian schools. This list of AAU-accredited institutions was transmitted to the *Prussian Kultusministerium* and corresponding ministers of other German states.

In 1917, the AAU published a slightly longer list for use by the registrars of American graduate and professional schools. In 1923, the association began to visit institutions as a part of its evaluation proce-dure, a process that absorbed most of the association's energies until 1948. In that year, after publishing a list of 283 approved institu-tions, the association went out of the accreditation business. Thus, America's first and only national system of accrediting institutions of higher learning had come to an end.

At the turn of the century, regional accreditation was beginning to emerge, a voluntary procedure that would have enormous significance in the self-regulation of American higher education. On March 29, 1895, representatives of a number of midwestern colleges and universities met in Evanston, Illinois. The final question on their agenda was: "Shall steps be taken looking to cooperation with the New England and Middle States Associations in securing greater uniformity in secondary instruction and in the requirements for admission to college?" [7] The answer was affirmative, and the organization that resulted was the North Central Association.

Academics accepted self-regulation partly because they feared outside control. In 1908, Edmund J. James, the president of the University of Illinois, warned that "the standardization of colleges was going on apace by agencies not wholly in sympathy with them" and that "if the educators desired to have a hand in that matter, it behooved them to act promptly and courageously." [8] In 1909, after some hesitation, the North Central Association adopted explicit standards for higher education institutions in its region. Thus began the movement that would cause a college to be answerable, not only to itself, but also to peers from other institutions of higher learning.

The North Central criteria were rigorous. Colleges were required not only to have 120 semester hours for graduation, but also to be able "to prepare their graduates to enter recognized graduate schools as candidates for advanced degrees." The criteria specified the exact level of endowment or tax support necessary to maintain this educational program, required that library and laboratory equipment be "sufficient," and specified that the construction and maintenance of buildings insure "hygienic conditions." The final standard was general: "the character of the curriculum, the efficiency of instruction, the scientific spirit," as well as the standards for awarding degrees and the general "tone of the institution" would be considered. [9] The North Central Association published its first list of accredited colleges in 1913.

By 1934, educators had growing doubts about the effectiveness of rigid standards, and the North Central Association, which had been the first regional group to adopt a checklist of requirements, became the first to eliminate it. Henry M. Wriston, then president of the North Central Association, announced that in the future the association would become "less and less a policing body and more and more an organization designed to encourage, to stimulate, and to evaluate." [10]

The pattern set by North Central was followed elsewhere in the country. The Association of Colleges and Schools of Southern States (which became the Southern Association for Colleges and Schools in 1961) issued its first list of accredited colleges and univerties in 1919, and the Middle States Association followed in 1921. The Northwest Association of Secondary and High Schools was established in 1917, and within several years adopted North Central's practice and standards of institutional accreditation.

When the AAU discontinued accrediting in 1948, 53 percent of the nation's colleges and universities had been accredited by a regional association.[11] That year, the percentage of institutions that were regionally accredited began to rise even higher as the Western College Association began accrediting. Four years later, the New England Association voted to begin formal accreditation of colleges and universities. By the 1950s, the six regional associations had become a national network for accrediting colleges and universities [12] with emphasis on "assisting institutions" rather than on rigid standards.

In due course, voluntary accreditation was legislatively affirmed. The Servicemen's Readjustment Act of 1944—the so-called "G.I. Bill of Rights"—was the key. Under the law, veterans were entitled to education benefits if they attended institutions "approved" by state education agencies, but no one was sure how an institution was to achieve this approved status. The Veterans' Administration itself had no authority to tell states how to carry out this responsibility. As a result, fly-by-night programs were created. Shocking stories of scandal and abuse began to circulate.

In 1952, the rules were tightened. Congress directed the United States Commissioner of Education to help state agencies determine eligibility by "publishing a list of nationally recognized accrediting agencies and associations which he determines to be reliable authorities as to the quality of training offered by an educational institution." [13] The commissioner's first published list of twenty-eight approved accrediting associations was drawn largely from the National Commission on Accrediting, the umbrella association of accrediting bodies.

During the past thirty years, the commissioner's authority to approve accrediting associations has been reaffirmed in at least twenty-five separate statutes. And as accreditation received official blessing, more and more associations sought federal approval. An office called the Division of Eligibility and Agency Evaluation in the United States Office of Education developed detailed criteria to decide which accrediting agencies the government should approve. By 1982, sixty-four associations—both regional and professional—were on the commissioner's (now secretary's) list (Appendix A).[14] Self-regulation in American higher education was now backed by the power of the state. The bureaucracy was kept busy evaluating the evaluators. And access to billions of federal dollars has been limited to institutions accredited by agencies on the approved list.

A marriage of convenience had occurred. The government needed a yardstick to determine which colleges were eligible to participate in federal programs. Rather than do the job itself, educational associations from the private sector—accrediting bodies—were designated by government to act as gatekeepers.

The movement for voluntary self-regulation in American higher education has been remarkably successful. Through regional associations, colleges and universities took the initiative in setting and enforcing standards. Ironically, in the course of this study we found that some college leaders have a casual, and sometimes cynical, attitude toward accreditation.

For many colleges—especially the more prestigious ones—accreditation plays no strategic role and on such campuses preparation for an accreditation visit is perfunctory at best. One administrator, reflecting on his experience as a member of an accreditation team, summarized the situation very well:

> Higher education does not take accreditation seriously enough. It is broadly criticized, readily kicked about, and otherwise ignored. Faculties and administrators from our most esteemed colleges and universities have not been active participants in the process.[15]

The academy is not alone in its failure to regulate itself adequately. Other professions—medicine, law, business—also seem unwilling or unable to establish and maintain high standards. Also as competition for money and students grows more intense, colleges may be still less willing, voluntarily, to impose high standards of conduct on themselves. Yet, if the integrity of higher education is to be preserved, the strengthening of regional accreditation is urgently required. If higher education cannot or will not regulate itself, then public agencies, commercial college guides for students, and the courts will move in to fill the void.

V

SPECIALIZATION: A HOUSE DIVIDED

A S KNOWLEDGE EXPANDED and new disciplines emerged, specialized associations were formed, not only to serve as a forum for ideas but also to protect the special interests of their members. When these professional bodies began accrediting colleges and universities, a powerful new force was added to the informal governance structure of higher education.

The American Medical Association was the progenitor of the specialized accreditation movement in this country. Organized in 1847, it was, from the first, concerned with the quality of medical education. Between 1875 and 1914, some 15,000 doctors educated in Europe returned to the United States, bringing with them new insights about the importance of clinical training and research.[1] Medical schools were challenged to improve their curricula and to tighten entrance and graduation requirements.

The 1910 Flexner report on medical education, sponsored by The Carnegie Foundation for the Advancement of Teaching, had a powerful impact. The number of medical schools was reduced from 155 to 80. "The weak schools literally melted away."[2] In making his inspection of medical schools, Flexner had an "ideal" in mind; it was embodied in the Johns Hopkins Medical School, described by Flexner as "the first medical school in America of genuine university type."[3] Johns Hopkins became the standard against which all other medical colleges would be measured.

The success of medicine in setting standards did not go unnoticed. The American Dental Association published its first list of accredited schools in 1918, and the American Bar Association issued its first list in 1923. Throughout the 1920s, associations in fields such as landscape architecture, library science, and music began accrediting programs and institutions. In the 1930s, chemistry, engineering, forestry, and social work followed. Between 1900 and 1949, forty specialized groups became involved in accreditation.[4] Today, fifty-one are on the list approved by the Secretary of Education.

Professional accrediting began with a noble purpose: to establish, on a national basis, educational standards and practices that assure minimum competency of graduates of accredited schools. But by the 1940s, the political power of the process was becoming clear. In 1931, Samuel P. Capen, chancellor of the University of Buffalo, commented:

> When the "standardizing" movement began, there were literally hundreds of institutions, colleges, academies, medical schools, law schools, and dental schools that were selling to the public—often at considerable profit to their backers—educational gold bricks. . . . No such brilliant success has ever attended any other movement in American education.[5]

Only eight years later, however, Capen reversed himself, decrying the fragmentation of academic life:

> I am against standardizing, any standardizing whatever, and against all accrediting. . . . The issue is plain. Is the American university system to be dominated by competitive blackmail, or is it to be conducted in accordance with the best judgment of the boards and administrative officers charged with this responsibility through charters and through legislative enactments? [6]

In 1940, according to the United States government's *Educational Directory,* Samuel Capen's own privately controlled University of Buffalo was accredited by two groups: the Association of American Universities and the Middle States Association. By 1980, the *Directory* reported that the now public State University of New York at Buffalo was accredited by *eighteen* separate organizations. Six additional organizations accredited the State University of New York Health Sciences Center at Buffalo. Buffalo's list of accreditations includes National Architectural Accrediting Board; National Association of Schools of Art; American Speech, Language and Hearing Association; American Assembly of Collegiate Schools of Business; American Psychological Association (clinical); American Psychological Association (counseling); and the list goes on.[7]

While professional associations moved to raise the standards of their profession, some groups also used the accrediting process to impose unreasonable and restrictive standards on the campuses.

The American Occupational Therapy Association, for example, spells out in detail how it expects to be involved in the administration of campus programs. The accreditation standards of the association include this telling statement:

> When the Director of the educational program is replaced, immediate notification shall be sent to the accrediting organization(s). The curriculum vitae of the new director, giving details of training, education and experience in the field, must be submitted. These credentials must be acceptable in order that the current accreditation status of the program be continued.[8]

The Council on Chiropractic Education goes one step further. This body, in its accreditation guidelines, sets forth budgeting standards as follows:

> It is felt that an institution depending upon tuition monies for more than 80 percent of its total educational and general expense is in a precarious position.[9]

And the American Veterinary Association calls for sweeping authority to review decisions of the campus:

> When an accredited or approved college contemplates fundamental changes in its administration, organization, association with its parent institution, curriculum, faculty, organization, instructional program, or stated objectives, the Council should be provided an opportunity to review the proposed changes prior to adoption.[10]

The Accrediting Bureau of Medical Laboratory Schools, now the Accrediting Bureau of Health Education Schools, requires that the institution being accredited provide intricate administrative detail:

> All accredited institutions are required to report the names of full-time and part-time instructors, listing their educational qualifications, affiliations, and other data the Bureau may require regarding the faculty members. Any changes in faculty shall be reported to the Bureau within 30 days.[11]

The American Assembly of Collegiate Schools of Business actually dictates, through accreditation, the advanced degrees the faculty must have:

> As a measure of the faculty's teaching, research, applied knowledge, and overall scholarly capability, at least 80 percent of the full-time equivalent academic staff . . . will possess qualifications such as the Ph.D., DBA, JD, or LLB, masters with professional certification such as the CPA, and appropriate masters degrees (or the equivalent).[13]

Specialized accrediting bodies often dictate detailed teaching load requirements. For the business schools the proposed faculty load is twelve credit hours; in chemistry it is fifteen contact hours; eight to nine contact hours are required for teachers of lecture courses in art. And, according to accreditation standards, the maximum faculty-student ratios must be 1:15 in journalism; 1:10 in dietetics; 1:14 in landscape architecture; 1:20 in forestry.[12]

Many specialized agencies even dictate the exact length of the academic program. Podiatry, requires that the minimum length of the professional curriculum "shall be four academic years. An academic year is defined as at least 30 instructional weeks."[14] The law schools insist on a total of ninety full weeks of work, defining a "class hour" as "a unit of classroom instruction of 50 to 60 minutes in duration. An additional fraction of a class hour may only be completed in increments of 10 minutes or more. Examples of acceptable units of instruction are 50, 60, 70, 80, and 90 minutes in duration."[15] The chiropractors require a minimum of 4,200 hours presented over eight semesters.[16]

31

The unevenness of specialized accreditation also should be noted. Why, for example, should some disciplinary associations accredit institutions while others do not. Why engineering but not physics or mathematics? Why business but not economics? Why social work but not sociology? Why journalism but not English?

We are especially concerned about the linkages between specialized accreditation and occupational licensure by state governments. Between 1870 and 1900, forty-six statutes licensing seventeen occupations were enacted. An even larger flood of legislation occurred between 1911 and 1915. During this four-year period, 110 statutes licensing twenty-four occupations were enacted. By 1952, seventy-five occupations were licensed by one or more states.[17]

Through this process, specialized associations, indirectly at least, also control key decisions on the campus. At least twenty-one specialized accrediting associations have persuaded states that graduation from an accredited program is necessary for licensure in that occupation. Today such licensing requirements enable specialized accrediting agencies to wield enormous power over higher education. Legally, the power to license rests with the state. In fact, specialized associations have been relied upon far beyond their founders' dreams to dictate legislation.

The state does, of course, have a stake in the health and safety of its citizens. And establishing state-controlled standards for practitioners in certain fields is crucial. Still, it is hard to believe that health and safety standards extend to all of the occupations that are now licensed by a state or local government, including real estate, private detecting, plumbing, and landscape architecture. It is even more difficult to believe that practitioners in twenty-one separate fields must graduate from an accredited program before they can even qualify to take the state licensing examination. Such specialized accreditation, when linked to certification by the state, has, to some considerable degree, weakened the authority of the campus.

The issue is not whether scholars should organize into disciplinary associations. Nor is the setting of standards being challenged. Rather, it is how detailed the oversight requirements should be and, in the larger sense, how these detailed requirements relate to the integrity of the campus and to the ability of each institution to control essential academic matters.

If specialized accreditation is used to protect the turf of a specific department against the larger interests of the institution, the campus becomes a holding company for special interests, receiving from each professional team its non-negotiable demands. Then, the integrity of higher education is violated by pressure from within.

PART THREE

IN SERVICE TO THE NATION

VI

THE STATE: FROM EXPANSION TO RETRENCHMENT

MIDPOINT IN THIS CENTURY, the nation's colleges and universities were called upon to serve more students and generate new knowledge. Old campuses were expanded. New campuses were built. Laboratories were refurbished, and massive numbers of students were enrolled. Almost overnight the relationship between higher education and government took a dramatic turn. Colleges and universities that had, for years, lived in relative isolation now found themselves caught up in national objectives.

State government took the lead in this expansion. In 1950, the states contributed $490 million to the operating incomes of public colleges and universities. By 1980 they were providing $17.6 billion annually.[1] From 1950 to 1980, enrollment in the public sector increased from 1.1 to 9.0 million students.[2] The number of public institutions more than doubled[3] and during the decade of the 1960s two-year colleges grew at the rate of nearly one each week.[4]

Private institutions also felt the impact of this expansion. Between 1950 and 1980, more than 465 new independent institutions were established, financed, in this case, mainly by nonpublic funds. Enrollment in the private sector more than doubled—from 1.1 to 2.5 million students.[5]

With this expansion, the governance structure of American higher education became more complex. From 1950 to 1970, many public colleges and universities were reorganized into multicampus "systems" with a single governing board. Some states organized several multicampus systems. Free-standing public institutions increasingly became the exception rather than the rule. Today, in twenty-one states, a single "consolidated" board governs all of public higher education in the state.

Statewide coordinating councils or commissions formed yet another tier of decision-making in higher education. As budgets and enrollments burgeoned, "coordination" became the code word for efficiency and rational planning. In some states, coordinating units were organized as early as 1940. By 1982, all but three states (Delaware, Vermont, and Wyoming) had a coordinating agency for higher education (See Table 1).

The authority granted to these coordinating boards varied greatly from state to state. In nineteen states, the agency has regulatory functions in specific areas such as budget review. Seven states have coordinating agencies that are advisory only. In the twenty-one states with a single consolidated governing board, the coordinating function is served by that board.

Master planning became the order of the day. By the end of the growth decade of the 1960s, thirty-eight states had adopted or drafted master plans. In the same number of states the higher education coordinating agency was given authority to prepare a consolidated higher education budget.

Meanwhile, statewide coordination was being pushed by Congress. The Higher Education Facilities Act of 1963 required that states participating in federal programs "shall designate . . . an existing state egency . . . or, if no such agency exists, shall establish such a state agency to coordinate plans with the federal government. . . ."[6] Similar provisions found their way into the Higher Education Act of 1965.

In the Education Amendments of 1972, section 1202 authorized the states to designate a new or existing state agency as the recipient of federal funds available for the improvement of postsecondary planning. This law inspired fifteen states to create new agencies. It also required that the coordinating agency be broadly "representative of *all* education."[7] Thus, through the 1202 commissions, private colleges and universities were given a voice in state coordination of higher education.

In the 1970s, growth slowed and budgets tightened in many states. "Avoiding duplication," "slowing proliferation," and "cutting out wasteful programs" became urgent new priorities even though no one seemed quite sure where the surgery should begin or end.

State budget officers and legislative oversight committees tightened their control over fiscal and administrative responsibilities traditionally controlled by presidents, vice presidents, and deans. State coordinating officers turned to the review of academic programs, a function historically controlled by faculties and accrediting associations.

What has been the impact of this new relationship between the campus and the state? With public officials increasingly involved in the oversight of higher education, has the integrity of colleges and universities been threatened?

The creation of new coordinating boards as intermediate units—standing between the campus and the legislature or governor's office—was a reasonable approach during an era of spectacular expansion. While campus autonomy in administrative matters was predictably restricted, the intellectual freedom of the nation's colleges rarely was challenged. The new planning structures and new accountability obligations were a small price to pay for the dramatic social and academic gains that were made because of state support.

Further, the results of our own survey of decision-making in higher education strongly suggest that control beyond the trustee level remains quite limited. In only eight states are government agencies involved in a significant number of the key decision areas that were studied. Presently, Pennsylvania, Connecticut, Florida, and New York are, in that order, the most restrictive.

Statewide planning, however, has changed the governance structure of higher education. America's colleges and universities are no longer viewed as wholly independent institutions. Instead, they have become "units" in a "statewide system." Private institutions often are included in this "integrated network" even though their location was frequently an accident of history and even though their outreach often extends far beyond the boundaries of the state.

Looking ahead, we see new dangers in the relationship between the campus and the state.

TABLE 1.
EVOLUTION OF COORDINATING PATTERNS WITHIN STATES

State	Before 1940	1940-1949	1950-1959	1960-1964	1965-1969	1970-1982
Alabama	I	I	I	I	III	IIIa
Alaska	IV	IV	IV	IV	IV	IV
Arizona	I	IV	IV	IV	IV	IV
Arkansas	I	I	II	III	III	III
California	I	II	II	III	III	III
Colorado	I	I	I	II	IIIa	IIIa
Connecticut	I	I	I	I	IIIa	IIIa
Delaware	I	I	I	I	I	I
Florida	IV	IV	IV	IV	IV	IV
Georgia	IV	IV	IV	IV	IV	IV
Hawaii	IV	IV	IV	IV	IV	IV
Idaho	IV	IV	IV	IV	IV	IV
Illinois	I	II	III	IIIa	IIIa	IIIa
Indiana	I	I	II	II	II	IIIa
Iowa	IV	IV	IV	IV	IV	IV
Kansas	IV	IV	IV	IV	IV	IV
Kentucky	III	III	III	III	III	IIIa
Louisiana	I	I	I	I	IIIa	IIIa
Maine	I	I	I	I	IV	IV
Maryland	I	I	I	III[1]	IIIa	IIIa
Massachusetts	I	I	I	I	IIIa	IV
Michigan	I	I	II	II[2]	III	III
Minnesota	I	I	II	II	III	III
Mississippi	IV	IV	IV	IV	IV	IV
Missouri	I	I	II	III	III	IIIa

I   No state agency
II   Voluntary coordination
III   Coordinating board; advisory powers
IIIa   Coordinating board; regulatory powers
IV   Consolidated governing board

	Before 1940	1940-1949	1950-1959	1960-1964	1965-1969	1970-1982
Montana	IV	IV	IV	IV	IV	IV
Nebraska	I	I	I	I	II	III
Nevada	IV	IV	IV	IV	IV	IV
New Hampshire	I	I	I	IV	IV	IV
New Jersey	I	I	I	I	IIIa	IIIa
New Mexico	I	I	IIIa	IIIa	IIIa	IIIa
New York	IIIa	IIIa	IIIa	IIIa	IIIa	IIIa
North Carolina	I	I	IIIa	IIIa	IIIa	IV
North Dakota	IV	IV	IV	IV	IV	IV
Ohio	I	II	II	IIIa	IIIa	IIIa
Oklahoma	I	IIIa	IIIa	IIIa	IIIa	IIIa
Oregon	IV	IV	IV	IV	IV	III^3
Pennsylvania	I	I	I	III	III	IIIa
Rhode Island	IV	IV	IV	IV	IV	IV
South Carolina	I	I	I	III	IIIa	IIIa
South Dakota	IV	IV	IV	IV	IV	IV
Tennessee	I	I	I	I	IIIa	IIIa
Texas	I	I	IIIa	IIIa	IIIa	IIIa
Utah	I	I	III	III	IV	IV
Vermont	I	I	I	I	I	I
Virginia	I	I	III	III	III	IIIa
Washington	I	I	I	II	III	III
West Virginia	I	I	I	I	IV	IV
Wisconsin	I	I	III	III	IIIa	IV
Wyoming	IV	IV	IV	IV	IV	I

1. Became a coordinating board with advisory powers (III) in 1962 and a coordinating board with regulatory powers in 1963.
2. Became a coordinating board with advisory powers in 1964.
3. A coordinating agency was established in 1975 to oversee all public and private educational systems, but the consolidated governing board also continues to operate for postsecondary education.

Source: This table has been adapted from Robert O. Berdahl, *Statewide Coordination of Higher Education,* Washington, D.C.: American Council on Education, 1971, pp. 34-35.

Our survey shows, for example, that when academic decisions are dominated by budget considerations, effective authority tends to move beyond the campus. In such matters as determining campus missions and establishing undergraduate, graduate, or professional programs, state officials become more active. In at least three states, the legislature now determines student-faculty ratios.

In several states, government agencies also have moved to evaluate and eliminate academic programs. This, we conclude, is a move in the wrong direction. If such program review is expanded, and if external bodies not only report their findings but actually terminate, reduce, or transfer programs, dangerous precedents will be established. Such actions by a state agency could, by accident or design, fundamentally change the mission of a campus through a process in which the governing board, the president, and the faculty are bypassed. Further, for the state to decide which programs are "acceptable" and "unacceptable" may open the door not only for *academic* oversight, but *political* oversight as well.

Educational quality is, of course, essential, and states have a right to call upon universities to review periodically their academic programs and report their findings. Also, state officials may join accrediting teams in their regular campus visits, and request accrediting bodies to make special visits to examine selected fields of study. In the end, however, the academy must assume primary responsibility for this function.

On quite a different front, we are troubled that the enrollment-driven budget formulas adopted during an era of rapid growth continue to be used during a period of decline. The facts are brutally simple. If enrollment declines, the costs to the college are not proportionately diminished. Classrooms must still be maintained and professors must still be paid. If enrollment-driven funding formulas are rigidly applied during a period of decline, the impact will be a sharp erosion in the quality of education.

Some states have considered new budgeting procedures that distinguish between costs that vary with enrollment, and those that are fixed. Ohio has developed new plans that would maintain between 70 and 75 percent of state funding for an institution even if its enrollment falls 40 percent. A proposal in Oregon relates funding not to the traditional average cost per students, but to the cost of maintaining educational quality based on funding levels in comparable states. We believe every state should develop budgeting procedures that go beyond the simplistic, enrollment-driven yardstick.

We are also disturbed that state governments often fail to reward efficient leaders. All too often, savings automatically revert to the state. Flexibility is denied, and money cannot be transferred from one budget category to another. In the process, incentives for efficiency are destroyed.

Again, a few states are breaking out of this counterproductive rigidity. In Colorado, the University adopted a system of performance budgeting that provides for internal review of the cost and quality of its programs. In response, the legislature eased its control, reducing the number of specific categories in the university's budget from seventeen to one.

If state control is too restrictive, and if uniform formulas are rigidly imposed, one of the most important qualities of American higher education—diversity within and among campuses—will be lost. Nell Eurich, in a comparative study of higher education systems, contends that strengthening diversity should be an explicit goal of statewide coordination along with the more traditional goals of efficiency and equity. She observes:

> If diversity is to be preserved and increased to provide for the untold interests and abilities of man—the great learning potential—then the also human tendency to organize affairs to the point of uniformity must be wisely controlled and examined carefully at each step to strengthen the differentiation within higher education systems.[8]

It would be ironic indeed if state supervision of higher education were to become unduly bureaucratic and heavy handed at the very time decentralization and self-regulation are gaining favor elsewhere. Increased oversight does not necessarily lead to greater efficiency and effectiveness in any organization, especially in higher education. In fact, if campuses are not actively involved when tough decisions must be made, authority is drained, priorities become confused, morale plummets, and efficiency declines.

Without question, the state's role in the expansion of higher education has been remarkably successful. Colleges have been chartered and budgets have skyrocketed. Clearly, the benefits of state support have far outdistanced the abuses.

We warn, however, that to impose suffocating requirements on colleges at a time when flexibility is required is the wrong prescription. In a climate of retrenchment, the nation's campuses must be given incentives to achieve efficiency in the management of their affairs. To cut back in both money and flexibility is to make a difficult situation almost hopeless.

VII

THE FEDERAL CONNECTION:
MORE STUDENTS, MORE RESEARCH

W HILE STATE GOVERNMENTS provided *general* support
for the nation's public colleges and universities, the
federal government, during the past forty years *targeted*
its support on two critical national objectives: expanding student
access and generating new knowledge. As federal funding massively
increased, Washington became deeply involved in the fiscal and administrative oversight of higher education.

The Servicemen's Readjustment Act of 1944—the G.I. Bill—
was a watershed. By 1956, the United States government had spent
about $5.5 billion on higher education for veterans.[1] Nearly 8 million
veterans eventually received training, and over 2 million of them
attended colleges and universities.[2] In spectacular fashion, higher
learning and the federal government had become inextricably inter-
locked.

In 1965, Congress passed the Higher Education Act. That law,
with its Educational Opportunity Grants and Guaranteed Student
Loans, further extended Washington's role in higher education. Expanding access became national policy. In 1972, Congress transformed
the act's benefits into direct entitlements to needy students. The Middle Income Student Assistance Act of 1978 made still more students
eligible for federal loans and grants. In 1981, federal student aid in
the Department of Education alone totalled over $6 billion.[3]

Even before the explosive impact of the G.I. Bill, the nation's universities were linked to the federal government on another front. In 1941, Vannevar Bush, a pioneer in computer science, former president of the Massachusetts Institute of Technology, and later president of the Carnegie Institution of Washington, took the lead in establishing what became the Office of Scientific Research and Development. The approach of this new agency was novel. James Conant, president of Harvard and a participant in the effort, wrote of it:

> I shall never forget my surprise at hearing about this revolutionary scheme. Scientists were to be mobilized for the defense effort in their own laboratories. A man who we thought could do a job was going to be asked to be the chief investigator; he would assemble a staff in his own laboratory if possible; he would make progress reports to our committee through a small organization of part-time advisers and full-time staff.[4]

As the war drew to a close, Vannevar Bush—in response to a request from President Roosevelt—urged a federal commitment to basic research in peacetime. Bush's publication, *Science, the Endless Frontier: A Report to the President on a Program for Postwar Scientific Research*, released in 1945, is the fundamental text for the modern partnership between government and university science. Bush wrote:

> The publicly and privately supported colleges, universities, and research institutes are the centers of basic research. They are the wellsprings of knowledge and understanding. As long as they are vigorous and healthy and their scientists are free to pursue the truth wherever it may lead, there will be a flow of new scientific knowledge to those who can apply it to practical problems in government, or in industry, or elsewhere.[5]

By becoming the university's major patron for research, the federal government assumed new obligations. The most obvious was financial. The level of federal support for university research increased from less than $40 million in 1940 to $138 million in 1953 to $3.4 billion in 1979.

What, in fact, has been the governance impact of the expanded

46

federal role in higher education? Has increased federal support threatened the integrity of the campus? If so, where have the threats been most acute?

We conclude that, tensions notwithstanding, the student aid partnership between government and higher education—from a public policy perspective—has been outstandingly successful. While there have been skirmishes from time to time, and while the administrative burden is severe, millions of students have been helped and the academic integrity of institutions has not been undermined. Most colleges agree that the paperwork is a small price to pay for the expansion of educational opportunity and the increase in student choice.

Still, there have been problems. As student aid became a multi-billion-dollar program, government oversight predictably expanded. In 1964, the General Accounting Office released a critical report on the student loan program. The title itself is revealing: *Weaknesses in Administration of Student Loan Programs Under Title II of the National Defense Education Act of 1958.* A year later, a House subcommittee announced a 16 percent delinquency rate under the National Defense Student Loan Program.[6] Poor institutional management was blamed.

Troubled by what appeared to be inadequate administration of student aid and embarrassed by sensationalized headlines about defaults on loans, Congress began to tighten the legislative screws. Two astute observers of the debate on the Education Amendments of 1972 wrote:

> The 1972 Act reinforces the mandate of the General Accounting Office . . . to audit federal education programs. . . . The GAO is also directed to 'evaluate' federal education programs and projects. . . . Finally, the law also incorporates provisions that seem to move federal policy in the direction of cost accounting standards.[7]

The fat was in the fire. Colleges and universities were discovering that federal support meant federal oversight as well. The Office of Education built a separate system for monitoring student assistance funds. Private collectors were hired by the government to track down defaulters. Campuses were required to secure outside biennial audits of student aid funds and report the findings to Washington.

In administering the G.I. Bill, the Veterans' Administration (VA) issued rules on everything from institutional eligibility to attendance records. Campuses were, quite properly, disturbed by these crude attempts to dictate how they should carry on their work. In 1976, Wayne State University sued the VA when the agency reduced benefits to veterans enrolled in the university's College of Lifelong Learning, a program that emphasizes independent study. The university's president, George E. Gullen, Jr., labeled the action a "severe and unwarranted intrusion into the academic governance" of the institution, arguing that the regulation "presumes that academic quality of a program is a direct function of classroom contact hours." [8] The Federal Court of Appeals, however, upheld the right of the VA to take the action challenged by Wayne State. The university was forced to modify its program.

The dramatic expansion of federal student aid programs also opened an old wound—how to determine which colleges are eligible for federal funds. While the government traditionally had relied on private accreditation agencies, this process did not weed out financially shaky and administratively careless institutions. Many colleges—even with accreditation—had high default rates on student loans. But if accreditation teams cannot measure fiscal integrity, who is to decide? The issue came to a head in 1980 when the Carter Administration proposed to sever the relationship between institutional eligibility and accreditation. The Department of Education itself would evaluate colleges, thus reintroducing the battle Kendric Babcock engaged in forty years before. Congress, like President Taft, rejected the proposal.

In 1982, Secretary of Education Terrel Bell acted unilaterally to weed out institutions with a poor track record in the administration of student aid. He declared that any previously eligible institution with a student default rate of 25 percent would be restricted in participating in the direct student loan program, irrespective of its accreditation status.

In assessing the impact of federal student aid on the nation's campuses, there remains one overarching issue. Today, hundreds of campuses receive much of their annual revenue from these programs. A network of federally-dependent institutions has been created and the distinction between public and private colleges has been blurred.

In 1978, federal student aid funds (excluding guaranteed loans) were equal to about 50 percent of the tuition revenues at public comprehensive colleges, and to more than 45 percent of tuition income at public two-year colleges.

At private liberal arts colleges, federal student aid, (again exclusive of guaranteed loans) was equivalent to more than 25 percent of the tuition revenues. In aggregate, this federal support represents about 13 percent of the total income of private liberal arts colleges—a level of dependence that would have startled private college presidents not many years ago.[9]

The governance implications of this dependency are profound. American higher education is only beginning to grasp the significance of having all campuses, in some measure, financially dependent on Washington. This may, in the long run, prove to be the most important governance issue to be faced.

We do not propose that the federal student aid programs should be restricted. Equality of opportunity must continue as the bedrock educational policy of this nation. We do suggest, however, that individual colleges monitor closely their sources of support, seeking to avoid a disproportionate dependence on federal aid. And we remind government officials that, in the administration of these programs, maximum flexibility and continuity are essential.

HOW ABOUT THE GROWTH of federal support for university-based research? What has been the governance impact of this program? Has academic integrity been threatened?

Once again, the relationship between government and higher education has been, from a national perspective, remarkably rewarding. Federally-financed research laboratories contributed greatly to the Allied victory. The development of radar to which the Massachusetts Institute of Technology made crucial contributions, may, alone have saved Great Britain from invasion. During the war, almost everyone agreed that the interests of both government and the university were well served by the nation's support of basic and applied research.

This comfortable relationship—too comfortable perhaps—between the federal government and the nation's leading universities was fostered at least, in part, by those who ran the program. Almost without exception, directors of federal research agencies came from university campuses. They understood the traditions of higher education. No one, not even a hard-headed politician, was inclined to challenge the system of peer review used to select projects and maintain quality control.

This is not to say that the relationship between government and the campus has been friction-free. Billions of public dollars could not be sent to the nation's universities without an occasional conflict over how the money should be spent. The annual "indirect cost" negotiation between a university and the government, for example, has often been a source of irritation. The university wants more support to cover so-called "hidden costs," while federal funding agencies have identified abuses and, understandably, are suspicious of paying for costs not directly related to the projects they fund. Today, institutional indirect cost rates vary greatly. Among the twenty largest National Institutes of Health grantees, the range is from a high of 63.8 percent to a low of 24.4 percent.[10]

Also, federal officials have repeatedly charged that university accounting and management are unsound. A 1978 General Accounting Office report concluded that campus procedures did not "provide a reliable basis to verify the validity of many direct costs charged to research, especially personnel costs" and that "many of these charges are not related to the specific grant charged."[11] Another General Accounting Office study held that universities did not have the inventory systems needed to avoid duplication in the purchase of equipment already available on the campus.[12]

In response to these charges, the Office of Management and Budget proposed in 1979 controversial new guidelines. Among other things, the proposed regulations, popularly known as Circular A-21 Revised, called for a reporting and categorizing of 100 percent of the activities of researchers supported by federal funds.[13] Academics were appalled. Such detailed requirements, they argued, reflected ignorance of the nature of research. One university medical researcher put the point bluntly: the government's "petty requirements" were a "dishonest ritual." [14] Also, A. Bartlett Giamatti, president of Yale University, commented that "some individuals in the government must misunderstand completely that it is impossible to segregate teaching from research from administration in doing basic research and to assign percentages to these false distinctions." [15]

The irony is that government's call for more detailed accounting procedures did not originate in the actual misuse of funds. In fact, during fiscal year 1977, the Department of Health, Education and Welfare audited $1.2 billion worth of research grants and contracts to institutions of higher education and found that only $13.2 million had been misspent or misapplied. [16] The "violations"—which included such technical matters as charging time or purchases to the wrong grant—accounted for a mere 1.1 percent of the total amount audited. By contrast, HEW's own error rate was estimated to be about 6 percent. [17] Government's real concern seemed to be that about $420 million of the $1.2 billion "was not adequately documented, as required by federal rules,"—not that there was clear evidence of abuse. [18]

Procedural problems such as these have caused friction. However, the fundamental question is this: To what extent has the research relationship between the federal government and the campus violated the integrity of the university? Has the independence of scholars—their right to conduct research and disseminate results freely —been threatened? We conclude that, with few exceptions, the federally-funded research program has been appropriately administered by agencies in Washington. Conflicting interests of government and science usually have been resolved in a spirit of cooperation. In short, we consider it a great achievement that so much public money has been channeled to the nation's campuses with so little interference.

However, several recent episodes have raised red flags that cannot be ignored. In the mid 1970s, there was vigorous debate over how best to regulate research on recombinant DNA. Both scientists and laymen were concerned that the creation of novel organisms could endanger public health. After a group of scientists declared a moratorium on this form of research, the National Institutes of Health developed guidelines for genetic engineering experiments. Government held, quite properly we believe, that it had an obligation to protect the rights, health, and safety of citizens. In principle at least, this obligation appeared to take precedence over a scientist's right to direct, without restriction, his own inquiry. Still, the government's original regulations, which were considered unduly restrictive, were modified as the university demonstrated its awareness of the health and safety issues involved and developed machinery to monitor itself.

HEW's move to protect the rights of human subjects also threatened to involve a federal agency too deeply in research. The agency's proposed regulations called for prior review of research designs, were also extended to research *not* funded by the government, and required prior consent of subjects even in studies with little or no potential harm. Such intrusive oversight would have threatened the integrity of higher education. In the end, government backed off, delegating enforcement, through a peer review process, to the academy itself.

Finally, there is the delicate issue of national security. During World War II, universities usually accepted secret military contracts without question. However, such contracts were heatedly debated during the 1960s, and, with the emergence of the nuclear freeze movement, they have become so again. Some scientists have refused, on principle, to engage in such investigations, arguing that it violates the whole notion of free and open inquiry. Questions surrounding this clash of fundamental values continue to be unresolved.

Today, for example, government officials fear that unrestrained publication of cryptography research could help scientists in other nations break our highly secret and sensitive codes. They also warn that visiting foreign scholars could carry away knowledge about such fields as robotics that would neutralize our technological advantage in emerging disciplines. Early in 1982, Admiral Bobby Inman, then deputy director of the Central Intelligence Agency, warned that unless universities allowed the government to review research results with military applications before they were published a "tidal wave of public outrage" would force the government to impose stringent restrictions.[19]

Research scholars on the other hand, emphasize that free discourse is the lifeblood of our scientific preeminence. William Carey, executive officer of the American Association for the Advancement of Science, warned that if proposed expansion of government classification of scientific research were adopted, "much of the normal discourse of science will be silenced and progress arrested. If we then doubled the federal dollars for basic research, I do not think it would make up our losses."[20]

In a move to mediate these conflicting interests, the American Council on Education developed procedures by which cryptography scholars voluntarily submit papers for review by the National Security Agency. The National Academy of Sciences decided to review government restrictions on visiting scholars to see if they were "workable and compatible with the general procedures for conducting unclassified research in an academic environment."[21] Conflicts between academic freedom and national security will never be completely resolved, but the work of these mediating agencies indicates how compromises can be fashioned.

This brings us back to the essential point. The most fundamental threat to institutions of higher learning is interference—either accidental or by design—in the actual conduct of research. When this occurs, the integrity of the institution is eroded. While the federal government has generally been respectful of the university's right to independence, we view with apprehension any move to introduce political ideology into the process of peer review, or to dictate the topics and the terms of research support. Such a policy undermines the very foundation of creative inquiry upon which the university is built.

In the days ahead, government's role in the conduct of research will grow more, not less, complex. As new knowledge pushes us further and further into inquiries that could profoundly affect the quality of life on earth, new tensions inevitably will emerge. Matters addressed by science increasingly will be moral and ethical in character, sometimes having practical, even life-and-death implications for the national welfare. Manipulation of genes involves researchers in the control of life forms. Biological control of crop pests also has disturbing military implications. Where is the line to be drawn? By whom?

Success in reconciling these potentially serious differences suggests the following: when the fundamental rights of the campus and the fundamental responsibilities of government collide, public officials have an obligation to pose the basic questions, develop general guidelines, and then give the university the opportunity voluntarily to regulate itself. Universities, in turn, have a responsibility to meet the challenge. Only a relatively few higher learning institutions have been significantly touched by these massive increases in public research funding. Still, those institutions involved are among the nation's most distinguished, and if their integrity is eroded the entire enterprise is threatened.

We conclude that the nation's research institutions, individually and collectively, must be fully accountable in the expenditure of research funds. However, we also conclude that they must vigorously resist any regulation that would impose limits on the conduct of research and weaken the integrity of the institution at its core.

VIII

CONGRESS, THE COURTS, AND CIVIL RIGHTS

W ITH ITS LANDMARK decision in *Brown* v. *Board of Education* in 1954, the United States Supreme Court launched a social revolution that would profoundly affect the control of higher education. A succession of sweeping laws guaranteeing equal opportunity to all Americans has had a substantial impact on the relationships among the academy, the federal bureaucracy, the courts, and society at large. Such laws and related court actions were required to overcome inequity toward members of minorities, women, and handicapped people, and to accomplish reforms that higher education had too long neglected or openly resisted.

The key legislative measure promoting equal rights was the deceptively brief Title VI of the Civil Rights Act of 1964, which outlawed discrimination on the basis of race, color, or national origin in "any program or activity receiving federal financial assistance."[1] The same act, under Title VII, also bars discrimination in employment on the basis of sex as well as the other categories. In 1965, President Lyndon B. Johnson issued Executive Order 11246 requiring all federal government contractors to take affirmative action to end discrimination. As amended in 1967, the order also forbade discrimination on the basis of sex.

At first, colleges and universities were exempted from the provisions of Title VII, but, in 1972, Congress amended the act to include higher education. In taking this step, Congress declared:

It is difficult to imagine a more sensitive area than educational institutions, where the youth of the Nation are exposed to a multitude of ideas and impressions that will strongly influence their future development. To permit discrimination here would, *more than in any other area,* tend to promote existing misconceptions and stereotypical categorizations which in turn would lead to future patterns of discrimination.[2]

The 1972 Education Amendments (specifically Title IX) barred discrimination on the basis of sex in educational institutions. A year later, Section 504 of the Rehabilitation Act prohibited discrimination on the basis of handicap in any federally assisted program or activity. As in the 1964 Civil Rights Act, these laws gave government the power to cut off federal funds to any institution found to be in non-compliance.

In the 1970s, federally mandated health and safety requirements were extended to the nation's campuses. Higher education also felt the impact of the consumer protection movement. In 1974, the so-called "Buckley Amendment" gave students the right to control their personal college records. It is at points such as these—where issues of individual rights and social justice intersect with long-established and deeply cherished traditions of academic governance—that the academy confronts some of its thorniest dilemmas.

This brings us to the fundamental question: In matters relating to the enforcement of individual rights, has an appropriate balance been maintained between public accountability and the integrity of the campus?

The point of departure for any discussion of these problems must be for institutions of higher education to acknowledge past failures to promote equality and to reaffirm their absolutely unwavering commitment to fairness and equity for all in matters of recruitment, hiring, and advancement. Colleges also should acknowledge that discrimination practices on some campuses have not been limited to faculty employment. They have included student recruitment, admissions, grading and class placement, too. Still, even among college administrators who acknowledge the urgent need for fair practices and strong civil rights enforcement, we encountered during our study sharp complaints about the enforcement methods used by federal officials. Academics are critical, for example, of government threats to cut off *all* funding if any of its requirements are not met. The punishment rarely fits the crime. Such a threat made sense as a weapon against the wholesale segregation of state school systems, but that may have been its only appropriate application.

As William McGill, former president of Columbia University, has pointed out, "a university with a faulty personnel management system or inadequate data reporting should not be placed in the same jeopardy as a state that creates publicly supported private academies in order to avoid desegregation."[3] The problem is that government seems to have few "intermediate range" sanctions it can legally impose. In fact, its "ultimate weapon" has never been used.

Colleges and universities also have been annoyed by what they characterize as the "presumption of guilt" by the Office for Civil Rights and other enforcement agencies. The federal government, they argue, all too readily assumes that institutions are discriminatory employers. To support their view, they point to such evidence as this passage from HEW's 1972 guidelines for implementing affirmative action requirements: "A *necessary prerequisite* to the development of a meaningful affirmative action program is the identification and analysis of *problem areas inherent in* minority and female employment."[4]

Similarly, Title VII of the Civil Rights Act of 1964 embodies the assumption that discrimination is likely to have occurred. To bring a Title VII case to court, the complainant, or the government, need only establish a *prima facie* case; the burden falls on the employer to prove that its policies are not discriminatory.

Commenting on the government's proposed revisions of affirmative action regulations, an attorney for the American Council on Education observed:

We continue to be troubled by the overall negative tone of the proposals. There is implicit in the language and the organization of the rules a presumption of guilt on the part of every covered contractor. . . . The presumption is . . . evident in the failure to include . . . any provisions describing the steps to be taken by OFCCP [Office of Federal

57

Contract Compliance Programs] when it finds no discrimination.[5]

There was, of course, good reason for government officials to be suspicious of some colleges where discrimination existed and affirmative action steps were ineffective. Still, other colleges have provided outstanding leadership in this essential field and more and more institutions have taken steps to overcome deficiencies of the past. This reality should be recognized by those responsible for civil rights enforcement.

The most significant points of tension in civil rights enforcement relate to the essential core—the freedom of faculty members to select, to evaluate, and to promote colleagues. Academics insist that this process must be uninhibited, possibly even confidential, while government officials claim that they must review the process to assure that no discrimination has occurred.

At the University of California at Berkeley in 1978 there was a classic confrontation. The Department of Labor sought to remove information from the Berkeley campus to determine whether certain academic appointments had violated civil rights requirements. A preliminary investigation by the department indicated they had. Berkeley officials challenged the removal of records on the grounds that once the documents were in possession of the federal officials, they would become "agency records" and therefore subject to public disclosure under the Freedom of Information Act. The university also argued that removing the records would undermine the freedom of scholars to make judgments about their colleagues—the heart of the academic enterprise.[6]

In a decision that seemed to leave the central issue blurred, Secretary of Labor F. Ray Marshall held in 1980 that the university was obligated to turn over to government any requested documents. On this principle he did not budge. But in deference to the university, the secretary (himself a former professor) also ordered that freedom of information regulations within the Department of Labor be interpreted so as to protect the documents from public disclosure.[7]

Neither party was reassured. The Department of Labor's regulations may be challenged in court, changed by another secretary, or completely ignored by regulation writers in other departments. In

58

addition, the Equal Employment Opportunity Commission, which also investigates discrimination in academic employment, has rules that would, under certain conditions, *permit* the disclosure of such records.

Institutions of higher education have also found themselves increasingly answerable to the courts on key issues of academic governance. In January 1970, the Women's Equity Action League filed a class-action complaint with the United States Department of Labor against all colleges and universities, charging violation of President Johnson's 1965 Executive Order. That action brought onto campuses government officials who launched wide-ranging investigations and sparked often heated discussions about alleged sex and racial discrimination.

In 1970, Kenneth Adams[8] and a coalition of black advocacy groups sued HEW, claiming that the department had "defaulted" in carrying out its desegregation responsibilities. In finding for the plaintiffs, the court ordered the department to call for new desegregation plans from the ten state higher education systems involved in the suit.

The universities involved[9] began negotiating with HEW's Office for Civil Rights in 1972, and some reached agreement. In 1977, however, prior agreements were put aside. The Adams plaintiffs returned to court, charging that the eight state desegregation plans the department had accepted in 1974 (two states had been referred to the Department of Justice for enforcement proceedings) did not meet the Department's own guidelines. The court, once again finding for the plaintiffs, ordered the department to develop new criteria for desegregation, specifying that an acceptable plan must also take into account the "unique importance of black colleges."[10]

In the new HEW guidelines, university officials were asked to discontinue academic programs to avoid duplication between black and white colleges, add new programs at black colleges to make them more attractive, revise budgets, plan new facilities, and set targets for minority interests. In an historic legal confrontation, the University of North Carolina challenged the right of government officials to impose such academic, curriculum, and programmatic changes that the university contended would not further civil rights and, furthermore, violated the integrity of the institution. In 1979, the United States District Court for the Eastern District of North Carolina ruled that there should be an administrative hearing on these issues but that the government could not cut off funds before the hearing was concluded.

In January 1980, in the case of *Keene State College* v. *Sweeney*, the Supreme Court ruled on the delicate matter of peer review. The high court let stand a lower court decision that had *overruled* a unanimous peer recommendation against promotion to tenure.[11] It was the case of Christine Sweeney, an associate professor of education at Keene State College in New Hampshire who, in the academic year 1972-73, applied for promotion to tenure. When her application was denied, she took her case to a faculty appeals committee, to the president of the college, and, eventually to a state commission and the courts.

In finding for Dr. Sweeney in 1978, the U.S. District Court of Appeals announced its disagreement with earlier judicial decisions in similar cases:

> We voice misgivings over one theme recurrent in earlier Title VII opinions: The notion that courts should keep "hands off" the salary, promotion, and hiring decisions of colleges and universities. This reluctance no doubt arises from the courts' recognition that hiring, promotion, and tenure decisions require subjective evaluation most appropriately made by persons thoroughly familiar with the academic setting. Nevertheless, we caution against permitting judicial deference to result in judicial abdication of a responsibility entrusted to the courts by Congress.[12]

At the University of Minnesota, attorneys have been called in to supervise academic employment. In settling a sex discrimination complaint, the university agreed to employ a "special master," or attorney, whose apointment was to be jointly approved by the institution, the complainants, and the court. In addition to reviewing hiring, promotion, and tenure procedures, the "special master" was given responsibility to conduct hearings on discrimination complaints after they have gone through an internal hearing process. Following the hearing panel's decision, the "special master" would submit in

60

writing, for the court's ultimate decision, "findings of fact, conclusions of law, and recommendations."[13] Clearly, a new voice was added to a process that historically was regarded as the sole prerogative of the university.

Finally, James A. Dinnan, a professor at the University of Georgia, went to jail rather than reveal his vote on a tenure decision in his department. The United States District Court ruled that the protection of the civil rights of the plaintiff was more important than confidentiality in the process of peer selection. The United States Supreme Court refused to hear Professor Dinnan's appeal.[14]

Given this sampling of administrative and legal confrontation, what lessons can be drawn? Has the integrity of the campus been weakened? We conclude that during the past fifteen years, the federal civil rights laws have pushed colleges and universities in the right direction, stirring an awareness on campus of the often deeply entrenched barriers faced by members of minorities and women. Higher education has been required, quite properly, to make moves toward equity—moves that had been far too long delayed.

It is also true that in the past the courts generally have deferred to the campus in academic matters. Indeed, Walter C. Hobbs of the State University of New York at Buffalo takes the position that court decisions, while imposing modest limits on institutional autonomy, have, in fact, reinforced the legal bases of academic freedom. He says that "both individuals within the academic enterprise and the enterprise per se . . . are truly the beneficiaries of a strong judicial bias toward academic liberty."[15]

But it would be naive to believe that litigation by persons who believe themselves aggrieved will fade away. For the foreseeable future, it is likely that the academy will not have fewer but more encounters with the courts. And recent decisions indicate that courts are not only likely to be more actively involved in academic matters, but more *activist* as well, involving themselves in procedures that traditionally defined the independence of the institution.

Unquestionably, there will continue to be occasions when the courts must step in to rectify grave injustices, but a strong presumption should always operate, as it has in the past, in favor of the preservation of hard-won academic governance procedures that have evolved over many centuries of institutional development.

The relationship between the campus and federal enforcement agencies is yet another matter. The failure of some campuses to push affirmative action programs has caused government officials to suspect both their methods and their motives. On the other hand, the continuing "presumption of guilt" by federal officials has bred tension. Also, inconsistency in government requirements, erratic procedures of enforcement, and the lack of due process arrangements have caused frustration and contempt. Most disturbing, perhaps, is the fact that the vision of giving full opportunity to every person has been overburdened by quarrels and confrontations, and praiseworthy ends have been obscured in conflicts over means.

There is no simple formula to guarantee that justice will emerge from these encounters, or that the integrity of academic governance will never be jeopardized. Federal and state enforcement officials should, however, be extremely circumspect in stepping into matters that historically have been resolved through internal governance procedures. Such intervention, even in the name of high principle, can lay the groundwork for long-range changes in the nature of our society that would be in the interests of none. In the end, the academy should be measured by *results,* not detailed procedures.

Finally, we deplore the suspicion and lack of trust that has sometimes been revealed by both academics and government officials. Academic governance, like most human activities, has as much to do with underlying attitudes as with formal structures, and achieving social justice should be viewed by all parties as an essential goal that unites rather than divides.

IX

LIMITS OF GOVERNMENT
REGULATION

I N OUR REVIEW of the control of higher education, we have
discovered conditions inherent in bureaucracy at both the state
and federal levels that limit its capacity to regulate the campus
effectively. This is not to suggest that government officials are not
well intentioned or that colleges and universities should not fulfill
their accountability obligations. Rather, we simply remind public
officials that there is a limit to the oversight functions government
can perform.

In many government agencies there is frequent turnover at the
top. Signals change as administrations change. Institutional memory
is short. Often, when a new administration takes charge, new legislation is introduced that changes the shape and character of existing
programs.

In the now-famous Adams case, the universities involved had
been negotiating for years with the Office for Civil Rights in the Department of Health, Education and Welfare (HEW). In some states,
accommodations had been reached. In 1977, when a new administration came in, and when HEW was placed under court order to reach
settlement, prior agreements were set aside. Universities were given
new compliance rules. As one young HEW lawyer put it: "This is
a new administration and we're not bound by what the others did."
In 1981, yet another administration came to Washington and, once
again, the enforcement strategy was changed.

When Harvard's President Derek Bok complained to the alumni of the university in 1975 about the federal government's "clumsy legislation . . . stifling bureaucratic requirements . . . erratic fluctuations" in funding, his anger had recently been stoked. Just before his speech, he had received a special delivery letter from the acting director of HEW's Office for Civil Rights. It warned that Harvard was about to lose millions of dollars in research grants if it did not revise its affirmative action plan in less than two weeks. Harvard's plan had already been approved by HEW's regional office.

Jerome Wiesner, former president of the Massachusetts Institute of Technology, once described how he had to scramble to replace government funding for a vast multiyear research project. Federal funds had been cut off because government priorities had changed. Such disruptions happened so frequently, Wiesner remarked, "I sometimes feel like a battered child."[1] The harsh fact is that many colleges have lost faith in government oversight, not because they reject the goals or resist their obligation to be accountable, but because the signals are so erratic.

Sometimes, lack of continuity in government action is simply the result of poor administration. On March 24, 1982, the *Chronicle of Higher Education* reported a major snag in the Guaranteed Student Loan program. "Colleges and banks have been unable to begin processing applications for loans to be used after July 1 because the Education Department has not yet issued rules governing the loan program after that date." Because the rules would apply a new limit to student eligibility, "anxious students cannot find out how much they will be able to borrow next fall—or if they are eligible at all."[2]

Government supervision is also limited because of its obligation to treat all cases uniformly. Such rigidity is not the creation of mindless bureaucrats who enjoy inducing pain and discomfort. Rather, it reflects the fact that a public agency, when enforcing duly adopted regulations, cannot grant an exception to one institution without granting the same privilege to all.

A grant application submitted to the United States Office (now Department) of Education was postmarked one minute after the deadline announced in the regulations. The reason for the late submission was compelling. Government lawyers ruled, however, that the

64

application had to be rejected. To accept the late application would require that new regulations be issued to give all other "late submitters" an opportunity for their case to be heard.

In drafting regulations, the concerns of agency lawyers often have little to do with either effective administration or the convenience of the client. Rather, the goal is to make sure the regulation will "stand up in court." Thus, those who participate in government programs confront rigid regulations written in a climate of "anticipatory litigation."

Further, government officials have a tendency to generalize policy from isolated "worst cases," and then impose that cautious standard on all. In 1972, a means test was imposed on the Guaranteed Student Loan program because one congressman repeatedly cited the example of a student who had admitted using his Guaranteed Student Loan to buy a "red Corvette."

Government oversight is further flawed by its chronic vulnerability to external political pressures. During our study, a former government official reported that members of Congress frequently urged that exceptions to regulations be made and criteria be ignored in order to secure funds for higher education institutions in specific Congressional districts.

In 1976, the parents of American students studying medicine abroad successfully lobbied for an amendment to the Public Health Service Act. The amendment provided that American students who had completed two years of study in a foreign medical school and could pass the first phase of the Medical Examiners test would be admitted to medical schools in this country. The Secretary of Health, Education and Welfare was given discretion to allocate the students to various American medical schools. The law transferred control of admissions to the government, and was so vehemently criticized by university leaders that it had to be quickly amended.

However, we conclude that the most serious problem encountered by higher education is the *cumulative* impact of government intervention. Taken by itself, any single action may not be unbearably intrusive, but the combined impact of many actions can nearly suffocate an institution. As public officials ask colleges and universities to defend endlessly their decisions, they inadvertently reshape the institution in fundamental ways. Priorities are shifted as faculty and administrators spend more time on paperwork than on academic planning.

In one year the University of California reported filing 229 "unique" reports with 32 separate federal agencies.[3] The president of another university recently complained that within a three-week period his institution had been subjected to compliance reviews by no fewer than four different federal agencies. Recipients of federal grants are now subject to 59 legislative and regulatory requirements regarding administration and social policy. Virtually all of them, directly or indirectly, affect colleges and universities.[4]

A recent report from Pennsylvania shows that the state's central government controls purchases over $1,000; all contracts; all civil service management; administrative classifications and pay telephone installations; computer configurations; consultant fees and honoraria over $2,000; and institutional memberships in national organizations.[5] The state also supervises such fundamental matters as academic program and formal planning, tuition, financial aid programs, and federal grants. This is simply bad management.

In Arizona and Nevada, the state legislature or its staff decides on student-faculty ratios.[6] And in Arkansas, a state agency in the executive branch decides on purchases costing over $1,000, the transfer of more than $5,000 between budget categories, and authorizing fund-raising campaigns for capital improvements.[7]

Such detailed supervision of campus activity may at first blush appear to be administrative only. However, the issue goes deeper. Trying to administer a college by remote control ignores principles of good management, reflects a climate of distrust, and assumes incorrectly that if centralized management is increased, efficiency will improve.

Further, such an ambitious range of bureaucratic oversight generates a workload that government itself cannot handle. Requests go unanswered, order forms are lost, mountains of unused data reports accumulate in cardboard boxes in government corridors, and threatened audit and compliance reviews are sporadically conducted. Simply stated, "efficiency" standards are imposed by inefficient organizations.

In 1977, Office of Education officials admitted that they did not know which students were in default on their government loans and acknowledged that students were not even being reminded that payments were due. That same year, Senator Daniel Moynihan asked HEW how many complaints its Office for Civil Rights had received and settled under each of its statutory jurisdictions. The department had to admit that the figures could not be supplied.[8]

Unhappily, the bottom line in the growth of government regulation is that there is no bottom line. Campus leaders, from presidents on down, feel caught in a confusing bureaucratic web that demands accountability, but provides few incentives for responsible decision making. As government oversight expands, and as more agencies intervene, it is increasingly difficult to know where decisions are and are not being made.

In summary, there are real limits to the government's capacity to regulate higher education. As public officials introduce more and more oversight requirements, the process becomes overburdened, contradictory, and finally incoherent. We conclude that improvement will not come from better management of the government's regulatory functions, although this is certainly a worthy goal to be pursued. Instead, the academy must rediscover more effective ways to regulate itself. It is to this theme we now return.

PART FOUR

REGAINING CONTROL

X

A GOVERNANCE FRAMEWORK
FOR HIGHER EDUCATION

I N THIS REPORT we repeatedly have called upon higher education to reaffirm and strengthen self regulation—not to isolate the campus from the larger community—but because control of the academic core is the one function the university may not lose without losing everything.

To call upon higher education to regulate itself may seem unrealistic, if not naive. In the days ahead, public agencies will be hard pressed for funds. Most colleges and universities will be asked to justify in full detail their budgets and expenditures. Competition will increase as campuses struggle for dollars and for students. Under these conditions, one might reasonably predict more bureaucratic control and less responsible behavior by the academic community.

Still, there is, we believe, a growing understanding that centrally mandated, formula-driven efficiency has its limits. There is recognition that local initiatives may well be more effective than layers of bureaucratic oversight and control. Further, the academy, with all its limitations, has had a long, successful tradition of self-regulation. Even by government's own assessment, colleges and universities, with few exceptions, have been good stewards of public funds.

This appears, then, to be the right moment, therefore, for the academy to strengthen its traditional decision-making machinery and add new accountability arrangements. In this section, we review the major conclusions of the report, outline recommendations, and suggest a governance framework for the future.

THE GOVERNING BOARD

Informed by our review of the history of higher education in Europe and America, we conclude that the governing board constitutes the keystone in the governance structure of higher education. Looking to the future, we also conclude that the role of this body will become more, not less, important. Internally, trustees set goals and resolve disputes—functions that will become increasingly critical as higher education moves from expansion to constraint. Externally, they are the connecting link between institutions of higher learning and outside authorities.

The paradox is that despite their authority, the role of governing boards remains ambigious. Decision making is spread among trustees, presidents, and faculty, and although the legal status of trustees has not changed, there is ambivalence as to how much power they should have. During the protests of the 1960s, there was, in fact, a strong minority opinion that governing boards should be abolished.

On some campuses, trustees operate in the shadows of the institution. They come to campus once or twice a year, remain marginally involved, and appear only ceremonially at homecoming and commencement. On other campuses, trustees meet more frequently but tend to get bogged down in routine details. Governing boards, according to one study, make an average of fifty-one separate decisions per meeting and about half of these decisions concern operational details.[1]

We believe a larger vision is required. In addition to the traditional functions of setting policy, electing presidents, and approving budgets and key personnel appointments, trustees also must participate in shaping educational priorities for the future and actively involve themselves in the review of the quality of the institution.

Strengthening the role of trustees starts with the board itself. Trusteeship, by definition, means fulfilling a special "trust"—representing the public interest without compromising the community of learning. Trustees, if they are to guide an institution wisely, should be fully and coherently informed about its functions.

Governing boards also must be properly constituted. Ideally, trustees are appointed because they have a broad perspective and because of their interest in the institution overall. Ex officio board appointments and special-interest membership on governing boards should be a matter of concern.

Respect for trustees is sustained by the quality of those appointed or elected, and by their ability to earn respect through the wisdom of their actions and their willingness to serve enlightened rather than parochial interests. To strengthen the trusteeship role, we make the following recommendations:

☐ The essential role of the governing board in American higher education should be reaffirmed and vigorously supported by all members of the academic community.

☐ Governing boards should be responsible for the overall policy of the institution and for the appointment of presidents and other major officers; approval of faculty appointments, at least at the tenure level; approval of major expansion of facilities; and approval of the budget.

☐ Trustees also have a special obligation to help assess the educational quality of the institution by participating in the campuswide review of academic programs.

☐ Governing boards should consult fully and frankly with all segments of the campus—administrators, faculty, and students—in the shaping of new policies and procedures.

☐ Trustees should be appointed or elected because of their appropriate experience and broad perspective, not as a political reward or because they represent narrow, special interests.

☐ The length of trustee service should be long enough—at least six years—to assure continuity of interest and direction and to protect board members from undue political pressure.

☐ Above all, trustees should be fully informed about the function of their institutions and faithfully interpret those functions to the public. They should vigorously defend their institutions against all efforts, from any source, to undermine the integrity of the campus.

In the end, the authority of boards of trustees will be sustained by the quality of those chosen as members, by the wisdom of their actions, and by their willingness to serve the general interests of the public while protecting higher education.

GOVERNANCE ON THE CAMPUS

We have noted in this report that a large share of the work and authority of academic governance is, quite properly, delegated by trustees to administrators, faculty and students. We conclude that if higher education is to regulate itself more effectively, campus decision-making structures need to be improved.

Traditional structures do not seem to be working very well. Faculty participation has declined, and we discovered a curious mismatch between the agendas of faculty councils and the crisis now confronted by many institutions. For example, we were told that the faculty senate at one ranking public university has not had a quorum for seven years.

The inadequate state of campus governance should not be attributed to faculty alone. Some administrators still appear to be too authoritarian or too bureaucratic to consult openly and honestly with colleagues. The chair of the faculty budgetary affairs committee at one major university reported a feeling of futility about the consultation process: "Our work on program review, many of us felt, was used as a shield for unpopular administrative decision-making and some of our most important suggestions were ignored."[2]

Also the breakdown of campus governance is perhaps an all too predictable reaction to hard times. Life on a campus in retrenchment becomes tense. At such an institution there is what Irving J. Spitzberg of the American Association of University Professors calls "a war of all-against-all."[3] As difficult as it may be to accomplish, we conclude

74

that collegial compacts must be renewed in order to handle urgent campus matters and improve relationships between the academy and the larger society.

Finally, a word must be said about the impact of collective bargaining. Clearly, faculty unionization constitutes a fundamental shift in campus governance. We believe, however, that collective bargaining will not violate the traditions of academic life if faculty members on campuses are in charge of the negotiations and if contractual agreements respect the freedom and professional judgments of individual teachers. It should be recognized that faculty senates and similar bodies are still needed to deal with the full range of academic and administrative matters that fall within their concern.

To strengthen campus governance, we make the following recommendations:

☐ The faculty at each institution, with trustee-delegated authority, should vigorously support a campuswide senate or comparable body to oversee all matters relating to the institution's academic core.

☐ In addition to traditional academic concerns, special consultative bodies of faculty, administrators, and students should monitor campus performance in response to the new public accountability mandates—fiscal integrity, social justice and consumer protection.

☐ A clear distinction should be drawn between the corporate authority of trustees and campus governance. If representatives of campus constituent groups are placed on governing boards, they should serve in an advisory capacity only.

☐ If collective bargaining is introduced, it should be conducted by the faculty on campus and should relate to such issues as compensation and due process while respecting the freedom and judgment of the individual teacher.

☐ Campuses with collective bargaining should also acknowledge the importance of other existing arrangements for faculty participation in campus governance.

☐ Colleges and universities may wish to convene governance convocations to consider ways more effectively to involve all members of the academic community in decision making on campus.

Today, there is a paucity of thoughtful debate about academic governance. If the larger interests of the institution are to be served, and if the public is to be assured that the academy can manage its own affairs, that debate must become more vigorous and more vital.

REGIONAL ACCREDITATION

Throughout this report, we have emphasized the importance of self-regulation. In doing so, we have viewed regional accreditation as a critically important part of academic governance.

The irony is that such accreditation has increasingly lost significance at the very time it is needed most. Among accreditors there is no agreement about the meaning of a college education, and the neglect of undergraduate education is especially disturbing.

While preparing this report, we heard that accreditation review often is little more than an empty ritual. Most discouraging, perhaps, many campuses downplay the importance of accreditation visits. Higher education leaders frequently decline to participate in the process.

Further, we found that regional accreditation has not responded satisfactorily to the new accountability mandates imposed by government agencies and the courts. Even though public obligations have increased, accrediting officials seem hesitant to accept expanded evaluation responsibilities. One key accreditation official took the following position:

> Accreditation cannot, by itself, serve as the basis for determining eligibility for federal funds; neither can it function as an arm of government in policing compliance. . . . Accreditation cannot allow itself to be used for purposes other than evaluating and encouraging *educational* quality, and the burden is always on the accrediting body to demonstrate that its criteria and procedures serve this ideal.[4]

76

Higher education quite properly opposes any government move to accredit institutions. But this threat can be contained only as regional bodies expand the scope of their authority and hold colleges accountable not only for academic excellence but also for good management, affirmative action, and consumer protection, too.

We conclude that the erosion of regional accrediting authority and prestige leaves a dangerous void. The integrity of higher education urgently requires that regional accrediting be supported and that its procedures be improved. To achieve this objective, we recommend the following measures:

☐ Senior officials at all colleges should fully support their accrediting associations and participate actively in their work. Serving on an accreditation team should be the equivalent of jury duty for every academic.

☐ Regional associations should do more than measure a college against its own objectives. They should also have their own clear standards of academic quality, giving special attention to the undergraduate college and to the meaning of liberal education.

☐ Regional associations should also hold campuses accountable for good management, enlightened personnel policies, and consumer protection—those areas of special concern to state and federal agencies and the courts.

☐ Accrediting agencies should develop clearly defined categories of institutional membership that are consistent from one region to another so the public can better understand the accreditation status of each institution.

☐ Information about the accreditation of colleges should be more accessible by the public. A summary of the results of each campus evaluation—excluding confidential personnel information—should be available to all concerned constituencies.

☐ A national panel should be established to serve as a "court of last resort" to receive appeals and to resolve conflicts when an institution believes it has been unfairly treated by a regional association. The Council on

Postsecondary Accreditation—the organization that brings together at the national level all recognized accrediting bodies—is an appropriate group to organize and maintain this appeal procedure.

Here, then, is our conclusion: Public confidence in higher education's ability to govern itself must be restored and government involvement in the academy diminished. To achieve this goal academic leaders must be willing, collectively, to set academic and public accountability standards and, through regional accreditation, participate in their enforcement.

SPECIALIZED ACCREDITATION

In our review of academic governance we found that one form of self-regulation—specialized accreditation—actually threatens the integrity of the campus.

The original goals of professional accrediting were estimable: to establish, on a national basis, educational standards, primarily in fields related to public health and safety. However, during the past fifty years, the list of accrediting bodies has grown from a small core to more than fifty associations. On some campuses a dozen or more visiting teams impose requirements that may compromise the authority of the trustees and undermine the overall priorities of the institution.

The issue here is not whether professional programs should meet high academic standards. It is, rather, how detailed those standards should be; how they should be enforced; and, most importantly, whether specialized programs are to fit within the larger purposes of the campus.

Looking ahead, tensions among departments and disciplines may increase as budgets tighten. In such a climate, professionals on campus may be even more tempted to abuse accreditation, using the process not to protect the public and promote excellence but to gain leverage in the competition for limited resources.

We are especially troubled that at least twenty-one specialized accrediting associations have been linked to occupational licensure by the state. Through such arrangements, they wield enormous power over higher education by controlling entry into the professions, and giving states strong influence over academic matters. The role of the state in occupational licensing should be to certify results, not to control the process of education.

To fit specialized accreditation more effectively into the overall governance of higher education the following recommendations are proposed:

☐ Standards for specialized accreditation should focus on outcomes, and campus evaluations should be conducted with full respect for the overall mission of the institution.

☐ Colleges and universities should not invite to campus any specialized accrediting agency whose criteria for membership are so intrusive or detailed as to weaken an institution's own authority over teaching and research.

☐ Specialized accreditation teams should coordinate their visits with regional associations, and, whenever possible, such collaboration should involve sharing information and preparing combined summary reports.

☐ State governments should reexamine the link between occupational licensing and specialized accreditation. In some cases, alternate routes to licensure, such as formal examinations or practical experience should be provided. In other cases, the link between licensing and accreditation should be broken altogether.

Clearly, professional associations will continue to play an important role in the self-regulatory structures of higher education. We share their interest in maintaining excellence in the quality of the professions they serve. We urge caution, however, in the proliferation of accrediting associations and in the creation of restrictive standards that erode the integrity of the campus.

LINKAGES WITH STATE GOVERNMENTS

In this report, we have talked about the core of higher learning—the obligation of the university to protect the essential functions of teaching and research. But agencies of the state also have an essential core—the obligation to protect the rights of citizens and to oversee the use of public funds. Good governance will acknowledge and keep in proper balance both of these essential claims of the academy and the public.

State officials have generally respected the independence of the campus. Today, however, under the pressure for accountability, the trend is in the opposite direction. Some state agencies have become deeply involved in educational matters, including the evaluation of academic programs.

State fiscal control also has tightened. The review of higher education budgets may include the governor's budget director, three or four legislative committees, the state auditor, and the purchasing department, just to name a few. Frequently, what begins as accountability ends up as chaos and confusion.

In the government of higher education, a division of labor must be maintained. States have an obligation to develop long-range plans, authorize new campuses, develop missions for each institution, set enrollment goals, and provide adequate support. And state coordinating boards created to guide expansion have an equally important role to play in a period of possible contraction. While closing foundering public campuses is much more painful than building new ones, it is, we conclude, an obligation state governments should fulfill.

However, good management requires that decisions be made as close as possible to the point where they will be carried out. Good management also requires that effective performance be rewarded. Permitting colleges to retain savings, for example, will, encourage good leadership and save money. As the late Stephen Bailey cogently observed: "Unless states provide incentives for quality improvement, a Gresham's law is bound to predominate." [5]

Above all, special effort must be made to protect diversity both within an institution and among campuses as well. And authority over teaching and research and the review of academic programs must be kept with the academy itself.

We conclude that, in the days ahead, a more effective relationship is required between the campus and the state. To clarify and improve state activities in higher education, we recommend that:

- [ ] State governments—working primarily through statewide coordinating boards—have the responsibility to plan and provide basic support for a comprehensive system of higher education.

- [ ] While holding colleges and universities fully accountable for the use of public funds, states should encourage good management by permitting administrative decisions to be made as close as possible to the point where they will be carried out.

- [ ] In fiscal matters, state governments should create broad categories of expenditures rather than line item budgets.

- [ ] In academic matters, the integrity of the campus should be fully protected. State officials should not involve themselves directly in the review of academic programs. Rather, they should call upon higher learning institutions periodically to assess such programs and report their findings.

- [ ] State coordinating agencies should also work closely with regional accrediting associations to evaluate the performance of each campus by providing relevant information and encouraging members of their staffs to serve on evaluation teams.

- [ ] Diversity should be a primary goal of statewide coordination. This objective should be given special priority during periods of contraction.

In our review of the state role in higher education, we conclude that much has been accomplished with little threat to the integrity of the campus. Nevertheless, new tensions have emerged and these recommendations, if adopted, will improve coordination and accountability while reducing threats to the integrity of higher education's essential academic core.

THE FEDERAL CONNECTION

As federal support for higher education skyrocketed, colleges and universities were, quite predictably, called upon to be more accountable for their use of public funds. The relationship between Washington and the campus became much more complex. Still, in our review of the growth of research or student aid support we found few examples where federal oversight of these programs was excessive.

If federal involvement in higher education has been relatively benign, how is it that there has been, until recently at least, so much complaining about government intrusion? The answer lies, at least in part, in what we call "the cumulative impact." One regulation may not be restrictive, but many regulations quite literally smother an institution.

Clearly, a new approach is needed. To clarify the relationship between federal agencies and the nation's campuses we propose that new government-university forums be created to improve communication, resolve differences, and move toward policy consensus. As a beginning, we suggest two such bodies: one for research, the other for student aid.

There are precedents for what we have in mind. The National Science Foundation, the National Institutes of Health, and other government agencies have long used ad hoc advisory boards from the academy. The American Council on Education also has established an Office of Self-Regulatory Initiatives, with a national advisory committee to help settle conflicts over such matters as the administration of student aid. The National Academy of Science now has a committee called Government-University Relations in Support of Science that is exploring the forum idea.[6] These are, we believe, moves in the right direction.

One final point. We note in this report that the federal government has, for thirty years, relied on the academy itself—through voluntary accreditation—to determine which colleges are eligible to get federal support. This procedure is not perfect but it is better than having the Department of Education evaluating colleges and involving itself more deeply in the accredition of the accreditors—functions that we conclude are better left to the academy itself.

Now that Washington's role in higher education is being challenged, we believe the historic partnership must be reaffirmed. And, if higher education is properly to meet its responsibilities in administering federally funded research and student aid, new arrangements are required. We, therefore, recommend:

☐ The federal government has an obligation to support higher education programs—such as research and student aid—that are truly national in character and that transcend the needs and interests of one state or region.

☐ Public officials, in their supervision of federally-funded research and student aid, should limit their control of higher education to the fiscal oversight of such programs.

☐ To improve such oversight, the National Academy of Sciences, should establish a government-higher education research forum to exchange ideas, search for agreement on research policy and resolve disputes over the administration of existing programs. Such a forum should be organized in consultation with appropriate federal agencies and professional bodies.

☐ The American Council on Education, working with the Department of Education, should also establish a government-higher education student assistance forum to exchange ideas, search for agreement on policy, and, resolve disputes over the administration of student aid programs. The Council should also enlarge the work of its Office of Self-Regulatory Initiatives.

☐ Policy guidelines developed by the American Council on Education's self-regulation project and by the new forums recommended in this report should be considered for adoption at every institution of higher learning to which they apply. Further, such guidelines should be used by accrediting teams to assist in the evaluation of individual campuses.

☐ In determining the eligibility of colleges to participate in federal programs, the Secretary of Education should use regional accreditation as the basis for approval.

☐ The preparation of an approved list of regional associations should be a function of the Council of Postsecondary Accreditation, not the federal government.

The founders of this nation were wise to restrict the role of the federal government in the control of American higher education. The nation's leaders have also been enlightened in recognizing that there are certain educational objectives that can best be served by federal support. Reconciling this important principle—federal support without federal control—has created a need for new procedures to resolve conflicts as they arise. Our recommendations have been designed to meet the challenge.

PROTECTING INDIVIDUAL RIGHTS

Protecting the rights of individuals is one of the most sensitive and most essential issues we confront in this report on the control of higher education. The right of the university to decide who is to teach confronts the right of the individual to be employed, promoted, or dismissed without prejudice. In such matters, who controls the campus?

Higher education must not retreat from the goal of equal opportunity, and we call upon colleges and universities to affirm an absolutely unwavering commitment to equity for all. Such a commitment will go far, we conclude, to resolve tensions in the troubled arena of civil rights enforcement.

But the methods of monitoring compliance also need review. Government standards are sometimes too specific and at other times too vague. Enforcement ground rules change from one administration to another. Most disturbing, has been the inclination of government officials to impose procedural requirements on the campus that threaten traditional academic prerogatives of the institution. Further, with over 3,200 colleges and universities to be monitored, government cannot do the job alone.

To strengthen self regulation in this important matter we support a recent suggestion that equal opportunity councils should be formed within each university and college, building upon higher education's tradition of peer review. The successful institutional review boards mandated by the Department of Health and Human Services to monitor the use of human volunteers in federally funded research provides a model. These boards have protected human subjects while reducing the need for a vast enforcement machinery within the bureaucracy itself.

The equal opportunity councils we have in mind would extend the work of affirmative action committees by monitoring the hiring, dismissal, and promotion with the institution.[7] Such councils will not overcome the poor employment opportunities caused by declining resources and enrollments. Still, equality of opportunity is required during bad times as well as good. And we conclude that colleges and universities should now seize the initiative and develop strategies that will effectively fulfill their legal and moral obligations. To achieve these ends the following recommendations are proposed.

☐ Protecting individual rights is a public accountability obligation that must be met by every higher learning institution.

☐ In fulfilling this mandate, colleges and universities should vigorously reaffirm their commitment to equality of opportunity by having clearly stated goals with detailed plans for implementation.

☐ Higher learning institutions should form equal opportunity councils to monitor both faculty and nonfaculty hirings, dismissals, and promotions. Council membership should include campus personnel and professionals from other campuses as well.

☐ The findings of the equal opportunity council should be examined by regional accrediting committees and made available to appropriate government enforcement agencies.

☐ While new self-monitoring arrangements for the achievements of equality of opportunity are essential, in the end, a campus should be judged by goals and results rather than detailed procedures.

A LOOK AHEAD: THE CAMPUS AND THE CORPORATION

Throughout higher education's history, universities have had to negotiate the terms of their independence with the most powerful institutions of the day. At first, they were influenced significantly by various
religious bodies. For early American colleges, preparing ministers and
transmitting the faith to a new generation were top priorities. Later, as
the nation-state grew strong, religious issues faded, and higher education increasingly became engaged in the public agenda, establishing a
close relationship to the states and, later, to the federal government
as well.

What about the future? Looking ahead we expect that federal
and state agencies will continue to play important roles in shaping
the mission and influencing the governance of higher education. There
will be a renewal of church influence at a cluster of private colleges,
but this shift will not be enough to overcome the earlier decline.

The most dramatic governance issue of the future, we believe,
will be one we have not yet mentioned in this report—the connection
of higher education to the corporate world. Businessmen have long
served on governing boards, and have exerted influence as wealthy
benefactors. As early as 1918, Thorstein Veblen wrote a trenchant
and often hilarious critique of the way corporate and commercial
values were penetrating the academy.[8]

Today, however, corporate political and economic power is on
the rise, and higher education will increasingly find itself negotiating
less with government bureaucrats, and more with giants of the business world. Increasingly, academic decisions are being shaped by
decisions in corporate board rooms.

The connection between higher education and major corporations—in both research and curriculum decisions—imperils colleges
and universities in much the same way as the church and the state
have threatened university integrity in the past. And preoccupation
on the part of the academy with the priorities of business and industry
may mean that the larger social mandates highlighted in this report—
equality of access to education, fiscal accountability, social justice—
will be compromised.

As we have stressed, academic governance is important not as
an end in itself but as a means of helping the academy fulfill its

overarching social obligations. We agree with Derek Bok, president of Harvard University:

> Education and research may not be the most visible or heroic means of striking at the evils of society. But taken as a whole, they represent the surest way by which academic institutions can resolve the moral dilemma of continuing to enjoy the quieter pursuits of learning in a world filled with suffering and injustice. If universities pursue this course with enough energy and determination, even the angriest critics may eventually come to appreciate the full weight of their social contribution.[9]

President Bok's comment suggests what we believe to be the fundamental question: If colleges and universities become too closely linked to corporate interests, can they continue to ask society to grant them the special and privileged status that the academy has historically enjoyed? The issue is a profound one, and we believe that the larger implications of the burgeoning corporate connection are just emerging.

The most important possession of colleges and universities is not their endowments, nor facilities, not even the faculty, administrators, and trustees. The possession that is important above all others is integrity. In the end, the structure of governance must protect the ability of higher education to carry on, with integrity, the essential functions of teaching and research.

XI

A RENEWAL OF LEADERSHIP

THIS REPORT HAS focused on the legal structures and administrative procedures that connect higher education, government, and the larger society. Unquestionably, such structures and procedures must be shaped with great care and repeatedly reviewed. But, in truth, they can only provide the framework for achievement, not achievement itself. Like all human institutions, the academy can be no greater than the human beings who comprise it. For all the attention to flow charts, master plans, and program reviews, the educational enterprise ultimately depends upon people.

Governance guidelines in themselves have no animating power. In its most authentic sense, governance is simply the process by which people pursue common ends and, in the process, breathe life into otherwise lifeless forms.

The best measure of the health of the governance structure at a college is not how it looks on paper, but the climate in which it functions. Do those involved see some point to what they are doing? Do they believe their efforts can make a difference? Is there a sense of excitement? Is the leadership confident of its aims and goals, without being isolated from either the larger society or the particular institutional community on whose behalf leadership is being exercised?

Whether higher education is to remain socially accountable and intellectually independent will be determined by the quality and spirit of its leadership, including presidents, trustees, deans, and individual members of the faculty.

Unfortunately, too many higher education leaders, from presidents on down, feel almost overwhelmed by demands of the bureaucracy that call for accountability but provide few rewards and give campus leaders little freedom to make their own decisions. Even trustees feel pressured and confused, their own governance function almost hopelessly constricted within a complicated bureaucratic grid.

The ever-increasing role of outside agencies in campus matters is gradually wearing down internal governance structures. As leadership is diminished, power and initiative flow even more rapidly to bureaucracies outside. Under such circumstances, administration too often means simply responding to an impersonal system, flowing along on a ceaseless tide of forms, reports, and computer printouts. As Harold Enarson, former president of Ohio State University, once put it in a moment of exasperation: "I could once say decisively, 'the buck stops here.' Now it never stops." [1]

This destructive cycle must be ended. The governance initiative must return where it belongs: to the campus itself. But structural and administrative reforms, like those proposed in this report can only go so far toward achieving this goal. What is most required is no less than a rebirth of leadership in higher education.

Quite obviously, the steps to such a renewal of leadership, cannot be spelled out in a series of recommendations. Yet some of its characteristics can be suggested. It must be a leadership that can take the initiative in prodding colleges and universities to define their own academic standards and social obligations rather than waiting passively for such standards to be imposed by others. It must be a leadership that can redefine, in contemporary terms, the fragile tradition of academic freedom. It must be leadership that will forcibly remind those within the academy that independence and self-governance can survive only if they are willing to shoulder the burden of making it not merely a matter of pious rhetoric, but a living, working reality. It must, in short, be leadership of vision and creativity that can define and defend the spirit of the academic enterprise.

If such a new spirit of confidence were to emerge in higher education, we are convinced that many of the problems and frustrations that have been the concern of this report would dramatically shrink in importance. They would not vanish, but they would cease to be so stiflingly oppressive as the academy once began to define its own purposes and revitalize its historic governance traditions. Whether such a rebirth of leadership is possible may well be the central question facing American higher education in the years ahead.

APPENDICES

APPENDIX A:

ACCREDITING AGENCIES APPROVED BY THE UNITED STATES DEPARTMENT OF EDUCATION

APPENDIX B:

SURVEY OF HIGHER EDUCATION DECISION MAKING

APPENDIX A

ACCREDITING AGENCIES
AND ASSOCIATIONS

Approved by the United States Department of Education

Regional Institutional Accrediting Associations

1. Middle States Association of Colleges and Schools
2. New England Association of Schools and Colleges [1]
3. North Central Association of Colleges and Schools [1]
4. Northwest Association of Schools and Colleges
5. Western Association of Schools and Colleges [2]
6. Southern Association of Colleges and Schools [1]

National Institutions and Specialized Accrediting Bodies

1. Committee on Allied Health Education and Accreditation
2. National Architectural Accrediting Board, Inc.
3. National Association of Schools of Art and Design
4. American Association of Bible Colleges
5. National Accreditation Council for Agencies Serving the Blind and Visually Handicapped
6. American Association of Blood Banks [3]

[1] The association has separate commissions for colleges and universities and for vocational institutions.

[2] Separate commissions operate for four-year institutions, junior and community colleges, and vocational institutions.

[3] Accreditation is done in cooperation with the Committee on Allied Health Education and Accreditation.

7. American Assembly of Collegiate Schools of Business
8. Association of Independent Colleges and Schools
9. The Council on Chiropractic Education
10. Association for Clinical Pastoral Education, Inc.
11. Council for Non-Collegiate Continuing Education
12. National Accrediting Commission of Cosmetology Arts and Sciences
13. American Society of Cytology [3]
14. Joint Commission on Dance and Theater Accreditation
15. American Dental Association
16. The American Dietetic Association
17. Accreditation Board for Engineering and Technology, Inc.
18. Society of American Foresters
19. American Board of Funeral Service Education
20. Accrediting Commission on Education for Health Services Administration
21. National Accrediting Agency for Clinical Laboratory Sciences [3]
22. National Home Study Council
23. Foundation for Interior Design Education Research
24. Accrediting Council on Education in Journalism and Mass Communications
25. American Society of Landscape Architects
26. American Bar Association
27. American Library Association
28. American Association for Marriage and Family Therapy
29. Accrediting Bureau of Health Education Schools
30. American Association of Medical Assistants [3]
31. American Medical Record Association [3]
32. Liaison Committee on Medical Education of the Council on Medical Education of the American Medical Association and the Executive Council of the Association of American Medical Colleges
33. American Academy of Microbiology
34. National Association of Schools of Music
35. Joint Review Committee on Educational Programs in Nuclear Medicine Technology [3]

94

36. American Association of Nurse Anesthetists
37. National Association for Practical Nurse Education and Service, Inc.
38. National League for Nursing, Inc.
39. American Occupational Therapy Association [3]
40. National Association of Trade and Technical Schools
41. American Optometric Association
42. American Osteopathic Association
43. American Council on Pharmaceutical Education
44. American Physical Therapy Association
45. Joint Review Committee on Education Programs for Physician's Assistants
46. American Podiatry Association
47. American Psychological Association
48. Council on Education for Public Health
49. Association of Advanced Rabbinical and Talmudic Schools
50. Joint Review Committee on Education in Radiologic Technology [3]
51. Joint Review Committee for Respiratory Therapy Education [3]
52. Council on Social Work Education
53. American Speech-Language-Hearing Association
54. Joint Review Committee on Education for the Surgical Technologist
55. National Council for Accreditation of Teacher Education
56. Association of Theological Schools in the United States and Canada
57. American Veterinary Medical Association
58. New York State Board of Regents

THE CARNEGIE SURVEY
OF
HIGHER EDUCATION
DECISION MAKING

T O OBTAIN A CLEAR impression of the current state of academic governance, The Carnegie Foundation for the Advancement of Teaching conducted in May, 1982, a survey of decision making in higher education.

Our survey instrument listed 39 decisions under three headings: academic, personnel, and administrative. We did not attempt to be exhaustive. Instead, we selected decisions we considered to be representative of key policy areas.

Our survey also listed 12 locations of decision making, and the respondents were asked to identify the locations which held effective authority for each of the 39 decisions. *Effective authority* was defined for the respondents as "the agency whose decision generally stands and usually is not reversed."

The survey was sent to four respondents in each of the fifty states:

☐ The chief executive officer of the state's flagship university or university system

☐ The chief executive officer of a public four-year institution

☐ The chief executive officer of a public two-year institution

☐ The head of the state's higher education agency.

96

The last category overlapped the first because in six of the responding states, the state public university system is also the state higher education agency. In all, we mailed out nearly 200 questionnaires and received responses from 76 percent of the institutions and agencies surveyed, that is, from state higher education agencies in 41 states; from 41 flagship universities;[1] from 42 four-year colleges, and 26 two-year institutions.

In the report of the data that follows, the 39 key higher education *"decisions"* are listed vertically on the left side of every page. The four types of universities, colleges, and agencies from which the responses came are repeated under each of the "decisions."

The 12 *"Locations of Decision-Making"* are listed horizontally across the top of the tables.

Responses of the chief executive officers of the various types of institutions surveyed are numerically clustered *under* the various locations of decision-making.

[1] In six instances in which a respondent was both a flagship institution and the state agency, responses are included for both types of respondents. Although the numbers are roughly equivalent for state agencies and flagship institutions, they do not always include agencies, and institutions in the *same* state.

Numbers of higher education agencies and institutions assigning "effective authority"

ACADEMIC DECISIONS	Depart-mental level	Faculty senate or council, campus level	Adminis-tration at the campus level	Govern-ing board, campus level	Faculty senate or council, multi-campus system	Adminis-tration, multi-campus system
1. Defining campus mission and objectives						
Higher Education agencies	—	1	3	5	—	1
Flagship institutions	—	—	3	5	—	5
Four-year institutions	—	—	7	7	—	1
Two-year institutions	—	1	2	9	—	—
2. Setting campus admissions standards						
Higher Education agencies	—	8	15	8	—	—
Flagship institutions	2	11	13	1	3	2
Four-year institutions	1	9	10	5	—	—
Two-year institutions	1	2	12	3	—	1
3. Determining course content & objectives						
Higher Education agencies	38	2	1	—	—	—
Flagship institutions	34	6	—	—	1	—
Four-year institutions	33	8	—	1	—	—
Two-year institutions	17	4	2	—	2	1
4. Setting student-faculty ratios						
Higher Education agencies	3	—	20	1	1	2
Flagship institutions	5	1	21	—	—	2
Four-year institutions	3	2	19	2	—	—
Two-year institutions	—	1	15	3	—	4
5. Establishing minimum faculty-student contact hours						
Higher Education agencies	8	—	19	2	—	1
Flagship institutions	12	2	17	—	—	1
Four-year institutions	3	1	23	—	—	—
Two-year institutions	—	—	15	4	—	4

for making selected decisions to units within higher education and state governments.

Governing board, multicampus system	State coordinating agency	State department of education	Governor's office	Other state executive branch agency	Legislature or its staff	Multiple response	Not applicable
16	7	—	—	—	—	8	—
17	2	—	—	—	—	8	—
17	4	1	—	—	1	3	1
7	2	—	—	—	2	2	—
7	1	—	—	1	1	—	—
6	2	—	—	—	1	—	1
12	3	—	—	—	1	—	1
5	1	1	—	—	—	—	—
—	—	—	—	—	—	—	—
—	—	—	—	—	—	—	—
—	—	—	—	—	—	—	—
—	—	—	—	—	—	—	—
3	2	—	—	1	5	—	4
1	1	1	—	1	3	—	4
7	4	1	—	1	3	—	—
1	—	—	—	—	1	—	1
2	—	—	1	—	—	5	3
2	—	1	—	—	1	4	1
5	3	1	1	—	2	3	—
2	—	—	—	—	1	—	—

	Departmental level	Faculty senate or council, campus level	Administration at the campus level	Governing board, campus level	Faculty senate or council, multi-campus system	Administration, multi-campus system
6. Accepting research funds from external sources						
Higher Education agencies	6	—	24	5	—	2
Flagship institutions	3	—	27	2	—	5
Four-year institutions	—	—	29	3	—	3
Two-year institutions	1	—	12	7	—	2
7. Setting degree requirements						
Higher Education agencies	4	21	3	5	1	—
Flagship institutions	13	17	6	1	2	—
Four-year institutions	5	24	5	3	—	—
Two-year institutions	1	6	7	2	—	2
8. Deciding content of institutional self-study for regional accreditation						
Higher Education agencies	3	5	32	—	—	—
Flagship institutions	3	2	30	1	—	4
Four-year institutions	3	8	29	2	—	—
Two-year institutions	2	4	13	—	—	6
9. Deciding whether to seek specialized accreditation for particular programs						
Higher Education agencies	7	—	26	—	—	1
Flagship institutions	7	1	26	—	—	2
Four-year institutions	7	2	27	—	—	1
Two-year institutions	4	1	16	—	—	4
10. Establishing new undergraduate programs						
Higher Education agencies	1	2	5	5	—	—
Flagship institutions	6	5	8	1	1	1
Four-year institutions	1	5	5	4	1	2
Two-year institutions	—	6	5	1	—	2

Govern-ing board, multi-campus system	State coordi-nating agency	State depart-ment of educa-tion	Gover-nor's office	Other state executive branch	Legis-lature or its staff	Multi-ple res-ponse	Not ap-plicable
3	1	—	—	—	—	—	—
3	—	—	—	—	—	—	1
4	1	—	—	1	—	—	1
5	—	—	—	—	—	—	—
3	1	—	—	—	—	—	3
—	—	—	—	—	—	—	1
2	2	—	—	—	—	—	1
5	1	2	—	—	—	—	—
1	—	—	—	—	—	—	—
—	—	—	—	—	—	—	1
—	—	—	—	—	—	—	—
—	—	—	—	—	—	—	1
1	—	—	—	—	—	6	—
—	—	—	—	—	—	4	1
1	—	—	—	—	—	4	—
—	—	—	—	—	—	1	—
16	10	1	—	1	—	—	—
11	7	1	—	—	—	—	—
13	8	2	—	—	1	—	—
7	4	—	—	—	1	—	—

	Depart-mental level	Faculty senate or council, campus level	Adminis-tration at the campus level	Govern-ing board, campus level	Faculty senate or council, multi-campus system	Adminis-tration, multi-campus system
11. Establishing new graduate or professional programs						
Higher Education agencies	—	2	3	4	—	1
Flagship institutions	5	5	7	2	2	2
Four-year institutions	—	4	3	4	1	1
Two-year institutions	—	—	—	1	—	1
12. Reviewing and eliminating existing undergraduate programs						
Higher Education agencies	—	3	11	6	—	3
Flagship institutions	2	2	21	1	1	—
Four-year institutions	2	5	17	4	—	—
Two-year institutions	1	3	8	2	—	2
13. Reviewing and eliminating existing graduate programs						
Higher Education agencies	—	2	9	2	—	1
Flagship institutions	1	1	16	1	1	—
Four-year institutions	1	3	13	3	—	—
Two-year institutions	—	—	1	2	—	—
14. Adding or discontinuing an academic department or division						
Higher Education agencies	—	1	16	9	—	3
Flagship institutions	2	2	19	1	—	3
Four-year institutions	—	2	18	9	1	1
Two-year institutions	—	—	13	4	—	3

Governing board, multi-campus system	State coordinating agency	State department of education	Governor's office	Other state executive branch agency	Legislature or its staff	Multiple response	Not applicable
17	11	1	—	1	—	—	1
11	6	7	—	—	—	—	—
14	10	2	—	—	1	—	2
3	3	—	—	2	—	—	16
14	4	—	—	—	—	—	—
12	1	1	—	—	—	—	—
12	1	1	—	—	—	—	—
6	1	1	—	—	—	—	2
15	5	—	—	—	—	6	1
12	1	1	—	—	—	7	—
12	3	1	—	—	—	4	2
4	—	—	—	—	1	—	18
11	1	—	—	—	—	—	—
12	1	1	—	—	—	—	—
10	1	—	—	—	—	—	—
5	1	—	—	—	—	—	—

PERSONNEL DECISIONS	Departmental level	Faculty senate or council, campus level	Administration at the campus level	Governing board, campus level	Faculty senate or council, multi-campus system	Administration, multi-campus system
1. Appointing senior campus administrators						
Higher Education agencies	—	—	16	13	—	2
Flagship institutions	—	—	15	5	—	7
Four-year institutions	—	—	20	9	—	—
Two-year institutions	—	—	7	11	—	2
2. Hiring new faculty members						
Higher Education agencies	24	—	13	3	—	1
Flagship institutions	18	—	20	2	—	—
Four-year institutions	13	—	22	4	—	—
Two-year institutions	2	—	16	3	—	3
3. Granting faculty tenure and promotions						
Higher Education agencies	2	2	20	4	1	—
Flagship institutions	2	—	14	1	—	6
Four-year institutions	1	—	20	6	—	—
Two-year institutions	—	—	6	8	—	2
4. Determining academic salary schedules						
Higher Education agencies	—	—	14	6	—	4
Flagship institutions	5	—	14	1	—	6
Four-year institutions	—	1	17	3	—	3
Two-year institutions	—	—	5	8	—	4
5. Setting rules on outside income for faculty members						
Higher Education agencies	1	—	13	9	—	3
Flagship institutions	—	3	17	1	—	5
Four-year institutions	—	1	15	6	—	1
Two-year institutions	—	—	8	7	—	5

Governing board, multicampus system	State coordinating agency	State department of education	Governor's office	Other state executive branch agency	Legislature or its staff	Multiple response	Not applicable
10	—	—	—	—	—	—	—
14	—	—	—	—	—	—	—
11	—	—	—	—	—	—	2
6	—	—	—	—	—	—	—
—	—	—	—	—	—	—	—
1	—	—	—	—	—	—	—
2	—	—	1	—	—	—	—
2	—	—	—	—	—	—	—
6	—	—	—	—	—	6	—
9	—	—	—	—	—	9	—
9	—	—	1	—	—	5	—
4	—	—	—	—	1	1	3
11	1	1	—	1	1	—	2
9	—	—	—	1	1	—	3
12	2	—	2	2	—	—	—
5	—	—	—	—	4	—	—
11	—	—	—	1	—	—	3
10	—	—	—	—	—	—	5
14	1	—	1	1	—	—	2
3	—	—	—	—	—	—	3

	Departmental level	Faculty senate or council, campus level	Administration at the campus level	Governing board, campus level	Faculty senate or council, multi-campus system	Administration, multi-campus system
6. Authorizing out-of-state travel for faculty members						
Higher Education agencies	12	—	27	—	—	—
Flagship institutions	16	—	24	—	—	1
Four-year institutions	8	—	31	—	—	—
Two-year institutions	3	—	15	3	—	5
7. Allocating vacant faculty positions among departments						
Higher Education agencies	—	—	39	—	—	—
Flagship institutions	—	—	38	—	—	2
Four-year institutions	—	—	42	—	—	—
Two-year institutions	2	—	20	1	—	3
8. Negotiating with unions for collective bargaining agreements for academic personnel						
Higher Education agencies	1	—	10	2	—	7
Flagship institutions	—	—	2	—	—	13
Four-year institutions	—	—	7	2	—	5
Two-year institutions	—	—	5	8	—	3
9. Determining affirmative action targets for academic hiring						
Higher Education agencies	—	1	32	1	—	1
Flagship institutions	2	—	28	—	—	9
Four-year institutions	3	—	32	1	—	—
Two-year instiutions	—	2	10	5	—	6
10. Adjudicating faculty grievances						
Higher Education agencies	—	3	23	3	—	3
Flagship institutions	1	10	15	1	—	4
Four-year institutions	1	2	25	2	—	3
Two-year institutions	—	—	16	2	—	2

Governing board, multi-campus system	State coordinating agency	State department of education	Governor's office	Other state executive branch agency	Legislature or its staff	Multiple response	Not applicable
1	—	—	—	1	—	—	—
—	—	—	—	—	—	—	—
1	—	—	—	1	1	—	—
—	—	—	—	—	—	—	—
—	—	—	—	—	—	2	—
—	—	—	—	—	—	1	—
—	—	—	—	—	—	—	—
—	—	—	—	—	—	—	—
5	—	—	1	2	—	—	13
3	—	—	—	1	—	—	22
10	1	—	2	—	—	—	15
3	—	—	—	—	—	—	7
2	2	1	—	—	—	—	1
2	—	—	—	—	—	—	—
1	3	1	—	—	—	1	—
2	1	—	—	—	—	—	—
2	—	—	—	1	—	6	—
2	—	—	—	—	—	7	1
3	—	1	—	—	—	3	2
3	—	—	—	2	—	—	—

ADMINISTRATIVE DECISIONS	Departmental level	Faculty senate or council, campus level	Administration at the campus level	Governing board, campus level	Faculty senate or council, multicampus system	Administration, multicampus system
1. Setting campus enrollment levels						
Higher Education agencies	—	—	12	7	—	3
Flagship institutions	1	—	14	—	—	5
Four-year institutions	—	—	24	2	—	—
Two-year institutions	—	—	15	4	—	5
2. Determining affirmative action targets for enrollment						
Higher Education agencies	—	—	22	5	—	3
Flagship institutions	—	—	25	—	—	4
Four-year institutions	—	—	28	1	—	—
Two-year institutions	—	1	12	3	—	6
3. Setting tuition levels						
Higher Education agencies	—	—	—	9	—	1
Flagship institutions	—	—	1	6	—	4
Four-year institutions	—	—	3	7	—	—
Two-year institutions	—	—	2	10	—	3
4. Allocating revenue from non-state sources (indirect cost reimbursement, auxiliary enterprises)						
Higher Education agencies	—	—	23	5	—	3
Flagship institutions	—	—	19	1	—	9
Four-year institutions	—	—	27	2	—	2
Two-year institutions	1	—	14	4	—	4
5. Approving departmental budgets						
Higher Education agencies	—	—	37	—	—	—
Flagship institutions	—	—	35	1	—	2
Four-year institutions	—	—	39	—	—	1
Two-year institutions	—	1	18	3	—	3

Governing board, multicampus system	State coordinating agency	State department of education	Governor's office	Other state executive branch agency	Legislature or its staff	Multiple response	Not applicable
10	4	—	—	2	—	—	3
11	1	1	—	—	4	—	4
7	3	—	—	1	—	—	5
1	—	1	—	—	—	—	—
4	3	1	—	—	—	—	3
5	2	—	—	—	1	—	—
3	3	1	—	—	—	—	6
2	1	1	—	—	—	—	—
22	2	1	—	—	5	—	1
25	2	—	—	—	3	—	—
22	2	1	—	—	5	—	2
6	2	1	—	—	2	—	—
2	—	—	—	1	1	5	1
4	—	—	—	—	1	4	3
5	—	—	—	2	—	2	2
3	—	—	—	—	—	—	—
3	—	—	—	—	—	—	1
2	—	—	—	—	—	—	1
—	—	—	—	—	—	—	2
1	—	—	—	—	—	—	—

	Departmental level	Faculty senate or council, campus level	Administration at the campus level	Governing board, campus level	Faculty senate or council, multi-campus system	Administration, multi-campus system
6. Establishing guidelines for budget development						
Higher Education agencies	—	1	11	1	—	6
Flagship institutions	—	1	12	1	—	17
Four-year institutions	—	1	21	1	—	6
Two-year institutions	—	—	10	6	—	5
7. Making purchases over $1,000						
Higher Education agencies	1	1	31	—	—	1
Flagship institutions	9	1	23	—	—	6
Four-year institutions	4	—	30	—	—	1
Two-year institutions	—	—	14	5	—	4
8. Transferring more than $5,000 between budget categories						
Higher Education agencies	—	1	18	3	—	3
Flagship institutions	—	1	25	—	—	6
Four-year institutions	1	—	18	1	—	2
Two-year institutions	—	—	11	5	—	2
9. Assigning space and facilities to specific academic programs						
Higher Education agencies	—	1	37	—	—	1
Flagship institutions	—	1	37	—	—	2
Four-year institutions	1	—	39	—	—	—
Two-year institutions	1	—	20	2	—	2
10. Building or habitat a campus facility						
Higher Education agencies	—	1	6	6	—	3
Flagship institutions	—	1	11	3	—	7
Four-year institutions	—	—	8	4	—	4
Two-year institutions	—	—	5	9	—	6

Governing board, multicampus system	State coordinating agency	State department of education	Governor's office	Other state executive branch agency	Legislature or its staff	Multiple response	Not applicable
11	4	1	2	2	1	—	1
7	—	—	1	—	—	—	2
8	1	—	—	2	—	—	2
5	—	—	—	—	—	—	—
2	—	1	—	4	—	—	—
1	—	—	—	—	—	—	1
—	—	—	1	4	—	—	2
2	—	—	—	1	—	—	—
4	—	2	1	6	—	3	—
5	—	—	1	—	—	2	1
5	1	1	—	6	—	4	3
2	1	1	—	—	1	3	—
1	—	—	—	—	—	—	1
—	—	—	—	—	—	—	1
—	—	—	—	—	—	—	2
1	—	—	—	—	—	—	—
12	6	1	1	2	3	—	—
12	1	—	2	—	3	—	1
11	2	—	3	1	7	—	2
4	1	—	—	—	1	—	—

	Departmental level	Faculty senate or council, campus level	Administration at the campus level	Governing board, campus level	Faculty senate or council, multi-campus system	Administration, multi-campus system
11. *Authorizing fund-raising for capital improvements*						
Higher Education agencies	—	—	14	8	1	1
Flagship institutions	—	—	13	6	1	9
Four-year institutions	—	—	16	10	—	1
Two-year institutions	—	—	6	13	—	2
12. *Establishing or closing branch campuses*						
Higher Education agencies	—	—	—	3	1	—
Flagship institutions	—	—	1	3	1	2
Four-year institutions	—	—	2	3	—	—
Two-year institutions	—	—	2	10	—	2
13. *Offering courses and programs off campus*						
Higher Education agencies	1	2	24	2	—	1
Flagship institutions	2	3	17	1	—	7
Four-year institutions	5	—	24	1	—	—
Two-year institutions	1	—	17	2	—	5
14. *Determining specific reductions required by mid-year budget cuts*						
Higher Education agencies	—	1	28	4	—	2
Flagship institutions	—	1	27	1	—	8
Four-year institutions	1	—	34	—	—	—
Two-year institutions	—	—	16	5	—	5
15. *Use of year-end campus budget surplus*						
Higher Education agencies	—	1	21	6	—	2
Flagship institutions	1	1	18	2	—	8
Four-year institutions	—	1	27	1	—	1
Two-year institutions	—	—	8	9	—	6

Governing board, multicampus system	State coordinating agency	State department of education	Governor's office	Other state executive branch agency	Legislature or its staff	Multiple response	Not applicable
11	—	1	1	2	1	—	1
10	—	—	—	—	1	—	1
6	1	—	1	—	1	—	6
4	—	—	—	—	1	—	—
14	7	—	—	—	10	6	—
14	2	1	1	—	3	6	7
15	6	1	2	—	5	2	6
6	2	—	—	—	2	2	—
3	7	—	—	—	—	—	1
4	4	1	—	—	1	—	1
5	2	3	—	—	—	—	2
—	—	1	—	—	—	—	—
4	—	—	—	—	—	—	2
1	—	—	—	—	—	—	3
2	1	—	—	1	—	—	3
—	—	—	—	—	—	—	—
1	—	—	2	5	1	—	2
4	—	—	1	—	2	—	4
3	—	—	1	3	1	1	3
1	—	—	—	1	—	—	1

113

INSTITUTIONS AND AGENCIES PARTICIPATING IN THE SURVEY OF DECISION MAKING IN HIGHER EDUCATION

State Education Agencies

Alabama Commission on Higher Education
University of Alaska Statewide System
Arizona Board of Regents
Arkansas Department of Higher Education
California Postsecondary Education Commission
Connecticut Board of Higher Education
Delaware Postsecondary Education Commission
Florida Department of Education
Georgia Board of Regents of the University System
Hawaii State Postsecondary Education Commission*
Idaho State Board of Education
Indiana Commission for Higher Education
Iowa State Board of Regents
Kansas Board of Regents
Kentucky Council on Higher Education
Louisiana Board of Regents
University of Maine Board of Trustees*
Maryland State Board for Higher Education
Massachusetts Board of Regents of Higher Education
Michigan State Board of Education
Minnesota Higher Education Coordinating Board
Mississippi Board of Trustees of State Institutions of Higher Learning
Montana Board of Regents of Higher Education*
Nebraska Coordinating Commission for Postsecondary Education
University of Nevada System*
New Jersey State Board of Higher Education
New Mexico Board of Educational Finance
New York State Education Department

* Institutions counted as both flagship institutions and state education agencies.

114

Board of Governors of the University of North Carolina*
North Dakota State Board of Higher Education
Ohio Board of Regents
Oklahoma State Regents for Higher Education
Oregon Educational Coordinating Commission
Pennsylvania Office of Higher Education
Rhode Island Board of Governors for Higher Education
Texas Coordinating Board, College and University System
Vermont Higher Education Planning Commission
Virginia State Council of Higher Education
Washington Council for Postsecondary Education
West Virginia Board of Regents
University of Wisconsin at Madison*

Flagship universities

University of Alaska
University of Alabama
University of Arizona
University of Arkansas
University of California
University of Colorado
University of Connecticut
University of Florida
University of Georgia
University of Hawaii*
University of Idaho
University of Illinois
Indiana University
University of Iowa
University of Kansas
University of Kentucky
University of Maine*
University of Maryland
University of Minnesota
University of Mississippi
University of Missouri
University of Montana*
University of Nevada System*
University of New Hampshire
University of New Mexico
State University of New York
University of North Carolina*
Ohio State University
University of Oklahoma

Oregon Department of Higher Education
University of Pennsylvania
Rutgers, the State University of New Jersey
University of South Carolina
University of South Dakota
University of Tennessee
University of Utah
University of Vermont
University of Virginia
University of Washington
University of Wisconsin at Madison*
University of Wyoming

Four Year Institutions

Alabama A & M University
Angelo State University (Texas)
Armstrong State College (Georgia)
Bemiji State University (Minnesota)
California State College (Pennsylvania)
California State University Hayward
Central Washington University
Delaware State College
Delta State University (Mississippi)
East Central University (Oklahoma)
Eastern Connecticut State College
Eastern Illinois University
Florida Atlantic University
Francis Marion College (South Carolina)
Henderson State University (Arizona)
Keene State College (New Hampshire)
Lyndon State College (Vermont)
Mesa College (Colorado)
Miami University (Ohio)
Murray State University (Kentucky)
New Mexico Highlands University
North Carolina Central University
Northeast Missouri University
Northern Michigan University
Northern Montana College
Northern State College (South Dakota)
Purdue University Calumet (Indiana)
Radford University (Virginia)
Salisbury State College (Maryland)
Shepherd College (West Virginia)

State University College at Cortland (New York)
Tennessee State University
University of Nevada, Las Vegas
University of Hawaii at Hilo
University of Maine at Presque Isle
University of Wisconsin at Stout
Valley City State College (North Dakota)
Washburn University of Topeka (Kansas)
Wayne State University (Nebraska)
Weber State University (Utah)
Western Oregon State College
Worcester State College (Maine)

Two-Year Colleges

Austin Community College (Minnesota)
Bossier Parish Community College (Louisiana)
Central Community College (Nebraska)
Clark Community College (Nevada)
College of Southern Idaho
Colorado Mountain College
Community College of Beara County (Pennsylvania)
Community College of Rhode Island
District One Technical Institute (Wisconsin)
East Central College (Missouri)
Gainesville Junior College (Georgia)
Greon River Community College (Washington)
Horry Georgetown Technical College (South Carolina)
Howard Community College (Maryland)
Isothermal Community College (North Carolina)
Lake Region Community College (North Dakota)
Miles Community College (Montana)
Niagara County Community College (New York)
Northern New Mexico Community College
Pearl River Junior College (Mississippi)
Polk Community College (Florida)
Solano Community College (California)
South Plains College (Texas)
University of Kentucky Community College (Kentucky)
Yavapai College (Arizona)
Waubonsee Community College (Illinois)

NOTES

I. THE ESSENTIAL MISSION

1. *Sweezy* v. *New Hampshire,* 354 U.S. 234, 263 (1957).
2. Leff, Gordon. *Paris and Oxford Universities in the Thirteenth and Fourteenth Centuries* (New York: John Wiley and Sons, Inc., 1968), p. 25.
3. *Ibid.,* p. 82.
4. *Ibid.,* pp. 18-19, 94-95. Rashdall, Hastings. *The Universities of Europe in the Middle Ages* 3 volumes, 1895. Edited by F. M. Powicke and A. B. Emden, (London: Oxford University Press, 1936), Vol. I, pp. 8-10.
5. Hofstadter, Richard, and Metzger, Walter P. *The Development of Academic Freedom in the United States* (New York: Columbia University Press, 1955), p. 11.
6. O'Neil, Robert M. "God and Government at Yale: The Limits of Federal Regulation of Higher Education." *Cincinnati Law Review,* 1975, Vol. 44, No. 3, p. 545. (Emphasis added.)
7. *Ibid.* (Emphasis added.)

II. THE AMERICAN TRADITION

1. Hofstadter, Richard, and Smith, Wilson (Eds.). *American Higher Education: A Documentary History* 2 volumes (Chicago & London: The University of Chicago Press, 1961), Vol. I, p. 11.
2. *Ibid.,* p. 36.
3. *Ibid.,* p. 50.
4. *Ibid.,* p. 211.
5. Tewksbury, Donald G. *The Founding of American Colleges Before the Civil War,* 1932. Reprinted (New York: Arno Press and the New York Times, 1969), p. 152.
6. Glenny, Lyman A., and Dalglish, Thomas K. *Public Universities, State Agencies, and the Law* (Berkeley: Center for Research and Development in Higher Education, University of California, Berkeley, 1973), pp. 17, 18.
7. *Ibid.,* p. 20.
8. *Ibid.,* p. 46.

III. GOVERNANCE ON THE CAMPUS

1. Vesey, Laurence R. *The Emergence of the American University* (Chicago: Phoenix Books, 1970), p. 57.

2. Rudolph, Frederick. *The American College and University: A History* (New York: Vintage Books, 1962), p. 165.

3. Cowley, W. H. *Presidents, Professors and Trustees: The Evolution of Academic Government* (San Francisco: Jossey-Bass, 1980), p. 80.

4. Calculated from: U.S. Bureau of the Census. *Historical Statistics of the United States, Colonial Times to 1970, Bicentennial Edition, Part 1* (Washington, D.C.: 1975), pp. 382-385. Also Baldridge, J. Victor, *et al. Policy Making and Effective Leadership* (San Francisco: Jossey-Bass, 1978), p. 253.

5. Brubacher, John S., and Rudy, Willis. *Higher Education in Transition. A History of American Colleges and Universities, 1636-1976* (New York: Harper & Row, 1976), pp. 365-366.

6. In Hofstadter, Richard, and Smith, Wilson (Eds.) *American Higher Education: A Documentary History,* 2 volumes (Chicago and London: The University of Chicago Press, 1961), Vol. II, p. 756.

7. *Ibid.* Vol. II, p. 775.

8. Duryea, E. D. "Evolution of University Organization" in James A. Perkins (Ed.) *The University as an Organization* (New York: McGraw-Hill, 1973), p. 25.

9. Veysey 1970, p. 392.

10. In Hofstadter 1961, Vol. II, p. 865.

11. *Ibid.,* Vol. II, p. 872.

12. In *American Association of University Professors Policy Documents and Reports* (Washington, D.C.: AAUP 1977), p. 43.

13. *Ibid.,* pp. 43-44.

14. Douglas, Joel M. with Kramer, Stephen. *Directory of Faculty Contracts and Bargaining Agents in Institutions of Higher Education* (New York: The National Center for the Study of Collective Bargaining in Higher Education and the Professions, Baruch College, City University of New York, January 1982, Vol. VIII), p. 64.

15. *NLRB* v. *Yeshiva University,* 444 U.S. 672 (1980).

16. Calculated from data in Baldridge, J. Victor, Kemerer, Frank R., and Associates. *Assessing the Impact of Faculty Collective Bargaining* (Washington, D.C.: ERIC-AAHE Research Report No. 8, 1981), p. 20.

17. Mason, Henry L. "The 1966 Statement Revisited," *Academe* January-February 1982, Vol. 68, No. 1, p. 4A.

18. Wilson, Logan. *American Academics Then and Now* (New York: Oxford University Press, 1979), p. 113.

IV. REGIONAL AND NATIONAL ASSOCIATIONS

1. Selden, William K. *Accreditation: A Struggle Over Standards In Higher Education* (New York: Harper & Row, 1960), p. 26.
2. *Ibid.*, p. 35.
3. Brubacher, John S., and Rudy, Willis. *Higher Education in Transition: A History of American Colleges and Universities, 1636-1976* (New York: Harper & Row, 1976), p. 358.
4. Rudolph, Frederick. *The American College and University: A History* (New York: Vintage Books, 1972), p. 436.
5. Selden 1960, p. 47.
6. *Ibid.*, pp. 47, 48.
7. Davis, Calvin Olin. *A History of the North Central Association of Colleges and Secondary Schools, 1894-1945* (Ann Arbor, Michigan: The North Central Association, 1945), pp. 5, 6.
8. *Ibid.*, p. 59.
9. *Ibid.*, pp. 60-62.
10. Selden 1960, p. 41.
11. *Ibid.*, p. 106.
12. *Ibid.*, pp. 37, 38.
13. PL 82-550, Part VI, Section 253 (a) (4).
14. *Nationally Recognized Accreditation Agencies and Associations* (Washington, D.C.: U.S. Department of Education, April, 1982), pp. 9-17.
15. Levine, Arthur E. "Reflections on Accreditation." Unpublished Article, March 1982.

V. SPECIALIZATION: A HOUSE DIVIDED

1. Shyrock, Richard Harrison. *Medical Licensing in America, 1650-1965* (Baltimore: The Johns Hopkins Press, 1967), p. 46.
2. Capen, Samuel P. "Professional Education in America," in *The Management of Universities* (Buffalo: Foster and Stewart, 1953) in Orlans, Harold and Associates. *Private Accreditation and Public Eligibility* (Lexington, Massachusetts: D.C. Heath, 1975), p. 142.
3. Flexner, Abraham. *Medical Education in the United States and Canada. A Report to The Carnegie Foundation for the Advancement of Teaching.* (1910; reprint ed., Boston: The Merrymount Press, 1960), p. 12.
4. Grimm, Karen L. "The Relationship of Accreditation to Voluntary Certification, 1964-1971," in National Commission on Accreditation, *Accreditation of Health Education Programs, Part II.* Staff Working Papers (Washington, D.C.: NCA, 1971), pp. 1-11.
5. Capen, Samuel P. "The Principles Which Should Govern Standards and Accrediting Practices." *Educational Record,* April 1931, Vol. 12, No. 2, p. 95.

6. In Cowley, W. H. *Presidents, Professors, and Trustees: The Evolution of Academic Government* (San Francisco: Jossey-Bass, 1980), p. 156.
7. U.S. Office of Education. *Educational Directory.* Bulletin, 1940, No. 1 (Washington, D.C.: Government Printing Office, 1939); Smith, Carolyn R., and Davis, Geneva C. *Education Directory, Colleges and Universities, 1980-1981* (Washington, D.C.: National Center for Education Statistics, 1981), p. 286.
8. Accreditation Committee. American Occupational Therapy Association. *Program Evaluation Guide Professional Program in Occupational Therapy* (Rockville, MD: AOTA, n.d.), p. 12.
9. Council on Chiropractic Education. *Educational Standards for Chiropractic Colleges.* (Des Moines: CCE, August 1981), p. 66.
10. American Veterinary Medical Association. *Accreditation Policies and Procedures.* (Schaumberg, IL: AVMA, May 1982), p. 7.
11. Accrediting Bureau of Health Education Schools. *Accrediting Manual for Medical Laboratory Technician Education Programs* (Elkhart, Ind.: ABHES, 1979), p. 20.
12. American Assembly of Collegiate Schools of Business. *Accreditation Council Policies, Procedures and Standards, 1980-1981* (St. Louis: AACSB, 1980-81), p. 31; National Association of Schools of Art. *Handbook* (Reston, VA: NASA, 1981), p. 38; American Council on Education in Journalism and Mass Communication. *Accredited Journalism and Mass Communications Education* (Columbia, Mo.; ADEJMC, 1981), p. 7; American Dietetic Association. *Essentials for Coordinated Undergraduate Programs in Dietetics With Self-Study Guide* (Chicago: ADA, 1982), p. 6; Society of American Foresters. *Standards and Procedures for Accrediting Institutions for the Teaching of Professional Forestry* (Washington, D.C.: 1976), n.p.
13. AASCSB, p. 29.
14. Council on Podiatry Education. *Criteria and Guidelines for Colleges of Podiatric Medicine* (Washington, D.C.: American Podiatry Association, August 1980), p. 8.
15. American Bar Association. *Standards and Rules of Procedure for Approval of Law Schools and Interpretations* (Chicago: ABA, August 1981), pp. S305, I305.
16. *Educational Standards for Chiropractors* 1981, p. 39.
17. Council of State Governments. *Occupational Licensing Legislation in the States* (Chicago: CGS, 1952), p. 22.

VI. THE STATE: FROM EXPANSION TO RETRENCHMENT

1. Calculated from Grant, W. Vance, and Lind, C. George. *Digest of Education Statistics, 1979* (Washington, D.C.: National Center for Education Statistics, 1979), p. 131; National Center for Education Statistics. *Bulletin 81-362,* December 1981, p. 10.

2. Calculated from Grant and Lind, 1979, p. 90; Dearman, Nancy B. and Plisko, Valena White. *The Condition of Education, 1981 Edition* (Washington, D.C., National Center for Education Statistics, 1981), p. 164.
3. Calculated from Hodgkinson, Harold. *Institutions in Transition* (New York: McGraw-Hill, 1971), p. 51; Dearman and Plisko, 1981, p. 162.
4. Calculated from Grant and Lind, 1979, p. 101.
5. Calculated from Hodgkinson, 1971, p. 51; Grant and Lind, 1979, p. 90; Dearman and Plisko, 1981, pp. 162, 164.
6. Higher Education Facilities Act of 1963, Public Law 88-204, Section 715.
7. Education Amendments of 1972, Public Law 92-318. Section 196, adding Section 1202 as an amendment to Title 10 of the Higher Education Act of 1965.
8. Eurich, Nell. *Systems of Higher Education in Twelve Countries* (New York: Praeger, 1981), p. 140.

VII. THE FEDERAL CONNECTION: MORE STUDENTS, MORE RESEARCH

1. Olson, Keith W. *The G.I. Bill, The Veterans, and the Colleges* (Lexington, Ky.: The University Press of Kentucky, 1974), pp. 43, 101, 124. Henry, David O. *Challenges Past, Challenges Present* (San Francisco: Jossey-Bass, 1975), p. 60.
2. Olson 1974, pp. 43, 101, 124; Henry 1975, p. 60.
3. Data supplied by Office of Planning and Budget, U.S. Department of Education.
4. Conant, James B. *My Several Lives* (New York: Harper & Row, 1970), p. 236.
5. Bush, Vannevar. *Science—The Endless Frontier,* 1945. Reprinted (Washington, D.C.: National Science Foundation, 1980), p. 12.
6. Applied Management Systems. *Study of Program Management Procedures in the Basic Grant and Campus Based Programs, Final Report, Vol. I. The Institutional Administration of Student Financial Aid Programs* (Silver Spring, MD.: AMS, May 1980), pp. 2-27.
7. Gladieux, Lawrence and Wolanin, Thomas R. *Congress and the Colleges* (Lexington, Mass.: D.C. Heath, 1976), pp. 228-229.
8. *Oversight Hearings on All Forms of Student Federal Financial Assistance.* Subcommittee on Postsecondary Education, Commtttee on Education and Labor, U.S. House of Representatives (Washington, D.C.: Government Printing Office, 1977), p. 551.
9. Tabulated by The Carnegie Foundation for the Advancement of Teaching using unpublished data from the Office of Student Financial Assistance, U.S. Department of Education.
10. Brown, Kenneth T. "Indirect Costs of Federally Supported Research," *Science,* April 24, 1981, Vol. 212, No. 4493, p. 415.

11. U.S. Comptroller General. *Federally Sponsored Research at Educational Institutions—A Need for Improved Accountability* (Washington, D.C.: General Accounting Office, August 18, 1978), pp. i, iii.

12. U.S. Comptroller General. *Minimum Requirements Are Needed For Colleges and Universities to Justify Research Equipment Purchases* (Washington, D.C.: General Accounting Office, May 11, 1978).

13. Office of Management and Budget, Executive Office of the President. *Circular A-21 Revised* (Washington, D.C.: February 26, 1979), pp. 22-25.

14. Roark, Anne C. "Academic Researchers Protest Rule Requiring Strict Accounting of Time." *The Chronicle of Higher Education,* October 20, 1980, Vol. 21, No. 9, pp. 1, 15.

15. Giamatti, A. Bartlett. "Science and the University." *Science,* November 28, 1980, Vol. 210, No. 4473, p. 984.

16. U.S. Comptroller General. *Need for More Effective Audits of Federal Grants and Contracts Administered by Institutions of Higher Education* (Washington, D.C.: General Accounting Office, July 19, 1979), p. 4.

17. Roark 1980, p. 15.

18. U.S. Comptroller General 1979, p. 4.

19. McDonald, Kim. "Official Warns Universities Face Increased Threat of Soviet Espionage." *The Chronicle of Higher Education,* April 7, 1982, Vol. 24, No. 6, pp. 1, 21.

20. McDonald, Kim, "Proposed Changes in Secrecy Rules Alarm Scientists," *The Chronicle of Higher Education,* March 17, 1982, Vol. 24, No. 3, p. 1.

21. Biemiller, Lawrence. "National Academy to Monitor Curbs U.S. Proposes for Visiting Scientists," *The Chronicle of Higher Education,* March 10, 1982, Vol. 24, No. 2, p. 110.

VIII. CONGRESS, THE COURTS, AND CIVIL RIGHTS

1. 42 U.S.C. 2000d (1964).

2. Senate Committee on Labor and Public Welfare, Senate Report No. 92-415, 92nd Congress, 2d Session, p. 12. (Emphasis added.)

3. McGill, William J. "The University and the State," *Educational Record,* Spring, 1977, Vol. 58, No. 2, p. 144.

4. Office for Civil Rights. Department of Health, Education and Welfare. *Higher Education Guidelines, Executive Order 11246* (Washington, D.C.: OCR, 1972), p. J-1. (Emphasis added.)

5. Guthrie, R. Claire to Joseph Hogan, (Acting Director, Division of Program Policy, U.S. Department of Labor), March 24, 1980, p. 1.

6. *U.S. Department of Labor* v. *University of California, Berkeley.* Decision and Administrative Order of the Secretary of Labor, Case No. 78-OFCCP-7, 4. September 1980; *U.S. Department of Labor* v. *Regents of the University of California,* Case No. 78-OFCCP-7, 4 October 1980 (unpublished consent decree).

7. *Ibid.*

8. Kenneth Adams was an elementary school student and his was the first name in the list of plaintiffs filing suit.

9. The states involved in the original suit were: Louisiana, Mississippi, Oklahoma, North Carolina, Florida, Arkansas, Pennsylvania, Georgia, Maryland, and Virginia.

10. *Adams v. Califano,* 430 F. Supp. 118 (D.C. 1977).

11. *Keene State College v. Sweeney,* 439 U.S. 24 (1978).

12. *Keene State College v. Sweeney,* 569 F. 2d 169, 176 (1st Cir. 1978). By then, Dr. Sweeney, by unanimous vote by the Faculty Advisory Evaluation Committee, had been promoted to full professor.

13. *Rajender* v. *The University of Minnesota,* Civil Action No. 4-73-435, in the District Court for the District of Minnesota, Fourth Division, August 14, 1980, p. 9. On July 24, 1982, a federal district court granted nearly $2 million in fees to the attorneys who won the case. The fees awarded were triple the actual charges in order to discourage discrimination, the judge explained. *The Washington Post,* July 26, 1982, p. A5.

14. *In re Dinnan,* 661 F. 2d 426 (5th Cir. 1981), *cert. denied,* 50 U.S.L.W. 3962 (June 8, 1982).

15. Hobbs, Walter C. "The Courts." In Philip C. Altbach and Robert O. Berdahl (Eds.) *Higher Education in American Society* (Buffalo: Prometheus Books, 1981), p. 181.

IX. LIMITS OF GOVERNMENT REGULATION

1. Weisner, Jerome B. "Universities and the Federal Government: A Troubled Relationship." *Chemical and Engineering News,* December 11, 1978, p. 35.

2. Hook, Janet. "Bureaucratic Tie-Ups Delay Student Aid," *The Chronicle of Higher Education,* March 24, 1982, Vol. 24, No. 4, p. 13.

3. Cheit, Earl F. "Benefits and Burdens of Federal Financial Assistance to Higher Education." *The College Board Review,* Spring 1977, No. 103, p. 17.

4. Office of Management and Budget. *Managing Federal Assistance in the 1980's* (Washington, D.C.: OMB, March 1980), pp. 20-26.

5. American Association of State Colleges and Universities. *Memo to the President,* December 29, 1981, p. 8.

6. The Carnegie Foundation for the Advancement of Teaching. Survey of Decision Making in Higher Education. Spring 1982.

7. *Ibid.*

8. Rabkin, Jeremy. "Office for Civil Rights," in James Q. Wilson (Ed.) *The Politics of Regulation* (New York: Basic Books, 1980), pp. 345, 349.

X. A GOVERNANCE FRAMEWORK FOR HIGHER EDUCATION

1. Paltridge, James Gilbert; Hurst, Julie, and Morgan, Anthony. *Boards of Trustees: Their Decision Patterns* (Berkeley: Center for Research and Development in Higher Education, University of California, Berkeley, 1973), pp. 17-18.
2. Brown, Mary Ellen. "The Experience of One Committee (Or, What is the Sound of One Hand Clapping?)," *Academe* January-February, 1982, Vol. 68, No. 1, p. 7A.
3. Spitzberg, Irving J. "Report of the General Secretary to the Sixty-eighth Annual Meeting of the American Association of University Professors, June 25, 1982, p. 6.
4. Young, Kenneth. "New Pressures on Accreditation," *The Journal of Higher Education* March/April, 1979, Vol. 50, No. 2, p. 135.
5. Bailey, Stephen K. "State Perspective on Retirement," address to the Third Annual Invitational Seminar for State Higher Education Officers and members of Statewide Coordinating and Governing Boards of Higher Education, Colorado Springs, CO., August 4, 1981.
6. Correspondence with Donald S. Fredrickson, M.D., Scholar in Residence, National Academy of Sciences, August 20, 1982.
7. Fishbein, Estelle. "The Revolution Against Regulation: From Rhetoric to Reform," December 3, 1981 (unpublished address)
8. Veblen, Thorsein. *The Higher Learning in America.* (New York: Sagamore Press, 1958).
9. Bok, Derek. *Beyond the Ivory Tower: Social Responsibilities of the Modern University,* (Cambridge, Mass. Harvard University Press, 1982) p. 309.

XI. A RENEWAL OF LEADERSHIP

1. Enarson, Harold. "Quality and Accountability: Are We Destroying What We Want to Preserve?" *Change* October 1980, Vol. 12, No. 7, p. 9.